PARALLAX

WORKS BY JEREMY ROBINSON

The Didymus Contingency
Raising the Past
Antarktos Rising
Kronos
Beneath
Pulse
Instinct
Threshold
Fracture
Torment
The Last Hunter
Insomnia
SecondWorld
Project Nemesis
Ragnarok
Island 731
Nazi Hunter: Atlantis
Prime
Omega
Project Maigo
Refuge
Guardian
Human After All
Savage
Flood Rising
Project 731
Cannibal
Endgame
MirrorWorld
Herculean
Project Hyperion
Patriot
Apocalypse Machine
Empire
Unity
Project Legion
The Distance
The Last Valkyrie
Centurion
Infinite
Helios
Viking Tomorrow
Forbidden Island
The Divide
The Others
Space Force
Alter
Flux
Tether
Tribe
NPC
Exo-Hunter
Infinite2
The Dark
Mind Bullet
The Order
Khaos
Singularity
Hunger: The Complete Trilogy
Nemesis
Point Nemo
Good Boys: The Lost Tribe
Good Boys: Unleashed
Kingdom
Good Boys: The Visionary
The Sentinel Trilogy
Artifact
30Seven
Parallax

PARALLAX

JEREMY ROBINSON

Cover design by Jeremy Robinson

ISBN: 979-8-3470-1220-6

Published in 2026 by Podium Publishing
www.podiumentertainment.com

Norah Robinson,

For always being interested in what I'm working on . . .

even if you're too afraid to read them.

PARALLAX

PROLOGUE

Todd Richard thought he was a normal person.

Then two men in black suits showed up at his apartment door. Neither of them mentioned an agency, but he knew they were from the government. Who else could know so much about his life? They knew everything, from his social security number to his recent dreams, and the only other person who knew about those was his therapist.

These men had access to every aspect of his life, and that frightened him more than the guns they carried on their hips.

They said he'd been selected for a top-secret program for people with his 'gifts.' He had no idea what they were talking about, and they didn't elaborate. They just demanded he come with them. Where? They wouldn't say. How long? Silence. No one outright threatened him. They didn't need to. Only a fool would think they had a choice in the matter.

So Todd let the men escort him to their black SUV. They drove to a private airfield where a nice business jet waited. After boarding, they flew for five straight hours.

When he tried to check his location on his phone, it was taken.

When he tried to look out the window, it was closed.

Secrecy was king.

When the plane touched down, Todd lost his patience and lifted his window shade. In the two seconds before the shade was closed again, he saw a distant sign and managed to read the words 'Grand Canyon National Park Airport.'

"The Grand Canyon?" he asked, more confused than ever. "Are you sure you have the right person?"

Neither man responded. They weren't outwardly hostile, but their unwavering stoicism was beginning to weigh on him. The plane taxied for three minutes before coming to a stop and powering down. When they exited, Todd found himself in a hangar where another black SUV waited for them.

He sat in the back seat. The two men sat in the front. When the driver started the vehicle, his comrade turned around, handed Todd a hood, and said, "Put it on. Now."

Todd was close to tears now. He felt like one of Ulysses' men, sailing toward the irresistible Sirens' song—and death.

But it was worse than that. He hadn't been promised anything. There was no carrot dangling in front of his face. He'd just gone along with these men. Didn't put up a fight. Didn't even complain much. He was just . . . placid.

And Todd Richard was not a placid man. He was prone to bar fights. His intelligence was kept in check by a deep well of rage. Conflict resolution was usually worked out with fists and a jail cell. Following these men across the country wasn't just out of character, it was unthinkable.

But even that realization couldn't overcome his willingness to comply.

The hood went on, and they drove for thirty minutes.

He was blind during the drive, the walk that followed, and what he assumed was an elevator ride that went down for a long time. When the elevator opened, the hood was peeled off.

"Walk," one of his guards said.

"You have a name?" Todd asked.

The second guard gave him a shove and repeated the first's order. "Walk."

So, he did. They gave him directions, navigating a series of tunnels that looked like they'd been constructed during the Cold War. Like they could survive a nuclear strike. And maybe they could. They were deep underground. He was sure of it.

He stopped when the tunnel ahead ended at what looked like a large bank vault.

"What's that?" Todd asked.

"To your right," one of the men replied.

He turned to a door that he hadn't noticed. It was a normal door. Unlabeled. Todd took the handle and noticed that neither man had moved to follow him. "Not coming?"

One of the men raised his eyebrows at Todd. Said nothing, but the grim expression was enough.

"Okay, okay," Todd said. "Shit."

He turned back to the door, feeling more unsure about why he was listening to these men but still following their every command, request, and suggestion. No matter how much he didn't like something, he felt compelled to comply.

The door opened to a room that looked like a stereotypical interrogation room. Metal table. Two chairs. A large two-way mirror. Otherwise empty. He stepped inside the room and the door closed behind him.

"Take a seat," a voice said.

He obeyed.

"Do you know why you're here?" the voice asked.

"Am I supposed to?"

"Tell me about your dreams."

Todd ran his hands over his shaved head. "They're not exciting."

"Humor me."

"I see . . . places." Todd shifted uncomfortably. He wouldn't admit it, but his dreams scared him. Not because of the content, but because they were almost tangible. "They feel real, but some of them are too strange to be real."

"Strange, how?"

"I don't know. Like movie sets. Places that don't look real."

"Be more descriptive please."

Todd sighed. His dreams were notoriously difficult to describe. "Some are like caves. Rock walls. Pretty boring. But others look like . . . a kaleidoscope. Like I know there's something there, but the view is shattered and moving."

"What do you see in the shards?"

"It's the same thing . . . but different. Like looking at a house and seeing the land before it was built, the construction, and the changes it might go through when different families live there. New siding. Different shingles. Shifting trees and plants."

"Like you're seeing several moments in time, all at once."

Todd snapped his fingers. "Yes. That. Exactly like that."

He waited for a reply, but none came. "Are you going to tell me what this is about now?"

The silence that followed lasted for two minutes but felt like an hour. Todd folded his arms on the table and lowered his head. He closed his eyes and felt himself relax.

"Still with me, Mr. Richard?"

Todd flinched and sat up. He felt like he'd been sleeping but wasn't sure. Nothing felt real. "I-I'm here."

"When dreaming, do you see people, and if so, do you communicate with them?"

"What? No."

"And when you're awake, can you see other locations like when you're sleeping?"

"I haven't," Todd said. "That doesn't sound like a real thing."

"Do me a favor," the voice said. "Close your eyes and try. Tell me what's behind that bank vault you saw."

"You're serious?" Todd asked.

"Wouldn't have flown you here if I wasn't."

Todd shook his head, closed his eyes, and felt himself relax like he'd just taken a few shots of absinthe.

"This is stupid," he mumbled, as his thoughts began to wander. He should be at work. Would probably be fired. He imagined his boss in the office, pounding on his desk, furious that Todd hadn't shown up for work. His boss cursed at the office manager who told him. Swatted his pen holder, making a mess that he then demanded the manager clean up. Shouted at the man about not being able to control their employees. Threatened to fire the manager along with Todd. And then, Todd's boss put a hand to his chest. He looked uncomfortable. Sweaty. Todd grinned at the idea of his asshole boss having a heart attack because of him. The boss pitched forward, vomited, and then fell to his side.

"Todd."

Todd gasped out of his imagination. "Huh? What?"

"Tell me what you saw."

Todd grinned. "Not behind the door, if that's what you were hoping for."

"Tell me what you saw."

"I was thinking about how my boss would react to me not showing up today. He's kind of a loose cannon. I pictured him shouting and having a heart attack."

"I see."

Silence followed. "Any more questions?"

More silence.

He was about to put his head back down when, "Mr. Richard, how would you like a new job?"

"What are you talking about?"

"I'd like to hire you."

"For *what?*" Todd asked. "I'm an environmental engineer pushing paper for a company that has nothing to do with the environment or engineering. I don't have a lot of hirable skills."

"That's not accurate," the voice said. "Not remotely." The voice snickered like he had made a joke. If he did, Todd didn't get it.

"Can you please just be straightforward with me?" Todd asked, losing patience.

"I suppose you deserve that much," the voice said. "I believe you have certain abilities that make you useful to my organization and you might very well be the one person that can help us achieve our goals."

"What organization? What goals?"

"Not important," the voice said. "What *is* important is that your boss just died from a heart attack, exactly as you described, in Rhode Island, more than two thousand miles away."

"What the fuck? Are you serious?"

"Always," the voice said. "Mr. Richard, I'm afraid I need an answer now. No more questions. You will be compensated very well.

All will be revealed after we've reached an agreement. Your answer?"

Todd didn't hesitate. "Yes. Obviously, yes."

The door opened. The two suits entered. One of them approached the table and slapped down a thirty-page document.

"This is an employment and non-disclosure agreement. You can read it if you like, but you *will* be signing it. And the sooner you do, the sooner you get your answers."

The man beside him pulled a retractable pen from his pocket, clicked it open, and held it out.

Todd stared at the pen for a moment. Then he took it, turned to the last page of the document, and signed his name.

"Very good, Mr. Richard," the voice said. "Welcome to the Parallax Initiative. You won't be disappointed."

1

This is stupid."

"Silas, *you're* stupid," my sister, Sara, replies. She's on the phone, thousands of miles away in Mechanic Falls, Maine, where we're both from. Small town. When we were young, the place to be was Cumby's, aka Cumberland Farms. And now? Still Cumby's.

"Your face is stupid," I say.

"My face has seven hundred thousand followers on Insta," she says.

"I'm not sure that's because of your face," I say. She doesn't argue the point because she knows it's true. Her profile started growing when her fashion sense changed from jeans and flannel to tights and anything that reveals 'the girls.' Mom and Dad hate it, but she's making bank. From ads. From sponsors.

Easy money. Hell, if I got the good looks genes she did, I might do the same. But not me. My shaggy, unkempt head and faceful of brown hair doesn't turn many heads. I've got the body of an athlete, because I played soccer through high school and college, but my scruff is a sexy-time roadblock. Intentionally. I'm not interested in whatever the female version of a TLC 'scrub' is called. Booties get lumpy. Boobs eventually sag. But brains? Brains are forever.

Unless you get Dementia . . . or Alzheimer's . . . or just really old, I guess. But by then, who cares?

"Look," she says. "Do you want to make friends or not?"

I lean around my car's steering wheel and turn down the air conditioning. I'm not used to the Arizona temperature shift between day and night. Here in Tusayan, a small town just south of the Grand Canyon, it was ninety degrees today. Tonight, it's fifty-five. A thirty-five degree temperature change in just a few hours. This place makes no sense. "Honestly, I don't know. Don't have a great track record in the friend department."

"Oh, boo hoo. So sad, Silas. The mistake you made in your youth was being friends exclusively with jocks. I get that you were part of that world, but you and I both know your IQ doesn't really jibe with the 'yah brah, let's score some tail' crowd. Friends with brains, remember? That's the plan. And that's why you are going to the Gandalf Club."

I know she's messing with me, but I can't stop myself from correcting her. "Ganzfeld Collective."

"Whatever," she says, "they sound like your brand of smart and weird as shit."

"Yeah," I say, looking at the flyer I found, taped to a light pole, outside the hotel I'm working at for the next few months. Tusayan is a resort town right next to the only airport around. Lots of people in and out, staying here for a week max because the town is just seven miles from the Grand Canyon Village. Not a lot of opportunities to make actual friends. But there are technically five hundred and fifty official residents here. Come November, half of them will disappear for the winter, but some people stick around for the whole year. I'll be one of them this year. Next year? I doubt it.

The flyer has a photo of three guys in the middle. They're not wearing *Ghostbusters* uniforms, but the pose and slogan—'We're ready to believe you!'—are clear callbacks. The guys look youngish. Around my age. Early twenties. Two of them are black. Look like brothers, and hopefully that's not me being racist. The third guy is whiter and scruffier than me. Kind of scrawny, too. The flyer is an invitation to their 'collective,' which meets on Wednesday nights, inside what looks like a double-wide mobile home.

Hard to say from where I'm sitting, parked in my car, across from the house. All the homes here appear to be trailers. Some are the mobile sort. Others are here to stay.

The flyer didn't provide a lot of information aside from a list of keywords.

Astral Perception.

Telepathy.

Clairvoyance.

Remote viewing.

Telekinesis.

I'm not really into mind powers or alien conspiracy theories, but this is the closest thing to a science-minded group of people I'm going to find in a resort town full of folks working in the hospitality industry.

That's an asshole thing to think. I'm currently *in* the hospitality industry. I clean dishes. Sometimes toilets. I'm not exactly living the life of an intellectual.

"Silas!" Sara shouts, like she's said my name a few times already. "You're zoning out again."

I blink out of my thoughts. "Sorry. Nervous, I guess."

"It's hard for grown, mature men to make friends," she says, sincere until she smiles. "So, you shouldn't have any trouble. If they're too weird, just bail. Send me a text and I'll call you. You can pretend it's work calling."

"A plate-washing emergency," I say.

"Just don't tell them what you do."

I sigh and look at the house. The yard is the same as everything else in this part of the world—dirt. It's a nice reddish-brown during the day, but a nightmare when it's windy. There's a lone ponderosa pine beside the home. Tusayan is technically situated in a forest, but the pines, junipers, and piñon pines are so sparse, no one in all New England would look at this parcel of land and think it was forested.

I glance at the car's clock. I'm ten minutes late. Haven't seen any other cars coming or going. "Okay, I got this."

"It's a nerd club," Sara says. "Not a sorority. They'll just be glad you're there."

I smile. “Thanks, little sis.”

“Any time, old man.”

Before I can say goodbye, she goes all movie-phone on me and hangs up. I’m more of a ‘Later. Seeya. Okay, bye. Yup. Bye,’ kind of guy. I open the car door to the cool night air. Grab my NASA sweatshirt, step out into the street, and put the hoodie on. Wrapped in geek comfort, I close the car door and head for the house.

I debate whether to do this until I reach the door.

Lift my fist to knock.

Put it down.

Lift it again.

The door opens before I get a chance to knock.

On the other side of it is the younger of the two black men from the poster. He’s wearing cargo shorts and a retro *Thundarr the Barbarian* T-shirt. What stands out most is his big toothy smile. “Hi,” he says. “Hello. Are you here for the Ganzfeld Collective?”

“Is there any other reason to be here right now?”

“Uh, yes. Yes, there is. We ordered pizza. Pepperoni for me. I always get pepperoni. Do you like pepperoni?”

“Love it,” I say, squinting at the man, trying to figure him out. His positivity is almost overwhelming. His enthusiastic speech hits as forced, but it feels genuine after it sinks in. He’s either pretending to be excited or is working really hard at not being too excited.

Pretty sure it’s the latter.

“That’s great. That’s great that you love pepperoni. What’s your name?”

“Silas,” I say, holding out my hand. “Silas Keene.”

“Silas Keene. I’m glad you’re here, Silas Keene.” He shakes my hand vigorously.

“Just ‘Silas’ is fine,” I say. “What’s your name?”

“Chuck Jones,” he says. “Hey, Silas Ke—just Silas—do you have a special ability?”

“Don’t think so,” I say.

"Oh, that's too bad. That's too bad, Silas. But maybe you just don't know about it, right? That would be good, Silas. If you didn't know about it, but we could help you find out about it."

"How would you do that?" I ask.

He opens his mouth and takes a deep breath. A loud voice saves me from what I think would have been a long-winded, repetitive spiel about mental abilities. "Chuck! What you doing, man?"

"Hey, Darius. I'm talking to Silas Keene. Just Silas."

"Silas?" the voice says, and then the man it belongs to pokes his head around the wall just beyond Chuck. He blinks in surprise when he sees me. "You're here for the . . ."

He looks doubtful, like I've come to the wrong place. But I definitely haven't, because this guy is the older black man from the flyer.

"Ganzfeld Collective," I say with a nod. "Yeah."

"Hey Silas," Chuck says. "Do you know why it's called the 'Ganzfeld Collective,' Silas?"

I looked it up, so I actually know the answer to this question. "Ganzfeld is German for 'entire field.' In parapsychology—what you all are interested in—the Ganzfeld experiment is a method for testing extrasensory perceptions like telepathy and remote viewing."

Chuck's mouth hangs open when I finish. "Yes. Silas, yes. That's exactly right, Silas." He turns to Darius. "Did you hear that, Darius? He knew the answer. Josh said no one would know, but Silas knew—" He looks back to me. "—didn't you, Silas?"

I slow-nod. This all feels very surreal and nothing like I'd imagined while sitting in the car.

"Come on in, man," Darius says, motioning for me to enter, despite Chuck still standing in the way. "Chuck, let him in."

"Okay, Darius, I'll let Silas in. Hey Silas, are you excited to be tested?"

"Huh?"

"The Ganzfeld test, Silas. Everyone who joins has to take the test. To find out if you have extrasensory abilities. I don't.

Josh doesn't. Darius hasn't taken the test. I told him that's not fair—Didn't I, Darius?—but he won't take it."

"Because I'm an adult," he says. "And Silas doesn't need to take it, either."

Chuck's face twists up in what looks like fear, but it's hard to read. His excitement over the idea of someone coming—I think I'm the first—and taking the test got his hopes right up to the top, really fast. The idea of me *not* taking the test looks like it might break him.

Good thing I'm a nice guy. "I'll consider it."

He heaves a sigh. "That's good, Silas. That's good. You know why? Because you might have an ability and never know. And don't worry, Silas. It doesn't hurt. Mmm. Umm. Except for the shocks. Those hurt a little bit. Josh says they hurt a little bit. They made me cry, Silas. I didn't like it. Not at all."

He steps to the side, and waits for me to enter, holding his massive smile while I get past my growing apprehension and step over the threshold.

2

The next ten minutes are a wordy tour of the double-wide, including things I really don't need to know, like who sleeps where, whose room has the bikini babe posters (Josh), whose room has no posters (Darius), and whose room is plastered with posters from *The X-files*, *The OA*, *Akira*, *Firestarter,* and *Stranger Things*. I could have guessed the last one was Chuck's room without being told.

The tour ends in the kitchen, where Darius, and who I assume is Josh, wait.

"Hey," Josh says, like he's known me his whole life. In person, he's even scruffier and scrawnier than he looked in the flyer.

The kitchen is well stocked with a lot of familiar items. Bottles of water, small cans of soda, bagged snacks. It's a smorgasbord of resort snack items. I smile at the haul and say, "Someone works at the BWPG."

That's short for the Best Western Premier Grand Canyon Squire Inn. It's a mouthful and the closest thing to a full-fledged resort in town. Has a full bar, bowling alley, and an arcade. They cater to families and large groups, hence the large variety of snack foods. It's not the nicest place in town. That honor goes to The Grand Hotel at the Grand Canyon. High-end Western lodge vibes. The enormous lobby has a stone fireplace. It's also where I work.

"Naw, man," Josh says. "Better than that. We're in the food and beverage delivery business, servicing all the hotels." He sweeps his hand out over the snack foods and drinks laid out on the counter. "This is . . . a tax."

"You don't think someone is going to notice?" I ask.

"Pff. You work at a hotel. If a pallet came in with a box missing, would you know? Would you even think to look at the packing slip, or notice it was missing? We're not the only ones skimming snacks, BTW. If you don't have a hoard at your place, you're one of the few." He squints at me. "You're not a narc, right?"

I smile. "Not at all. Just jealous. The only food I can take while washing dishes is the pre-chewed variety."

"Gross," Chuck says, "Silas, that is gross. You don't do that, Silas? Right?"

"Not even if I was starving," I say.

"Good. That's good, Silas."

"You going to introduce yourself?" Darius asks Josh.

Josh rolls his eyes. "Josh Conaway." I open my mouth to respond. "I know who you are."

"You do?" I ask.

"*Josh . . .*" Darius's tone is a warning.

It doesn't work. "I did a background check during your tour. Good news: you're clean. No criminal record. No record of government employment. A little sporty for my taste, but I won't hold that against you unless you start talking about all the goals you scored and times you got MVP trophies."

I know I should feel offended, aghast, and violated, but I'm really just impressed. "And what about you?" I ask. "Seems a little unfair that I don't—"

He picks up three folders from the counter and hands them to me. "Dossiers on each of us. Not a lot in them because we're basically all goody-two-shoes."

"Except for the snack tax, Josh," Chuck says. "That's against the law. Josh, that's stealing."

"You don't like it," Josh says, "feel free to stop eating the chips."

Chuck looks at the nearby bags of Ruffles. "But I like the chips, Josh."

Josh gives a thumbs up. "Then we're copacetic."

"Copacetic. That's a funny word, Josh. Josh, I don't know what that means."

"Don't sweat it, little bro." Darius pats Chuck's shoulder. "He doesn't know what it means, either."

"Ha. Ha." Josh is about to make some kind of comeback when there's a knock on the door. Chuck and Josh duck a little, hiding behind the kitchen's island and peeking over the top.

Darius rolls his eyes. "It's the pizza."

"You don't know that," Josh says.

"What if it's *them*, Darius?" Chuck asks.

"Who, exactly, are we worried about?" I ask.

"The SUV people," Chuck says. "They're watching us, Silas."

Darius shakes his head. "Someone with a black Chevy Suburban has been parking in the street. These two struggle with the idea that the driver might be visiting a neighbor."

"They've parked across the street, every Wednesday night, for the past three weeks," Josh says. "Windows are tinted, and they're parked directly across from the house so we can't see the license plate without going outside and exposing ourselves."

"Could be a regular hookup," I say.

"A what?" Chuck asks.

"Like a friends-with-benefits kind of situation. People schedule that stuff. Might just be someone getting lucky every Wednesday."

"Huh," Josh says, thinks on it for a moment, and then scoffs. "People don't do that."

"You'd do it if you could find a willing partner," Darius says.

"Yeah, but that doesn't mean it's a normal thing that people do. Just . . . give me a second to make sure the perimeter is secure." Josh rolls across the floor, scrambles back to his feet, and then makes for the room with the bikini posters. He's gone for thirty seconds before casually returning. "It's the pizza."

He heads for the front door, opens it, and receives the pizza. Before closing the door, he leans out and scans the street in both directions. Then he's back with three large pizzas, which he places on the island. He turns to me. "That little Hyundai yours?"

"What, you didn't see my lease in the background check?"

Darius bursts out laughing. Chuck does, too, but he has a hand over his mouth and isn't making a sound. Josh raises his eyebrows and waits.

"Yes, it's mine. No tinted windows, and I'm sure you can see the Maine license plate from here."

His paranoia is over the top, but amusing.

"Think fast," Darius says, holding a stack of paper plates in his hand. He whips them out like shuriken. The first curves toward Josh, who tries to catch it, but misses. The second biffs Chuck in the forehead. The third arcs toward me. I casually reach out and pluck it from the air.

"Wow, Silas! You caught it!" Chuck claps like a performance of Hamilton has just finished.

"He got lucky," Josh grumbles, picking his plate up off the floor.

Darius throws a second plate at me, and it's really not that hard to catch it. I've played ultimate frisbee. This is easier.

"Whoa!" Chuck says. "I don't think you're right, Josh. You're right a lot of the time, but not this time. He caught two plates, Josh. Two."

"It's not a pattern until—"

Darius does me a solid and throws a third plate. I guess it's coming this time, so I'm ready for it. I spin around and catch it behind my back.

Chuck thrusts his arms over his head and jumps up and down. "Yes! Yes! Yes!"

Darius and I are laughing, and it feels good. Josh gives me a squinty glare. "Interesting." He snaps his finger. "Pizza now, then we're testing this guy."

"It's just normal reflexes," I say.

"Bullshit," he says.

I toss a plate at Darius without looking. He catches it.

Chuck's jaw drops.

"Since when can *you* catch a plate?" Josh asks, and I realize that I might have just blown Darius's cover as a super nerd. I know a fellow former athlete when I see one. His posture is straight. His shoulders are thick. Slender, despite the mounds of snack food and pizza. Probably works out before Josh wakes up.

"Got lucky," Darius says, opening a box and dragging a cheesy slice onto his plate.

"Uh-huh," Josh says, not buying it. He moves the cheese pizza to the side, opens the second to reveal a pepperoni, which he also moves. He opens the last to reveal what I assume is some kind of meat lover's abomination. Can't even see the cheese. It's always the skinniest guy who has the worst diet. He drags three slices onto his plate, which is two slices too many. He takes the plate and retreats to the living room couch like a jaguar protecting his kill.

The next ten minutes pass in silence. It's the pizza-bro code. No talking. Just consumption. Four, maybe five bites for the slice, a swig of soda, followed by the crust, another swig, and the pattern repeats.

Chuck and I tag team the pepperoni into oblivion. Darius gives up on the cheese pizza after three slices. Josh devours his entire pizza and follows it with a bag of chips.

When the bag of chips disappears, Josh sucks on all ten of his fingers and turns to Chuck. "C'mon, let's get ready."

The pair disappear into Chuck's bedroom.

"Should I be worried?" I ask Darius.

He shakes his head. "It's harmless."

"What about the shock?"

He smiles and waves my concern away. "That's only if you get the answer wrong."

"Uh . . . huh." I glance toward Chuck's bedroom door and then back to Darius.

"You're wondering what's up with Chuck?"

"Sure *you're* not a mind reader?" I ask.

"Chuck was in an accident three years ago. Was riding his bike when a drunk driver hit him. He was in a coma for a month. When he woke up, he was like he is now. Still smart. Still funny.

But his speech had changed, and—" He smiles. "—he's always happy. Even when he shouldn't be. But he's also too quick to trust, naïve, and easy to take advantage of. Before the accident . . . he was a lot like you."

Oof. I wasn't sure what Chuck had going on, but I imagine it hasn't been easy on him, or Darius. He's a good brother.

"What about Josh?" I ask.

Darius chuckles. "He was born like that. You'll get used to him. Assuming you're sticking around."

I smile. "Yeah . . . yeah, I think I am."

Look at me now, Sis. Three new friends!

"Okay!" Josh shouts triumphantly, entering the living room with his hands full of equipment I don't recognize, some kind of headgear, and twisting coils of wires. "It's Ganzfeld time!"

3

You really don't have to do this," Darius says, looking down at me.

I'm laid back in a comfortable recliner, waiting for the test to start. Not sure why I need to be so comfortable to answer questions, but I'm just going with the flow. Chuck's excitement is contagious.

"Not a big deal," I say. "Feel like a kid again."

Darius smiles. "It does feel like that, doesn't it? An initiation to the inner circle of friendship." He shakes his head and chuckles. "Chuck and I met Josh when I was seven. Chuck was six, but we were already little tribal assholes. Made him jump in the ocean with no clothes on. He stayed in the cold water for five minutes, until we started shouting 'shark.' We've been friends since."

"My childhood friends made me climb a cliff," I say. "In hindsight it was insane. Could have died. But we're still friends, too. Don't live together, though."

"Three Musketeers," he says. "That's us."

"And you're not from Arizona," I say.

"Hell, no. Virginia."

"Fellow East Coasters." I hold up a fist, and Darius bumps it. "You miss the ocean?"

"Every damn day," he says. "I'm not a fan of this dry-ass landscape, but living near the Grand Canyon sounded fun, and I'll be honest, the constant flow of young, adventurous women that come through here is a nice perk. We'll be gone next year. Probably to the West Coast for a year. We're working our way around the country while we're young."

"Solid plan," I say.

"Why are you here?" Darius asks.

"Honestly, I'm doing the same thing. On my own."

"Running from a dark past," he jokes.

I smile. "From an ex."

"Uh-oh. That bad?"

"Only my sister and parents know where I am. New phone. New email. The ex turned out to be . . . possessive."

"Oh shit." He's getting a kick out of my story, and why not. Crazy women are horrible when you're with them, but I can laugh at the whole situation from a safe distance.

"She scratched another girl's face for looking at me. Jumped out of the car and tackled her on the sidewalk. Scratched her up like a cat."

"Oh *shit!*" He's laughing now.

"Yeah. The girl was twelve."

"Oh," he says, serious now. "Shit."

"Yeah."

Chuck clears his throat. He and Josh have been sitting here this whole time, waiting and listening. Chuck's patience is gone. "Um, Silas, we're ready to begin the test now. Is that okay with you?"

I adjust in the recliner, getting comfortable. "I'm good to go."

"That's good, Silas. I'm glad it's okay with you. Do you, do you consent to the testing process, Silas?"

I glance at Darius. He scrunches up his face and nods.

"Sure," I say.

"That's good, Silas. Thank you, Silas." Chuck stands over me and holds up two white objects. "This is a ping-pong ball. It's cut in half. I need to put them over your eyes."

"I thought you were just going to be asking me questions," I say.

Josh stands beside Chuck, positioning an unlit light on a pole. The bulb is red. "The Ganzfeld test isn't a fixed set of questions. It's a procedure, not a quiz." He turns on the red light and then tilts his head up toward Darius. "Lights."

Darius does as instructed and turns off the lights, first in the living room, and then in the dining room. All that remains is the red light, casting a hellish glow.

I nervous-laugh at the strangeness of it all. "If one of you puts on a goat head mask, I'm out."

Chuck is aghast at the thought.

Josh shoots me a skeptical glance, as though trying to deduce whether or not I've had real world experience with the kind of people that would wear a goat's head.

"Silas, we don't use a goat's head," Chuck says after recovering from his shock. "That doesn't sound good, Silas. We would never do that."

"That's good," I say. "I'm glad."

"I'm glad that you're glad, Silas. Are you ready to start now?"

"Let's do it," I say, and close my eyes.

"Okay, Silas," Chuck says, his voice closer now. "I'm putting the ping-pong halves over your eyes now." He's gentle about it, and whispers, "Yes!" when he's successfully completed the task.

"In a minute I'm going to put headphones over your ears," Josh says. "They're going to be playing pink noise."

"Pink noise?" I ask. "Is that like the *Barbie* movie soundtrack?"

"Funny," he says, without a trace of humor. "You know what white noise is?"

"Sure," I say. "A fan makes white noise."

"Right," he says. "Pink noise is similar to white noise, but the signal contains an equal amount of energy per octave. Low frequencies are louder. Higher frequencies are softer. It's a deeper, more balanced sound. More like steady rainfall. Wind through trees. A distant waterfall."

"So . . . relaxing," I say.

"Exactly," he says. "The point of all of this is to put you in a relaxed, low sensory environment. Which is why no one is going to fart."

"That only happened once, Josh," Chuck says. "I won't do it again, even though we just ate a lot of pizza. That makes all of us gassy. Does pizza make you gassy, Silas?"

I smile and the ping-pong ball halves over my eyes shift a little. "I tolerate lactose just fine, thank you."

"That's good, Silas. Silas, I won't fart in your low sensory environment."

"I appreciate that."

Josh clears his throat and continues. "Darius is going to be the 'sender.' He's going to go into his room and look at a picture or video. Silas, you're the receiver. Just relax and open your mind to what's being sent."

"So, am I supposed to see what he's seeing, or—"

"We can't tell you what you're supposed to see. Odds are you'll see nothing at all. All you need to do is speak freely. Free-associate. Tell us everything you see and feel, even if you think you're imagining it. And when I say everything, I mean *everything*. Don't filter it. When we're done, we'll show you four images, and you can choose what best matches what you received."

I raise a hand. "What's free-associating?"

"Say whatever comes to mind. No judgment. No analysis. If you think about a cheeseburger, a chinchilla, a crying baby, whatever, just say it all out loud. Don't edit yourself. Don't try to be right, because there is no right."

"Okay, I get it."

"Hey, Darius," Chuck calls out. "Are you ready, Darius?"

From behind a closed door, Darius shouts, "Good to go."

"That's good, Darius. Thank you, Darius."

"Here come the headphones," Josh says, and he places them over my head. The pink noise is strangely and quickly relaxing.

"Let your mind wander," Josh says, his voice softer and muffled, but still clear enough to understand. "Focus on the first thing that comes to your mind. Keep talking, even if it doesn't make sense."

I'm physically comfortable, but speaking my raw thoughts to strangers is a foreign experience. I decide to get started with a memory. The moment the pandora's box of my childhood is opened, I start speaking. "Old Orchard Beach. Ocean Park. Warm sand. Big waves." I smile. "It's a good day. I . . . can smell sunscreen. Coconut scented. I'm under the water, swimming for the bottom. Goggles on my face. There's a sand dollar. Size of my hand. I pick it up. Want to take it home. But I feel bad for it. There used to be more of them. Chocolate ice cream. Shuffleboard. Flip flops.

"More sand. Red sand. An orange rock face. It's warm. Inviting. There's water. I can hear it.

"A river. Lazy river. There's a crayfish in it. Swims away from me, but now I'm afraid it's going to pinch my toes. Rope swing. The feeling of gravity pulling me down.

"I'm falling."

A shiver runs through my body.

"Keep going, Silas." Chuck's voice is soft. "You're doing great, Silas."

I feel a jolt but keep speaking. "I land in bed. My room. Comic book posters on the walls. Drawings. I'm embarrassed. Afraid people will see my room. Will know I'm not cool. My black and white TV. I got it from the trash. A dumpster. It's green. There's a raccoon inside. Smells like trash. Rotting food. Also pine.

"In the woods. Searching for treasure. The coins are chocolate.

"Like Easter chocolate, but worse. Sara complains about it. She throws the coins in the air. She's . . . jumping up and down. Back on the beach. There are rocks. Jagged. The kind with tide pools. The color yellow. Three triangles. Two with the pointy side up, one with it down. Smiling. Happy. Talking.

"I don't smell the beach. I can't hear the waves.

"I feel . . ." I sneer. "This is wrong."

"Whatever it is," Josh says. "Just spit it out."

I try to shake the feeling, but it's just increasing. I flail out of the experience, pulling the headset off my head while the ping pong ball halves fall off. "What the fuck?"

Josh and Chuck, lit in stark red light, stare at me with wide eyes.

"What did you see?" Josh asks, whispering. "What did you feel?"

"Hey," Darius calls out from his room. "We done?" He steps into the living room, sees my face and says, "Whoa. What happened to you?"

Josh crosses his arms. "What were you looking at? Which of the four pictures?"

"What four pictures?" I ask, happy to forget what I just experienced.

"A skyscraper, a jungle, an elephant, and Jupiter," Darius says.

Chuck throws his hands in the air. "You're not supposed to tell him!"

Darius is lying. I'm no CIA operative, but it feels obvious to me. "You weren't looking at one of the photos."

The way his head snaps to me confirms it.

"What were you looking at, Darius?" Chuck asks. "Huh? This test is important. We can't—"

"Hold on, hold on." Josh holds out his hand, silencing everyone. He turns to me. "*You* tell us what he was looking at."

I replay the last bit of what flitted through my mind. Yellow triangles. The pieces slowly coagulate until I recognize what I'm seeing as a five second video clip, posted to Instagram last summer. Caused an epic argument with my parents. I look at Darius, kind of seriously, and ask, "Were you just looking at *my sister?*"

4

What?" Darius says. "No. I don't even know your sister."

I notice he didn't say he didn't know I had a sister.

Chuck crosses his arms. "What *were* you looking at, Darius?"

Darius glances to the right. "It was . . . uh . . ."

Chuck stomps a foot. "Darius!"

"Fine," Darius says. "I was looking at the 1989 *Sports Illustrated Swimsuit Issue*. It was the 25th anniversary. Kathy Ireland on the cover."

"Mm," Josh says, not sounding convinced. He turns to me. "Can you show us an image of what you thought it was?"

"It's a video," I say, "and don't ask me to play it. Not going to happen."

"Agreed," Josh says, like we've just finished a parlay to avoid a battle.

I take out my phone, open Instagram, head to my sister's profile and start scrolling back. That video was Sara's first viral, and it got her hooked. There have been hundreds of posts since, all in various states of 'tasteful' undress. I'm not comfortable scrolling through all this shit, but at least they're not trying to look over my shoulder.

When I find the video, I tap it to open and immediately pause it. The image frozen on screen is my sister sitting on rocks at the beach, dressed in a yellow bikini. In the ten seconds to follow, she jumps up and pretends to slow motion jog at the camera.

I feel embarrassed for her just thinking about it. But she's a modern woman and she's making money from this silliness. A hell of a lot more money than I am scrubbing dishes.

I turn the phone around and two sets of eyes widen in surprise. Darius doesn't react much. Could be because he's just been looking at Kathy Ireland. Could be because he's seen this already and happens to have an encyclopedic knowledge of swimsuit issues.

"Whoa, Silas," Chuck says. "That's your sister, Silas? She sure is beautiful. I would like to date someone like that, Silas. I used to be a stud, you know. Now girls mostly laugh at me. Do girls laugh at you, Silas?"

My heart goes out to the guy. Like his brother, Chuck's a good looking guy, but his mannerisms and speech make him stand out in a way that can make a lot of people feel uncomfortable.

"Pretty sure girls laugh at all of us when we can't hear them," I say.

"Bros before hoes, Silas. That's why they say that, right? Bros before hoes."

That gets everyone laughing.

"Yeah, man," I say. "Bros before hoes."

"That's good, Silas." He lifts his hand to dab me up. I oblige and we clap our hands together. Our cupped palms clap loudly. It's the perfect dab and gets an "Oooh!" out of everyone.

Chuck's laugh is goofy and infectious.

I glance at Josh. He's stopped laughing. Is looking at his phone, eyes wide.

Darius spots him, too. "What's up?"

Josh turns his phone around, showing us an image of the 1989 Swimsuit Issue cover. Sitting on a rock by the ocean is Kathy Ireland—I'm assuming—wearing a yellow bikini. It's not exactly the same image, but the similarities are impossible to ignore.

"Do you know what this means?" Josh says.

Chuck raises his hands. "I think it means that Silas's sister should be on the cover of a magazine."

I smile. She'd love that compliment.

"No, dumbass," Josh says. "It means it *worked*." He points at me. "*He* worked! He saw what Darius was looking at. Transplanted a more familiar image, but he saw a woman in a yellow bikini and Darius was looking at a woman in a yellow bikini!"

"I'm sorry," I say. "What does this mean?"

"It means you can remote view," Josh says, voice a whisper. He's stunned. Blindsided by the revelation.

I'm far less impressed with myself. "It's a coincidence."

Josh nods. "Maybe. We'll need to do more tests—" He shoots a look at Darius. "—and *everyone* needs to take it seriously."

Darius raises his hands. "Okay, okay. How was I supposed to know someone was actually going to have powers?"

"I don't have powers," I say.

"Right," Josh says, surprising me, but then adds, "We call them abilities."

I sigh. "Okay, what tests do we need to do to convince you I don't have abilities?"

"The same tests to convince me you do." He smiles. "We'll repeat this test and take it seriously, then—can we call your sister and have her look at something?"

"As long as no one hits on her," I say. She knows I'm here, what the group is, and would be thrilled to hear I'd been accepted by a group of weirdos. "I'm serious. You need to swear an oath."

Chuck raises his hand. "I swear on . . . do we have a Bible?"

Headshakes all around. "I swear on the life of my dear brother, Darius—"

"Hey!" Darius says.

"—that I will not seduce Silas's sister."

"Good enough," I say. "But why my sister?"

"We need to test your range," Josh says. "Seeing into the next room is one thing. Seeing something on the other side of the country . . . that's some CIA level shit."

"CIA?" I ask.

"Sure," Josh says. "Do you not know . . ." He sighs. "Buckle up. It's time for an education."

He puts his hands behind his back—easy for a guy so skinny—and then paces back and forth in the small living room. "I know it sounds bonkers, but the CIA has been balls-deep in remote viewing longer than any of us have been alive. I'm talking millions of dollars funneled into a secret spy program. In the 1970s, they got spooked after receiving intelligence about the Soviets experimenting with 'psychotronic warfare.' Psychic stuff. It was the Cold War, and we couldn't have the Ruskies get a leg up—even if it sounded crazy—so the CIA dove headlong into psychic research.

"They recruited military personnel, civilians, and more than a few legit weirdos. Like crystal-hugging hippies. Their testing was crude by comparison. They gave subjects a set of coordinates—like the average person can make any sense of the numbers—and asked, 'What do you see?' Most people washed out very quickly.

"But there were some who excelled. They could look at a set of coordinates and see what was there. They'd say something like, 'I see a dome-shaped structure. Metal. Satellite dish. I smell diesel.' The CIA would later get visual intel of the target area, and every detail was right, down to the presence of spilled fuel. It was groundbreaking research, man.

"They called it Gondola Wish, Grill Flame, Center Lane, Stargate. Like the movie, yeah, but nothing to do with traveling to other worlds. They couldn't decide on a codename, but they all agreed on one thing—the human mind could be weaponized.

"It didn't always work. People got stuff wrong. But it worked enough that it made people uncomfortable. One guy described the inside of a top-secret Soviet base so accurately that they assumed the guy had cheated, that he was just reciting leaked information. Nope. He was just a guy in a basement room with a notebook, able to see inside enemy bases. Then again, there were people who described aliens wearing masks, leading people into lakes. Total hogwash. So, even though some people got things right, the intel could never be trusted. Couldn't risk people's lives on it. Couldn't act on it.

"By the mid-nineties, the CIA flipped psychic abilities the double bird and walked into the horizon. So they say. I think it's bullshit. They just went deeper and darker. No way they'd walk away from the potential power they'd witnessed. They just wanted the world to think they did. This is my theory, BTW. Private contractors. Deep black budgets. Need-to-know buried deeper than the government's collection of 1980s cheese. For real. Millions of pounds of faux-cheese product are buried in limestone caves beneath Springfield, Missouri.

"Anywho, these programs exist today. Of that, I have no doubt. And that is why none of us—not one of us—is going to mention this to anyone outside this room—"

"Except for my sister," I say.

Josh snaps his fingers. "Except for her. And even then, only over a secure chat. You have Signal?"

The expression on my face communicates that I have no idea what he's talking about.

"We can get it," he says. "If any of you posts about this online, I'm gone."

Darius scrunches up his face. "Because . . ."

Chuck looks suddenly serious. Turns around and heads for the door.

"Because the time it will take for men in suits to come knocking will be measured in hours. And when they get here, you don't want to be. Feel me? They will disappear you and put you to work." Josh turns to me. "You think our testing is extreme?" He shakes his head. "No, thank you."

Chuck is on his tippy toes, looking out the high window on the front door. "Guys . . ."

"Now," Josh says, "we need to—"

"Guys!" Chuck ducks down, back against the door. "Guys, they're back!"

Josh dives over the couch and rolls to the window. He splits the blinds with his fingers and looks outside for just a second. Then he yanks his hand back and ducks beneath the window. "He's right."

"You know, some things are actually coincidences," I say.

"I don't believe in coincidences," Josh says.

"Yeah," I say, heading for the front door. "I don't believe in being a chicken-shit." When I open the door, Chuck gasps.

Josh says, "What the fuck, dude?"

Even Darius sounds concerned. "*No bueno,* man."

I glance back at Darius. "You could have done this weeks ago."

"Right," he says, rolling his eyes. "A black dude approaching a nice car at night in an area where white tourists have money and 911 on speed dial. I don't think so."

Can't fault him for that logic and can't pretend I know what that feels like. So, I drape myself in white privilege and stride toward the black SUV with dark tinted windows. It looks more and more ominous the closer I get, but my pride is on the line now. No backing down.

I stop beside the driver's side window, lift a fist and knock on the glass.

5

I knock on the glass a second time. Nothing happens and I wonder if no one is inside. That's the most likely scenario, after all. The owner of this admittedly *sus* looking vehicle is probably visiting a friend. I look at my reflection in the tinted glass. I really need to shave soon. Looking a little unruly, even for a dishwasher. I turn around expecting to see my three new friends standing in the doorway. Instead, the door is closed.

A sliver of light draws my attention to the large living room window. Three slivers of light, actually, each of them partly blocked by a head. "These guys," I whisper, and turn back to the SUV.

Where my reflection should be is someone else's face, looking at me through a pair of glasses. "Hi."

The sudden transformation of my face into someone else's hits me like an electric jolt. Every muscle in my body spasms, sphincter to face. I flail a step back. In that moment of involuntary twitching, I realize that I've made a fool of myself, and I attempt to lessen my embarrassment by saying something humorous. "Holy flying spaghetti monster!"

"Praise be his name," the woman inside the SUV says, looking at me with stoic eyes. She's not smiling. Her eyebrows are raised slightly. But her eyes . . . So dark brown they're nearly black. I feel like I can see good humor in them. Then I'm past the event horizon of her gaze, and mesmerized by the darkness that reaches out, takes hold of my heart, and squeezes.

"Mm," she says, freeing me from her Medusa eyes. "We'll see."

"We'll see what?" I ask, seeing the rest of her for the first time. She's East Asian, but I'm not great at seeing the subtle differences between Japanese, Chinese, Vietnamese, and the rest. I've learned that some people take offense if you guess wrong, so I don't even attempt it, even in my thoughts.

Her face is both adorable and serious. Her nose is flat. Her lips full. Straight black hair cut in a chin-length bob frames her round face. She's polished. Maintains a neutral expression. I can feel her observant eyes flicking over me, evaluating every part of me . . . while I do the same to her.

"I'm sorry," I say, attempting to collect myself. This woman isn't what I'd have considered my type, but something about her has me feeling flustered.

"Who are you?" she asks.

"Silas—*hey*, who are *you?*"

"'Silas Hey' is a weird name." There's not even a hint of a smile on her face, but the tone of her voice says she's mocking me.

"Ha, ha, ha. You're hysterical." I'm layering sarcasm like lasagna, but I'm not lying. Her deadpan, straightforward humor combined with a face that is both intimidating and pinchable cute, is a unique juxtaposition. "C'mon, man, these guys in there think you're a government spy."

The slightest grin suggests she thinks that is uproariously funny.

"Can you blame them?" I ask. "You park out here every week, in a black SUV with tinted windows."

"I'm not fond of being seen," she says.

"Well, you're seen now," I say, "so what's the deal? Why are you here?"

She thinks on the question for a few seconds, pushes her glasses up, and then sighs. "Probably the same reason you are."

"You have no friends and thought three guys interested in psychic phenomenon might be the smartest and most interesting guys in town, despite the fact that they're putting up actual flyers and live in a double-wide?"

Her smile widens a few millimeters, but the distance feels as broad as the Grand Canyon is long.

"You left out their criminal empire," she says.

I try to show no expression on my face and purposefully glance up and to the left—a sign that I'm telling the truth. "I have no idea what you're talking about."

"Impressive," she says. "But looking to the left as a sign of truth has been debunked. People look all over the place when they're telling the truth and when they're lying, which you just did."

"Prove it," I say.

"You have Cheeto dust on your T-shirt."

My mind flashes back to the bag of Cheetos I snacked on when Josh was telling me about the CIA. Bad move, but Cheetos are hard to resist. When I was done, I wiped my fingers on my shirt once before thinking better of it. I glance down and see four, subtle orange streaks.

She's smart and observant. Feels like I'm having a slap fight with Chuck Norris in his prime. "You have a name, smarty-pants?"

"Ami Sato," she says, and waits for a reaction.

"Silas Keene," I respond and offer my hand to shake.

She takes my hand but doesn't shake it. She just holds it gently while looking up into my eyes. A surge of nervous energy leaps out from hiding and kicks me in the gut. When her thumb gently rubs my hand, it takes a supreme mental effort to not pull back.

I have never met a woman so confident and forward.

Honestly, it's intoxicating.

I stand there, once again turned to stone in her gaze, immune to the effects of time. I'm not sure how long I stay still, but I don't break out of the trance until she lets go of my hand.

"You have potential," she says. "More than you know."

I have no idea what she's talking about but say, "Thanks . . ."

"What are they like?" she asks, tilting her chin up toward the house.

I glance back and spot three sets of eyes between the blinds. "A little weird, but so am I, and no offense, so are you."

"Oh, I'm the weirdest, by far. What else? Are they loons?"

I shake my head. "Conspiracy theorists? Sure. Crazy? Nah. Chuck and Josh are true believers. I think Darius, Chuck's older brother—"

"You don't need to explain who's who," she says. "I've done my research."

"The criminal empire," I say. "Right. Well . . . they're good guys. I'm still getting to know them, but they'd probably be loyal friends. Trustworthy. Earnest. Like, *really* earnest."

"How's the testing going?" she asks. "Any of them have . . . abilities?"

I squint at her. "You sure you're not with the government?"

She digs into her pants pocket, and I notice her clothing for the first time. Tight yellow T-shirt and jeans. Again, she's not exactly supermodel material—maybe five feet tall and no sizable . . . uh, feminine features. But the confidence with which she rocks the tight clothing, combined with her mesmerizing face, has me flustered.

Her hand snaps up. There's a business card between her fingers.

I pluck it free and look it over.

First thing I notice is the familiar red crown logo and long ass name: Best Western Premier Grand Canyon Squire Inn.

Beneath it is her name: Ami Sato.

And then her title: General Manager.

"Holy shit, you run the BWPG?"

The nice vehicle and her knowledge of the snack theft ring suddenly make sense. I replay our conversation and feel confident that I never actually acknowledged that the Cheeto streaks were from stolen snacks. "Why are you *really* here?"

"You're a loyal guy, huh?" she asks. "You just met them tonight, right?"

"Loyal to a fault," I say.

"You know," she says, "if I wanted them arrested, they'd have been locked up months ago."

"*Months* ago?"

"I'm very observant," she says. "Was on to them after the first snack heist. But I'm more interested in their extracurricular activities."

"So, you sit out here every week and what?" I lean to the side and try to look into the SUV's back. "Spy on them? You have some listening equipment or something?"

"Despite being in a position of power in a town that largely exists only to serve the business I run, my degrees, and my phenomenally charming personality—" She says that last bit sarcastically, acknowledging that the truth is the exact opposite of what she's said. "I'm not accustomed to joining clubs, making friends, or talking about a subject that is . . . personal to me. Also, I'm not stupid. None of them have criminal records, but I'm a small woman and they're three men."

"They're harmless," I say.

"Said every neighbor about every serial killer ever."

I smile. "Point taken. Well, I can protect you."

Her eyebrows rise. "I don't know you, either, Silas."

"C'mon," I say. "We have a connection, right?"

One of her eyebrows drops. "A connection, huh?"

I shrug. "Or something."

"That magical word web you weave must catch all the girls, huh?" More sarcasm but it's the kind of positive jab friends make. The connection is real, and she knows it. "Your soft dishwashing hands seal the deal."

"Hey, you—"

"Had the sheriff run your plates for me," she says and nods. "No criminal record. Lots of sports related articles in the local paper. Boring as shit social media accounts that haven't been updated in years. Not helpful, by the way, but I respect the resistance to doom scrolling. The big mystery is why you moved here. Top of your class in college. Could have a solid job, but chose dishwashing in the middle of nowhere, and cancelled your phone plan. Who are you hiding from?"

I'm stunned into silence. I can't decide if I'm impressed by her resourcefulness or offended by the invasion of my privacy. Before I can decide, my mouth opens and I answer honestly. "Crazy ex."

"Figured," she says.

"What's that supposed to mean?" I ask.

"Guys like you are easy targets for crazy chicks. A few months of love bombing and your loyalty will make you put up with anything. She probably started out lovely and then was dancing the Macarena with Schrödinger's cat."

My face scrunches up.

She puts one palm forward like she's doing the dance. "Is she amazing?" She lays out her second palm. "Is she a psycho hose beast?"

I chuckle at the *Wayne's World* reference. "Before I left, both hands were psycho hose beast."

"We're going to have to work on your predictability, Silas," she says, and I feel nervous again, because it suggests we're now, at the very least, pals.

"I'd like that," I say.

"Yeah, you would," she says, and her window rises between us until I'm left looking at the reflection of my goo-goo-eyed face in the glass. I force my expression back to the closest I can get to manly man and then leap back when the door opens. All five feet of Ami slides out of the front seat. She lands on the pavement and slams the door closed behind her. With a key fob tap, the vehicle locks. She looks up at me. "Okay, studmuffin, let's get this over with."

I watch her strut away toward the house where three sets of blinds suddenly close. She lifts a hand and snaps her fingers. I scurry to catch up and, for the first time, I feel happy about moving to this crappy resort town in the middle of nowhere.

6

Ami sits in a chair across from the rest of us, all crammed onto the small couch. There's a coffee table between us, covered in the wrappers of contraband stolen from the hotel she manages. She doesn't mention it. She's too busy looking into our eyes, one at a time.

Introductions were brief when she entered. Just names really. I explained who she was, why she was here, and why she'd been outside the house for the past few weeks. Josh wanted proof she didn't work for the government, but I pointed out that proof could be faked by the government and said we'd just have to trust her. For now.

Then, she took over. Told us where to sit. Told us to think of three things: a color, a word, and an image.

Now we're just sitting and waiting.

I'm last in line and feel the same surge of nervous energy when our eyes meet. She winces slightly and looks a little embarrassed. Then she leans back as though pondering for a moment. "You guys are . . . interesting."

"That a compliment?" Josh asks. "Or are you making fun of us?"

"Compliment," she says, and then with her perfected deadpan, adds, "For three of you." Before Josh can respond she pulls out her phone, turns it on, and taps the screen a few times. She turns the phone around and slides it onto the table between us.

"What's this?" Darius asks, taking the phone.

"NDA," she says. "I plan on having a long and lucrative career. So, everything I talk about here is confidential."

"Would be anyway," Josh says. "We don't narc on our own."

"No offense, but I'm not yet one of your own," she says. "Just hold your thumb against the screen. It will scan your print and work as a signature."

"That's cool," Chuck says. "Hey Ami, you can be one of our own if you want to. I think that would be nice, Ami. Because you can trust us. We're good guys. Even Josh."

He nearly gets a smile out of her, but she holds on to her serious image like a sloth clinging to a tree in a tornado.

"Hey," Josh says, and takes the phone from Chuck. "This is probably full of legalese that your primate mind won't—"

Chuck takes the phone back from Josh. "We don't have all night, Josh. You're a slow reader. It took you six months to read *The Others* and not because it's bad."

Josh rolls his eyes. "Yeah, well, not all of us were blessed with the ability to read like Lieutenant Commander Data."

"That's not nice, Josh," Chuck says, still smiling. "You know why I can. You know why—"

Darius elbows Josh and gives him a wide-eyed, brow-lifted stare.

"Sorry, man," Josh says. "I'm sorry. That was shitty."

"It was shitty. It was." Chuck smiles wider as he scrolls through the long form on the phone. His eyes flick back and forth, but I can't fathom reading that fast, let alone absorbing and understanding it all. "But I forgive you, Josh. I forgive you. Because we're friends. I'm sorry, too, Josh. I shouldn't have said you read slow."

Josh waves him off. "You're just telling the truth."

Chuck shrugs. "I don't know how to lie." He lifts the phone. "This is fine. We just need to not tell anyone what she tells us, and that's our rule anyway." He holds his thumb on the screen and the phone dings. He passes the phone to Josh.

"You're sure?" Josh asks.

Chuck nods. "I'm sure, Josh. It's fine, Josh."

"What happens if we break the NDA?" Josh asks.

"Nothing that will make you happy," Chuck says. "But that's the point. Right, Ami?"

She doesn't answer. Doesn't need to. We all know the purpose of an NDA.

Josh grunts. "Fine." He places his thumb on the screen until the phone dings. He passes it to Darius.

"I know Chuck already signed this, but we've already acknowledged that Chuck isn't really capable of lying. If someone asks him—"

"I can't lie, Darius, but I *can* stay quiet. I'm good at keeping secrets, Darius. That's why you and Josh trust me."

"Yeah, but this is different," Darius says. "There aren't consequences if you talk to people about what we do here, even if it's supposed to be secret."

"It's the same, Darius," Chuck says. "I keep secrets. And you want to know why you can believe me, Ami? Because I can't lie, Ami. And I'm saying I can keep secrets."

"Sound logic," Ami says and raises her eyebrows at Darius.

"Fine." Darius presses the screen with his thumb. It dings and he tosses the phone across the couch to me on the far side. I look Ami in the eyes and press the screen with my thumb. She waits for the chime with a flat expression and when it comes, she holds out her hand. I give her the phone.

She scoots back in her chair, crosses her legs, and then her arms. She looks at each of us and then points at Darius. "Red, shlong, shark."

Darius's eyes widen.

She points at Josh. "Violet, onomatopoeia, Cacodemon."

"Bullshit," Josh says. "Bullshit."

He's stunned. She's right again. But . . .

"What is a Cacodemon?" I ask.

Josh leans around Chuck to look at me. "Have you played *Doom*?"

I nod.

"They're the cycloptic horned floating meatballs," he says.

"That's obscure," I say.

"No shit," he says, looking spooked.

Ami points at Chuck. He smiles wider and rubs his hands together, ready for his turn. "You . . . You are an asshole."

Chuck squeal-laughs and bounces in his seat.

"Glaucous," she says. "Sounds like something an owl would cough up, but it's blueish-green-gray."

"The color of the waxy coating on grapes and plums," Chuck says. "Some bird feathers, too. I also like fuscous, coquelicot, and smaragdine. What's next, Ami? What's next?"

She sighs, closes her eyes and speaks slowly. "Floccinaucinihilipilification. Like I said, asshole."

Chuck claps. "That's a word. Can you even believe that's a word?"

"Don't need to know what it means," Josh says. "Never going to use it. Don't want to hear it again."

"What's my image, Ami?" Chuck asks.

She rolls her eyes again. "Pretty sure this one was a memory. Darius giving Josh a wedgie."

Chuck bursts out laughing. "That was last week!"

Josh throws up his arms and flops back on the couch. "Man! I take back my apology!"

Chuck continues laughing until Ami turns to me and points. He falls quickly silent.

"Orange," she says. "Won't say. If you're lucky."

"What does that mean, Ami?" Chuck asks.

Holy shit. I didn't take this seriously. After thinking of a color, my mind just kind of wandered. I barely remember what I was thinking, but it might have had something to do with Ami's body in a state of undress—the object and image. "Hey, looking into the mind of a twenty-two-year-old man is risky at best."

Darius slaps a hand on his forehead. "You dirty dog!"

Chuck finally understands the implications. "Oooh!" He claps his hands. "Silas and Ami sitting in a tree—"

Ami snaps her fingers and points at Chuck. He clamps his lips together.

"It wasn't a tree," I mumble.

She snaps her fingers and points at me.

"Do you guys know what this means?" Josh asks.

"Yes, yes, I do, Josh." Chuck bounces in his seat. "It means that Silas and Ami are—"

Josh puts a hand over Chuck's mouth. "What? No. It's means that *three* of us have psychic abilities!"

"*Three* of us?" Ami asks. She and I both turn to Josh. The trio hasn't been honest.

Chuck raises a hand. "You see? I *am* good at keeping secrets. Josh, you're not good at keeping secrets."

"So, which of you—"

Ami cuts me off. "It's Chuck."

"Me! It's me!" He breathes heavily, like he's just finished a triathlon. Keeping it to himself was work, but he had me fooled.

"What can you do?" I ask him.

"Chronesthesia," he says.

I scratch my head. "Isn't that when you see music in color?"

"That's Chro*m*esthesia. One letter is different. Chro*n*esthesia means I can see the future, Silas." Chuck flashes the biggest smile I've seen so far. "And the past."

7

I gag, choke, cough a half dozen times, and then manage to get a question out. "I'm sorry, what?"

"It's true, Silas," he says. "I don't lie. I can see different times."

"Bullshit," Ami says.

"Says the lady who can read minds," Josh says. "We didn't question your ability."

"Because I demonstrated it in a tangible way that couldn't be refuted," she says. "You didn't have a choice but to believe me. And I still haven't seen what *you* can do." She points at me. "You guys better not just be fucking around."

"No," Chuck says. "We don't fuck around, Ami. Not with this. That wouldn't be nice, and I'm a nice guy. I'm a nice guy, Ami."

The anger in her eyes dulls to her normal resting bitch face.

"We've been straight with you," Darius says. "No reason for Chuck to lie about it."

Ami crosses her arms. "Okay, then. Explain. How does it work? What do you see?"

"I don't know how to make it happen," Chuck says. "Sometimes it's like a dream. Sometimes it's like I'm there. That doesn't feel good, Ami. But I only see where I am."

"So, no getting tomorrow's Powerball numbers?"

"Believe me," Josh says, "we've tried. He slept in front of the TV for a month, hoping to get a flash of the numbers."

"All I saw was a Sarahsaurus," Chuck says.

"And that is?"

Chuck looks confused. Like everyone should know what a Sarahsaurus is. I'm guessing it has nothing to do with me calling my sister that during her period. Man, she hates that.

"It's a dinosaur," he says. "A sauropodomorph—" Chuck looks at me. "That's a long-necked plant eater."

"Like a brontosaurus," I say.

"Yes, yes, Silas. Like a Brontosaurus, but eighty million years earlier. They were some of the first longnecks." He closes his eyes. "It was gray and covered in mud. If it sat down, it would have looked like a rock. Except for the spines on its back. They rippled with each step. But it didn't sit, Silas, it walked right past."

He points to the living room wall. "Right over there." He closes his eyes and tilts his head toward the ceiling. "There was a river, too. And, and a volcano, waaaay over there." He points to the front window without looking. "There weren't any trees, but there were lots and lots of ferns and other big plants. The dirt was red. The sky was blue and dusty. Some hills. Lots of water."

"We looked it up," Darius says. "This area was part of a flood plain when Sarahsaurus was around. The soil was red. Water everywhere. Exactly like he described it. And before you ask, no, he didn't know anything about this area that far back and had never heard of a Sarahsaurus."

"No one has heard of Sarahsaurus," Chuck says. "Even though they've been found in the Painted Desert and Petrified Forest. Those are to the east of the Grand Canyon, but close enough."

"And how long ago did the Sarahsaurus live here?" Ami asks.

"Early Jurassic," Josh says.

"Whoa," Ami says.

I raise my hand. "For those of us—*me*—who aren't obsessed with *Jurassic Park* or dinosaurs in general . . . How many years ago was the early Jurassic?"

Josh leans around Chuck and looks me in the eyes. "One hundred ninety million years ago."

"Okay," I say, leaning back. "Oookay. That's . . . a lot."

"Anything more recent?" Ami asks.

"Oh yes, Ami," Chuck says. "Lots. Ami, this house burns down. I saw it on fire, but I don't know when."

"Have you tried to control it?" she asks. "Like really tried?"

"If you know how to control Chronesthesia," Josh says, "Let us know."

"I try, Ami," Chuck says. "All the time."

She nods. "I believe you, but maybe there are some things you haven't tried."

"Maybe, Ami." Chuck nods enthusiastically. "And now that we're friends, you can help me."

She nods again. "I'd like that."

"Sorry if this is too private," I say, "but . . . could you see through time before—"

"Oh no, Silas," Chuck says. "I was more normal than Darius."

"Hey," Darius says.

"It's okay." Chuck leans across Josh and pats his brother's knee. "The world needs normal people, too."

Darius offers an exaggerated frown. "Thanks."

Chuck has a hard time not laughing when he says, "N-not everyone c-can be special, Darius." Then he bursts out laughing and the rest of us can't help but join in. Normal laughter is infectious. Chuck's uproarious hee-haw laugh makes resistance futile.

"Okay," Ami says after everyone calms down a bit. "Okay. Assuming I take your claim at face value and believe you can see different times . . . I'm left with one question."

Everyone waits for the question.

She turns to me and asks, "What can *you* do?"

I'm surprised when one of the guys doesn't answer for me. Instead, all heads turn in my direction.

"Well," I say, feeling profoundly vulnerable and stupid. I'd never admit this to anyone outside this room and only do now because two out of four of them also have some weirdness going on in their brains. "Apparently, I can remote view."

"And you discovered this . . . when?" she asks.

"Just before you rolled up and The Lone Gunmen over here freaked out."

"Harsh," Josh says, "but in this house, a comparison to the Gunmen is a compliment of the highest order."

"For the record," Darius says, "I have no idea who 'The Lone Gunmen' are."

Josh and Chuck gasp in unison and turn toward Darius.

"*The X-Files*," Josh says. "The three guys that help Mulder."

"All I remember from *The X-Files* is Scully—hubba hubba—and that disgusting episode that made me question whether or not you two were monumental pervs." He leans forward to look around Josh and Chuck. "This family in Pennsylvania, man. They kept their limbless, deformed mother on a sliding board under the bed! And they . . . did things to her. Like breeding things." He shivers. "Fuck's sake. Just thinking about it is going to invert me for the week." He glances at Ami. "Sorry."

She shrugs. "I thought that was a good episode. Disturbing, sure, but an interesting take on human depravity, family values, and gothic horror."

"Oookay," Darius says, and then to me. "Good luck with this one."

"What?" I ask. "Huh?"

"Can we focus, people?" Chuck asks. "It's getting late, and Ami asked a serious question. I think we should show her . . . and do a second test for confirmation. Right, Ami? We should do a second test."

"Thank you, Chuck," she says. "I appreciate your ability to stay on task."

"Thank you. Thank you, Ami. I'm glad you appreciate that I can stay on task. Are you glad?"

"Totally," she says.

"I'm glad you're glad, Ami. That makes me happy." He turns to me. "We should do the Ganzfeld test again. But this time—" He reels around and thrusts a finger at Darius. "—*you* have to take it seriously."

"He was looking at a swimsuit issue," Josh says, which gets a shoulder slap from Darius. "Hey, I'm just being accurate!"

"Don't sweat it," Ami says. "I'll go in the other room."

Josh's eyes widen. "You know the Ganzfeld test?"

"I know a lot," she replies. "I'll look at something of my own. Where should I go?"

"My room is the safest," Chuck says. "Ami, you don't even want to know what you might see in their rooms."

She stands. "I can imagine. Which door?"

Chuck points toward his room, which is immaculate and completely lacking in suggestive or outright blatant sexually charged imagery.

She heads for the door and looks back to wink at me. "See you in there."

When the door closes behind her, Chuck nudges me and whispers. "Sitting in a tree."

"Yeah, yeah," I say. "We'll see. Unless you've seen it in the future."

"No, no I haven't, Silas. But I have a feeling." His smile is goofy.

"Okay," Josh says, standing over me, two halves of a ping-pong ball in his hands. He taps them together. "You know the drill. Let's prove you can do this and then use it to find out what people get up to behind closed doors in their hotel rooms."

8

Thresher shark," I say. "Just a flash of it. Taking a fish. Then it's gone, leaving a swirl of water. Salt water. Seaweed. The coast. An inlet. A river. Savannah. Spanish moss. Chiggers."

"You can't say that, Silas. You can't say that."

I flinch out of the stream of consciousness. "Huh?"

"You can't say that," Chuck says.

"Say what—oh, *chiggers*. Yeah, everyone has that reaction the first time they hear it. They're tiny bloodsucking mites that live in the Spanish moss in Savannah, Georgia. Probably lots of other places, too, but that's where I was when I was told not to touch the moss because of the chiggers. Being in the South, I assumed it was a racist term, but apparently it's just an unfortunate rhyme."

"Good to know," Darius says. "You were about to get smacked."

"Can we be serious?" Josh says. "He needs to stay in the zone, or this won't work."

"Okay." I take a deep breath, let it out, and try to let my mind wander again. And it wanders right into dangerous territory. Because I'm picturing Ami in a partial state of undress. She's looking at me with those killer eyes. I'm drawn to her, and when I get close, she smiles in a way I have yet to see.

"What are you seeing?" Josh asks. "We can see your face twitching. We know you're seeing something."

No way in hell I'm letting these guys in on my fantasy life, so I block Ami out of my mind and focus instead on Chuck's room. I see flashes of the space but they're just indistinct memories of my tour.

My mind flits back to Ami.

I'm not sure this is going to work with her on my mind. I'm supposed to be seeing what she's looking at in the next room, not giving myself a half-mast salute.

So I lie. "A pile of rocks." The words trigger a memory and I'm off to the races again. "Gravel. Sand. A huge mound of sand. Cold and wet. I'm on top of it. Police come. I run. Wet pine needles. Dry pine needles. Warm sun. Hot sun . . . on red rock. Not red. It's dark . . . and flakey. Reflecting the sun. Ahh, it's mica. A lot of mica. But this is different. There's pink underneath it. Above it is . . . a wall of stone. Cake layers. Brown and dark reddish-brown. Chocolate cake. Black Forest Cake. Sara's birthday."

"Can you tell me more about the rocks?" Josh asks, voice calm and guiding. "Look closely."

I see the stone just as I did the first time, but in greater detail. "There's a slab of it, lying on smaller stones. Mixed colors. But the big one is mica. Has mica in it. No . . . It's mostly mica. Flakey and delicate. I want to peel it apart." My attention shifts to the rock wall behind it. "There's a wall of stone behind it. The cake." I mentally approach the stone. "It's grainy." I imagine my hand against it. "Coarse. I can see grains of sand in it. There are layers of red, orange, and pink. It's cracking. Shattered. Flakes are falling away . . . The fuck?"

"What is it?" Josh asks.

"Skin," I say. "The wall beneath the stone is skin." I lean in close and reach out to touch it. My imaginary hand never reaches it.

The skin snaps open.

There's an eye.

I gasp and relay the information. "There's an eye in the wall. The iris is red. It's . . . looking at me. What the fuck is this?" I gasp again when one by one, five more eyes open. They move as one, looking left and right before settling on me. "There are six eyes. They're looking at me. They're—"

I grasp my head as a headache rips through my temples and into my eyes.

The headphones and ping-pong halves fall away when I sit upright and open my eyes, desperate to get away from the experience. “What was that?” I ask, feeling angry and violated. “What the fuck was that?”

Josh raises his hands. “Hell if I know, man.”

“Sorry,” I say, realizing I’ve directed my reaction at the wrong person. That shit came from inside me. From my own brain. “Must have been from a movie I saw and forgot.”

“Didn’t sound like something you’d forget, Silas.” Chuck looks concerned. “You sounded really afraid. I don’t like it when people sound afraid. I don’t like it.”

“Sorry,” I say again. “I just . . . it felt *real*.”

“What felt real?” Ami asks, returning from Chuck’s bedroom. She’s got a slight grin on her face and a twinkle in her eye. Then she notices my expression and gets serious again. “What happened?”

“He saw something,” Darius says. “And I don’t think it was anything you were looking at.”

“What was it?” she asks.

“Eyes,” I say. “Red eyes. Six of them, in stone, staring at me.”

“And then?” Josh asks. “You never said what happened at the end.”

“Pain,” I say. “In my head. My eyes. And . . .” I try to remember that last moment. “I heard words.” I replay the final moments over and over until I can see them clearly, without emotion. “It was a voice. A whisper.”

“What did it say?” Darius asks.

“My name.” I do an impression of the voice in my memory. “*Silas Keene.*”

“That’s ominous,” Darius says.

“It was just in my head,” I say.

Chuck shakes his head. “You don’t know that. You don’t know that, Silas. If you can remote view, it might have been real . . . Well, maybe not real because rocks don’t have eyes. But it might have been something that isn’t you.”

"Whatever it was, I'm done for tonight." I fake a yawn despite actually feeling wired. "I think I need to sleep."

And get a drink.

"Agreed," Josh says, "but I think we should reconvene tomorrow night, assuming we all have to work."

Everyone agrees.

Part of me says to put it off a week, but I also recognize that there is some genuine strangeness going on—with me, maybe Chuck, and definitely with Ami. This is the most interesting thing to happen since I moved here from home. Hell, it's more interesting than pretty much everything at home, too. Plus . . . I want to see Ami again. And I did what I came for—made friends. No reason not to hang out again.

"I'm going to do some research tonight," Josh says. "On the rocks, and the eyes. See if there's any historical or indigenous overlap. Try to make sense of seeing something metaphorical while remote viewing. By the way, you saw the rock wall both times you remote viewed. You didn't linger on it the first time, but I made a note to ask you. Didn't seem to fit with the rest of your associations."

The moment he says it, I know he's right. It was the same stone face both times.

"Might be something's on your mind. Might mean you're drawn to something real somewhere."

"Drawn to a rock wall," I say. "Yeah, I don't know about that."

"We'll figure it out, Silas," Chuck says. "We're friends now and this is what friends do. Right, Silas?"

I nod. His view of the world is pure and noble. I appreciate it. "Yeah."

"I'm glad you think so, Silas. I'm glad." He offers his fist, and I bump it, which thrills him.

"Tomorrow at seven," Ami says. "Anyone mind if I bring real food, or do you feel like manly pirates when you eat the snacks stolen from my hotel?"

Darius, Josh, and Chuck share a three-way glance-fest as they realize that they've been busted by the manager of the biggest hotel they service, making her the person they've ripped off most.

Chuck is about to respond, but Josh cuts him short by snapping his fingers. "Not a word."

Chuck purses his lips.

"Don't worry," Ami says to him. "I won't ask you directly."

Chuck sags in relief.

"But I'm not about to eat pilfered snack foods for dinner," Ami says.

"Right. Yeah. Sure." Darius isn't sure what to say. Their delivery business is in jeopardy. They're probably looking at jail time for the silliest of all crimes. What they don't know is that Ami has no intention of turning them in. "Bring whatever you want. Can we give you money for it?"

Ami huffs a laugh, shakes her head, and turns to me. "Walk me to the car?"

"Sure," I say, and follow her to the front door. She exits without another word. I glance back at the guys. Chuck is giving me an enthusiastic two thumbs up while making a kissy face.

Darius sees him and gives his shoulder a smack. "Chuck!"

"Hey, hey," Chuck says, laughing. "I know true love when I see—"

I quickly close the door behind me and spin around to see if Ami heard. She's halfway across the street, out of earshot, but . . . she's also psychic so that might not matter. Still, it wasn't me who said it. I'm just feeling more emotionally exposed than usual.

She doesn't wait for me to catch up. The SUV beeps and she opens the door. Climbs inside. Starts the hybrid engine.

I stop by her window, once again looking at my reflection until the window descends and I'm face-to-face with Ami.

"What are you doing?" she asks.

"I thought I was walking you to the car," I say.

"What? No. That's obviously code. Even Chuck got that."

"Code . . ." I say, catching on but afraid to presume.

"Get in the fucking SUV," she says. "You're coming home with me."

9

"You can relax." Ami glances over at me in the passenger's seat, gripping my knees. I've been with girls before. I'm a recent escapee from a relationship. But something about Ami is next level. Knowing that she might hear my thoughts about her is unnerving, especially when my thoughts are of a carnal nature.

I'm attempting to clear my mind, doing the work of a celibate monk.

"I'm not listening to your thoughts," she says.

"How did you know I was worrying about that?"

"Deduction. Also, obviously." She takes a left turn. "But it only really works if I'm looking in your eyes."

"Is that why I feel like I'm sinking into a comfortable abyss when you look in my eyes?"

She smiles. Blushes. "That's something else, I think."

"So, when we first met . . ."

She nods. "I heard you. And felt what you did."

"And?"

She chuckles. "I haven't been entirely honest with you and the guys. I'm not just psychic. I'm also an empath. I can feel what you're feeling. It's confusing sometimes. Easy to mix up other people's emotions for my own. But that's not the worst of it. Hearing what people think and feel about you can be devastating."

"I have a hard time believing anyone would think negatively about you," I say.

"I know you mean that, so thanks," she says, "but I'm a twenty-three-year-old Japanese American woman in a position of power—at least in this strange little nook of the world. People resent me. Think I'm a freak. Wonder who I blew to get my job. I don't encounter many pleasant thoughts or feelings about me on a daily basis."

I frown. "That . . . sucks. I once overheard friends talking about me behind my back, to some girls, about me being funny looking. I can't imagine hearing shit like that straight from people's minds."

"I hope you're not still friends with them," she says.

"Nope."

"Good, because you're handsome."

Been a while since I've been complimented. Feels good.

"Under all that hair. Why do you hide your face?" I don't have to say anything. She gets a whiff of my emotions and puts two and two together. "A girl said something, right?"

"The ex, yeah."

"Bitch."

"Yeah," I say, sinking into my seat. Thinking about her is like poking a salt-coated finger into an open wound.

"For what it's worth, I'm kind of glad she chased you all the way out here." She shoots me a smile, which I already know is a rare gift from Ami. "I mean, what are the odds that I would meet a guy with a good heart, a kind face, and abilities in the same category of 'what the fuck' as mine?"

"We have yet to conclusively prove that I have an ability to see things in other places. A rock wall with eyes . . . that can't be real. And the first test was . . . flawed. Also, I'm not sure how I feel about it. Being that different—"

"Is overwhelming. Paranoia inducing. Lonely."

"But how can it even be real? It makes no sense. I'm nothing special. Why would my mind be able to do anything like that? Chuck, I get. His brain was altered by an accident. But mine . . ."

She shrugs. "I thought I was normal until I realized my accurate guesses about what people were thinking and feeling weren't guesses at all. It feels imaginary, right? Until poof! Epiphany. It's real. Not fantasy. Not lucky guesses."

"But *how?*"

"I'm still getting to know you," she says, "but you seem like a smart guy. On a scale of one to ten, how are you with science talk?"

"Eight," I say. "Smart enough to understand. Not smart enough to come up with my own theories. Or at least not smart enough to know how to prove hypotheses."

"Have you heard of Orchestrated Objective Reduction theory?" she asks.

"Don't have to be a mind reader to know I haven't, because who the hell has?"

"It's the best theory I've found that allows for minds like ours to exist. Doesn't explain why some people are different but at least allows for extra-sensory experiences."

She glances at me, probably gauging whether I'm following and interested.

"Go on," I say.

"Think of it as a compelling, but still unproven, framework rooted in quantum consciousness—the idea that the mind isn't just neurons firing in a brain, but something entangled with the very fabric of reality. Okay, so there might be microtubules inside neurons, right? And they're not just physical structures. And in the wet, noisy soup of your brain, they're . . . doing weird physics—which is really *all* physics until we understand it.

"People think of the brain as a machine—a computer—doing all the processing locally, but . . . it might be more like a radio, tuned into the quantum hum of the universe. The microtubules are the antenna. It's a quantum system capable of things like non-local awareness, entanglement, and maybe even time symmetry—where information doesn't just move forward in time, but backward as well. Which, let's be honest, sounds a lot like what Chuck experiences.

"So, if consciousness is both quantum and non-local, something like remote viewing can be explained as your brain tapping into an entangled state. Your neurons are tuning into information in the universal cloud. In fucking spacetime. So, you're not really seeing a place, you're resonating with it, and your brain is translating that information in ways you can understand—sight, smell, touch, whatever."

I'm seriously reconsidering my eight out of ten rating. I'm getting the gist of what she's saying but not understanding it all.

The SUV jolts to a stop, and I'm kicked out of my thoughts. We're in the Best Western's parking lot. Didn't even notice where we were going. Assumed Ami had a house.

She sees the confused look on my face. "I don't like waking up early. I don't like commuting, even just for a few minutes. And I don't like shitting in bathrooms that aren't mine. Also, free housecleaning."

"You live in a hotel room?" I ask.

"Hotel room? No. I live in the goddamn Presidential Suite. I'm here for the experience, not to save money. This girl has standards." She climbs out of the SUV and closes the door behind her. Through the closed door, I hear her muffled voice. "Let's go!"

The cool desert night suits me. It's the only time of day that reminds me of home. Clean, cool air is plentiful in Maine. Not so much in the arid Southwest. I breathe easy and follow Ami toward a side door.

"Back to the smart talk," she says. "You were wondering why only some people can access extrasensory abilities. There are a few possibilities. First, it could just be structural differences in people's microtubule arrangements. Sounds wonky, but it's basically the same reason one brother can be a beefcake football player, and the other is a scrawny nerd. Some people are born with physical differences that allow them to do things other people can't. And it's not just physical. People with genius IQs can do things you can't."

"And you," I say, feeling defensive.

"If I weren't also a genius, sure."

Can't tell if she's screwing with me or not, but there's no denying her ability to understand and digest scientific concepts is a solid ten out of ten.

She holds up two fingers. "Second possible reason. The average brain contains all kinds of mental filters, but some people's are reduced or non-existent."

"Like autistic people," I say.

"Exactly," she says, "or in the case of Chuck, a brain injury that removes the filters."

She pauses at a door with a keypad beside it. Punches in a code and when the lock beeps, she lets herself in. "Hope you're okay with stairs."

"My body was born with above average physical abilities," I joke.

She looks me in the eyes. "We'll see."

Then she's moving up the stairs. I follow her and for the first time notice how tight her jeans are, and that she's—how does Sara put it?—'packing it in.' She's not looking back and can't see my eyes, so I don't bother adjusting my gaze. Nearly miss her lifting three fingers.

"Third possible reason," she says. "Altered states of consciousness."

"Psychedelics," I say.

"Sure," she says, "but that feels like cheating to me. Meditation can get the job done, too. That's why they had you in headphones and ping-pong balls, which is hysterical by the way. A sleep mask would have worked just as well. A fever could get you there, too. But these methods are temporary. The truly gifted have access at will."

"So, Chuck and I—"

"Need to practice," she says. "You just found out tonight, which has to be a mind-fuck. And Chuck . . . Chuck has other challenges." She opens the door at the top of the third flight of stairs. A quiet hallway with a plush red carpet is on the other side. There's a door directly across from us. She places her phone close to the door's keylock and it snaps open.

We enter her hotel room, and she's right, it's not a room. It's a suite. Has a kitchen, living room, and bedroom with a king-size bed. It's immaculate and organized, but there's one corner of the living room that stands out. There's a desk with a computer, and not just any computer. I know a gaming machine when I see one. I'm about to ask about it when Ami turns around and shuts me down with those big black eyes.

"I want you to know this up front," she says. "I've never done this before. Not once in my life. I've only known you for a few hours, but that first time you looked me in the eyes . . . I felt what you felt, and I heard your thoughts. No one has ever reacted like that to my face. It felt . . . amazing. And—" She smiles. "You're still doing it now."

"You're doing it to me," I whisper, feeling nervous again.

Then all thought melts from my mind, I place my hands on her soft cheeks, lean down, and kiss her. When I finish, she steps back with mischief in her eyes. She reaches down, takes hold of her shirt, and peels it off, up over her head.

My eyes widen. "Holy shit."

She looks down at herself. "C'mon, I'm not that—"

"I saw you," I say. "In the room. You . . . you had your shirt off! That was real? I thought I was fantasizing about you."

"Incredible," she says, truly impressed that I was able to see her in the next room. But then the look of mischief returns, and she backtracks toward the bedroom. "Want to see the rest?"

10

The rock wall in front of me is red and gritty, like dried blood on sandpaper. I've never seen that, but I imagine it would look like this. Not sure why I'm looking at it. Not sure where I am. But I'm locked in on the rock. Because it's important. I don't know why, but it's like how I felt the first time I saw 2B from *NieR: Automata*. Yeah, I know, weird taste.

Weirder still is how I ended up with a very traditional looking babe for a girlfriend. Blonde hair, ponytail, cheerleader, shallow, and a controlling bitch. Such a stereotype. But that was the circle I lived in back then. 'Jocks and knocks,' the boys would say, shortening 'knockers' to 'knocks.'

Life at home was a different story. My room wasn't full of bikini babes and sports heroes. It was comic books, novels, and video games. I've always been a closeted nerd. The drive to be popular can do that to a guy.

But I'm reformed now.

And staring at a rock wall.

Why am I here? Where am I?

I turn around and the rock wall is still there. Odd . . .

The wall follows my gaze. I look up. Rock wall. Look down. Rock wall. It's like a 3D print of the rough texture has been strapped to my face. I can't look away.

Because it wants to be seen?

Or . . . it wants to see me?

The stone bulges and cracks. Six eyes snap open inside the stone!

Red irises.

I've seen this before. I've been here.

When was that? Why can't I remember anything? The day. How I got here. Where I'm going. I have a horrible feeling I'm late for work but can't . . . ugh, I can't move.

I'm paralyzed.

The eyes look me up and down, scrutinizing.

And then, a whisper. "*Where . . . are . . . you?*" Reminds me of that alien in *Independence Day*, in the steamy lab, speaking through Data's body. It's inhuman. Otherworldly. Not the same voice that said my name last time.

Nope, nope, nope, I think and try to look away. But those eyes remain locked in front of me. I try to close my eyes but can't.

"*Where are you!?*" the voice whisper-shouts.

"Ahh shit!" This voice comes from somewhere else. I know this voice but can't put a face to it. All I know is that it is a welcome distraction, and I turn my full attention to it, hoping it will repeat.

"Aww, c'mon! Can you believe this shit?"

My eyes snap open. I'm in a bed. White sheets. Comfortable. Must be twelve hundred thread count minimum. Much nicer than my bed.

"Pick up the sword! Yes!"

Ami's voice fully returns me to the world of the waking. I sit up, thinking about the dream. It was the same rock wall I saw when remote viewing. The same eyes. I was kind of hoping I'd be able to forget that strange sight, but my subconscious has other plans.

My conscious mind fights back, remembering what happened before I fell asleep. Traditional hot girls get all the guys who are fooled into the belief that those women, sculpted and made up to perfection, will also be the pinnacle of sexual ability, desire, and passion. Truth is, they're usually just controlling and selfish lovers.

Ami put them all to shame. She was . . . I don't know. Supernatural. She *can* hear thoughts and feel others' emotions, so it probably wasn't hard for her to suss out exactly what I like most. Might be an unfair advantage, but she also knew *how* to move, and had an appetite to match mine—when I was sixteen.

I don't know when I fell asleep, but it was while Ami was showering.

Speaking of, I'm feeling a bit . . . tacky in my nethers. I should jump in the shower before getting ready for—*Shit*. Work! I scan the area around me. No phone. No clothes. I slide out of the bed, hoping to not be spotted buck naked as I search the floor.

My clothing is part of a pile, mixed with Ami's attire from the previous night. Looks like she kicked it all into a heap. I separate my clothes and search my pants pocket. The phone is right where it should be. I tap the screen and . . .

I sit back on the bed, deflated. I'm so screwed. It's 10am. I should have been at work three hours ago, cleaning dishes during the breakfast rush. But there are no texts from my boss, which is both strange and ominous. She usually texts if I take too long dropping a deuce. I swear she has a camera in the bathroom, watching me on the toilet, doom scrolling on TikTok.

I start working on my sob story to keep from being fired. I could be sick. Puking. Could fake an injury. I shake my head. A dishwashing job isn't worth the pain, even if it's on purpose.

Truth is, there isn't a thing I can say or do to stop myself from being fired. That's pretty much set in stone. I've seen guys fired for putting spoons where the forks go. She's not going to let this slide, even if I had a good excuse. And faking some kind of traumatic experience would be a stretch, because last night . . . Holy shit.

I gather my clothes and head for the bathroom, which catches me off guard. I used it during the night, but the lights were out, and I was half asleep. I didn't fully comprehend its size, its marble counters, tile floor, double sink, standing shower, and whirlpool tub. If I could afford this place, I'd pay for it too.

I lean out of the bathroom and shout, "Hey!"

"Morning," Ami shouts back. "Sleep well?"

"Too well," I say. "Pretty sure I'm jobless now."

"Ha!" she says. "Beware my cooch charisma!"

I laugh. *What the fuck?* Sounds like she's in a good mood, though, and I'll take some credit for that.

"You mind if I take a bath?" I ask.

"It's all yours, princess. Your breakfast is already cold. So, go for it."

Princess? Breakfast?

I could get used to this.

The bath is exquisite. The jets massage my body and loosen my sore muscles. Got a workout last night. I nearly fall back asleep, but then Ami is shouting again.

"Die! Die, asshole, die!"

What is she doing? Curiosity pulls me from the tub. I towel off and put my day-old clothing back on. Feel like a grub, but what can I do? I stroll out of the bedroom on wobbly legs.

She notices. "Right? I'm sore in places I didn't know had nerve endings."

I laugh, probably harder than I should, but seeing her once again dressed in a T-shirt and panties pokes the sleeping bear that is my libido. Two things distract me from her petite body: The first is a tray of food. Eggs. Pancakes. Fruit. Milk. Water. OJ.

The second is the game she's playing on her PC. "You're using a Titan Flame Blade?"

She pauses the game as her jaw drops. She slow-turns to me, wide-eyed. "You play Shadowborn?"

"Level twenty-nine Dark Mage."

"The evil path is so fun, right?"

I pick up the tray of food, and place it down on the PC desk, taking the chair beside Ami. "So fun. What's the point of being able to do anything if you act like it's real life?"

"Right?" she says, unpausing the game. "And yeah, I like the Titan Flame. It's not the most powerful weapon in the game, but—"

"—it sets people on fire," I say with a gleeful grin. "I know."

"I was reading up on the game stats. Seventy-seven percent of players follow the evil path. But the guy who made it all, who came up with all these evil things to do? He plays on the path of light and goodness. Boring AF."

"Guessing he knows which one pays off the most in the end, right?"

"Depends on your perspective," she says. "If your goal is to win, be the hero, get the girl, and feel good about your eternal soul, I guess the good path makes sense. But if you want to have fun? To create chaos, sow destruction, and conquer the world . . . Well, there's only one path that works—in the game and the real world. Am I right?" She holds out a fist, and I bump it. "Damn straight, I'm right. Now, watch this."

She slides off her horse beside a family of villagers. The fiery Titan blade lights the scene, making the NPCs cower in fright—because they know Ami has killed other villagers. Because her in-game reputation precedes her. I imagine it does in the real world, too, but without the need for violence.

I shove a whole slice of bacon in my mouth. It's been drizzled with maple syrup, and not the bullshit corn syrup stuff peddled by Log Cabin and Mrs. Butterworth's. This is the real thing. As a New Englander, I can tell the difference between the two like a cop can taste the potency of cocaine by tasting it . . . which might not be a real thing. Could just be another creative decision by a writer who didn't bother doing the research. Like shooting a gas can makes it go boom. Or enhancing blurry footage. Or weapon silencers—sorry, 'sound suppressors'—being whisper quiet.

I forget all about my gripes when I taste the pancake with the aforementioned maple syrup. "This is amazing," I say, still chewing. "Way better than the Grand. Is this what you guys serve guests?"

Ami laughs. "Hell, no. They get the cheap stuff, same as you. But, this is what the staff here gets. I know I'm not the most outwardly likeable person. But if you supply people with good eats, they'll love you even if you're rocking a level forty RBF."

"For the record . . ." I take another bite. ". . . mmm . . . I liked you before the food."

"And for that," she says, "if you need a new job—"

My phone rings. Habit forces me to pluck it from my pocket and look at the screen. I'm expecting my parents or Sara. They're pretty much the only people who call me these days. So, I'm surprised when I see 'Three Amigos' on the caller ID. Then I remember I let Chuck put his number in my phone.

"Weird," I say, holding the phone up so Ami can read it. "These guys are impatient."

"Well," she says, "answer it!"

Wasn't sure I wanted to, but I do as I'm told and put the phone to my ear. "Taco Bell customer service. How can I—"

"Cut the shit, man." It's Josh and he sounds genuinely upset.

"Sorry," I say, clearing my throat and tapping the speaker phone button so Ami can listen in. "Everything okay?"

"Can you guys just come in?" he says. "You weren't supposed to be back until tonight, but now you're just sitting out there and it's starting to freak us out."

In the background, I hear Darius shout, "Not me. Just them!"

"What . . . are you talking about?" I ask.

"You're parked in front of the house," Josh says. "I'm looking at you right now. Black SUV. Tinted windows."

Ami pauses her game. Looks concerned.

"Josh," I say, "please believe me when I tell you this. We are not parked in front of your house."

"Bullshit," he says, and rather than debate the fact, I tap the FaceTime icon on my screen. "See for yourself."

Josh's face appears on screen. He looks nervous. Chuck is with him. Darius is in the kitchen, eating a bag of chips. And on their screen, they're seeing me holding the phone out, so it captures Ami, me, and the computer screen behind us.

"Fuck," Josh says, switching to the phone's front facing camera. I see the blinds as he approaches them. He cracks them open and places the phone in the gap. Daylight washes out the camera, but it adjusts and focuses, revealing a black SUV parked across the street. The camera snaps back to a view of Josh again. Chuck and Darius are now close, both concerned.

"What should we do, guys?" Chuck asks, wringing his hands together. "It's not Wednesday. No one should be here. I don't like this. I don't like this, Darius."

"Guys," Ami says, and it's clear the three of them are about to start panicking. "Guys!"

She has their undivided attention now. "I'm assuming you have a back door?"

"Yes," Chuck says. "Yes, we do, Ami."

"Use it," she says. "Run."

11

Now what?" Josh asks. He's already out of breath, probably more from panic than being out of shape. But that will compound his exhaustion soon enough. The video feed is choppy, and mostly red dirt as they run from the back of the house. I get the occasional glimpse of Darius and Chuck. They all look worried.

"Run until you can't," Ami says, cool and collected. A natural problem solver. Probably why she's able to manage a large hotel at her age. She's out of my league in so many ways. "Then . . . just walk. Casually. Like you're three nerds out for a stroll. And yeah, you might look like penguins on an African savannah, but you'll draw less attention. Not that anyone should be home right now. Most everyone in town will be at work, at the hotels. Which is where you need to head."

"Hate to break it to you, but we're not in nearly good enough shape to—"

Darius pokes his head into frame. "Speak for yourself."

"I'm not in shape, Darius," Chuck says. "I don't like this. Darius, I don't like this."

"Just keep moving, Chuck," I say. "We're on our way." I glance at Ami to make sure I haven't overstepped. She gives me a nod and slides out of her chair, hustling to the bathroom. "You're going to be fine. It will take us just a few minutes to get there."

"I hear an engine," Darius says.

"Shit!" Josh shouts. The camera shakes all over the place. Impossible to see what's happening. "Is it them?"

"I can't see, Josh. I can't see!" Chuck's horrified voice cuts deep.

The call ends.

I'm on my feet and heading toward the door when Ami joins me. She's fully dressed now, her face dead serious. Snags her wallet and keys on the way to the door. Then we're rushing down the stairs, across the parking lot, slamming the doors of her SUV.

The engine roars. Definitely not a hybrid. The AC blasts, quickly fending off the morning heat that will climb five degrees every hour until the sun sets. Tires screech over the pavement and the back end of the massive vehicle swings around as we scream onto the road.

Ami is taking this seriously.

Life and death seriously.

She knows something I don't. And she notices me staring at her or hears my thoughts. One or the other.

"What?" she asks.

"You already know what," I say.

A slight grin confirms she's busted. "I can't shut it off, you know."

"Not concerned about that," I say. "But I'd like to know why you're driving like Speed Racer trying to rescue Chim-Chim from the Yakuza about to sell him to an Indonesian zoo."

"You have something against Indonesia?"

"What? No. They have a zoo there. Nicknamed 'the zoo of death.'"

"Sounds bad," she says.

"That's the point," I say. "Stop dodging the question."

We bang a hard left. I'm pressed into the passenger's window and leave a print of my forehead behind when we straighten out. There are just a few streets between us and the guys, but they're all sharp. I take hold of the 'oh shit' handle and apply a vice grip.

"Look," Ami says. "You're new to this stuff, right? Extrasensory perception. Telepathy. Remote viewing. You've heard of this stuff before, but never researched it, yeah?"

"Yeah . . ."

"Well, if you had . . . If you knew that most of what reads like government conspiracies were all real, you'd know that the program changes names but has never gone away. The government seeks out and disappears people like us. It's why I've never told anyone about what I can do—until last night. And this morning there's a vehicle, like this one, parked outside their house? Not a coincidence."

"You were parked outside their house for weeks in the same kind of vehicle."

She looks at me like I've just claimed the solar system is actually a swirling toilet. "Not the day after one person proves she can read minds, another can remote view, and a third can see forward and backward in time."

Good points all around, but I've never once in my life thought that the U.S. government might have any kind of interest in me, beyond whether I'm filing my taxes. And even then, they wouldn't care if I did because they have to pay all the withheld money back.

"And you think that if the guys are caught, they'll be taken away to some black site and never seen again?"

"I think Chuck is easy to write off because of his brain injury. I don't think the government will hold them indefinitely. But I do think all three of them will talk—even Josh. They're not professionals. They won't be able to resist professional coercion. Or torture. Most people would spill the beans at the suggestion of pain. And Chuck . . . they could just put someone nice with him, gain his trust, and he'd be an open book."

"So . . . you're worried about us?"

"I'm worried about all of us, dumbass!" She yanks the wheel to the right and if not for the handle I'm clinging to, my face would have wound up in her lap. Two more turns and we're there. Not sure if my right arm will still be attached, but—

My phone rings. I release the handle, dig the phone from my pocket, and look at the screen. Three Amigos. I answer it. "You guys okay?"

"We're hiding behind some trees," Josh whispers. "East side of the neighborhood. Haven't seen the SUV, but we can hear them searching the streets. They're probably in the house, too. Where are you guys?"

"You'll probably hear us in—hold on!" I drop the phone in my lap and grab hold of the handle again just in time to be whipped around the next turn. The tires screech and the SUV wobbles back and forth as we finish the turn. Most people would have flipped a top-heavy SUV making that turn, but Ami handles the vehicle like she's done it before. I pick up the phone. "You hear that screech?"

"Yeah, that you?"

"Yeah, inbound. Thirty seconds." I lean forward and look through the windshield. I can see the street they're on. One side is houses, the other, a smattering of short Ponderosa Pines. I spot Chuck crouched behind one, arms wrapped around his knees, rocking a bit. "Okay, I see you. Be ready to jump in when we pull up."

"You should slow down," Josh says, "or they'll hear you coming."

I'm about to relay the information to Ami, but she's already doing it, taking the last turn into the neighborhood like we're out for a Sunday drive.

"You see us?" I ask.

The phone disconnects. I'm worried for a moment, but then Chuck, Darius, and Josh emerge from the trees, speed-walking toward us. We stop in the street, and they pile in and close the doors. Then Ami does a calm three-point turn and we start our exfil—yeah, I play *Call of Duty*, too.

In the back seat, all three guys turn around, looking out the back window.

"You can go faster now," Josh says.

"No, I can't," she responds.

I look forward and notice the sheriff's cruiser passing in the other direction, no doubt looking for the source of the screeching tires. Ami gives a smile and a wave. The man returns it like they're pals. I suppose that makes sense. If there's trouble at her hotel, she's the one he'll have to speak to. Actually, the sheriff ran my plates for her, so they must be friendly.

"Hey, Ami," Chuck says. "This is a nice car, Ami. I like it."

"I'm glad you like it, Chuck," she says, adopting some of his mannerisms. It seems to put him at ease.

"But I didn't like what happened before," he says. "It's too hot outside to run. And I didn't like being chased."

I feel like a little skepticism is warranted. "We don't know that they were—"

"Oh yeah?" Josh says, pointing out the back where a second black SUV races toward us. "Here they come!"

Ami floors it, and we're pinned to our seats like we've just gone plaid.

"Whooaaa!" Chuck shouts.

His mouth is smiling, but his eyebrows are turned up. What must that be like? Looking happy even when you're frightened?

We all lean to the left as we work our way back out of the neighborhood.

Behind us, the second SUV speeds by the sheriff. Lights flash and the car spins around in hot pursuit of our pursuers. This time, Ami cuts corners, kicking up a cloud of red dust. Not sure if she's trying to hide where we're going, but it keeps me from seeing out the back.

"Where are we going?" Darius asks. "It's not like this town is very big. Not a lot of places to hide."

"Just hold on," Ami says, making a hard left that slams Darius and me into our windows.

"Holding on," Darius says, face squished against the glass. When we hit a straightaway and jump from thirty to sixty miles per hour in a few seconds, we get clear of the dust, and I can see the SUV behind us—stopped. The sheriff didn't just pull them over, he cut them off and forced them to stop.

They fade into the distance, and we make a right turn *away* from the Best Western. I glance at Ami, but she doesn't notice. She's focused. In the zone. But maybe she can still 'hear' me. I decide to put it to the test and start intentionally thinking loud affirmations in her direction.

You got this, girl!

You can do it, champ!

Go get 'em, tiger!

Her lips twitch up on the side. The briefest of smiles.

I'm about to think something dirty when she slams on the brakes in front of a ramshackle house. Looks like it could have been here before the rest of the town. She turns into the dirt driveway, heading for what looks like a barn.

"What's this?" I ask.

She doesn't look pleased about answering, but says, "I grew up here," before exiting the car, leaving the rest of us to look at each other, dumbfounded.

"Okay," Josh says, "show of hands. How many of us think this is *sus*?"

All three in the backseat lift a hand and turn to me. I don't want to lift a hand. I like Ami. A lot. But this place is definitely *sus*. And there's no way I can hide that feeling from Ami, so I raise my hand, too.

12

Ami shoves the large barn door to the side, revealing a white Jeep Gladiator with big ass tires. She climbs into the Jeep, starts the engine, and reverses out of the building. She parks behind the house while the rest of us watch from the SUV, like a gang of befuddled meerkats. Then she returns, climbing back into the front seat. She looks at each of us and then says, "Later."

She pulls the SUV into the barn and parks. "Let's go." She gets out and waits by the open barn door.

"This is bullshit," Chuck says. "Darius, this is bullshit."

Darius nods. "Yeah, it is."

"I don't know guys," Josh says. "We were basically pretending, right? Goofing around. Cautious, educated, but we were playing checkers without knowing we were in a game of chess. I think Ami just knew what game she was playing and was prepared." He shakes his head, disappointed. "I should've planned better. Should have had contingency plans."

"There was no way to know—"

Josh holds up a hand, silencing Darius. "I'm just saying, we know what game we're playing now, yeah? The stakes are real. We don't know who is after us, but it's probably the government, and they don't have a good track record when it comes to people with extrasensory abilities. So, let's up our game. And I think we should trust Ami, until she gives us a reason not to."

"I trust Ami," Chuck says. "Ami is nice. She's nice. Right, Silas?"

"Silas is biased," Darius says. "Ain't you?" He shoves my shoulder. "We all saw you, dog. Didn't realize you were a player."

"I'm not," I say. "She's just . . ."

"Don't need to know what you see in her," he says. "We all have our types, and she had your dick on a leash from the moment you saw her."

They all have a laugh, and I feel my face burning. Glad my shaggy beard hides it, but I'm also keenly aware that it needs to go. I've been living the bachelor life for a while but am feeling the need to tidy up my face.

"Hey, let's go!" Ami shouts.

"Still playing checkers," Josh grumbles at himself and hurries from the car.

"Let's bounce!" Darius says and exits from the other side, leaving Chuck in the middle and me in the front seat.

"Hey, Silas?"

"Yeah, Chuck?"

He's looking at me. Has a strange look in his eyes.

"Everything will be okay, Silas. I know it's scary. I'm scared, too. But, everything will be okay."

Not sure if he's genuinely trying to comfort me, or if this is some kind of self-soothing. *Doesn't matter,* I decide. I'll take it. "Thanks, Chuck. I believe you."

"That's good, Silas. I'm glad you believe me."

"Now, let's go, or Ami is going string us up by our nuts."

His eyes widen comically. "That wouldn't be nice, Silas. Not at all. I like my nuts!"

I laugh and exit the SUV. "Keep it to yourself. I don't need to know about your nuts."

Chuck gets out on the far side, slams his door shut, and then scoots past Ami with his hands cupped over his junk.

"Really?" she says to me, holding onto the barn door.

I shrug. "You are walking the dark road."

"Good point," she says. "Now if you value your nuts, help me with this door."

I take hold of the old wooden slab and pull. Takes more effort to pull it closed than I thought it would. Even with Ami pushing on the other side. It grinds and bumps over its rusted track, but it gets there. After the door *thunks* into place, Ami heads for the old house.

"No lock?" I ask.

"If you were a thief in Tusayan, would you stop to look inside that piece of shit?" She smiles back at me. "Besides, I'm pretty sure we've already got the only three career criminals in town with us."

I smile at that. She's probably right. "You really grew up here?"

"Until I was thirteen," she says.

"That why you're friendly with the sheriff?" I ask.

She nods. "He and my father played cards at our place on Saturday nights." She motions to the house. "This place. Didn't look like this back then, but, well, time isn't kind, right?"

"And your job at the hotel?" I ask.

"That was all me," she says. "Best Western doesn't give a shit if you're a local or not."

"Why come back?" I ask.

"Same reason you're here. Needed a reset. And, even though this is basically a shithole with hotels for Canyon-Gawkers, it's still home to me." She waves the guys gathered by the back door out of the way. They step aside and she pulls open the screen door, which screeches loud enough to make me wince. Then she waves her hand in front of the door, like Obi Wan to a Stormtrooper and says, "Abracadabra."

With a shove, the door opens.

"Seriously?" I ask.

"Most valuable thing in here is dust," she says. "And I wouldn't mind if someone took it. Now get inside." She holds the screen door open and motions for us to enter. We do as we're told, entering a kitchen that still has a table and chairs, but like Ami said, it's coated in dust.

She follows us inside and locks the screen door with a hook and eye latch. Then she closes the inner door and locks the deadbolt.

"Should I get the front?" I ask.

"That one is locked," she says. "Water works. Toilet works. We have power, but let's keep the lights out."

"Right," Josh says. "Awesome. Great. Ahh . . . what should we do?"

Glad he's humble enough to admit he has no idea what to do. A lot of guys would just try to take charge. And since I'm equally clueless, I turn to Ami for the answer. As do Darius and Chuck.

"I swear, men get all the credit, but I'm pretty sure we'd still be in the stone age without a woman around to tell you what to do." She takes a seat. Doesn't bother dusting it off. "We have two priorities, right? Survival and intel. We need to stay hidden and figure out what the hell is going on. Everyone have their phones?"

All four of us men pull phones from our pockets.

"I have my phone, Ami," Chuck says. "I have a lot of games, Ami."

"Phones on the table," she says, taking hers from her back pocket. She tilts her head to a cabinet and says, "Aluminum foil."

Josh's eyes light up. He gets it. "You're going to make a Faraday cage? Block the signals?"

"Sure," Ami says.

Josh returns with the foil. Ami tears off a sheet and starts shaping it into what looks like a cookie sheet.

"Ami," Chuck says, "when you said survival—"

"I meant 'hidden.'" She places her phone on the foil sheet. "We don't know what they want with us, but when it comes to SUVs with tinted windows, better safe than sorry, right?" She shoots Josh a smile.

"Exactly," he says.

"So, we'll stay here as long as we can, which without food is two to three days. Hopefully they'll think we've left town and move on. But the moment any of you three—" She points to the Three Musketeers. "—attempts to resume your lives, they'll know about it and come back. So, we need to figure out what they want and, if possible, give it to them."

"If not?" Darius asks.

"Know anyone who can forge an ID and get you passports?" She lets the question hang for a moment, places two more phones on the foil, and then says, "Darius, you're on guard duty. Watch the street. Anyone shows up, stay low and come tell me with a whisper. No shouting." She levels a finger at me and sweeps it around to everyone. "No shouting."

I hold up a boy-scout salute and nod. "Copy that."

"Chuck, I want you to chill for now. Take a load off. The beds are still here. Still have blankets. Just flip the pillow and take off the top blanket. Should be good to go."

"But I'm not tired, Ami," he says. "I'm not tired."

"Not sleep," she says. "Just relax. You need to do that, right?"

I hadn't really noticed how jazzed Chuck is, but now that she's pointed it out, he seems nervous and twitchy, wringing his hands together. And she's feeling all of it amplified because of the way her brain works. Getting him to calm down might be as much for her as it is for him.

Darius places his hand on Chuck's arm. "She's not wrong, Chuck. That was a lot."

"It was a lot," Chuck says. "Okay, Ami. I will try to calm down. Square breathing." He gets to his feet and steps into the hallway, searching for a bedroom. "Square breathing." He takes a deep breath and walks out of sight.

"What about me?" Josh asks.

Ami places the last two phones on the foil. "You . . . are going to help him . . ." She points at me. ". . . remote view the people chasing us. See if we can find out what's going on. If they're interested in us because of what we can do, they might have people doing the same thing to find us."

"Shit," Josh says. "You're right. What are you going to do?"

Ami stands with the foil holding the phones stretched between her hands. She walks across the kitchen and opens the wall mounted microwave. Places the phones inside. "I'm going to see if I can tag along for the ride."

"Tag along?" I ask.

"I let you in my pants, you let me in your brain." She smiles. "Seems like a fair trade."

"*I knew it*," Josh whispers, then his jaw drops open as Ami starts the microwave and it fills with crackling blue electric arcs and sparks, destroying all five phones.

13

Try to relax," Josh says.

"Emphasis on try," I say, folded arms resting on the kitchen table. I close my eyes and lean my head on my arms. I fell asleep like this more than once in high school, but I was exhausted from late nights, soccer practice, and boredom. I'm a little sore from last night's extracurricular activities, but I slept well and late. More than that, the temperature outside is creeping up on a hundred. We have all the shades pulled inside, but this place is an oven, and I've got rivulets of sweat leaking from my pits and running down my sides.

If this place didn't have running water, we'd resemble a buried pharaoh's sunken, leathery, flaking, parchment corpse by morning. Makes relaxing difficult.

"Thinking we should wait until tonight," I say.

"Man up, Silas," Ami says, patting my back and then regretting it. "Yuck." She wipes the sweat from my back into my hair. "I get why you want to wait. It's so hot in here, I don't even want to think."

"We could put on the AC," Darius says from the living room.

No one knows if the air conditioning even works, but after noticing the place had central air, the heat became even more unbearable.

"Air conditioners make noise," Ami says, "and if we want the people looking for you three—"

"Us three?" Darius says. "*Us* three?! I'm not psychic. I can't see anything that ain't in front of me. They're not looking for me."

"Feel free to tell them that," Ami says. "Now quit whining. You're not helping."

"This isn't going to work," I say, feeling more agitated with each passing moment.

"Hold on," Ami says and leaves the kitchen.

"She's not wrong, you know," Josh says. "Sooner we get answers, sooner we can leave this shithole. If there's even a chance you can get some info, you have to try."

"We don't even know if what I see is accurate. I saw red eyes in a stone wall. That's not real."

"Not everything you see is surreal," Josh says.

Ami returns holding a broad chunk of cardboard. "You saw me in the bedroom."

"He did?" Josh asks.

"One correct answer is not a reliable pattern," I argue.

"Two correct answers," Darius says from the other room.

"The yellow triangles?" I ask. "I didn't even see what I thought I saw."

Darius appears in the kitchen doorway. His eyes are locked on the floor. "Yeah, you did."

Silence follows and lingers for a few seconds.

"You're going to need to elaborate," Josh says.

"I'd rather not," Darius says.

And he doesn't need to. Because I remember what I saw, and what I thought it was. "You were looking at my sister!"

"On the plus side," Darius says, "your sister's a hottie. Honestly, she's crispy compared to Kathy Ireland."

My irritation turns to laughter. "You're a bastard. And what the hell does 'crispy' mean?"

Darius flashes a smile. "She's so hot, she's crispy . . . like cooked. Like us, in this house, without the AC running."

"Hey." Ami snaps her fingers and points to the living room. "Darius, living room. Silas, chill out and focus."

"I told you, it's too—"

A breeze washes over me, cooling my wet skin. I turn toward the source and find Ami waving the cardboard up and down.

"Can't do this all day, so get to it."

I smile. Her resourcefulness is just one more thing to like about her.

She rolls her eyes. "Enough with the goo-goo stare. Head down. Eyes closed."

I do as I'm told and find relaxing infinitely more possible with the breeze on my back. "What should I focus on?"

"You got a good look at the SUV, right?" Josh asks.

"Yeah."

"Focus on that," he says. "If you can find it, you'll find them. Hopefully."

I play back the events of the day, right up to the point when we were speeding away from the black SUV. It's nearly identical to Ami's, but there is one clear difference—the grill. Ami's Chevy Suburban has a black grill. The government vehicle has a silver grill, and centered near the top, a red logo. I didn't see it clearly, but only one car brand sports a red logo like that and makes giant, gas-guzzling SUVs. GMC. Which makes the vehicle a Yukon. Extra large, like all good things in 'Murica.'

I didn't actually see the SUV for very long. The time between when the Yukon first showed up and the sheriff had stopped it was maybe ten seconds. But I know what a Yukon looks like, and not many people drive black vehicles in the desert. Not sure why Ami does. At least the Jeep in the garage is white.

Yukon, I tell myself. Black GMC Yukon. I picture it. Focus on it. Let my mind drift. I see it behind us, speeding to catch up. I see it stopped, the sheriff's cruiser in its way. I see it in a parking lot. Baked by the sun. It's a familiar lot.

I must twitch or something because Josh says, "Tell us what you're seeing. Stream of consciousness, remember? Just let the words flow."

"Parking lot," I say. "The Yukon is parked."

"Can you look around?" Josh asks.

"I know where I am," I say. "Best Western parking lot."

"Focus on the drivers. Men in suits, probably. Feel them looking for you and then reverse course to them."

"They're in the lobby, talking to the receptionist. Two men. Black suits. Ties. Sunglasses. *Men in Black*–type shit. Feels . . . feels like that might just be me projecting."

"That's fine," Josh says. "Keeping thinking about them. Try to see where—"

I gasp. "I'm inside Ami's suite, but something is different." The image is blurry. I take a deep breath and feel the cool air washing over me. Then I see it. "It's a mess. They've gone through everything. The computer . . . they're sitting at the computer."

"Men in Black?" Josh asks.

"No. They . . . they look normal. Like they're on vacation. Cargo shorts. One is wearing a Hawaiian shirt. The other has a T-shirt. I can see the shape of a gun under it."

"Get closer," Ami says. "What are they doing?"

"Looks like . . . trying to crack your password."

She scoffs. "Good luck with that, assholes."

"Do you see anything else that might—"

I don't hear the rest of Josh's question. I feel a presence and turn toward it. "There's a third man. He's leaving the bedroom. He's . . . wearing a white suit. Looks expensive. Has pale skin. Bald."

The man pauses and turns toward me.

My breath catches.

"What is it?" Josh asks.

"His eyes. They're red. They're—"

The man smiles and speaks, "There you are."

"Gah!" I flail and topple to the floor. Lying flat on my back, staring up at the water-stained ceiling, I gasp for air. "He saw me . . . He fucking saw me!"

"*Who* saw you?" Ami asks.

"The guy in white," I say.

"The bald guy?"

"Yeah," I say, "but . . . but . . ." I clench my eyes shut, but can't erase the vision of his gaze, frozen in my mind like the after-image of a flash bulb. When I realize why, I cover my face with my hands.

"What is it?" Ami asks.

"He's looking back! He can see us!" He knows who the rest of them are by now, but my identity might still be a mystery. "I can feel him watching."

A sense of calm washes over me. A third presence has arrived. In a flash, the man is gone. The connection is broken. I pull my hands off my face to find Ami leaning over me, hand on my forehead.

"Was that you?" I ask.

She nods.

"Holy shit," Josh says. "I've heard about people who could mirrorlink, but I didn't believe it."

"Mirrorlink?" I ask.

"It's like a remote viewing feedback loop. An ESP dogfight. Two minds observing and reacting to each other across a distance. Like a temporary mental entanglement."

Ami nods. "I helped untangle you."

"I didn't know you could enter people's minds," Josh says. "That's . . . invasive."

"And why I don't do it," Ami says. "Hearing surface thoughts is passive. I can't stop it. Deeper thoughts, secrets, plans . . . I can't hear that stuff unless people are actively thinking about it."

"But you could," Josh says, "if you wanted to?"

I interrupt them. "This is interesting, but . . . there's more."

I have their full attention now. And we've been joined by both Darius and Chuck in the kitchen doorway. "He saw me. And he spoke to me. He said, 'There you are,' like he'd been looking for me. But that . . . that wasn't the worst part. It was his eyes . . . They're red. And each eye had two irises and pupils." I turn to Josh. "Could he see me when I was remote viewing?"

Josh shakes his head. "I think it's fair to say I'm out of my depth here. I could be wrong. But . . . unless you're astral projecting, you'd just be an invisible presence. And even if he somehow visually perceived you, I don't think you'd look like you.

Maybe an energy field or something. But not a full body and face."

"But when he mirrorlinked me?" I ask.

"It's possible," Josh says.

"But I doubt it," Ami says. "He'd be more interested in where we are than what you look like. He'd have gone outside. Looked at the house. Didn't have time to do much more than that."

"So, we need to bug out?" Darius asks, sounding hopeful.

"It's not a good thing," Ami says. "These aren't the kind of people we want to face on the open road."

That sounded ominous.

"His eyes." I tell her. "They were the same. The ones I saw in the rock wall. That was him, looking back. That's how they found you guys."

"Hey guys," Chuck says. "We should go. I think we should go. I don't want to stay here." He turns to his brother. "I don't want to see a man with four red eyes, Darius."

"Neither do I," Darius says.

"That's good, Darius." Chuck turns to Ami. "I'm glad you don't. Ami, we should leave."

"Chuck," I say, watching the way he's nervously fidgeting, like he knows something we don't. "Did you see something?"

He grows increasingly irritated, wrapping his head in both arms, clawing at his hair. "Need to leave. Need to leave! Need to leave, now!"

14

Chuck's terrified insistence lights a fire under the rest of us. We're speeding away in the Jeep Gladiator thirty seconds later. He doesn't calm down until we reach the end of the street and turn right.

Like Ami's SUV, this Jeep also has dark tinted windows, and it looks a lot like the adventurous vehicles tourists like to rent. Makes them feel like—I don't know, like they're outdoorsy, as they drive to the Grand Canyon and gaze into its abyss without ever actually setting foot inside it.

I'm sitting in front with Ami. The guys are in the back. We've instinctually all taken the same seats we had in the SUV, the way people do.

Ami drives casually, following the speed limit, using her blinkers. Nothing to make us stand out. She's not just smart, she's . . . I don't know. Experienced?

"How do you know how to do this?" I ask her.

"Do what?"

"Be sneaky. How to hide. Where to hide."

She gives me a confused look. "Are you serious?"

Getting a strong vibe that I shouldn't be serious. That I should already know, but I'm confused, afraid, and trying to make sense of anything that's happening.

"You walk the dark path," she says. "What do you do to gather resources, just pillaging?"

"What?" She's talking about Shadowborn. "No, I—hold on. Are you serious?"

She shrugs.

Ami is applying gameplay techniques to real life. There are some resources in game—certain foods, herbs, potions—that are only available to those on the light path. Because those on the dark path don't farm the land and forage for resources. We steal what we need but can't steal everything. Acquiring certain rare items requires deception, disguises, and misdirection. In game, I have five different safehouses where I keep my clothing, weapons, and shapeshifting spells that allow me to walk around town as a commoner, hero, or even a damsel.

"Holy shit . . ." I shake my head, smiling. "We're so screwed."

"It's worked so far," she says.

"Unless you have a Portal of Artinor or a Wandering Sword, we're going to run out of luck." I don't know if I should laugh or scream, but there's one thing I'm certain of. "We need to get the hell out of Dodge."

"That's the plan," she says.

Josh leans forward so his face is between the seats. "So, we haul ass south on sixty-four, then take forty . . . where? East or west?"

"Neither," Ami says. "Not yet."

"Uh, Ami," Chuck says. "We need to leave, Ami. We need to go far away."

"Care to share what you saw?" she asks him.

He folds his arms and presses his mouth shut.

"It might be important, Chuck," she says. "Might save our lives."

Chuck moans uncomfortably. He's distressed and bottling it.

"Give him a fucking break," Darius says.

"If he knows something—"

"If he knows something, he'll tell us when he's ready. He doesn't process things the way other people do. If he saw something bad, he would have lived it like it was real, right? So, ease the fuck off."

Ami nods. "Makes sense. Sorry, Chuck."

Chuck doesn't respond. He's lost in thought, eyes flicking back and forth. He's going through something, that's for damn sure.

Ami stops at an intersection and suddenly tenses, looking to the right. I follow her gaze and spot two black SUVs tearing toward us. Ami grips the wheel but doesn't hit the gas. Instead, she waits. The rest of us in the car shrink down, despite being hidden by the dark glass.

The SUVs tear through the intersection, running the stop sign, and screeching around us. They speed away toward Ami's old home. After they pass, Ami turns right and drives away, still following the speed limit.

"Can't go south," she says. "It's the obvious way out of town."

Josh, a bit breathless, responds, "Sixty-four north, to eighty-nine. North or south? There's not a lot of ways out of here, you know."

She nods. "We can't drive out. They'll watch sixty-four in both directions."

"We don't even know who *they* are," Darius says. "What if they're the good guys? What if we're not actually in danger?"

"Says the guy who thought better of knocking on a car window at night," I say.

"Yeah, well, I'm just saying, the U.S. government isn't all bad, right?"

Ami looks at Darius in the rearview while Josh and I shoot him, 'Are you serious?' glances.

"Okay, fine. They don't have a great track record with—"

"With people who can do things they logically shouldn't be able to do?" Josh asks. "The public track record is on par with the Soviets. Whatever is still secret is worse. Way worse. MKUltra is the public face of what the government did while researching extrasensory perceptions, and that included LSD, electroshock, and sensory deprivation. The subjects weren't volunteers. They used hospital patients, prisoners, and CIA employees. Think we know everything about that program? Think again. Most of the records were 'destroyed' in 1973. The depravity of people with blank checks and no regulation is boundless.

"Between 1932 and 1972, the U.S. Public Health Service experimented on six hundred black men in Alabama. 'Bad blood,' was the diagnosis, even though the doctors knew it was syphilis. And treatment was withheld, to observe the effect of syphilis on the human body—even after a cure had been found. Men died, and went blind and insane, and they unknowingly transmitted the disease to their wives and children.

"Not enough? Operation Sea-Spray. 1950. The U.S. Navy sprayed bacteria over San Francisco, simulating a biological attack . . . But it wasn't a simulation. It was an actual biological attack on American citizens."

"Fuck me," I say. "What bacteria?"

"Serratia marcescens," Ami says.

Josh nods. "That's the red shit."

"Bacillus globigii," Ami says. "That was the second one."

"They caused urinary tract infections, respiratory infections, festering wounds—" Josh starts.

Ami chimes in again. "Endocarditis. Sepsis. And an outbreak of Serratia infections."

"People died," Josh says, and turns to Darius. "And no one, in any of these cases has *ever* been held accountable. Human experimentation. Murder. Torture. These things are war crimes, and the U.S. government performs these experiments on its own citizens. Only a fool would believe it's not still happening."

"Well," Darius says, face flat. "Thank you for that, Encyclopedia One and Encyclopedia Two. I'm now primed to shit myself."

"Not the worst idea," Ami says. "Would probably prevent them from taking you into custody."

"Fun," he says. "So much fun." Then to Josh he asks. "If all this is true, why the hell did we put up a flyer advertising we were interested in this shit?"

"I believed it was possible," Josh says. "I didn't *know*." Josh looks down, energy sapped. "I'm sorry, guys. I—"

"Don't sweat it," Darius says, back to being supportive. "No way you could have known, because honestly, I never believed any of it was real. Still having a hard time accepting it."

When we turn onto Route 64 North toward the Grand Canyon, Ami floors it. The Gladiator roars and surges forward. I watch the speedometer twist its way toward one hundred miles per hour. At that speed, we'll reach the Grand Canyon Village in about eight minutes. I decide not to question the speed. If a nefarious government agency really is tracking us, they might have access to law enforcement, security cameras, and maybe even satellite imagery. I have a hard time believing those kinds of resources would be used to find a couple of Professor X wannabes. But Ami seems to know more about this than the rest of us, except maybe Josh, and she's running like the Road Runner if Wile E. Coyote got access to the Speed Force.

"Grand Canyon Village," Darius says. "Then what? Switch vehicles and try to run?"

"Ditch vehicle," Ami says, "and hit every ATM we can find. Take out as much cash as we can." She turns to me. "Except for you. Get a hoodie. Hide your face. Avoid every camera, store, and bank. Right now, your identity is a mystery. Hopefully. We'll let them see us, in the cameras. They'll know how much money we took. Then we buy a shit ton of travel food and gear. Make it look like we're running on the road. Buy everything on traceable credit cards. Create a narrative for them to follow. Then we do the opposite."

"You want to *stay* in the Village?" I ask.

"Hide," she says. "Two days later, we borrow a car, drive back to Tusayan, pool our money, and you—" She points at me. "—will book a private flight somewhere none of us have ever been."

"And then?" Josh asks.

"Then?" Ami shakes her head. "I have no idea. I've never done this before."

"Could've fooled me," Darius says.

"Yeah, well, my brain doesn't work like other people's." Ami's foot presses the gas pedal to the floor. We're approaching one twenty. Good thing this road is thirteen miles of flat, straight pavement.

"They're bad guys," Chuck says. "They're bad guys. They're bad guys."

All attention shifts to Chuck.

"They're bad guys," he says, and before anyone can ask him to elaborate, he does. "They found us at the house. They found us. The pale man with four red eyes. He . . . he shot Silas." He looks at me, tears in his eyes, smile on his face. "Silas, he shot you. In the head. Silas was dead. You died, Silas. That's what I saw. That's why we had to leave. I'm glad you're not, dead, Silas. I'm glad."

"I'm glad, too, buddy," I say, trying to sound calm while being internally flabbergasted by the possibility of Chuck not only being able to *see* the past and the future, but being able to alter future events. Ho. Lee. Shit.

15

You okay?" Ami asks, taking a seat on the bench beside me. We're seated outside the lodge where we've got two rooms, one for the guys, and one for Ami and me. The rooms are old and a bit musty but still cost a pretty penny because of their proximity to the Canyon. We're seated just twenty feet from the edge.

This was also our only option if we didn't want to be seen on security cameras. Security in the lobby was a mirror that allowed the receptionist to see us when her back was turned. She never actually looked. It's also the only place in town that would take cash—no questions asked—as long as we made a personal donation to the receptionist's college fund. Our hush-hush rooms cost us an extra hundred dollars. Small price to pay if it keeps us hidden from the people who, in an alternate timeline, shot me in the head.

Which I assume is the reason for Ami's check-in.

"Dandy," I say, watching a red-tailed hawk riding the thermal updrafts, eyes on the canyon floor far below. The setting sun makes it glow against the darkening sky. Like a phoenix.

Ami sits next to me. Can't help but grin when I look at her. Not because I have feelings for her—that's still a work in progress—but because of what she's wearing. We spent a few hours shopping for clothing as covertly as possible. At first, I went in alone, avoiding cameras, but not too worried because my identity is probably still unknown. I bought five sets of Grand Canyon themed hoodies, baseball caps, and sunglasses. We could conceal our identities while posing as tourists. But we matched too much. While in disguise, everyone picked out their own outfit, meant to both throw off attempts to identify them, and also blend in.

Ami chose to blend in by standing out. Her small size, combined with a bright pink hoodie with fluffy ears, makes her look like a kid. Anyone looking for a group of adults wouldn't give her a second glance. I'm dressed like my old Maine self. Cargo shorts. Black T-shirt. Open plaid flannel. It's one of two essential uniforms for New England men. The second replaces the shirt with a hoodie.

The only flaw with our disguises is that if anyone spots Ami and me being affectionate, or even entering the hotel room together, they might call the cops on account of our apparent age difference—and when they confirm our identities and ages, the jig is up. We'd be on the run again. So, we keep our distance in public and enter the hotel room separated by at least twenty minutes from each other.

"You don't look dandy," she says, pulling her legs up to her chest and hugging them. The day's heat is dissipating quickly, leaving a chill in the air. In an hour, it'll be too cold to sit outside.

"It's part of my disguise. Grumpy '90s grunge wannabe." I open my flannel shirt to reveal the Nirvana T-shirt beneath. "Remember?"

She flashes a peace symbol with her fingers and winks at me while sticking her tongue out of the side of her mouth, playing her role to perfection.

I laugh. "That might be the most disturbing thing I've seen in the last two days." I look at her again and a memory surfaces. "You ever read that novel . . . What's it called? *The Darkness*?"

"*The Dark*," she says. "Of course."

"You're dressed as Bree?" I ask.

She nods. "Demon Dog is the bomb." She squints at me. "Don't tell me you're dressed as Laser Chicken."

"Sans the skirt," I say, "but not on purpose. I always dress like this."

"Good book," she says.

"Good book," I agree.

Silence settles over us, and it's not uncomfortable. Only thing that would make this moment better is if I had my arm around her . . . and people weren't chasing us.

After five minutes of silence, I ask, "What do you think of Chuck's vision?"

"Of you getting shot in the head?"

"Uh-huh."

She thinks on it for a moment. "It's a mind-fuck is what it is. Because we'll never know if he actually saw a possible future, or if he imagined a worst-case scenario and got nervous."

"But we saw the SUVs. They were headed to the house."

She tilts her head up and blows her breath into the cool air, creating a plume of fog. "Which is why I think we should listen to him if he gives another warning—until he gets something wrong."

"So . . . where is our chartered flight going to take us?" I ask, still dubious about the plan.

"We need to leave the continental United States," she says. "Find someplace remote."

"So, what? Alaska?"

"Still on the continent," she says.

"Right. Hawaii?"

"Too much military there. I'm thinking Puerto Rico. Rincón is nice. Chill beach life. Lots of expats. Laid back. No one is going to ask for our IDs. We can get cash-paying jobs."

"And how long do you imagine we'll have to live like this?" I ask.

"Until we save enough to get new identities. There's got to be someone in San Juan that can do it."

Seems like a flimsy plan, but I don't have any ideas of my own.

"I need to let my family know what's going on," I say.

"You can't call them."

“I can use a payphone,” I say. “And leave out details that would connect me to . . . all this. They need to know I’m going to be out of touch.”

“That’s sweet of you, but we need to stay—”

“You don’t understand,” I say. “I talk to my sister nearly every day. My parents, once a week, at least. We’re tight. If I just disappear, they’ll raise the alarm, call every agency that will listen. They’ll have posters up by next week. If we want to keep my identity a secret, we need to call them off.”

“You’re a lucky guy,” she says. “Not many people get a family like that.” The tinge of sadness in her voice suggests she’s not one of the fortunate few. “Okay, you get a phone call, but it needs to be quick and free of details, names, places, and dates.

“Now I just need to find a payphone,” I say.

She huffs. “You’d have an easier time finding the Ark of the Covenant.” She digs into her pink sweatshirt pocket and pulls out a cheap looking cellphone.

“What the—”

“Burner phone,” she says. “It’s safe to use.”

I take the phone and stare at the keypad.

“You don’t know their numbers, do you?” she asks.

“Who memorizes numbers anymore? I’ll get it.” I dial four numbers, erase them, and dial again. When I’m done, I stare at the digits, trying to imagine what they’d look like on an iPhone screen. “This is right. I think this is right.”

Ami shrugs and waits.

I hit the call button. After five rings, my sister picks up. “Hello?” She’s confused by the unknown number. I’m tempted to screw with her, but I need to make this quick.

“Hey, Sis.”

“Silas? What number are you calling from?”

“Well, that’s part of what I need to tell you, and you need to tell Mom and Dad, okay?”

“Oookay . . .”

“I’ve met someone.”

"No shit? That's awesome. What's her name? Where's she from? What's she look like? Send me a pic. Is she there right now? Can I say 'hi?'"

"Slow down, Beavis," I say. "I'm taking a trip with her. Can't say where because we don't know yet. But we're going off grid. Going to take a break from the world."

"*She* didn't find you, did she?"

"No," I say, understanding Sara is talking about the psycho ex. "But I just need to get away—farther away. Clear my mind. Have some fun."

"Do you know how long?" she asks.

"No idea."

"Wow. Geez. Sounds like this could be serious. Why haven't you mentioned her before now?"

Because I met her yesterday, I think, and then say, "Didn't want to get your hopes up."

"Well, is she at least pretty?" she asks.

I look at Ami. She's listening in. "Gorgeous."

Ami rolls her eyes.

"She's totes there, isn't she? I know you, man. You were looking right at her when you said that. Can she hear me?" Sara doesn't wait for a response. "Hey girl, listen up. You better do right by my big bro, or I'll hunt you down, you feel me?"

I thought Ami might reply, but she's still being super careful. Could the government recognize her voice? Is that a thing?

"She's nodding," I say, as Ami taps her wrist like she's wearing a watch. "Listen, I need to jet. I'm going to be MIA for a while but having the time of my life. So, tell Mom and Dad to chill. I'm good. Loving life. Having an adventure. I'll call when the time is right. But it could be a long time."

"Swear you're not in trouble?" Sara asks.

"Double pinky swear." I hate having to lie to her. My sister and I are close. If she was here, in person, I'd tell her every detail. But over the phone . . . that's a risk I can't take. And not just for myself. If the people chasing us knew who I was, they could use my family to get to me. Can't let that happen.

"Okay, well, don't get her preggers."

I smile. "I'll try. Hey, I'm sorry, but I need to go."

"I'm jealous," she says. "I need to travel and sow my wild oats soon. Wherever you're going, I hope you have the time of your life. And don't worry about Mom and Dad. If I have to lie to calm them down, I will."

"Love you," I say.

"Back at you, big bro."

I hang up the phone and just look at it. I feel like I've just said goodbye to my sister for the last time. Like I'll never see her, or my parents, again.

"You'll see them again," Ami says, showing off that thought-hearing, empathic brain of hers.

"I'd feel a little more confident in that statement if it came from Chuck," I say.

She raises her eyebrows at me. "Well, I got something Chuck doesn't have."

"Oh yeah? What's that?" I ask.

"Tits," she says.

I bark a laugh. She is impossible to predict.

She stands and heads for the door that leads directly to our room. She gives me a wink. "Wait twenty minutes." Then she's inside, closing the door behind her.

I glance back and forth. There are a few other people outside who might have seen us and might see me go to the room with her. This is going to be a long twenty minutes.

Just two minutes pass before I notice a pair of guys, totally out of place, wearing black suits. They approach people one at a time, showing them a handful of photos. When the people shake their heads, the two men move on. I'm about to retreat to my room sixteen minutes before I'm supposed to, but am stopped when the two men spot me, flag me down, and approach.

16

I turn my face away from the two men as they approach, trying to act like I don't give a shit. When it's clear that they won't be diverting, I'm glad that I shaved the beard. If I'd been seen by the pale man with four eyes in two sockets, he'd have described my face with a beard.

"Excuse me, sir," the taller of the two men says. "I'm Special Agent Stephens. This is Special Agent Keller. We're with the FBI."

That gets my attention. When I turn to look at them, I come face to face with an FBI ID. Stephens flips it closed and pockets it. "Mind if we ask you a few questions?"

"Go for it," I say, trying to act casual, but not too casual because then I'm trying too hard and won't look casual at all. God, I feel like I'm going to shit myself. I've never been more nervous in my life.

"What are you doing here?" Keller asks.

"Enjoying the view," I say and then offer up some details I wasn't asked for, which could expose the lie, but I'm not really thinking things through. "At the Grand Canyon. On vacation. Road trip."

"Who are you with?" Stephens asks.

"Rolling solo across the U.S." I sit up a little straighter. "You guys looking for someone?"

Stephens glances at Keller and then asks, "What makes you think that?"

"Saw you showing photos to those other people. Also, isn't that what the FBI does? Look for bad guys? It's not like you'd be out here asking people what they thought of the *John Wick* franchise."

Keller cracks a smile. "He's got a point."

"Mm," Stephens says, far less charmed by my attempted joke. He digs into his pocket and takes out the photos I saw him showing around. He holds them out to me. "Have you seen any of these people?"

I take the photos and am greeted by what is clearly a social media profile pic of Darius. He's smiling awkwardly, wearing a football uniform and holding a football under one hand, his helmet in the other. The glory days. Looks a lot younger than he does now. He's either one of those people who just never updates their profile pics, or he opened the account and then abandoned it.

I flip to the next photo. It's Chuck. Candid. He's got his arms around two girls. Looks confident. Charming. The girls framing him look up at his face, totally enamored. This is Chuck before his accident. I feel bad that it changed him so much, but I also suspect I wouldn't like the Chuck in this photo nearly as much as I do the man I now call a friend.

The next photo is Josh. It's an actual mug shot. He looks disheveled. Hair's a mess. Bags under his eyes. He's either been studying all night, every night, for a week, or he's blitzed on something. Like the other two, the photo is years old.

Josh probably convinced the other two to reduce their online presence. That these guys are using old photos of all three suggests there isn't anything newer available.

"What's up with this guy?" I ask about Josh, curious if they actually know anything about the guys, or are just looking for faces in photos.

"Arrested for possession with intent to distribute," Keller says.

"Distribute what?"

"Marijuana," he says.

Well, that's not a big deal. It's legal in most New England states, and like half of all states. But I do my best to look slightly shocked. "Well, I haven't seen—"

I switch to the next photo. It makes me forget what I was about to say . . . because it's Ami, looking very professional, surrounded by the same FBI ID that Stephens flashed. I spot her name. Ami Sato. At least that isn't a lie. I swallow, choke, and then cough for a good twenty seconds. It's not fake, either. Gives me time to come up with a reason for stopping in my tracks.

"Sorry, sorry," I hold up a hand, coughing one last time. "I just wasn't expecting the last person to be one of you guys. Or . . . pretty. What's the deal with these four anyway? Are they like escaped cons rolling with a corrupt agent?" I widen my eyes. "Is she working for a cartel?"

"We aren't at liberty to say." Stephens crosses his arms. "Do you recognize her?"

"I'd remember her if I'd seen her," I say. "She's cute."

"Cute?" Keller says. "You have strange taste."

I nearly nut tap the guy. His crotch is within range and during my life as a jock I perfected a mean cobra strike for any of the guys that needed straightening out. Lightning quick and just enough contact to drop a man to the floor without endangering his future as a father. "What can I say, I like 'em nerdy."

And she does look nerdy. And it's not just her unique bowl cut hair. She's wearing a pair of glasses as well. Pretty thick, too, given the way her large eyes are shrunk.

But the real reason for my comment is to hide my abject shock at Ami being with the FBI. "Is she an agent, like you guys? Is she dangerous?"

"Former agent caught helping these guys move product." Stephens says, a blatant lie. "She look dangerous to you?"

"Not remotely," I say with a forced chuckle. "You guys have a card or something? In case I see any of these guys?"

Keller produces a business card. Looks official. FBI logo. Address is for a field office in Phoenix. And a phone number. "If you see them, don't approach. Just call."

I nod. "Got it." The card feels like a million pounds in my hand. "Can I text? Like if they're close enough to hear me call?"

"Sure," Keller says, confirming a suspicion. The phone number on the card is not an office phone. It's a cell phone. *His* cell phone.

"Coolio," I say, and pocket the card.

"You have a good night, sir," Stephens says and turns to leave.

"Will do," I say, doing my best to remain chill. I sit back and watch the pair leave from the corner of my eye. Then I remember something a friend told me. His father was a cop who said they can always tell who is guilty because they avoid looking at the police. Innocent people look directly at police, wondering what's going on. People who avoid looking at police are usually hiding something.

And I am hiding a lot.

So I turn and watch them leave. Before walking around the corner of a building, Keller glances back. I give him a casual wave, and then they're gone. I linger for ten more minutes in case they return. Better for them to see me unruffled than discover I've bolted the moment they were out of sight.

But they don't return. The Grand Canyon Village is home to about two thousand people and even more tourists. They'll have a lot of ground to cover and people to interview.

Positive that the coast is clear, I stand, stretch, and then meander back to my room. I open the door, slip inside, and close it behind me. I sigh and lean back against the wall, eyes closed. I no longer feel like I'm going to shit myself, but I definitely need to pee.

"What took you so long?"

I flinch at Ami's voice.

"Geez, you okay?" she asks.

"I'm not sure," I say, and head to the bathroom. I close the door behind me, drop my pants, and sit on the toilet. I've been made fun of for my preference to sit while peeing, but I dare any guy to place paper towels around their toilet, take a standing piss, and have a gander at how much of it ends up on the floor. On the wall. On the heater. And the plunger. And anything else beside the toilet. Standing to pee outside? Nothing better. Feels like a connection to our ancestors who might have peed on a tree daily. But inside? Nah. Leave that Neanderthal shit for the out of doors. Also, sitting lets you scroll on the phone and avoid confronting people about their former lives as an FBI agent.

"You okay?" Ami asks. She's at the door.

"Hard to pee when someone is listening," I say, and then realize she's not listening to me pee. She's listening to my thoughts.

I focus on the first song that comes to mind and start blaring the lyrics in my head. *Goodness, gracious, great balls of* . . .

"Jerry Lee Lewis? Really? You know he married his thirteen-year-old cousin, right?" She's not even hiding it. Must have heard my thoughts when I came in. Felt my fear. She knows something happened.

I finish taking a leak, because I don't actually care if she can hear me. I wash my hands, look in the mirror, and hardly recognize myself. The beard had grown on me. Ha. When I open the door, she's sitting on the side of the bed, arms crossed. "Okay, spill it. What happened?"

I cross my arms to match hers and meet her gaze. "How about you spill it, Special Agent Ami Sato."

17

Her deadpan expression doesn't flinch. "Who told you that?"

I answer honestly. "Two guys pretending to be agents. Stephens and Keller. They had pictures of Darius, Chuck, Josh, and you. But *your* photo was on an FBI ID."

"Maybe it was fake," she says.

"*They* were fake. Your ID was real, because showing people a photo of an FBI agent muddies the waters. It raises questions. Suspicions. Like who the hell is this lady, really? They're using it because it's all they have."

Ami is quiet for a moment and then relaxes. "Okay, fine. Busted." She raises her hands. "Guilty as charged."

"So, are you FBI now, or are you—"

"I lasted about two weeks," she says. "Top of my class at Quantico. Excelled in all areas of the job. Became an active field agent at twenty-two, which is mostly unheard of, and two weeks later . . . two fucking weeks . . . I heard something I shouldn't have. Because it wasn't said aloud. My SSA—Supervisory Special Agent Ronny Kreel—was selling child pornography on the dark web. I caught him remembering he needed to upload a new batch of photos to his anonymous clients.

"But I had no real evidence to take to the higher ups. No way to get a warrant or prove that what I overheard was real. So . . . I faked it. Planted incriminating evidence that suggested something was amiss."

"What did you plant?" I ask, curious despite also suspecting this is all bullshit.

"Photos of kids. Normal photos if they were your kids, but strange for a forty-year-old single man to have in his pocket. Suggestive, but not explicit. That combined with me claiming to have overheard a conversation was enough to get a warrant. He was running a big operation. More than just porn. Drugs. Guns. Everything black market, and well-protected because of his inside information. He'd also get advanced warning if anyone ever started looking into his covert online activity. But he wasn't ready for someone who could read minds and was willing to fight dirty. He's in jail now. Will be for a long time."

"And you're no longer with the FBI because . . ."

"The powers that be figured out that the initial evidence was planted and correctly assumed it was by me. They didn't tell anyone. Couldn't. Ronny would have walked. But . . . they couldn't let me stay either. Rather than being fired, I quit, moved to a place no one in the FBI would visit, and everything else you know about me is true."

"Why didn't you tell me?" I ask.

"In exchange for a recommendation letter from the FBI, I signed an NDA. I'm not trying to be deceptive or covert, but I'd rather not be sued by the government."

"Well, I think the government might want to do worse than that to us now," I say.

"Not the whole government," she says. "There are a lot of good people doing good things in most agencies. It's the secret programs that operate without oversight that we need to worry about. They do what they want, to whoever they want."

"And what agency is after us?" I ask.

"I have no idea," she says. "But they seem well funded, and that makes them dangerous . . . because we're *not* well funded and will eventually run out of resources."

"I'm not sure I believe a word you've said."

"Yeah, well, I wouldn't believe me either," she says.

"We need to tell the guys." I take a step toward the door.

She intercepts me. "Not happening."

"Yes, it is." I attempt to walk around her, but she steps in front of me, placing a hand on my chest.

"I'm not going to warn you again," she says.

"When did you warn me a first time?" I ask and then shake my head. "You know what, screw this. You're like a hundred pounds tops and we both know I can lift you up without a—whoa!"

I have no idea how I ended up on my back, but here I am, on the floor looking up at the ceiling, gasping for air. "What . . . the . . . fuck?"

Ami stands over me. "You can't tell them. If you do, they won't trust me. And if they don't trust me, I can't keep them safe."

It's a fair point, but how do I know she really wants to keep us safe?

"If I wanted you dead," she says in response to my thought, "you'd be dead already, and I wouldn't be staying in this shitty hotel. If I wanted to turn you in, or make a deal for my freedom, it would be done. I don't waste time, and I hope to hell, I didn't waste my time with you."

"Why?" I grunt.

"Because I like you, asshole." She offers a hand. I take it and she pulls me up, manhandling me a second time, despite her size.

"What was that?" I ask. "Kung-Fu?"

"Krav Maga," she says.

"And that is . . ."

"Israeli military close quarters combat system designed for real-world down-and-dirty street violence," she says. "When you're my size, it's the only fighting style worth knowing. I'm an expert in eye-gouges, groin strikes, throat jabs, joint breaks, and weapon disarming. No points. No forms. No belts. Just neutralize and survive. End fights before they begin."

"Well, you're good at that," I say, "but for the record—"

"You weren't going to fight me," she says. "I know."

"Then what was with the flip-shit?"

"I was proving a point," she says, and looks me in the eyes. "You guys are screwed without me. If you tell them I was FBI, they'll run and won't last more than ten minutes."

"And me?"

"You . . . could be okay, not because you're skilled or smarter. They just don't know who you are." She thinks on that for a moment. "Actually, you might just want to leave. Go back to Maine. You could be free and clear."

I shake my head. "*Could* isn't good enough for me to risk my family. And I don't abandon friends."

"You just met us," she says. "And despite our . . . intimate proximity . . . you don't owe me anything."

"First, *intimate proximity*? Who says that? Second, friends are friends. Ten years or two days. Doesn't make a difference to me. You guys are good people, and . . . this is my fault. They saw me in the remote viewing. That's how they found the guys. And from there, you."

"There was no way to know that was even possible," she says. "I've been studying extrasensory perceptions for a long time, and caller ID and location tracking are new tricks to me." She pauses to rub her forehead. "Look, if you're going to stay, great. But you need to follow my lead, and that means you need to trust me. And trust needs to be earned."

"You want to play twenty-questions or something?" I ask.

"I want . . . to try something."

"Is this a kinky something, because I don't know if—"

"Not this time," she says. "I'm going to give you access."

"To . . . ?"

"Me. My mind. My thoughts."

I sit on the bed across from her. "How do I know you're not just going to curate what I see?"

"I'm not Professor X," she says. "I haven't mastered telepathy. Not even close. It just kind of happens."

"But you've done this before?" I ask.

"I've thought about it," she says. "But it's kind of hard to test something that's secret."

"Right. So, mind meld?"

"That's the idea." She sits cross-legged on the bed and motions for me to scoot closer. "You have the ability to project your mind.

You're a transmitter. I'm a receiver. If we can establish a connection, the flow of unfiltered information would give you access to my thoughts, experiences and, most importantly, my intentions."

Transmitter and receiver . . . There's a sexual analogy to joke about there, but I keep it to myself. Well, I attempt to keep it to myself. Ami's smirk suggests she heard each and every joke edit that bounced through my head.

"This doesn't seem like a great idea," I say.

"I need you to trust me."

"Will you have access to my mind as well?" I ask.

"In theory." She nods. "You have anything to hide?"

"Actually," I say. "No. I'm pretty boring."

"You're far from boring," she says, holding out her hands.

This feels . . . weird. I just found out she'd been lying to us about the FBI. Lie of omission, which isn't the worst kind of lie, I suppose. But now I'm giving her full access to my mind? Sure, it's under the guise of me seeing into *her* mind, but it's a big ask, especially when my former relationship was the mother of all mind-fucks.

But here's the thing, I really want to trust her.

I want to know everything about her.

Because, even without Chuck's ability, I can see a future with her in it. So, I'll take the risk.

"Can you please stop thinking nice things about me?" she asks, cheeks flush. She shakes her open hands. "Let's do this."

I take her hands. They're soft. "Now what?"

"You're the remote viewer," she says. "Focus on entering my mind and I'll focus on opening—you're right, this sounds super sexual. But we were pretty good at that, so let's just roll with the analogy and try to connect on the same level."

I close my eyes and focus on the mind of the woman sitting across from me and feel . . . nothing. So, I use the technique taught to me by Josh and start saying everything that comes to mind. "FBI agents. Guns. Conspiracy. *The X-Files*. Dana Scully." The image of Scully in my mind shifts from a redheaded white lady to Ami's face and hair. I smile at the shift, and forget to say it aloud, because I'm no longer speaking. Because I'm sitting on a couch, watching *The X-Files*. Sitting next to me is ten-year-old Ami Sato. She looks over at me and says, "Hi, Silas. Are you ready?"

18

Ready for what?" I ask.

Young Ami shrugs. "To look for whatever you're looking for. Whatever you need to trust me. You're on a self-guided tour. Recognize the house?" She motions at our surroundings.

At first, I don't see anything familiar. The living room is comfortably furnished. The TV is large. There are paintings on the wall. Southwestern motifs. It looks like a nice place to grow up.

Then I notice the layout. It's familiar. I stand from the couch and step toward the kitchen. The table is the same. Microwave, too. This is the house she took us to, proving that part of her story was true.

I suppose that should be the goal—confirming her history, which means we'll need to visit the FBI. But I'm not ready to leave yet. I head back to the couch where Ami is engrossed in the show.

"Mind's eye," she says. "Season 5, Episode sixteen. Remember it?"

"Not really," I say, and realize she remembers it enough to replay the episode in her mind. It might not be a conscious choice—I have no idea how any of this really works—but Mulder and Scully are on screen, speaking lines that sound vaguely familiar.

I sit back on the couch. "What's this one about?"

Little Ami kicks her legs and says, "The blind woman who witnesses a murder through the killer's eyes."

"Like a mirrorlink gone wrong," I say.

"Mmhmm," Ami says, watching the TV.

On screen, Dana Scully says, "A split consciousness whereby a person has a certain level of visual ability but they're not aware that they're actually seeing."

"Right. I remember this. The blind lady telepathically linked to her serial killer father. She kills him in the end, right?"

Ami crosses her arms. "Spoilers!"

"Sorry! I thought—"

Young Ami bursts out laughing. It catches me off guard because I've never actually seen her laugh. Subtle smiles, a huff here and there, but a laugh? She was a carefree kid . . . who really liked *The X-Files*.

"I wanted to be Scully," she says, revealing that there's no such thing as a private thought while our minds are connected. "She's why I joined the FBI. Imagine my disappointment when I discovered that there wasn't a division for weird shit. No *X-Files*. No FCP-style unit. Given my secret abilities, I had hoped for something more. But . . ." She shrugs. ". . . it was all a pipe dream. Until you showed up, knocking on my car door."

I can feel her emotions. She's being honest and earnest. She'd been seeking a connection to people like her. Like us, I guess. As a kid, she found it in Mulder and Scully. As an adult, she hoped to find their real-world counterparts, but discovered there was no *X-Files* equivalent and that her boss was a dark web pedo trafficker.

I blink and we're no longer in Ami's living room. We're in a large, bustling office. Ami is still with me now but is an adult wearing a power suit and a security badge with the letters F, B, and I on it.

The transition from one location to another was sudden but not jarring. In fact, I feel calm. Before I can think the thought, Ami says, "We're connected. You're seeing all this for the first time, but it feels like a memory, right?"

"Yeah, but how—"

"I'm theorizing," she says. "Confidently. Stuff like this just makes sense to me . . . and I've been thinking about it my whole life."

"You've been able to do this since you were a kid?" I ask.

"Since I was born. And no, you don't want to experience what that was like, emerging from your mom's vagina and getting struck by everyone's emotions and thoughts with no idea what was actually being said."

"You can *remember* that?"

"Right now, I can, yeah. And it's fucking weird. In the real world, thank God, no." Ami tilts her head for me to follow her. "C'mon, let's get this over with."

I hustle after her, but we're no longer interacting. This is a memory on replay. She's holding a stack of folders. Looks thrilled to be here. We walk through a maze of cubicles and then hallways. We take an elevator up two floors and then navigate a few more turns before stopping in front of the door. I recognize the name on the door: Ronald Kreel.

Ami lifts a hand to knock and then freezes.

Then I hear what she does.

It's a murmuring at first, like you'd expect from a ghost haunting an insane asylum. Doesn't sound like words, because it's not. It's thoughts. And then images. I'm in Ami's head listening to someone else's thoughts and feeling his emotions.

And it's dirty. So fucking dirty.

His primary love isn't drugs or illicit sex. It's money and power. He is so full of himself, it's nauseating. A grandiose narcissist if there ever was one. I get images of the children, weapons, and drugs he's helping traffic around the world. I get glimpses of the conversation taking place on his personal phone. Feel his complete disregard for all human life save his own.

I can't remember feeling more disgusted in my life.

And I'm not the only one feeling it. Ami is scowling. Her hand trembles. She's struck by a wave of young faces, crying and pleading for freedom. Her hand lowers to her hip and the gun holstered there. She's about to kill him, when she thinks better of it.

She's an FBI agent. One of the good guys. She doesn't murder. But she knew there and then that she would do anything to bring Ronny down.

And she did.

All it cost was her lifelong dream of being an FBI agent.

Emotion boils up inside. A familiar righteous anger. At Ronny and . . .

I'm standing in the woods.

Familiar woods. Tall pines. Maples and oaks. Lumps of granite here and there. I'm home. This is Maine. And I recognize this path. It loops out to and around a pond. I came here as a kid. Loved it. Until . . . I look down at my wrists and spot a familiar bracelet. A gift . . . which I wore for a single week, making this moment easy to identify.

"No," I say, turning to my right where she—

It's Ami standing there, head twisting around as she scans our surroundings. "It's beautiful here. The air is so . . ." She breathes deep and smiles. "We don't get air like this in Arizona."

"We shouldn't be here," I say.

"I'm not steering this ship," she says. "You brought us here. Maybe not on purpose, but some part of you wants us here. Or . . . wants to show me?" She grows serious, feeling my emotions. "What happened here?"

The answer comes from someone else.

"You know, I just *can't* with you anymore," Shelly says, getting in my face, stabbing her finger at my eye. "Is it really too much to ask? Huh? I told you I didn't like Andrea Phillips, but nooo, you still had to talk to her."

"I said, 'hi.'" The words come from my mouth, unbidden by my present-day self as I relive the experience.

"Oh, you admit it, then! Are you screwing her, too?"

"What? No. I just don't think—"

"You don't *think?* Yeah, I know you don't think. Because if you did, we wouldn't be having this conversation, would we?" She pulls at her hair and screams at the sky. "My god, the shit I have to put up with."

She laughs. "I told Jacky and Brianna about this crap you pull. They think I should break up with you. They think you're pathetic. I've tried with you, you know that, right? Had to fix the way you dressed. The way you styled your hair. Everything about you was flawed until you met me. And *this* is how you thank me? By fucking around with Andrea?"

I shrink in on myself, melting into a pliable mass of easily manipulated, emasculated sludge. Still, I attempt to defend myself. "I didn't do anything."

"Well, you're going to do something now, aren't you?"

That catches me off guard. If she's looking for sex in the woods—not uncommon after she acts like this—I'm not sure I'll be able to perform. "W-what do you mean?"

"You're going to tell her you don't like her. You're going to tell her she's ugly and fat."

"I-I can't do that." Not only is it not true—Andrea is thin and pretty—but I'm not a fucking monster.

"I'm sorry, *what* did you say?"

"I can't do that," I repeat, feeling good for putting my foot down.

She laughs again. "I'm sorry, do you think you have a choice?"

"I'm not an asshole," I say, firmer now.

Her glare staggers me back a step. "Did you just—I think you did . . ."

"Did . . . what?" I ask, growing nervous again.

"Call *me* an asshole?"

"What? No, I—"

I don't see the slap coming, but I sure as shit feel it. Shelly is athletic. Strong. And she doesn't hold back. The unexpected impact knocks me to the side. I catch hold of a young birch. It keeps me upright, but I'm stunned into silence.

"Oh. My god. Are you crying?"

I'm not, but she's acting like I am. Will tell everyone I cried. The fallout from saying hello to an old friend is going to haunt me for months. But I'm going to make like Tom Petty and not back down. "Andrea used to be my friend. I'm not going to purposefully hurt her feelings to make you feel better about yourself."

Holy fuck.

I'm screwed.

Why did I say that? Why did I say anything?

I learned long ago to nod and agree. Nod and agree. Nod and agree, and placate, and compliment, and satiate her need for reassurance—because she's the greatest and needs to be told that non-fucking-stop.

The anger is new. Feels good. Feels right.

And then she says it. The statement I've been waiting for, that she has used to shut down every argument for the past month. "You know what? Maybe we should just break up."

She's expecting me to cringe at hearing this. To one-eighty and beg for forgiveness. God, I've been so pathetic and weak. But I made a promise to myself last time it happened. That the next time she said those words, 'Maybe we should just break up,' that I would respond with a single word.

"Fine."

She flinches. "What?"

"If you want to break up, that's fine." I'm stoic now, hiding my emotions, putting all my energy into standing my ground. The second I falter, I'll fall apart, and old habits will take hold.

Shelly's inability to back down from something she's said locks her into agreeing, but she won't go without taking her pound of flesh. Worse, she will destroy every relationship I have—with lies and accusations. But it will be worth it. I already feel the weight of her on my life lifting.

Then she punches me in the gut. I'm strong and have fast reflexes. So, my stomach is clenched to absorb the blow, as it does the next twenty. Frustrated by my lack of outward pain, her twenty-second punch redirects toward my face.

I catch her fist in my hand and say, "Not my face."

She staggers back, her world crumbling as she suffers her worst fear—rejection. But I don't feel bad for her. She's . . . the worst. The thought makes me smile. She barks a sob and runs off in a huff, probably already thinking about who to put her hooks into next.

When she's out of sight, I drop to my knees and cry.

Warmth wraps around me, soothing my pain. It's Ami, I realize, and I accept her affection.

"I'm sorry," she says. "That . . . was horrible. What a cunt."

I laugh through my tears and lean back, only to discover that we're no longer in the woods. We're back in our room at the Grand Canyon. And I'm crying for real. We look at each other for a moment, and then she wraps her arms around me and, for the first time since that day in the woods, I cry about the years-long hell that chased me out of Maine.

19

I wake in the morning feeling lighter. I hadn't told anyone the details of the day, or about the bruises on my torso that took more than a week to fade. Not even Sara. She'd have gone to war on my behalf, and all I really wanted to do was escape.

And I did, for a bit. But now . . . I don't know what will happen if we're caught, but I feel like it will be worse than Shelly's unstable rage.

"You feeling okay?" Ami asks. She's standing in front of the bathroom door, freshly showered, naked, and toweling off.

"Feeling better now," I say, smiling.

"Seriously," she says. "That was rough. I felt what that was like for you."

"At least she wasn't a human trafficker."

"Ronny was scum of the earth, but it was my job to stop people like him. It was unexpected, and cost me my career, but it wasn't . . ." She frowns. "You went through years of emotional torture and control. It would have broken most people."

"I feel broken," I say.

"But you're not. I felt that, too. You're stronger than you give yourself credit for, and I'm willing to bet she wasn't like that early on in the relationship."

I stare at the ceiling. "Not overtly, but in hindsight there were tells. Even the affection and compliments she showered me with. It was all to get my guard down and make me feel dependent on it—desperate for more, willing to put up with her behavior because if I didn't, the love—which was really just control—would be withheld."

"Love bombing," Ami says.

I turn back to her. "Huh?"

"It's called 'love bombing,'" she says. "It's a form of psychological control employed by narcissists. It's especially effective on empathic people. And I don't mean like me. I sense people's emotions. I don't take them on. It's usually followed up with devaluation, gaslighting, isolation—from other friends—and if you step out of line, the silent treatment aka: stonewalling. The list of tactics employed by people like Shelly is long but well documented."

"Is there like a narcissist playbook or something? How do they know to do these things?"

"Learned from parents." She pulls on a fresh pair of underwear, which helps me pay better attention. "Instinctual. Trial and error. Over time, she'd have seen what worked and what didn't and adjusted to your vulnerabilities."

"So . . . what is it called when someone accuses you of something you didn't do?" I ask. I have lingering questions from my time with Shelly.

Ami scrunches her face. She doesn't like the question—or the answer. "With a narcissist, there's a good chance it's projection." She spots my blank expression. "That's when you accuse someone of something that you are doing. It offers relief from whatever guilty conscience they have, and keeps you so focused on proving your innocence that you don't notice the signs of their transgressions."

"So, when she accused me of screwing girls . . ."

Ami shrugs. "Assuming you didn't, and never actually gave a reason for her to think you were, it's . . . probable."

I rub my eyes. "Such a mind-fuck."

"For what it's worth, I won't cheat on you." She grins. "I'd break up with you first."

It gets a laugh out of me, but then I hear the subtext. "For you to cheat on me, we'd have to be . . ."

She throws a T-shirt on, hiding her expression—and body—from me. "We're a good team. Like Batman and Robin but less inappropriate in bed."

I'm laughing again. "That's just wrong."

"Is it?" she asks, crawling onto the bed, straddling me and then lowering her face over mine. "Imagine it. Me dressed as Robin. You as Batman. Tell me that doesn't turn you on."

She's fucking with me, but she *would* look cute in a Robin costume. "I'd prefer Shaggy and Velma."

She furrows her brow and purses her lips. "You know . . . in terms of accuracy—"

"I know, right?"

She leans down and kisses me. It's not passionate. Just soft and comfortable and lingering. When she leans back up, I say, "Zoinks." She leans back down, and I think the next kiss is going to be the kind that leads to something there isn't a Saturday morning cartoon analogy for.

A knock at the door freezes Ami in place.

We lock eyes, both of us serious. She rolls off me, slips into her pair of shorts, and opens a drawer.

"You going to smack someone with a Gideon Bible?" I ask.

But it's not a Bible she pulls out.

It's a small pistol.

"How long have you had *that?*" I ask, trying to remember if we stopped anywhere that sold firearms . . . to people paying in cash . . . without showing an ID.

"Since we left my apartment," she says. "Tucked into the back of my pants—now shorts. You guys aren't super observant."

"To be fair, if I'm looking at your backside, my eyes are a little lower than your belt line."

She rolls her eyes and motions to the bathroom with her head. "Get dressed. I'll answer the door."

While she approaches the door, gun in hand, I grab my heap of clothing and scurry to the bathroom, dressing as quickly as I can while hoping the evidence of our near coital mingling fades before I need to exit.

I hear Ami open the door and the chain lock snap tight. A moment later, it's unlocked. Must be the guys.

I finish dressing and give myself a bulge check. After a quick shake of the leg, everything looks normal enough. As an extra layer of caution, I carry a towel in front of me when I exit the bathroom.

Standing in the room with Ami is Josh. He's wearing a baseball cap backward and a pair of aviator sunglasses. It's very not Josh, but I gotta be honest, it's a better look than his usual disheveled nerd-core. His muted pink Cuban Guayabera shirt with patterned vertical stripes isn't very subtle, but most American vacationers are easy to spot, wearing fresh, bright clothing like it's the first day of middle school. He fits the stereotype.

He takes the sunglasses off when I give him a sheepish wave, towel still in place. He looks tired. Bags under his eyes are a shade darker than usual.

"Sleep okay?" I ask.

He grunts. "Chuck snores. So does Darius. It's like trying to sleep in a room with an ornery elephant seal and a leaf blower having an argument."

"Ouch," I say, and sit on the bedside, towel on my lap.

"They'll be over in a minute," he says. "Following the rules."

"Good," Ami says. "And FYI, today is going to suck. We need to stay in the rooms as much as possible."

He nods. "Of course. And tomorrow, we fly." His smile is slight, but present. "Honestly, it's all kind of exciting. It's like being Jason Bourne or something, without all the fighting and killing. On the run from a government agency. I'm finally going to have some street cred."

"Street cred won't go very far in a black ops federal prison," Ami says. It's a joke, but the effect on Josh's grin is apocalyptic.

He sits on the bed beside me. "What's with the towel?"

"I find the texture soothing," I blurt. Makes no sense. The towels are as soft as a hedgehog's back.

"Weird," he says and flops back onto the bed. Doesn't spot Ami shaking her head and rolling her eyes at me.

I lift the towel, do a quick crotch-check and, no longer needing it, toss it at her. The towel wraps around her head. Josh and I have a good laugh at her expense. My laughter is cut short when the towel reverses course and strikes my face.

"Ugh!" I stand and start spinning the towel. "That's it, little miss, I'm gonna—"

There's another knock at the door, but it's not the casual triple tap Josh used. It's a constant stream of gentle, but rapid-fire knocks that doesn't stop until I open the door a crack. It's Chuck, wide-eyed and frightened. "Open the door. Open the door. Open the door."

He's pushing on it, keeping me from undoing the chain lock again.

"Chuck!" I whisper-shout, snapping him out of his panic long enough to say, "I can't unlock it when you're pushing on it!"

He eases up just enough for me to undo the lock. Then he shoves the door open, lunges inside, and slams it shut behind him. Josh steps in front of him and takes hold of both arms. "Breathe, Chuck. You know how to do it. C'mon."

Josh starts slow breathing, pausing between inhaling and exhaling. Chuck follows right along. Looks like something they've done before, a routine for panic attacks, which I imagine was part of having visions of the past and future before understanding what he was seeing—like the vision of their home burning down, not knowing if it was real, not knowing if Darius and Josh were in the house. Now Chuck knows better. The vision could be of something that happens thirty years in the future.

That means the fear in his eyes isn't about a vision of the distant past or future. It's either a near-future event featuring one of us—like me getting shot in the head—or it's something that's actually happening in real time.

"Okay," Josh says. "Nice and easy. Tell me what's bugging you."

"Outside," Chuck says, swallowing air. "Outside, Josh. I saw them. I saw them."

"Saw who?" Ami asks.

Chuck looks at me. "Bald man. He was a bald man, Silas."

"Dude," Josh says. "There are a lot of bald men—"

"His—his skin was white. And not like your skin, Josh. Like paper. *White* white. And, and, he had no eyebrows, Silas. He's wearing a suit. And he's not alone. One of the—one of the men with him is wearing a Hawaiian shirt. Silas, you said you saw that yesterday. A Hawaiian shirt, Silas. You said that. I remember you said that, Silas."

"Easy," I tell him, feigning a Zen-like calm. "Where did you see them?"

"Outside." He looks me in the eyes, and his terror makes me queasy, because I suspect he's going to tell me—

Ami beats us both to the punch. "They're questioning Darius."

20

Ami winces. Shakes her head. "I know who's speaking, but I can't hear them. Any of them. Not even Darius. It's all jumbled—it's . . . I think he's blocking me. The bald guy."

"Is that even possible?" I ask.

"No one really knows what is and what isn't possible when it comes to the human mind," Josh says. "Extrasensory abilities have been considered pseudo-science for so long that the only people willing to research it are the government. People used to make fun of a person's UFO experiences, but now we know UFOs are real. Call them UAPs if you want. Doesn't change the fact that the government was willing to cover everything up, even if it meant destroying people's lives. It's the same shit. Cover it up, contain exposure, consolidate power."

"Okay, okay," I say. "I get all that. But now isn't the time for a debate. We need to do something."

"What can we do?" Josh asks.

Chuck shakes his hands. "Darius is in trouble. My brother is in trouble, Josh. I don't know what to do. I don't know what to do!"

I cup a hand over his still smiling mouth, heart breaking for the guy. "I do. But you need to be quiet."

I wait for him to nod and turn to Ami, who looks ready to object to me doing anything at all. "They don't know my face. I've already been cleared. They have no reason to suspect me."

"And what do you think you can do?" she asks.

"I can distract them," I say. "I can de-escalate."

"And if that doesn't work?" Josh asks.

"I can kick like a motherfucker and run like a bitch."

"And you have the strategic mind of a hot dog," Ami says.

"No one wins by doing nothing," I say and open the door.

Before I can exit, Josh grabs my arm. "Wait." He picks up my sunglasses and hands them to me. "Don't let him see your eyes."

"Windows to the soul?" I joke.

Josh frowns. "Yes."

I don the sunglasses and say, "Window shades applied." Then I step into the morning sun. I close the door behind me and stretch like I'm happy to be alive and oblivious to the men standing in the walkway two doors down. I grunt loudly like someone who isn't afraid of being spotted.

The men have noticed me. I catch a glimpse of the faces turned in my direction. Two of them are familiar. Agents Stephens and Keller. They're no longer dressed in suits. Keller is wearing a Hawaiian shirt. I saw him dressed like this when I was remote viewing. Stephens is dressed casually but is wearing pleated shorts and a tucked in pink polo shirt. Looks like he was born with a silver spoon in his mouth and a bug in his ass.

I touch my toes and grunt like it's hard to do. While upside down, my eyes flick to the bald man. I nearly laugh. He's a caricature. Skin so pale he must be an albino. He's bald and I don't see eyebrows. He's wearing sunglasses, so I can't see if he really has four eyes. His white suit, skin, and western-style fedora glow in the sunlight, making him hard to look at for very long, even with sunglasses on. The band on his fedora, his shirt beneath his suit jacket, and his shoes are the only things that aren't bright white. They're all black.

He looks like a Bond villain. Like he shops at Nefarious Bad Guys 'R' Us. He's not physically imposing. Maybe a foot shorter than me. Poor posture. But that's not really what makes him scary. It's his brain and what he might be able to do with it.

I stretch my calves one at a time and then bounce on my toes. And it's not all an act. I've spent enough time running to know how important stretching is. If we have to run for it, I don't want to pull a hammy.

With a pep in my step, I whistle "A.I. Girlfriend" by Custodians and walk toward the three men and Darius, who sees me coming, but doesn't react. Smart. What I do next, might not be.

I wave and smile. "Hey! Keller, my man. How's it going?"

The bald man's frown directed at Keller is subtle but carries the impact of a gunshot. All three men turn to face me, turning their backs to a terrified Darius.

"And you are?" the bald man asks.

"Holy shit, dude," I say, maintaining my chill, oblivious act. "You sound like an agent. I mean, not like these guys. Not FBI. More like in *The Matrix*. You know. 'Mr. Anderson.'"

The bald man turns to Stephens, asking a question without speaking. And I don't think he's using telepathy to do it. His body language screams, 'Who is this buffoon?'

Stephens clears his throat. "We questioned and cleared him last night, sir."

"I gave him my card," Keller says, "in case he spotted one of our persons of interest."

"And yet, here he is," Baldy says, "two doors down from a 'person of interest,' oblivious."

"Distracted, yes," I say. "Flighty? Debatable. Oblivious? That stings, man."

"Mm," he says. "And you are . . . ?"

"Silas Keene," I say and offer my hand. "Also, I think what you guys do is sick. Hey Keller, do you think I have the chops to be an agent?"

No one answers. My hand hangs there. "And you are?"

I'm pushing it but trying to stay in character—which is a guy who has absolutely no fear of the FBI. "And *you* are? C'mon man, don't leave me hanging."

The man doesn't shake my hand but does offer his name.

"Paul Morrow," he says.

"Don't you mean 'Special Agent Paul Morrow?'"

"*Dr.* Paul Morrow."

"Dr. Morrow? Kind of gives Kevorkian vibes. Like Marrow. Which is *awesome!* What's a doctor going door to door for? Do those guys you're looking for have spicy crotch rot or something?" I lean around Morrow and ask Darius, "Yo, my man, you got coital eczema? Sizzle drip? Type 3 urethral spongiformitis? Whatever it is, keep that shit *away* from me."

Darius says nothing but picks up on the subtle shift in the word 'away.' He takes a slow step back toward his door. The rooms have windows out the building's far side. If he can get inside and lock the door, he should be able to get out and make a run for it before these guys can run around. I just need to hold their attention for a few more seconds.

Before I can think of what to say or do next, Morrow laughs.

Stephens and Keller share a nervous glance. Morrow is definitely in charge, and their fear of him is visceral . . . and concerning. He points at Darius. "This man is insignificant." His finger rotates around to me. "This is the one we want."

"Sir, he's a—"

Morrow tilts his head in Keller's direction, silencing him. Then he turns to face me while Darius slips back into his room and closes the door. Not sure he realizes that the plan needs to change now that I've been made.

Morrow turns to me and lowers his sunglasses.

I flinch back.

His eyes look the same as they did in the remote viewing—red and two pupils and irises in each eye. "Do I frighten you, Mr. Keene?"

"Hell yes, you do."

"Good," he says. "Then we won't have a problem, will we?"

I feel an itch in my forehead. Not on my head, like from a mosquito bite. Inside my head. The intensity increases. I feel like a hooked fish being dragged toward a fate I don't want.

A quick slap to my own face shakes the hook loose and refocuses me. "Listen, Dr. Evil, I don't know what the hell you're after, but you're not going to get shit from me."

He grins. "Intriguing." He looks at Keller. "His casual demeanor is a ruse. His heart is pounding. He is terrified."

"*He* is trying to implant thoughts in my head," I say. It's a joke, but then I realize that's exactly what's happening. His brain is different, too, and he's had a lot of practice. "But hey, I can be honest. I'm freaking out. My ass crack is sweating like the Colorado running through the Grand Canyon."

Keller fights a grin.

It disappears when Morrow takes a step away from me and says, "Take him."

As Stephens and Keller circle around in front of Morrow, I back up a step. "Guessing you two aren't actually FBI agents?"

"Sorry," Stephens says, slipping on a pair of brass knuckles. "How much can I hurt him?"

"Broken bones," Morrow says. "Avoid his head. I want him alive and awake."

Who the fuck are these guys? I think to myself and then follow through with step two of my plan. I kick hard, aiming for Stephens's nuts. Despite looking like a stick in the mud, he's no slouch. Blocks my kick with his brass knuckled fist. I reel back from the strike, hissing in pain, wondering if he's broken anything in my foot.

He steps in close and strikes faster than I'd have guessed was possible. He drives the brass knuckles into my gut. I drop to the walkway, gasping for air.

A short, Asian angel of death appears over me, handgun aimed at Stephens's head. "You so much as clench your sphincter and I will put a bullet between your eyes."

Behind Stephens, Keller starts drawing his pistol. Ami doesn't have the shot, and as soon as she diverts her aim, Stephens will attack. But she doesn't need to do anything. Darius charges out of his room, strikes Keller from behind, and slams him into the building on the walkway's far side. The pistol falls to the concrete. Darius snatches it up and levels it at Morrow. "Okay, you freaky-ass bitch. Time for you to talk."

Morrow smiles.

21

Morrow raises his hands, but his grin never falters, like he's still got control of the situation. But we're in charge now. Well, Ami is. She frisks Stephens and takes his pistol. Does the same to Morrow, but he's not carrying.

She hands Stephens's pistol to me. I've fired rifles in the woods back home. A handgun just once. I don't know much about them. Couldn't tell you what kind of weapon I'm holding. Looks boring. Probably some kind of standard issue thing. And heavy. But I know how it works and that's what's important at the moment.

Not that I want to shoot it.

Definitely don't want to kill anyone, even if they're *no bueno*. I just don't have that kind of killer instinct. Hell, I let Shelly beat the shit out of me. A single backhand would have ended her attack and would have been justified. I'm a feminist after all. Anyone who strikes another human being shouldn't complain when karma swings back. But having power doesn't mean you need to use it.

Plus, taking the high road can be more painful for the asshole trying to trigger you. I think there's a Bible verse about that. *Being nice to an asshole is like heaping hot coals on their head.* That's an extreme paraphrase, but I think it's accurate.

But if you're being nice heaping hot coals . . . are you actually being nice?

Question for another time.

"Who are you?" Ami asks, directing the question at Morrow.

He remains silent and unruffled.

"Why are you following us?" she asks. "And don't try to pass yourself off as FBI, or any other three letter acronym."

"You would know," Stephens says with a chuckle. "Your two weeks at the bureau makes you an expert?"

"Two weeks is longer than any of you idiots." Ami is getting angry. Mocking her past with the FBI is the wrong approach for anyone not wanting to get shot. "You didn't follow a single protocol. Your attempts at blending in are laughable. You're going door to door instead of having local PD do it for you. And your pistols—" She points at the weapon in my hand. "What is that? A CZ Shadow 2?" She laughs. "It's a range toy, *tacticult* weapon. You guys are private mall ninjas, hired as heavies for . . ." She turns her full attention to Morrow. ". . . this guy."

"I look forward to your assessment," he says.

"You're a freaky-ass sonuvabitch," Ami says, taking off his sunglasses, revealing his four eyes in two sockets.

He flinches and squints at the sun. Light sensitive thanks to his albinism.

"I don't like his eyes," Chuck says. "Ami, I don't like his eyes!"

"Easy, buddy," Josh says, rubbing Chuck's back. "He's just different. Doesn't mean he's scary."

"Not scary?" Morrow says. "Now I'm insulted."

"So, what are you?" she asks. "Independent morons moonlighting as a government agency? Or black budget morons moonlighting as a government agency?"

"I think you know the answer to that question," he says. "Why else would you change your clothing, pose as tourists, and take out cash . . ." He glances at Chuck, who's standing behind me with Josh, wringing his hands together. ". . . to charter a private flight to Puerto Rico."

Okay. So. He can read minds, too. But I don't think he's just hearing thoughts. I think he's digging for information. I felt him try the same on me, but I was able to push him out. Chuck is an easier target.

"Eyes on me," Ami says, whacking Morrow in the side of the head.

He clenches his jaw, trying to hide his emotions, but it doesn't take an empath to know he's pissed.

"Here's what's going to happen," Ami says. "You're going to explain yourselves, tell me who you're working for, and if I sense a lie—and I wouldn't test me—I'm going to put a bullet in the leg of the person bullshitting me. Then I'm going to call my pals at the FBI—who know what I sacrificed for them—and see what happens when they find three assholes with fake IDs harassing citizens."

Morrow's creepy perma-grin broadens, showing teeth. "Oh, I like you."

"We aren't telling you shit, bitch," Stephens says. A moment later, he's on the ground clutching a bullet wound to his thigh.

Ami wasn't bluffing. While the rest of us lower our hands from our ears, she says, "Now you're on the clock. How long until the police show up? You might have a get out of jail free card, but they're going to take one look at your IDs and lock you up."

"There's nowhere you can run that I can't—" She whacks Morrow in the head with her pistol, this time drawing blood.

Man, am I glad Ami is on my side.

She turns the pistol on Keller. "Who do you work for?"

Keller's face screws up. I think he's trying to respond—but can't. Is he just terrified, or is Dr. Morrow actually preventing him? I wouldn't have believed it two days ago, but I've seen some shit that is making me reconsider the fundamental laws of reality.

She adjusts her aim toward his leg. "Who do you work for?"

She's about to pull the trigger when I lean in close to her ear and whisper, "I know we need the info, but I'm not sure he can talk."

Ami glances at me, eyes widening slightly. She gets it, maybe because she's intuitive, maybe because she's also getting a whiff of my thoughts.

Relief washes over Keller when Ami redirects her weapon at Morrow. "I'm asking the wrong person. Now, who do you work for?"

"You *won't* shoot me," he says, all four of his eyes vibrating as he glares at her.

She leans in closer, not backing down from his stare. "You're not getting in my head, Cosplay Caillou, so make like a dog, and speak. Who. Do. You. Work. For?"

The side of Morrow's nose twitches in a sneer. He's maintaining control but raging on the inside. Through grinding teeth, he says, "The Smithsonian."

I have a good laugh at that. "You want us to believe you work for a museum?"

My laughter fades when I look around for someone to share the laugh with, point at Morrow, and say, "This guy!" But no one else finds the answer ridiculous. Only Darius looks as clueless as me, and he's preoccupied by the gun in his hand, aimed at Stephens.

"What am I missing?" I ask.

"Uhh," Josh says, like what he's about to say is obvious and well known. "Most people think the Smithsonian is just a museum, right? Science. History. Natural wonders. Shit like that. But that's just a façade, man. The Smithsonian is a government-funded, quasi-federal entity with ties to the military, the intelligence community, and even high-level academia. And they've got a hidden mandate, man."

"Collect, suppress and control anything that challenges the accepted narrative of human history," Ami says.

Josh snaps his fingers and points at her. "That. Any time something strange is discovered—giant skeletons, anomalous artifacts, buried cities—they take over, remove the evidence, shut down investigations, and disappear witnesses. If the discovery was made public before they get there, they plant evidence, discredit everyone involved, and present the whole thing as a hoax.

"Did you know that there are hundreds of accounts from the 1800s and early 1900s about giant human remains? I'm talking like eight to twelve feet tall. Not the kind of thing that can be explained by genetics or even something like acromegaly."

"Acro-what?" Darius asks.

"Hormonal disorder caused by excess growth hormone resulting from a pituitary gland tumor," Morrow says.

"Most of those old reports end with, 'sent to the Smithsonian for further study,' and then poof! Gone. You know how many of those giant bones have been put on display? None. They're just . . . gone. And I don't mean hidden. In the 1930s, a former Smithsonian employee said that thousands of skeletons that didn't fit the established model of human evolution were destroyed. Incinerated. Erased from history.

"Because they're not officially a law enforcement agency, they operate with zero oversight. And they vacuum up history, displaying just one percent of the hundred and fifty million artifacts they've collected. They're a curation filter. The gatekeepers of history. And when something comes along that threatens the colonial, patriarchal, puritan, religious worldview of their founders, they cover it up, burn it down, and if it's something still active, still ongoing, like, oh, I don't know, people with psychic abilities? They make it disappear."

Josh steps around Ami and gets in Morrow's face. "Tell me I'm wrong."

Morrow stays silent, eyes vibrating back and forth.

He's trying to get in Josh's head.

Josh grits his teeth but forces a smile. "Hope you enjoy the lyrics to *WAP*, asshole, because I've got it running on repeat in my head. I might not have the gift, but I know more than enough to shut you down. So, look me in the eyes and tell me I'm wrong."

"I can't," Morrow says.

Ami slips her finger around the trigger. Adjusts her aim at Morrow's leg. I have no doubt she's about to pull the trigger.

Neither does Morrow. He grins, Kubrick-stares at Josh with his four red eyes, and says, "I can't tell you you're wrong . . . because everything you've said—is true."

22

Just so we're clear," I ask, "you're rounding up people with different minds because we don't fit the Smithsonian's preferred mold of human development?"

"Heavens, no," Morrow says. "On the contrary, we believe that people like us—" He levels all four eyes at me when he says this. "—are the future of human development. Our minds are evolving to a modern world. No longer bound to tasks of survival, our minds are free to branch out. Make new connections. We can experience and interact with the world in new ways. Scientists first noticed the subtle shift in the sixties, and now . . . now it's undeniable.

"Extrasensory perception, remote viewing, telepathy, telekinesis—it's all possible. Before you have fantasies about exploding people's minds with a thought—"

"*Mind Bullet*," Josh whispers. "Great book."

"—this is the real world, and abilities are currently limited, misunderstood and, even for the best of us, a work in progress."

"You've met other people like us?" Ami asks, not bothering to pretend she isn't gifted.

"Oh yes," he says. "Many."

"And where are they now?" she asks.

"Oh, here and there," he says. "Most of them work for me now."

Ami scoffs. "Please don't tell me this is your attempt at recruitment."

"I admit, we came in a little hot and heavy, but I'm not usually pressed for time. And . . . most people don't run." Morrow grins. "Then again, it's rare to find people like you two—" He glances from Ami to me. "—working together. How long have you been a team?"

He doesn't mention Chuck, which is good news. I push thoughts of Chuck far from my mind, just in case.

Ami looks at a watch she's not wearing and says, "Almost two days."

Morrow's eyebrows rise. "And already a formidable pair."

"Why are you recruiting people with abilities?" Ami asks, giving the gun a waggle, reminding everyone who is currently in charge. "Why go to all this effort for us?"

"We were completely oblivious to your existence until one of you . . ." He points at me. ". . . you, I suspect . . . had a look at our operation. It was just a glance the first time, but I saw you. There, and then gone. Had you not returned, tracing your location would have been impossible."

"The cliff face," I say. "The eyes."

He motions to his face. "Do they look the same in the mind's eye?"

I nod. "But there were six, rather than four."

"Guys," Ami says. "Can you please stop answering *his* questions?"

"May I have my sunglasses back?" he asks. "The sun is quite unbearable."

When his shades are returned and back over his eyes, I relax a bit. With all four eyes visible, he looks like some kind of super villain. Covered up, he's just a creepy dude who looks like he's going to audition for a remake of the "Smooth Criminal" music video.

"I'm going to ask a few questions now," Ami says. "First non-answer or lie gets a bullet. Understood?"

"Very much so," Morrow says, smiling. He's getting a kick out of all this. Doesn't fear for his life, or about the pain Ami could inflict. Suggests he knows something we don't.

"Why us? Why now? What's the rush?"

"Your proximity to our operation was fortuitous. We just became aware of you. We have an urgent need of people like yourselves." He grins. "I believe that answers all of your questions."

"What is the urgent need?" she asks.

"I'm afraid I can't say. You of all people understand the need for secrecy. In the same way you agreed to cover up your investigatory short cuts for the greater good, I must do the same. If our project was public knowledge . . ." He shakes his head. "Catastrophe."

"For you," I say.

He shakes his head. "For the world."

Ami squints at him. "Bullshit."

"You will learn, as you get to know me, that I do not lie." Morrow looks serious. No hint of a joke. "But you are free to think whatever you like, for now."

For now? The hell does that mean?

Ami points her pistol at his leg again. "Nor do I. Speak or limp, it's up to you."

"All will be explained in due time, but not here." He glances around. People have started to gather. "Not with all these ears. And certainly not when I have the upper hand."

"You do understand how a pistol works, yes?" Ami says.

"And I understand that while you've been playing Go Fish, digging for information, I've been playing Strategema." He waits for a reaction and gets blank stares. "Ahh, well. Not everyone can be a well-rounded consumer of media." He tilts his head toward his collar and says, "Make yourselves known."

At the far end of the walkway, two black SUVs converge, blocking our escape. The only way to get away is toward the canyon. But that's not an option, either. A black helicopter rises from the canyon, its rotor chop hidden until it's in the air above us.

Dust kicks up and swirls down the walkway. The helicopter turns its side toward us. A man in black stands in the open side door, hands on the trigger of what I'd call a minigun but which might be something else to people who know more about firearms. Don't need to know what it's called to understand it can cut me in half with the ease of a guillotine blade dropping on a worm.

"Weapons," Morrow says, holding out a hand.

"I could still kill you," Ami says, weapon now aimed at Morrow's head.

"Meh." Morrow shrugs. "I'm sure you might if it wouldn't result in the immediate, painful deaths of your friends."

Ami spins the gun around and places it in Morrow's hand. He turns to Darius and he does the same. Morrow turns to me next, and I shrug. "I feel like being petty." I toss the gun out over the Grand Canyon and it falls out of sight.

"Hey man," Keller says. "That was mine."

I feel a little bad for Keller. He strikes me as a normal guy who's in over his head working for douchebags. "It wasn't like an heirloom or something?"

He shakes his head. "But it *was* a custom build."

Ami rolls her eyes. "Like I said, range toys." She tilts her chin up at Morrow. "Lead the way, Casper."

"Somebody's trying to get cancelled," Morrow jokes and then turns to Stephens, who is on his feet but limping. "Take these three—" He points to Josh, Darius, and Chuck. "—to Topside."

"You're not splitting us up," Josh says, but clamps his mouth shut when Stephens points a pistol at him. "Splitting up and shutting up."

"We mean you no harm," Morrow says. "For now, we simply require your submissive obedience."

Ami glares but says nothing. I follow her lead.

"I don't like this, Darius," Chuck says. "I don't want to go with them. Darius, I don't want to—"

"Chuck," Morrow says. "Chuck, Chuck, Chucky. You have nothing to fear. I know this is all a bit strange, but if all goes well, you will have played a small part in saving the world from destruction. Your brain-injury might have left you diminished, but I believe you have a part to play yet. Would you like to help save the world, Chuck?"

“Uhh, yes. Yes. I would. That would be awesome. Darius, that would be awesome, right?”

Darius frowns, but says, “Super awesome.”

“Oh, good,” Chuck says. “I’m glad, Darius. I’m glad you think it would be super awesome.”

“Now then.” Morrow motions to the black SUVs and the Three Musketeers are led away by Stephens and Keller.

“What about us?” I ask.

Morrow points behind us. The black helicopter has spun around and landed, its side door open, the gunner now turned around, beckoning us to board.

Ami sighs and sags. Nudges me with her elbow. “C’mon. Let’s take the Mad Hatter’s carriage.”

“Oh,” Morrow says, following us toward the helicopter. “Wonderland is nothing compared to what you’re about to see.”

23

Aside from the helicopter's rotor chop, the flight is silent. We don't ask questions. Morrow doesn't offer any information. I don't even talk to Ami. I consider thinking thoughts to her, but Morrow is just as likely to hear them. So, I keep my eyes on the view, which is incredible.

I've never been on a helicopter before. The constant motion doesn't agree with my stomach, but the shifting lines of colorful stone strata keep my mind occupied so I don't worry too much about puking.

Then again, if I retch I'll make sure to do it in Morrow's direction.

The thought puts a smile on my face.

As we descend, the canyon walls close in on either side. Going to be a tight fit at the bottom. I lean close to the window and look down. We're only about a hundred feet up and the view below is . . . familiar.

I flinch when I realize this is what I saw in my first remote viewing sessions. This is the rock wall with the eyes, except the eyes aren't actually in the stone. They're in the head of the guy seated diagonally across from me. But he was here when I visited, and he detected me watching.

The mirrorlink.

Being abducted because I'm able to remote view is surreal. Terms like *mirrorlink* weren't part of my vocabulary until yesterday.

My knowledge of extrasensory abilities mostly comes from Professor X and Jean Grey. I am in over my head and, in the end, I doubt I'll be much use to Morrow.

And I don't know if that's a good or bad thing. Because if I'm not valuable, I'm a liability, right? I doubt they'll just let me leave. Best case scenario, I'll need to sign an NDA and be on my way. And I really hope that's what's happening with the guys.

Because the alternative is that they're already dead, and when I can't do whatever Morrow wants, I won't be far behind them.

Ami is a different story. She's known about her ability for a long time. Has researched and practiced. Doesn't mean she'll willingly help, though. So, this view of the canyon might be the last beautiful thing I see.

I decide to enjoy it, marveling at the layers of ancient history.

How far back are we at that bottom? I wonder.

"At the bottom? Two billion years," Morrow says, his voice clear over the headset I'm wearing. "Vishnu Schist and Zoroaster Granite. Building blocks of the old Earth, before the emergence of complex lifeforms, but long after the emergence of single-celled lifeforms. We humans like to think the world is ours, but bacteria have called this world home for billions of years, whereas we are the noisy, dirty new neighbors. At our current altitude . . ." He points at a band of dark red rock. "See the rusty looking band? One point nine billion years old. Photosynthetic cyano-bacteria led to the Great Oxygenation Event that killed off many anaerobic organisms and ushered in the dawn of complex cellular life. Eukaryotes—cells with a nucleus—emerged and would eventually give rise to plants, fungi, animals . . . you."

I'm not sure how to respond, so I'm just honest. "Wild."

Morrow nods. "Indeed. But you will be far less impressed by the day's end."

Not sure what he means by that, and he doesn't elaborate. Not wanting to appear too friendly with the enemy, I don't ask.

I glance at Ami. She hasn't moved since sitting down and crossing her arms. She's impossible to read, and I think that's intentional. She hasn't glanced in my direction once or shown any sign of affection. I suspect she's trying to hide our connection because it could be used against us, but . . . I'm much more of an open book.

I'm trying to hide my thoughts, but feelings are trickier. Just looking at her for a moment triggers a cocktail of emotions. No idea whether Morrow can detect people's feelings, but the subtle downturn of Ami's lips reminds me that she can, and she doesn't approve of my undisciplined emotional state.

To conceal my thoughts and feelings, I turn to the past.

My first kiss. It wasn't Shelly, thank god.

It was a girl named Penny. Last name, unknown. We were friends for a summer. That happens with kids sometimes. They show up in your life and then, for some reason, they just disappear. She was new to the neighborhood and only around on weekends—when her father had her. Not that he ever saw her. She was mostly with me.

We were kindred spirits, exploring the woods, setting things on fire, fishing, and talking about our favorite animated shows. Hers: *Adventure Time.* Mine: *Ben 10.* We both agreed that *Phineas and Ferb* was a solid runner-up.

It occurs to me that Dr. Morrow gives off 'son of Dr. Doofenshmirtz' vibes, and I chuckle.

Then I'm back in the memory. Walking in the woods. We'd known each other for three months at this point. Solid friends. All in person. No tech. No public online connection—her request. During the walk, she tripped and I caught her. She was wrapped in my arms, and we both froze. Felt like we were standing like that for minutes. Then, she kissed me gently and lingered for just a moment.

I was thirteen and it felt like magic.

As my eyes widened and my smile spread, we separated, and I danced around like a fool. She laughed and we continued our adventure for the rest of the day, holding hands. When we parted that night, a kiss goodbye.

What I didn't know was that it was a final kiss goodbye.

I never saw her again. When I returned the following weekend, new people were moving into her father's apartment, and I had no way to contact her. Still don't know what happened to her. That last day with Penny was one of the best of my life and, a week later, it became one of the most painful to think about. Even now. I miss her, not for the kiss or the potential for romance, but because she might have been the best friend I ever had.

"You could find her," Morrow says, confirming that he'd been listening in. Then again, I was kind of broadcasting my memories to hide my thoughts. Which means Ami heard it all, too.

I'm not worried about that. Ami knows how I feel about her and is emotionally mature enough to not feel intimidated by a memory. Then again, if Morrow is telling the truth, maybe she *would* have a problem with it.

"I've remote viewed all of three times? Maybe four?" I say. "That doesn't sound likely."

"There is nothing on, around, or in this planet that you won't be able to see, with practice. I can show you how."

Ami moves for the first time, turning toward me. "He's not wrong. I liked her a lot more than Shelly."

I chuckle. "Me too."

The helicopter jolts to a stop. I was so deep in the past that I didn't feel us slowing down or detect the shift in the rotor's pitch. As the blades' spin slows, Morrow removes his headset and leans forward. Waits for us to remove our headsets, then says, "Do what I say. Answer my questions. Take my tests. And when you are done, I will reveal all to you. At that point, you'll have a choice to make. Stay or leave." He grins. "But I have no doubt in the outcome. By this time tomorrow, you will think of me as an ally."

I don't bother responding. Ami stays quiet, too. No point in antagonizing the man while we're his prisoners. Preferably, things stay amicable. Not only will we be treated better, but he's more likely to reveal more than if we remain blatant adversaries.

That said, this plan will only work if he answers a single question. "Where are the guys? Are they okay?"

"That was two questions," he says. My inner monologue is playing like an audiobook in his mind. "But rest assured, 'the guys' are fine. They're being questioned. When they are cleared, they will be brought here." He turns to Ami and motions to his head. "Feel free to confirm."

She grimaces. "I'll take your word for it."

The armored and silent soldier, whose face is mostly hidden by a helmet and sunglasses, opens the side door and climbs out onto a concrete landing pad that has been painted to match the stone around it. From the air it would be invisible but, like most paintings, the illusion is ruined up close. It's impressive, but I keep it to myself.

Not that it matters.

You're in my head, right?

"I'm not," he says, climbing out behind me.

Ami exits last and claps me on the shoulder. "You just think really loud. If you want to avoid narrating life to the mind readers around you, pick a song and put it on repeat in your head."

"Better yet," Morrow says, "make it an annoying song and we will actively block you."

Odd, I think. *Why is he being—*

John Jacob Jingleheimer Schmidt

His name is my name too

Whenever we go out

The people always shout

"There goes John Jacob Jingleheimer Schmidt!"

Da da da da da da daaa . . .

Ami and Morrow both wince for a moment and then look back to normal.

"And just like that," Morrow says. "You're blocked."

"Why don't you normally have people blocked?" I ask.

"Tactical advantage," Ami says.

"Indeed," Morrow says. "You know the old adage . . ." He waves a hand in an arc. "'The more you know.' Now, please follow me."

Morrow steps away, but neither Ami nor I follow. We're not trying to be difficult, we're just mesmerized by the view. We're at the bottom of the Grand Canyon. The Colorado River flows past, just a few feet from the landing pad. On this side of the river is a rocky shoreline. On the river's far side, the cliffs rise quickly. And man, does it make you feel small. I've been to Manhattan. Have stared up at the walls of towering skyscrapers. But they are dwarfed by the Grand Canyon which, in some places, is a mile deep. Here . . . you could stack three Empire State Buildings on top of each other and still fit a 30 Rockefeller Plaza on top. Manhattan feels small in comparison. The canyon isn't just deep—it's prehistoric trench-of-the-gods deep.

"You can sight-see later," Morrow says. "Time is not on our side."

While the chopper finishes winding down and the soldier remains in place, Morrow leads us toward a flat wall.

"Is this like an 'open sesame' kind of situation?" I ask.

"It's more of an illusion," he says, "And not one created by me, or anyone living." He leads us to the side and what looked like a flat wall straight on slowly becomes an entryway hidden by a wall of stone that blends perfectly with the cliff face behind it. From the river, it would be easy to miss it.

"What's inside?" I ask.

"A world that predates modern human history," he says, and then steps into the vertical entryway carved directly in the canyon's solid rock wall.

I glance at Ami and she shrugs. Then she whispers, "Keep that song in your head. Belt it out now and then. Keep him from hearing you. At some point, we won't be useful, and he's going to kill us. We need to find out what's going on, and either get the fuck out—or kill him first. Can you fly a helicopter?"

"What? *No.*" I say, feeling more nervous than I was in the chopper. I don't want to kill anyone, even if they are a creepy four-eyed asshole who took us captive at minigun point.

Morrow leans out of the doorway, sunglasses off, red quad-eyes revealed. He waves for us to follow and offers a friendly, "This way, my fellow Espers."

24

I'm not sure what to expect inside the cave, but if you gave me an infinite number of guesses, I'd be a skeleton before guessing correctly. There are just three things that make sense in the fifty-foot tall, smooth-walled cavern on the other side of the cave entrance—two large lights in the ceiling, and a futuristic looking doorway.

That's where the normal world ends and the surreal begins.

Two forty-foot-tall statues flank the modern doorway. They're carved from the canyon rock and have the same strata layers as the walls behind them. They'd probably be hard to see without the two lights in the ceiling, each shining down and adding depth and shadow to the sculptures.

Each statue is of a giant seated man. They're similar but hold different objects in their hands. No idea what the objects are supposed to be. They're not wearing clothing and are somewhat muscular. They're like if Michelangelo sculpted a seated pharaoh.

Both men are stoic. Noble. Powerful. They wear different headdresses. One pointed and Pope-like. The other fans out like a clam shell. But there's one feature that stands out as odd—their eyes. At first glance, they appear Asian, but the slant is wrong. Instead, the lower lid is dominant, folding up on either side. As a result, the eyes are turned up . . . like smiles.

It's just enough to create a solid uncanny valley vibe. Human, but maybe not?

"You noticed the eyes," Morrow says. I don't think he's reading my mind, just looking at my unnerved expression as I stare up at the statues' faces. "They're human, if you're wondering about that. Their skeletal features and musculature are consistent with those of Homo sapiens. But there is a subtle difference around the eyes. In the same way people of Asian descent—" He motions to Ami.

"Thanks for pointing out that I'm Asian," she snarks. "I thought I was Irish."

"In the same way people of Asian descent have ocular features created by epicanthic folds and downward slanting palpebral fissures, this long-lost race of humanity has a positive canthal tilt and distinctive lateral epicanthic variants that I call the 'epimirth fold.'"

"I get it," Ami says. "Mirth. Smile. How long did you spend coming up with that? Look, this is all very interesting, but what in the hell is this place, and why did the U.S. government carve two naked dudes into the—hold on. This isn't like some Mason Illuminati shit?"

Morrow smiles. "You think *we* made this?"

"Native American tribes didn't have the ability to carve solid stone like this. Not even the Aztec or Maya, at the peak of their cultures, could have carved this stone with such precision." She runs her hand over the shin of the giant Pope. "It's smooth. Almost polished. And the height?" She looks up, shaking her head. "How did they get all the way up there? Impossible. This is modern."

Morrow grins. "There are several megalithic structures built by the ancients that still defy explanation. Theories abound, but they are impossible to prove and most theories just feel . . . wrong."

"I get it," I say. "No way people could move stones that weigh a bazillion tons by rolling them over logs. It doesn't make sense."

"It's almost like the knowledge of how it was done was forgotten . . . but known to ancient cultures all around the world.

A shared technique passed down by common ancestors who had long ago figured out how to create wonders."

Ami is agitated, acting like she's being taken for a ride. "But that kind of ancient construction knowledge didn't exist in North America."

"Yes and no," Morrow says. "You're correct that there are no giant block structures in North America, but there are several examples of massive cave systems being carved into stone faces. Mesa Verde. Canyon de Chelly. Montezuma Castle, which is neither a castle nor has anything to do with Montezuma. There are enough common features that we believe the inspiration for those early American dwellings came from the cave system we now stand in, which predates the arrival of modern humans from Beringia—the land bridge that connected Siberia and Alaska during the last ice age, when sea levels were much lower."

"Predates . . ." Ami shakes her head. "That was twenty thousand years ago, and what, fifteen thousand years before the pyramids?"

"Indeed," he says. "I appreciate your knowledge of ancient history. It is not in your profile."

"Guess you didn't get my streaming history," she says, eyeing the statues. "So, Dr. Morrow, how old *is* this place?"

"Keep in mind, this is an estimate. We could be off by several thousand years in either direction." He pauses for dramatic effect. Then says, "One hundred thousand years."

"One hundred thousand years," I repeat, putting a pinkie up to the side of my mouth, nearly making Ami laugh. Glad she got the reference, or I'd have looked ridiculous.

"That's just . . . stupid," Ami says. "You expect us to believe that this place was built by what—cavemen with stone tools, who magically appeared on this side of the planet, long before people figured out how to make boats? Where is the evidence?"

Morrow looks confused. Glances at me for confirmation that I understand the answer to the question. I decide to show him I do. "Ami, I think we're standing in it."

"Perhaps you'd like to hear the story of how this cave system was discovered?" Morrow asks.

"Let me guess," she says. "You were rafting down the river, on a routine expedition with Marshal, Will, and Holly?"

Morrow is confused again. So am I. "Who are—"

"Never mind," Ami says. "Point is, you're about to tell us an amazing story about how you—"

"I didn't discover this site, and the men who did are long dead."

"This feels like an impending info dump," I say. "Aren't we supposed to be doing something interesting to offset the boring unraveling of information?"

Morrow raises his eyebrows at me. "We're standing in a giant cave with two massive statues carved by a human civilization that predates recorded history by ninety-five thousand years."

"Fair point," I say and wait for him to continue.

He begins to pace, hands clasped behind his back. I brace myself for the mother of all info dumps. "April fifth, 1909. A story was published in the *Arizona Gazette*. The headline? *Explorations in Grand Canyon: Remarkable finds indicate ancient people migrated from the Orient.*"

"Long headline," I say.

He ignores me. "Two men are mentioned in the article. G.E. Kinkaid, an explorer who claimed to be working for the Smithsonian. And Professor S.A. Jordan, who oversaw the excavation. Now, Kinkaid was very vocal about the discovery, claiming to have discovered a vast underground city near Marble Canyon, along the Colorado River. He told of a massive cave system with hieroglyphs, statues resembling Egyptian gods, mummies, weapons, and strange tools. He also claimed that the entrance was high on the cavern wall.

"Some of his story was outright bullshit. The entrance is on the ground level, and nowhere near Marble Canyon, which is much farther downstream. I personally believe that these two details were misdirection to keep others from finding and pillaging his discovery. The rest of his claims . . . Well, he was simply misinformed, lacking modern technology, and suffered from a chronic case of no imagination.

"It's said that Kinkaid contacted his higher ups at the Smithsonian, who sent a team to excavate, and then . . . nothing. The story ends there, as far as the public is concerned. No more articles. No documentation at the Smithsonian. And neither man was heard from or seen ever again.

"They were disappeared," I say.

He shakes his head. "They were put in charge, and it didn't take long for them to understand that what they'd stumbled onto wasn't Egyptian, and it shouldn't be publicly known. For a long time, the remote location and illusion guarding the entrance was enough. In 1987, a group of rafters who ran aground stumbled upon the entrance, came inside unnoticed, and found themselves in a situation they could not survive."

"The Smithsonian killed them?" Ami asks.

"Hardly," Morrow says. "We will discuss the nature of their deaths, which weren't the first and nowhere near the last, later today. But the result of their unfortunate discovery was the 1987 National Parks Overflights Act, which banned low flying aircraft over the canyon, and set the tone for restricting sensitive areas—especially those with tribal or ecological significance—which can be anywhere we want or need. The 1988 Grand Canyon Backcountry Management Plan prohibits entry into unmapped caves and abandoned mines for safety, archaeological protection, and Tribal sovereignty—again, giving the Smithsonian a broad sword when it comes to cleaving away portions of the canyon from the public."

"And how do you fit into all of this?" Ami asks. "How old are you? Forty? You'd have been a baby."

"Not yet born," he says. "And I'm younger than I look." He holds his hands out to me, pleading for patience despite the fact that I'm actually fascinated by the story. "I'm almost done." He clears his throat. "I was brought on to the Parallax Initiative ten years ago, after graduating from the MKSearch program. Before you ask, MKSearch *is* a continuation of MKUltra with a deeper classification, better organization, and refined techniques. I was one of few to finish the program with my sanity intact. Mostly intact. They wanted me to explore the unreachable portions of the cave system, which is vast, using remote viewing. I was able to map the unreachable tunnels and catalogue their contents. In the end, we determined that this site was created specifically for people like me. Like *us*. Like those who made it so long ago."

He looks between us, making sure he has our full attention. "The genes that make our minds different are not a new adaptation, but a reawakening of a long dormant gene from a civilization of humanity's ancestors who were capable of creating marvels that break the known laws of physics." He grins. "Those ancient genes are awake in me, and in the two of you. And together . . . *together*, we will unravel their ancient mysteries by this time tomorrow."

"Or . . . what?" I ask.

He purses his lips and makes a popping sound to punctuate his single word reply. "Apocalypse."

25

Before we can ask what he means by 'Apocalypse', he steps up to the modern doorway and waits for a moment. I'm not sure if hidden sensors are scanning his biometrics or if some guy named Steve is watching through a camera. The result is the same. There's a *thunk* and then the hatch opens. The door looks as thick and sturdy as a bank vault. No one is getting in without permission or an Abrams tank.

And no one is getting out.

He doesn't look back. Doesn't wait for us to follow. Just heads inside, supremely confident that we will.

Ami takes hold of my arm. "We go in there, the odds of us leaving are close to zero."

"What's the alternative?" I ask her.

"I'm the alternative," says a deep voice from the cave entrance.

We look back. It's the black clad soldier, some kind of submachine gun aimed toward us. Looks like an MP5 from *Call of Duty*. The gun model doesn't really matter. It shoots bullets. Bullets put holes in people.

Ami deflates. If she had a plan, this guy's arrival ruined it. "C'mon." She pulls me toward the open hatch. "Look at it this way. At least we found each other before we died."

Her casually spoken sentence fills me with nervous energy. I knew we clicked. I know I find her irresistible. And I know I'd love to get to know everything about her. But what she just said?

Makes me think she feels the same way, which is honestly something I haven't been on the receiving end of since Penny.

So, as I step through the open hatch to my eventual demise, I do it with a smile on my face.

She must not have me blocked anymore, because she smiles up at me, chuckles, and shakes her head.

"What?" I say, looking down the hallway on the other side. It's straight, smooth, arched, and carved right out of the stone. The strata layers, looking a bit like bacon, streak the length of the tunnel, which ends at a second hatch. Morrow waits for us there, tapping a foot.

"Nothing," she says. "It's nice. Your lack of broseph mentality catches me off guard."

"Broseph?"

"You know," she says, "like 'dude, check the tits on that bitch' kind of stuff."

"How many guys actually talk like that?" I ask.

"It's not how they talk—though some of them do—it's how they *think*. You . . . you think with your heart. Might be what I like most about you. You're kind of a sap."

"Please stop," Morrow says. "I cannot take any more cooing."

"Well," I say, "now we know his weakness."

Morrow crosses his arms and waits. I notice his four eyes vibrating slightly.

John Jacob Jingleheimer Schmidt

His name is my name too!

He winces, clutches his eyes shut for a moment.

I smile.

That'll teach him.

Behind him, the hatch opens. He gave no indication that it should open. Is he communicating with someone telepathically? Is he triggering the door directly, with his thoughts? Seems more complicated than it needs to be. Most realistic option is Steve.

As we approach, he puts his sunglasses back on and steps through the hatch into a white, modern tunnel with white strips of light in all four corners. The omnidirectional lighting leaves no shadows and reflects off Morrow's white suit, hat, and skin, giving him an angelic appearance.

"Welcome to God's softbox," he says, and walks away from us.

We stick close to him this time, squinting in the bright light. I look down at Ami. She looks pale in the glow. Almost sickly.

"You look like a cadaver," she says, smiling up at me. I appreciate her ability to remain cool and humorous, despite the circumstances. Right now, it's all we can really do to not freak out.

"You look like Gollum with a bowl cut," I reply.

"You better not be making fun of my hair," she says.

"I love your hair."

"Oh my god, you two," Morrow says. "You're torturing me. You did hear what I said about an impending apocalypse, yes? Neither of you have asked or even *thought* about it."

"What I want to know," I say, "is what's up with the giant tube of bright light?"

"The light is meant to distract you from noticing the sensors scanning your bodies as you move through the tunnel and to perfectly illuminate you for the cameras capturing every detail, movement, and body language nuance. I prefer to think of it as a Near Death Experience tunnel. Normal life is at the beginning. The world beyond awaits, but your relatives aren't beckoning you forward."

"So, you *wanted* us to ask questions?" I ask.

He sighs. "Follow me. Feel free to not talk at all."

He leads us through a series of square hallways. There's no way to know if these are retrofitted original tunnels, or new construction. And the light becomes unbearable after just a few seconds. I close my eyes and place a hand against the wall to keep me on course.

I do the same thing on bright summer days when I've forgotten my sunglasses. If I've just left the grocery store or a movie theater and the sun's light feels unbearable, I find my car in the lot, identify any obstacles—people, cars, whatever—and then just close my eyes and walk. Probably looks funny to anyone watching me, but I'm pretty good at gauging distance and typically open my eyes just a few feet from my vehicle. The hallway is easy in comparison.

My thoughts wander, replaying the events from the past day. On the run. Buying clothes. Being questioned by Stephens and Keller. Our standoff, during which I held and pointed a gun at people. The helicopter ride. It's all surreal. Like I've been transplanted to the Matrix or something.

There is no spoon, after all. Extrasensory perceptions are suddenly part of the real world. Even crazier, I've got the gift. Now I understand what Neo must have felt like.

My imagination replays the Kung-Fu fight scene. In my mind, Morpheus hangs in the air like a bird of prey, about to descend on Neo. And then, he's engulfed in light. As the illumination spreads, Neo covers his eyes.

The light fades and I'm back in a tunnel, walking.

We left the modern tunnel while my eyes were closed. Weird. I look for Morrow ahead, but don't see him. I'm about to ask Ami where he went, but a voice calls to me from a tunnel branch ahead. "Silas!"

It sounds like Sara.

What is my sister doing here?

"Silas! Hurry!"

Not needing any more prodding, I sprint down the tunnel, passing a series of branches. I run through chambers full of statues and artifacts that are just a blur to me.

"Down here!" she shouts, and I catch sight of her running away from me.

"Sara! Slow down!"

She enters a chamber and runs out of view. I double-time it to the chamber and slide to a stop over the grit-covered floor.

Sara stands with her back to me, looking down at a glowing object held on a three foot tall pedestal.

"It's the most beautiful thing I've ever seen," she says.

"Sara," I say, catching my breath. "What the fuck? Why are you here? Why are you—"

My sister turns around . . . and is missing a face.

I fall back and scramble away from her.

"Don't be afraid," she says, jaw moving like she's actually speaking, her voice projecting despite the lack of a mouth. "Now, come here. We want to get to know you."

"We?" I ask, voice shaky.

My faceless sister steps to the side, revealing the pedestal and the object it contains. I don't know what to make of it. Looks like a football-sized, luminous pumpkin seed. The flat, white ones. Not pepitas, the superior snack variety. It's hovering vertically an inch above the pedestal.

"I'm talking to a seed?" I ask.

Sara cocks her faceless head to the side. "Silas, you're talking to the universe."

26

Silas," a different voice says.

My sister is gone. The pedestal, too. In fact, I can't see anything.

"Silas, open your eyes."

The voice belongs to Ami, and I do as I'm told. I only manage to open my eyes a sliver before I squeeze them shut again. "Too bright!"

"He's awake," she says.

"Awake?" I ask, looking up at Ami's concerned face, just a foot above mine. She forces my eyes open one at a time, looking in them. "Eyes are dilated. He might have a concussion." She looks me in the eyes. "What's your name?"

"You just said it like two times," I say.

"Need to hear you say it."

I roll my eyes. "Silas."

"Do you know where you are?"

"Not a fucking clue," I say. "Same as you."

"Fair," she says. "You said the light was too bright. Is it still?"

"Well, yeah, we're still in a tube of light," I say, "but . . . this is more, I guess. It's making me nauseous."

"What were you doing before you wound up on the floor?"

"I'm on the floor?" I turn my head to the side to confirm. "I'm on the floor. I . . . I was walking . . . with my eyes closed because it's so freakin' bright, but I had a hand on the wall."

I leave out the conversation I just had with my sister. If I walked headlong into a wall and knocked myself silly, then all of that was a dream.

"Do you have a headache?" Ami asks.

"Now that you mention it . . ." I nod.

"Dizzy? Nauseous? Lightheaded?"

I frown. "All of the above."

Morrow stands behind Ami, looking down at me with his four red eyes. He unnerves me into action. I push myself up and am suddenly on a tilt-o-whirl. "Oh, shit!" I turn away from Ami and puke on the floor.

Ami closes her eyes for a moment, composing herself. Then she looks up at Morrow and says, "Concussion."

The next ten minutes are a blur. Men in blue coveralls show up. Two of them pick me up and help me stumble-walk. A third has a bucket and a mop. I'm led through a series of hallways and am instantly lost. I'm vaguely aware of Ami and Morrow behind me. Then I'm in a room. How'd I get in here? I'm sitting in a chair, head down on my folded arms.

I feel myself drifting back into a dream.

Ami swats my shoulder. "Stay awake."

"Awake," I say. "Right. Feels like there's a carrot jammed in each of my eyes. Can someone hook me up with ibuprofen?"

"I asked for acetaminophen," she says. "Ibuprofen increases the risk of bleeding, and that's not something you want happening in your brain."

"Did I really hit the wall that hard?" I ask.

"I'm not sure what you hit," she says, "aside from the floor. You dropped like someone pulled your plug."

"Where are we now?" I ask.

"Looks like an interrogation room," she says. "Even has a two-way mirror, so don't do anything stupid."

"Right," I say. "No privacy. Not even in my brain."

"Huh?"

"I can feel you poking around," I say.

"You can feel that?"

"Feels like an itch . . . in my brain, that can't be scratched, so that sucks. What are you looking for anyway?"

"Trying to make sure you're okay," she says. "I'm not trying to see memories or anything. I'm not even sure that's possible if you're not actively thinking about something."

"So, then you're . . ."

"Listening to *how* you're thinking," she says. "Because I need you to not be a concussed fruit loop."

"I'm thinking clearly," I say. "It just hurts."

The door opens and Morrow enters holding two paper cups. He sits down across from Ami and me and places the cups in front of me. One has water, the other, two white pills. I don't bother asking what it is or what it's for. Seems obvious, and if it's actually LSD or something, he'll just lie and I'll take them anyway. I take the pills and drain the water. When I'm done, I shake the cup. "You guys offer free refills?"

Morrow removes his hat and places it on the table. His four eyes look me over. Feels like he's trying to intimidate me, which I don't appreciate, so I redirect the silence to a question I've been wondering since seeing his face. "What is up with your eyes?"

He doesn't look annoyed by the question. I bet most people ask right away. "Polycoria, the rarest of eye conditions. I believe I am one of just three living people with the condition."

"Three . . . in the world?" I ask.

He nods. "I am a collection of rarities—body and mind."

"How do you see? I mean, is it like an IMAX view of the world?"

"An accurate, but oversimplified comparison," he says. "In truth, I just see . . . more. Of everything. But I am not the only one at this table capable of seeing the mysteries of the universe." He looks at Ami, and I think I've just dodged being told I'm the chosen one. Then his gaze shifts back to me. "What did you dream?"

"Huh?" I know what he's asking, but I was kind of hoping that it wasn't important.

"It wasn't real," he says. "There is no reason to fear it, and no reason to hide what I already know to be true."

"What did you see?" The question comes from Ami this time.

"I saw a girl," I say.

"Who was she?" Morrow asks.

"Never seen her before," I say.

He grins. "Mr. Keene, it uses the face and voice of the person we trust most in the world. And we do not have time to collect more people."

More people. He's talking about using people as motivation to participate in whatever secret government bullshit is going on here. If they don't need 'more', they're talking about the guys. I haven't known them long, but right now, they're the only friends I've got—and I'm a loyal kind of guy. He's right. They'll be motivation enough.

"It was my sister," I admit.

"Go on," he says.

"She was here, in the tunnels. She led me through a maze that ended in a stone chamber." I'm leaving out a lot of details, but I don't think they matter. Pretty sure I know what he's waiting to hear. "There was a pedestal. And . . ." I glance at Ami. ". . . floating over the pedestal was . . . I don't know . . . a big pumpkin seed."

Morrow's smile grows wide. "Excellent. You're in tune."

"In tune with *what?*"

"We call it 'The Seed,'" he says, "but we have no idea what it is, what it wants, or what's going to happen."

"Happen . . . when?" Ami asks.

"Tomorrow," he says. "Your appearance was in the nick of time, as they say. I thought I'd be making the final run, but you two . . . You two are a unique find. Diamonds in the rough."

"*Aladdin*," I say.

Morrow is instantly confused. "What?"

"Diamond in the rough," I say, doing an impression of the giant tiger god. "It's a line from *Aladdin*."

Morrow squeezes his lips together, like he's trying to keep an ICBM from launching out of his mouth. "Wouldn't know."

"How do you know something is going to happen tomorrow?" Ami asks.

"A countdown," he says.

"Let me guess," I say. "It's transmitting a hidden signal—a repeating binary code acting like a countdown."

Morrow squints at me. "How did you—"

I throw my hands up. "C'mon, man! That's from *Independence Day*. Whoever cooked up the script for this interview really likes their 90s movies."

"There is no script, and I do not watch movies." Morrow leans forward, his face twitching. "It appears you need motivation, Mr. Keene. I was hoping to avoid this, but your lack of respect and attention have left me no choice."

He looks up at a camera mounted in the ceiling. Then he tilts his head toward the large two-way mirror.

The lights in the interrogation room go out, plunging us into darkness until . . . the lights on the other side of the large mirror turn on, revealing a cave wall where three roughed up men stand, hands cuffed, looking terrified. Darius. Josh. Chuck.

I stand from my chair. "What the fuck are you doing?"

"Motivating you," Morrow says, and then points his fingers like a pistol, first at Chuck. Then Darius. Then Josh. He pulls his hand trigger and says, "Kill that one."

27

"No, no, no, no!" Chuck shouts. I can't hear him, but his mouth is easy to read. He stands in front of Josh, blocking him with his body. He continues shouting, but it's impossible to make out. Darius tries to calm him down, but Chuck is inconsolable. I've seen him like this once before, when he foresaw my death.

Morrow glances back at Ami and me. He points to Chuck. "What's this?"

"He must have seen you through the glass," Ami said.

"Impossible," Morrow says. "Much more likely, you're protecting the imbecile."

"Asshole," I say. "He's not stupid."

"Well, he's not smart enough to stay quiet."

A man dressed in black, head to toe, walks in with a sound suppressed pistol pointed at Josh. He's blocked by Chuck, and then Darius.

"These three are close," Morrow says. "I think I'll keep Chuck. Peel apart his mind and find out what he can do. That is, unless one of you can tell me how he was able to know who was going to be killed."

Ami and I look at each other. Giving this guy any kind of information feels wrong, but I can't think of any other way to prevent one of the guys from getting shot.

"You don't need to shoot one of them for us to take you seriously," I say. "We know you'll do it."

Ami grips my forearm. Pretty sure she wants me to shut up. But I can't just let him kill Josh.

Morrow looks up at the camera. "Wait." His four eyes shift to me. "And how do you know that?"

"Chuck—"

"*Silas*," Ami says.

"He's going to kill Josh."

"He's going to kill all of us," Ami responds.

"Not true," Morrow says. "There is one sequence of events in which you survive."

"Go to the seed," I say. "End the countdown."

He snaps and points at me. "Save the world and you get to live."

I don't buy the 'save the world' bullshit. If there *is* a countdown, it could be for any number of things. Could be a 'low battery' signal for all we know. But working with him buys us time to figure out how to survive.

"We know you'll kill him because you already killed me," I say.

That gets his attention. "Explain."

"Back at our . . . safe house . . ."

"Ami's childhood home," he says.

"Yeah. You arrived before we left. Shot me in the forehead. You killed me."

"That's . . . not what happened," he says.

I wring my hands together, unsure about telling him anything, but not seeing any other option. "Because Chuck saw it. We left when we did to avoid that future where you killed *me*. Chuck sees the future. Randomly. It's not something he controls."

"He's a seer," Morrow says, eyes widening. "An oracle. I wasn't even sure it was possible." He smiles. "He might very well be what we've been missing . . . why the other teams failed."

"Other . . . teams?" Ami asks.

"You say he can't control it," Morrow says, "and yet he has foreseen the future deaths of his friends—twice. He might not know *how* to control it, but it appears to be keyed into his subconscious. Let's put it to the test, shall we?"

He looks at the camera. "Kill the older brother."

"No!" I say, and my voice perfectly matches Chuck, who's just exploded again and shoved Darius behind him. They're a mess. All of them. Terrified. Crying. Facing down death, each trying to protect the other. All the while, Chuck is smiling. The lower half of his face looks delighted, but the truth is visible in his eyes and upturned eyebrows.

"I'd say that's conclusive," Morrow says. "He's a canary in a coal mine. Let's see if there is a way around it." He closes his eyes.

"You don't need to do that!" Ami shouts, charging toward Morrow, fists clenched and ready to swing. He barely reacts, but it's enough. He pivots to the side, narrowly avoiding Ami's swing while planting a foot to trip her. She soars past him and collides with the wall.

Instinct drives me to attack. I make it two steps toward him when his four eyes lock on to mine and vibrate back and forth. A wave of pressure moves through my head, right to left, and my body follows it. I wind up lying on my side, on the table, unable to move.

All I can do is watch.

The man with the pistol approaches Darius. He and Chuck fight each other for the front position, each trying to save the other. Josh moves to the side, cowering down. He's separated. Unprotected.

"Josh," I whisper, with tears in my eyes.

Morrow closes his eyes again. A moment later, the gunman shifts his aim from Darius to Josh—and pulls the trigger.

28

Motherfucker!" I scream as Josh drops out of sight. Rage carries me toward Morrow. There's no plan. I'm just going to thrash him like a silverback gorilla that's just been flicked in the nuts.

I make it two steps.

Then I'm on the floor. On my back. Looking up at the ceiling. "The fuck?"

Morrow is above me, still looking through the two-way mirror. "Your anger is misplaced. I strongly advise you don't try that again. I am impressed by your loyalty to these people you've only recently met, and by the violence you intended to inflict upon me, but—"

"What did you do to me?" I ask, gently pressing a hand against a lump on my forehead. The lump isn't huge, but the slight pressure makes me wince. Going to be a bruise tomorrow.

"You tripped." Ami stands at the two-way mirror, her back to me. "Hit your head on the table. Rag-dolled onto the floor."

"Bullshit." I played sports long enough to know what I can and cannot do. I know my limits. I can manage a few steps across a room, blinded by rage or not. Morrow must have screwed with my equilibrium. Ami would know that, too. But she's not saying anything, so I decide to let it go.

Also, she doesn't seem upset, which means I don't have a full understanding of what happened. With some help from the tabletop, I grunt my way back to my feet. My head pounds as blood shifts in my body, forcing my eyes shut. When I feel balanced again and the pain dulls slightly, I open my eyes and look through the mirror.

Darius and Chuck are crouched on either side of Josh. He's crying and traumatized, curled up and holding his knees. But he's alive. And not wounded. There's a scratch on the stone wall behind them where the bullet struck. Morrow instructed the man to fire—but to miss.

He spared Josh's life, while giving us a taste of what it would feel like if he killed one of us. What it would feel like if we stepped out of line.

"You're an asshole," I say.

Morrow shrugs. "I do what it takes. There isn't time to ask nicely."

"Shit, man, you could have just offered us like a million bucks each."

He smiles at me, and I don't like it. "That approach doesn't get you past the second chamber."

"What's the second chamber?" Ami asks.

He looks up at the camera and says, "Bring them to the staging area."

Not sure why he doesn't just keep giving orders via mindpower. Maybe it takes a bigger effort than he lets on? Would be nice to think he's got limits. Attacking him physically isn't really an option, even if it feels like it. He didn't flinch when we had him at gunpoint, and I don't think it's because he knew backup was en route. It's because we wouldn't have been able to pull our triggers.

He grins at me and raises his eyebrows twice.

John Jacob Jingleheimer Schmidt

His name is my name, too!

I already hate that song, but the wince on his face confirms that it is still a good mind-rape deterrent.

"This way," he says, heading for the exit, which opens at his approach.

Ami pauses by my side before following him.

"I didn't trip," I say. "I don't trip. Angry or not."

"I know," she says.

"You have any idea what his limits are?" I ask.

She shakes her head. "And I don't want to put it to the test unless we have no choice."

"Worst case scenario?" I ask.

Ami frowns. "He lobotomizes us with a thought. Honestly, I don't know. I haven't pushed myself to those kinds of extremes. For all we know, both of us are more talented, or powerful—whatever you want to call it—than he is, but we're bound by a sense of right and wrong that he doesn't share."

"Onward and upward," Morrow calls out from the hallway beyond the doorway. "The world isn't going to save itself."

"Odds that we're really trying to save the world?" I ask her.

"That question I can answer without a shred of doubt," she says. "Zero."

With a growing number of questions that might never be answered, we follow Morrow into the maze of hallways. We turn right twice and left once. It's not a lot, but there are many hallways, all identical. Pretty sure I wouldn't be able to find my way out of here without taking the wrong route a dozen times.

"This place is a labyrinth," I say.

"Indeed," Morrow says.

"I don't mean like it's confusing," I say. "I mean like it's a literal labyrinth, laid out to confuse and redirect the people in it."

"I knew what you meant," Morrow says. "I believe the designers of this maze started these tunnels with a complexity equivalent of an eighth grade maze book. To weed out the dotards. When the tunnels were first discovered, there were skeletons here. Long before the Smithsonian became involved, these tunnels were discovered by several different parties. Ten thousand years ago. Two thousand years ago. The last group identified were dated to the late seventeenth century. None of them made it out alive. All of them starved to death."

"None of them thought to just make infinite right turns until they got out?" I ask.

He pauses by a closed door. "It's possible some escaped these early tunnels using that method, but it's just as likely that they progressed deeper in the labyrinth from which escape is impossible without an advanced mind."

"The tunnels didn't look like this when they were discovered?" Ami says.

"Quite right. These walls and floors are modern, which is only possible because this portion of the complex is unchanging. The rest, well, you'll have to see that for yourself." He faces the door, and it opens.

The space on the other side reminds me of the bridge on *Star Trek: Discovery*. It's all smooth lines, large glowing flat screens, and touch-screen desktop surfaces. Everything is digital and cool looking.

Morrow looks proud.

"This was you?" I ask. "All this flashy stuff?"

"All this flashy stuff helped us achieve what ninety years of our predecessors couldn't," he says.

"And that is?" Ami asks.

"Survive the first chamber. Over the years, we've pushed past the first two."

"Out of . . . ?" I ask.

"Four," he says, "not counting the tunnel systems, side chambers between them, and the final chamber in which the Seed is located."

"Do you have a map?"

"Impossible." He walks to a ten-foot long flatscreen table. With a few taps, a map appears. Pretty standard stuff. Eleven large spaces with tunnels twisting and crisscrossing. "Before we made this first map, I was able to confirm the number of major chambers using remote viewing. That's also how I discovered the Seed in the final chamber. Two chambers had been discovered via remote viewing before my arrival, but those men weren't nearly as skilled, and their minds had been largely broken by MKUltra's use of LSD."

He touches the screen with both hands and spreads them apart, zooming in on a patch of twisting tunnels. "I created this map with a personally selected team of remote viewers. Each of us followed a path until we had a clear picture of the labyrinth. The challenges faced in each chamber still needed to be overcome, but we knew the way from point A to point B . . . until we didn't. A day after the map was complete, the first team of Espers entered and became quickly lost. We lost contact a short time later and they were never seen again."

"Despite the map," I say.

"Indeed," he says, and then taps the screen, opening another map. It's the same style, but the layout is completely different. "We repeated the map-making process the following day and ended up with this. The labyrinth's layout changes completely at random times. Navigating requires a map-maker—someone who can remote view—on each team. The more gifted the remote viewer, the farther the teams make it."

"Make it forward," I say. "But not back."

"Does that intimidate you?" he asks.

I try to play it cool. "It's no different than Diablo. The original. The map layout for each subterranean level leading to hell changed every time you played. Impossible to remember the way through or create a map."

"And what was the solution?" Morrow asks.

"Hack and slash," Ami says, "until you find the right path."

Should have known she'd know the game. It's older than both of us, but a classic for fans of the genre, especially those who play Shadowborn, which uses similar randomized layouts for its underworld, cave systems, and root systems found inside the static open world.

"Perhaps that same technique will serve you well," he says.

"You going to give me The Grandfather?" Ami asks.

I raise a hand, "I'll take a Godly Plate of the Whale."

He looks at us like we've lost our minds.

"+150% armor class," I say. "+100 to life. Would help us—"

"Why are you not taking this seriously?" he asks. "You do understand that you and your friends will be entering the labyrinth in short order. Their lives, and yours, depend on your minds."

"So, train us," I say.

"Have you listened at all?" he asks, growing irritated.

"End of the world," I say, "Countdown. Blah, blah, blah."

He taps the tabletop a few times until a large countdown appears. Days, hours, minutes, seconds, all scrolling by. There are six hours until zero. "We do not know what will happen when this countdown ends, but it is the consensus of the most brilliant minds on this planet that it is one: unlikely benign, two: far beyond our capabilities, now or at any time in the near future, and three: world altering. Will it end all life on the planet? Maybe. And that answer should scare the shit out of you all."

"It scares me, Dr. Morrow," Chuck says. All three guys are standing inside the entryway, a gun leveled at their backs by the man meant to shoot one of them. "Dr. Morrow, it scares me, a lot."

29

Great, you're here," Morrow says. "Chuck, would you mind joining Silas and Ami?"

"What about us?" Darius asks, holding onto Chuck.

Josh stays quiet. He's shaking. Still in shock from his near-death experience.

"You'll all be together soon enough," Morrow says. "You have nothing to fear from me—as long as no one steps out of line or attempts to sabotage this mission." He leaves out the fact that he fully intended on killing one of them until Chuck showed his ability.

"What mission?" Darius shouts. "What the fuck is going on? I need answers, or—or—" His angry face goes slack. Beside him, Josh relaxes.

I don't ask what happened to them. I know. Morrow gave them an attitude adjustment. Made them relaxed and pliable. It's seriously not cool, but if everything Morrow said was true, then I understand the rush. Fate of the world and all that. But what are the odds he's telling the truth? If there really is some kind of ancient technology seed-thing at the center of a physics-bending maze, why would someone—or something—put it there to destroy the world at some future point?

Doesn't make sense.

Then again, a mind capable of technology like that probably wouldn't make sense to me.

"Chuck," Morrow says. "Please join Silas and Ami."

"It's okay, buddy," I tell him.

He looks to Darius and Josh. Darius offers a relaxed thumbs up. Looks like he's high. Feeling really good. It's a massive invasion of their minds, but at least he didn't make them flop over and hit their heads on the table.

Chuck leaves his brother and friend behind and stands between Ami and me. "H-hi, Ami. Hi, Silas. I-I don't like it here." He points at the man in the doorway, still holding his sound suppressed pistol. "H-He almost shot Josh."

"But he didn't," I say, placing a hand on his back, doing my best to reassure him. "We're all okay. And we're going to *be* okay." I hate lying to him, but I don't see a version of this where we fight our way out and live. Sometimes you just need to let the rapids take you and wait for the river to calm. I've never actually been in rapids, but it sounds like good advice. "We just need to do what Dr. Morrow tells us, and you'll be back home eating stolen chips."

"Excellent," Morrow says. "Now, I need you to come with me. One at a time. Who wants to go first?"

"This like a physical exam?" I ask. "You gonna check my prostate? Do a cup and cough?"

"I'll go first," Ami says, not amused by my attempt at humor.

"The bravest of the bunch," Morrow says. "This way." He leads her to a side door.

As Ami exits, she looks back at me and says, "Don't do anything stupid." Before I can respond, the door slides closed behind her.

"What do you think 'stupid' means?" I ask Chuck.

He shrugs.

Josh laughs and slides himself into a chair, high as a kite. "You're sooo stupid." He laughs again. "Stu-pid. Stupid. That's a funny word."

Darius cracks up laughing along with Josh, and I tune them out.

If I'm not supposed to do anything stupid, then maybe I'm supposed to do something smart? What would be the smart thing to do right now? If we start messing around with the touchscreens, looking for information, then the guy with the gun will see us. I think that would qualify as stupid. So, what can I—oooh. Right. That. I can look around without moving.

"We should probably try to relax while they're gone," I tell Chuck, and take a seat, facing away from the guard. Chuck does the same. In a subtle act of rebellion, I put my feet up on the workstation, fold my arms, and close my eyes.

My mind drifts. Concerns surface first. I worry about what my family will go through if I just disappear. I see them at home. Parents in the kitchen, making lunch, joking around. Sara is in her room, taking photos of herself in the mirror, making a kissy face.

It occurs to me now that I'm not imagining these things. I'm seeing them in real time, doing these things.

How many times did I think I was imagining things about people, but I was actually watching them? How many times did I worry about Shelly cheating on me . . . because I saw it happening? I wish I knew then what I know now. Would have saved me from a lot of pain.

I force my attention to the maze. I don't know what it looks like but imagine it's similar to the large entryway with its massive statues and layers of strata. I'm in a tunnel. Then a chamber. It's immense . . . and small at the same time. The shifting perspective makes me sick to my stomach.

Deeper, I think. *Where is the Seed?*

"Over here," Sara shouts to me. She's not running away this time. She's in an arched doorway, looking back at me. She has a face this time. "Welcome back. C'mon!"

She disappears into the doorway, and I follow. Inside is . . . I don't know. The space is blurry except for Sara and the Seed, hovering over its pedestal. It looks harmless. Innocuous. Like a snack for a really big bird.

"It's not a seed," Sara says. "Though we understand the comparison. We see it in your memories. Carving pumpkins for

Halloween—a strange ritual—but we feel the seeds in your hands. They're slimy. Pungent. And if the wetness dries, sticky. You performed this ritual for ten years of your life. And then stopped. Why did you stop?"

"Can't you just read my thoughts?" I ask.

"Yes," Sara says, "when our intellects are intertwined as they are now. But we prefer to hear your response. How you wish to be perceived—whether you lie, twist, or distort—tells us about your character."

"I got bored with it," I say. "Carving pumpkins."

"Interesting," Sara says, and the response makes me consider the question at a deeper level.

"I was made fun of," I say. "I loved carving pumpkins, but when people in high school found out that I carved pumpkins every year, they teased me relentlessly. For years."

"They?" Sara asks, raising an eyebrow.

"Why are you digging so deep on this subject?" I ask, growing impatient. "It literally doesn't matter."

She smiles. "If that were true, you wouldn't be emoting so fervently."

"Fervently?" I ask. "If you're going to impersonate my sister, you might as well try to match her vocabulary, too."

"Mm," Sara says. "Stop dodging the question, bro."

"Okay, that might be worse," I say. "And yeah, I know the answer. My friends teased me for a day. Shelly teased me for years. Any time my 'ego got out of check' she would bring it up—one of a hundred other embarrassing tidbits—in front of people and everyone would have a good fucking laugh at my expense. That what you wanted to hear?"

"The question and answer are insignificant," she says.

"Great," I say. "For some otherworldly intelligence, or fount of knowledge, or world destroying A.I. bomb, this seems like a horrendous waste of time."

"What would be a better use of time?" Sara asks.

"How about you just tell me what you are? Where you're from? What do you want?"

"You haven't earned that information," Sara says, "but you are nearly out of time."

"The countdown," I say. "That's real?"

"Very."

"Cool," I say. "Awesome. Just . . . awesome. Shit. So, what else do you want to know from me, huh? Should we do the trolley test? Let's say Sara is on one track and ten people are on the other. Would I move the trolley to the track with ten people to save my sister? Hell, yes, I would. What else?"

"Stop," Sara says. "You're almost out of time."

"The countdown," I say. "Got it."

"No, Silas Keene," she says. "The path ahead of you will break and remake you. You will be reduced to ash and rise again. You will beg for death, and may very well be granted that escape, as have all those before you. When that time comes, remember this conversation. Remember your sister. Remember Shelly. Remember who you were. And who you—"

"Wakey, wakey, heads and achey," Ami says, nudging me.

I gasp awake and nearly fall from the chair.

"You fell asleep," she says, wincing when she talks. "Chuck just finished his turn. You're up."

"What's he do?" I ask.

"Hard to explain," she says. "But it's going to leave you with a monster headache."

"You seem—"

"Placated?" she guesses. "Far from it. Feels like there's a gopher digging through my brain. Thinking hurts."

I look at Chuck. He's silent. Looks stunned. "You okay, bud?"

He doesn't respond. I'm not sure he even heard me.

"He's going to need a minute." Ami winces at her own voice, and then whispers, "It's a lot to process."

A whistle gets my attention. It's Morrow, standing in the magic doorway, waving me over. "Your turn."

To say I'm uneasy about this is the mother of all understatements. He's clearly done something to Ami and Chuck. Both are alive, but Chuck is on another planet, and Ami is in pain. That said, she didn't warn me away from what was about to happen. So, whatever it is must be either important or worth the pain.

"Tick tock," Morrow says.

With a sigh, I stand up and follow him into the unknown—something I suspect I'll be doing for the rest of the day, or until I die.

30

Morrow motions to a chair at the center of a small square room. "Have a seat." The walls are white and blank. Not a single decoration, light switch, or outlet. The only aberrations I can spot are dime-sized black spots centered near the ceiling of each wall. When the door slides closed, the seam disappears.

I'm instantly claustrophobic. "This is a bit sketch, don't you think?"

"Time is short," he says. "And we both know you will eventually sit, so skip the tit for tat, and let's press on."

I sit without another word. Ami would have warned me if this was dangerous. Then again, she wound up with a migraine. "So, what's the point of this?"

"Think of it as a cheat code," he says. "I was sixteen when I first started hearing thoughts, but I had no control over it. I couldn't sleep. Couldn't focus. Voices slipped in and out of my mind. At first, it was just mumbling. Then sentences. Then different voices, sometimes overlapping. After being treated for schizophrenia—with no effect—I came to realize I was hearing actual thoughts. Unsure what it meant, but infinitely curious, I anonymously posted my experience on Reddit, hoping that someone, somewhere might have answers."

He stands behind me, hands on my shoulders. Feels like I'm about to be molested. "I was recruited by MKSearch a week later.

That was the last time I saw my family, not that they cared. I was their albino, four-eyed son who heard voices. They were relieved when the police told them I was presumed dead, thanks to some evidence planted by the MK program. They had me in a van at the end of the driveway. Encouraged me to listen in. I heard my parents' words through the speakers. 'Oh no. Dear God. How could this happen?' All the things you're supposed to say when a loved one dies."

He squeezes my shoulders hard enough to hurt. "But I could also hear their thoughts. '*Thank god. We can finally save money. I can convert his bedroom into a craft room.*' MK made sure that I was happy to cut ties with my former life. And then, they spent the next few years breaking and remaking me. What started out as an uncontrolled ability to hear thoughts evolved into much more.

"I can hear and read thoughts. More than that, I can silence the noise. I can influence people's thoughts and emotions. Remote viewing lets me see the world without leaving home. What I cannot do is see the future. And despite my best efforts, Chuck still has no control over what he sees and was too afraid to plumb the depths of his mind for latent abilities."

I look up at him and find his four red eyes staring down at me. Instantly creeped out, I look away. "So, this is like a pep talk or something? You want me to try reading your mind?"

"I want you to be open. If you can manage that, we will reduce the decade-long process I went through to reach my current level of extrasensory competence to ten minutes."

"That sounds like it could be—"

"Traumatic," he says. "Yes. But we are no stranger to trauma. And when we are done, you will be more. Stronger. Able to use your mind in ways that would terrify those who have wronged you."

"Not really a vengeful kind of guy," I say.

"We'll see," he says.

"So, what's next? We going to look at Rorschach images, or—ouch!" I slap my hand to the side of my neck. "What was that?"

Morrow's hand lowers in front of my face. He's holding a small syringe, now empty. "I call it 'keyhole.' It's a perfectly safe combination of psilocybin, DMT, aniracetam, and oxytocin agonist. It will activate latent areas of the brain which, in gifted people, allows for clairaudience, precognition, telepathy, and more. It also allows for a strong mirrorlink, which will allooow meee toooo . . ."

His voice slows down and garbles. His hand splits into ten copies, each of them rising up, one at a time. I lift my hands and move them around, smiling as a rainbow of watercolor paint oozes from my fingertips and bleeds over reality.

The world transforms.

The room disappears.

Images flash on the walls and ceiling. At least, I think they're images. It's like watching a sixty-frame-per-second video where every frame is something completely different. Then, the images kaleidoscope, turning into floating shards of glass, each one of them displaying images faster than I can process.

My mind and body relax.

I smile.

And then, a voice. An angel, I think. "Do not be afraid."

"I'm not," I tell it.

"Open your mind. Become malleable. You are clay in my hands."

I'm crying. I think. "I am clay in your hands, God."

"Good," God says. "Now, I will remake you in my image, my son."

I become aware of everything and nothing, all at once. I feel the universe moving through me. I experience it through senses, old and new. I see five dimensions, moving forward and backward through eternity. Then six dimensions. Seven.

I feel bent and twisted. That's when I realize I no longer have a body. I'm a free floating, full torso, vaporous apparition, and I'm being molded. Reshaped. By God.

God!

I can't even believe it.

God. Like . . . GOD!

I don't go to church. Never have. But here I am, communing with the Almighty. How? *How?!* I attempt to ask, "Are you there, Jesus?" but the sound coming out of the mouth I no longer have is like a foghorn.

"I am that I am," a voice says, and then I see a deity, floating cross-legged and wearing a robe. But he's bald. Was Jesus bald? Could God be bald?! What? I mean, *what?* I start laughing at the idea of bald Jesus with a beard. He'd look like a backwoods rootin' tootin' conservative! How much would they love a bearded and bald Jesus wearing flannel, shooting an AK-47 into the air?

I laugh again. No, no, no. That's the literal opposite of Jesus. Right? My religious friend, Christopher Hinkle, tried to convert me one summer. Good 'ol Toph told me all about Jesus. About the ways he said to live. Turning the other cheek. Reattaching ears. Blessing everyone who didn't get a fair shake in life. The poor. The immigrant. The slave. It was the people in power who were fucked. The people who believed they knew best.

"I don't know shit, Jesus!" I call out, but my voice sounds like dripping water now.

"Almost done," a voice says, and it's not bald Jesus. I mean, it came from bald Jesus, but it just sounded like a normal dude.

"Bald Jesus," I say. "Why didn't I get Pokemon that Christmas when I asked for them?"

"Your impure thoughts made you undeserving," the not-bald Jesus voice says.

"Doppelganger!" I shout. "Also, I was six!"

"We're done," the voice says. "Open your eyes."

Feels like someone just cracked a smelling salt stick beneath my nose. I'm instantly awake and sober, clear minded and fully aware of my limited five senses again. I'm not sure if I miss that mind-altering experience, or if I'm terrified of ever returning to it. But I'm glad to be awake.

And . . . on the floor?

I'm in a fetal position, curled up tight and . . . sucking my thumb.

The fuck?

"Dr. Morrow?" I push myself up and find myself alone in the plain white room. "Hello?" I get to my feet, and a headache hits me like a sniper round, punching through my left temple and exiting from the right—taking half of my head with it.

I nearly fall back to the floor but manage to stumble to the wall where there was once a door. "Open up." To my surprise, the door obeys. The seam appears as the door unlocks and then slides open.

A wave of dizziness pushes me against the hallway wall. I stand still for a moment, eyes closed, trying to steady myself.

This is crazy. I don't like this. Raw nerves swirl in my gut. *This is dangerous. Darius could get hurt, like how Josh almost got shot. They were going to kill him. I saw it. I saw it!*

My eyes snap open.

What . . .

Those thoughts weren't mine. It was Chuck. I heard his thoughts!

I can hear thoughts!

I hold a hand out toward the lights in the ceiling and then crush my hand into a fist, trying to break the light with telekinesis. Nothing happens. Too bad. Would've been fun.

You going to stand out there all day?

It's Ami. In my head. Talking to me.

The headache goes away, she says. *After you pee. It's from the drugs.*

Hearing the word 'pee' reminds me that I've had to take a leak since the helicopter landed. "Where is the bathroom?" I ask aloud.

A mental map projects in my mind, courtesy of Ami.

Okay, this is cool, I think, following the map to a bathroom.

You'll change your mind when you can't stop hearing what people are thinking of you.

Will you teach me how to mute people? I think.

Of course. Just . . . go pee. We're almost ready to leave.

"Leave?" I say aloud, as the bathroom door slides shut behind me. "Where are we going?"

Have you been paying attention? she asks. *The Seed? The labyrinth? The end of the world?*

"You believe all that?" I ask.

You don't need to speak aloud, she says.

Right. Sorry. Do you believe everything he's told us?

Not because he told us, she thinks at me. *Because I saw what he knows.*

What he knows about what? I ask.

There's a pause and then her mentally projected voice makes me flinch as I'm about to lose my bladder. *Everything.*

31

"For real?" I say, holding up a white bodysuit that's one part armor and one part who knows what. Looks like it'll be form fitting and tight in places that haven't been explored by myself or a woman. The gray portions—over the chest, back, thighs, and crotch—are also vertically ribbed. For no one's pleasure. There's a Velcro nametape on the chest. "Richard."

"*Ri-chard,*" Morrow corrects me. "Last name. First name, Todd. Your predecessor. This was one of his spare suits."

"Do we get name tags?" I ask.

"We used the nametapes in case we had to identify a headless body. But if you die in there, no one will be following to collect your remains. The nametapes are not important anymore. The suit is. It will help keep you alive. It will regulate your body temperature, protect you from being impaled, and reduce the effect of shifting physics on your body."

I raise a hand. "Impaled?"

Morrow shrugs. "Forward thinking. We don't know what waits for you beyond the three previously explored chambers. But the suits are simply a support for the body, while the mind is pushed to its limits."

"What do you think?" Ami asks.

She's already geared up. Didn't see her change. As strange as the suit looks in my hands, its skintight fit looks . . . amazing on Ami.

"If we survive this," I say, "I'm going to need a calendar made of you in that suit."

"Ready!" Chuck announces. "Silas, you are slow."

"You two are clothes-changing ninjas," I say, and I'm confused about why they're both so eager to get started.

Ami places her hand on mine. "There is nothing we can say or do that will change anything that's about to happen."

She doesn't try to communicate anything mind-to-mind. Morrow is listening. Old fashioned senses are enough for me to know she's asking for trust. She knows what he knows. I don't know what that is, aside from 'everything,' but she's keeping a lid on what that is for now.

Probably because she doesn't want him to know she knows.

Or something.

What I do know is that I'm confused and disoriented. I'm taking in more of the world than I ever have before but have no idea how to process everything. It's left me in kind of a stupor, slow to think, slower to act. I decide to just follow Ami's lead. She hasn't steered us wrong yet.

I pick up my suit and notice that there's just one left on the table. "Think you forgot one. There are five of us."

"And only four of you are going," Morrow says.

"Where's my brother?" Chuck asks like he's just realized Darius hasn't been with us since I returned from having my mind peeled open like an orange and then slapped back together with scotch tape. "Where is Darius?"

"Nearby," Morrow says. "Safe. For now."

I get it. "Josh is coming with us. Darius is motivation. That about right?"

"Exactly right." Morrow lifts his chin toward a door. It slides open revealing Josh at gunpoint. Aside from a pair of tighty-whities, he's naked, and shaking.

The soldier in black behind Josh shoves him into the room. "Get dressed."

Josh makes eye contact with me for just a moment. He's defeated. Broken. Does as he's told, sliding into the white suit, which zips up in the front like my childhood pajama onesie.

"Fine," I grumble and strip down to my boxers. The white uniform is easy to put on. Conforms to my body but doesn't feel tight. When it's zipped up, I do a stretch test and find everything oddly comfortable. The feet have built-in protection over the toes, and hiking-boot style grip on the bottom. The gloves over the hands are flexible, soft, and yet . . . I place a hand on the table and punch it with the other. The moment my fist connects, the fabric goes rigid. I feel almost nothing. Certainly not pain.

"If you need access to your bare hands," Morrow says, taking my hand and turning it palm up. "There's a simple button on the wrist." He undoes it and peels my glove off and folds it back onto my forearm, where it sticks in place. I don't bother asking how it works, mostly because I don't care, but also because it doesn't matter.

"Where is my brother?" Chuck shouts.

"Easy," Josh says, hand on Chuck's shoulder. "I was just with him. He's cool. They have a waiting room kind of place. TV. Mini-fridge. Even a Switch. He's okay."

"And he will stay that way," Morrow says, "as long as you follow instructions and complete your mission."

Chuck wrings his hands together. "Dr. Morrow. What if we don't complete our mission? I don't want anything to happen to Darius, Dr. Morrow."

"If you fail, we will *all* die," Morrow says.

"Can we just get the fucking show on the road?" I say, losing patience with all the bullshit verbal foreplay.

"By all means." Morrow motions to a nearby table where four backpacks wait for us. "The packs contain food and water enough to keep you hydrated and energized for a day. There are knives, toolkits, and coils of dynamic rope. I suspect you won't need any of that, but better to have it and not need it, than need it and not have it. Most importantly, there are transmitter relay nodes, three to a bag. You will need to place one in each of the last three chambers so we can remain in contact."

"I thought contact was impossible," Ami says.

"Using traditional radio signals," he says. "Yes. It's quite impossible. We're using a network of ELF-band repeaters. Like nested WiFi extenders. The signal degrades quickly through all the rock—but each relay catches, stabilizes, and re-broadcasts the pulse. Slow, but reliable. And it works despite the shifting layout."

Three in each pack. He's sending each of us with enough to complete the job on our own if necessary. He doesn't say anything about it, but it's a subtle reminder that the path ahead is dangerous and has claimed the lives of everyone who's attempted to navigate the maze before us.

"Simply place a node on the floor and press the power button," he says. "We made them idiot proof." He looks at me with his four eyes. "So, you should have no trouble."

Ami snickers.

"Hey, what did I—"

"This way," Morrow says, exiting the staging area.

I motion for Ami to follow him first. "After you, smarty pants."

"I'm a smarty pants, too," Chuck says. "Sorry, Silas. You're smart too, Silas. But not a smarty pants." He laughs at my expense, and it's good to see. His nerves have settled some.

"For the record," Josh says, pausing beside me. "I think we're all idiots."

"You might be right about that," I say. "Hey, what you said about Darius. All true?"

He nods. "I left out the armed guards, but yeah. He's pissed about not being allowed to come, and worried about Chuck, but he got the easy job."

"Until we need motivating," I say.

"Yeah." He heads after the others, leaving me in the staging area by myself.

I close my eyes and think of my parents. A moment later, I'm there with them. In their bedroom. Watching TV. Watching smut!

Ugh! What the fuck?!

I snap out of the remote viewing session, which was surprisingly easy. Morrow hasn't explained what was done to my mind, but it seems to have enhanced, or unlocked, my remote viewing ability. If only there was a way to censor the results.

This is going to be a permanent mental scar.

Move it, Ami says in my head. *We're waiting on you.*

I hustle through the hallway and step through an open hatch that leads to a stone tunnel, striped with layers of stone. The ceiling is eight feet up and arched, carved out of the stone. It's not polished and shiny but feels like a book with a matte finish.

The others wait in a small chamber with dozens of alcoves carved into two of the walls.

"What's all this?" I ask.

"There were thirty-six mummified corpses, impeccably preserved in these loculi. The Smithsonian removed them long before any of us were born. They've never been displayed, though I've had the pleasure of seeing them. Biologically, they are no different from modern man. Nothing less. Nothing more. But we believe they were like us. That the genes awakening in us comes from them."

"And is any of this important to the journey ahead?" Ami asks.

"Not at all," Morrow says, and then motions to the door at the far end of the burial chamber. "But that is."

"Looks like another stone hallway," Josh says.

"That is what it looks like," Morrow says. "But the moment you step into it, the labyrinth layout will shift, the way back will no longer exist, and the only path available to you . . . is forward."

"Awesome," Josh says, deadpan, and heads for the tunnel. He's about to enter, when Morrow catches his arm.

"All together," he says. "Entering the maze individually will put you on different paths. Link hands and step over the threshold as one unit. Moving forward, it's recommended you stay together, but the labyrinth will not change again for you."

He opens his hand, revealing four earpieces that look like supercharged EarPods. "Wear these at all times. They're connected to the nodes and will allow us to communicate."

We each take one and place it in an ear. I flinch when the interior earbud expands and locks onto my ear. Won't be falling out, that's for damn sure.

I offer a hand to Ami. "Who's ready to start the last thing we'll ever do?"

Ami takes my hand. Josh takes her other hand and offers his free hand to Chuck.

"I didn't like that joke, Silas," he says. "I didn't like it."

"Sorry, buddy," I say. "Gallows humor. Can't help myself sometimes. Also, don't sweat it." I tilt my head toward Morrow. "This freakshow has been working with B-teams. We're the A-Team."

"I'm Faceman," Josh says.

"B.A. Baracus!" Chuck shouts, smiling. "Pity the fool. I pity the fool."

Josh turns to Ami with a shit-eating grin.

"You're obviously Hannibal," he says.

Ami raises her eyebrows at us. "I'm not saying it."

"You *have* to say it, Ami," Chuck says. "Ami, you're Hannibal. You have to say it." Chuck whispers, "I love it when a plan comes together."

"What . . . are you guys talking about?" I ask.

"What do you mean?" Chuck asks. "You said *The A-Team*."

"Yeah, like 'the best.' People say it in *Call of Duty*. A is better than B. What do *you* think it means?"

"*The A-Team* is one of the most iconic TV shows of the 1980s," Ami says, squinting at me.

"I'm *twenty-two*," I say. "Why would I know—"

"We all know," Chuck says, releasing some nervous laughter at my expense. "Silas, everyone knows the A-Team!"

I turn to Morrow, wearing my confusion like a wet poncho, arms up, hoping he'll be just as clueless as me.

"I am familiar with the series," he says.

“All right,” Ami says. “Let’s knock off the displacement conversation and get this show on the road.” She takes hold of my hand again, and pulls us toward the tunnel.

As we cross the threshold, Morrow says, “Good luck.” The ‘good’ reaches both of my ears through the air. But the ‘luck’ is heard just in my right ear, through the earbud.

32

The sound of Morrow's voice in the earbud, but not in both ears, spins me around. I gasp when my nose is nearly touching a flat stone wall. "Holy shit, he wasn't fucking with us."

My voice echoes in the tight stone tunnel, reverberating away.

Ami stands beside me and places a hand against the wall that wasn't there a moment ago. "I think everything he's told us was true."

"Is that like a psychic thing?" Josh asks.

She shakes her head. "An observation thing. I'm good at spotting lies, even if it's in a video, no ESP required. He's either telling the truth or doesn't know he's lying. That includes the fact that once we get past the third chamber, we have no idea what we're in for."

"I'm grateful for the support, Ms. Sato." Morrow's voice is clear but doesn't echo.

"Support is a generous word," she says.

"Regardless," Morrow responds. "Believing what I tell you from here on will help keep you—and all of us—alive to the end of the labyrinth."

I knock on the rock wall. "So, are you on the other side of this wall? If we blew it up, could we leave?"

Feels like a dumb question the moment I ask it, but he responds with, "That was one of the first things we tried. Alas, no. In our experience, the only way out is through."

"If there *is* a way out," Josh says.

"Indeed," Morrow says.

I rub my hands through my hair. "I mean . . . just . . . you know you *can* lie sometimes."

"Hey, guys!" It's Chuck, his booming voice bouncing off the walls a hundred times before fading. He's a hundred feet ahead, looking through an arched doorway. His face is glowing orange.

We hurry toward him.

"First door on the left," Ami says. "Glowing orange light."

At first, I'm confused about why she's telling us what we can see, but then Morrow responds, "Contains what we call the perpetual flame. I suspect it's been burning since the labyrinth was constructed. Of course, it's possible that one of the first to enter the maze lit the flame. There is no way to know. It wasn't until we developed the node technology that any information from within the maze could be recorded. There are ninety years of knowledge and experience completely lost to the maze."

"Were they all like us?" I ask.

"No," Morrow says. "Which is why none of them stood a chance. We know none of them made it past the first chamber, because once a chamber has been cleared, its effects on those who follow are dramatically reduced. You shouldn't have any trouble passing the first two."

He offers no encouragement regarding the last two.

"Look, Josh," Chuck says, pointing into the room. "It's upside down!"

"Oookay," I say, seeing the flame extending downward from a long post hanging down from the ceiling. Looks like a stone floor lamp, striped with stone strata. Everything in this place was carved out of the stone beneath the Grand Canyon's ledges.

"The flame was the first sign that physics are . . ." Morrow clears his throat. ". . . *distorted* in the maze."

"What happens if we go inside?" I ask, lowering my voice.

There's a slight crackle in my ear. "Responding to just you. The chamber is perfectly safe. It's a primer of sorts, for what is to come. A clue, perhaps, to the early teams. But right now, to the left of the door, are the remains of a team from the early nineteen hundreds. There are thirty-seven sets of remains before the first chamber. The first team under my command collected the dead and placed them in the side chambers. This is why you need to avoid them. I believe they would be detrimental to Chuck's psychological health."

"Well, that's nice of you," I say.

"Hardly," he says. "I believe Chuck's ability may be instrumental when passing through the fourth chamber."

There's another crackle, and I think he's now speaking to the group again. "Time is short. I must insist you continue on. You are not there to sightsee."

"You heard the man." I tug Chuck away from the door and urge him to press on. Josh links arms with Chuck and leads him away. Ami follows them, but glances back at me, quizzical. I motion for her to keep going and then dip into the upside-down flame room, looking to the left. I thought Morrow might be full of shit, but he was being honest. There are seven mummified bodies, held together by their clothing, stacked against the wall like firewood. Their dry, stretched skin pulls their mouths open. Laughing, eyeless sockets looking right through me.

An echoing cough snaps me back to the present. I duck back out of the room and spot Ami, waving at me to catch up. Takes just a moment to reach her. I tap my head, indicating that we should keep the conversation silent.

What were you doing? she asks.

Fact-checking Morrow, I tell her. *You're right. He's telling the truth.*

What was in there?

Bodies. Seven of them. Some of the OG explorers that came in here. And there are thirty more in the side rooms of the first tunnel.

"Hey," Ami says, getting Chuck and Josh's attention. "While I think Morrow is a tool, asshole, and little bitch—" She gives me a wink. "—I think he's been honest with us about what we're facing . . . and the time we have to make it through the maze. So, no side quests. If he says skip a room, we skip it. Understood?"

"I like side quests, Ami," Chuck says.

"Who doesn't?" Ami says. "But look at it like this. The side quests are for level thirty, and we just got here, so we're level one. We need to do some serious leveling, then, if we're still alive, we can come back and see what's up in these side rooms. Got it?"

"Got it, Ami," Chuck says, giving a thumbs up. "That makes sense, Ami. I like pretending this is a quest. I'm going to do that. It feels less . . . real. Not as scary."

The new rule is put into place just in time. We pass another open doorway. Inside is another post descending from the ceiling. This one has what looks like an upside-down birdfeeder at the end. From a hole in the floor, a column of water rises upward into the bowl. The water flows over the edges and defies gravity by flowing up and out of sight.

Feels a little like I'm in a *Ripley's Believe It or Not* museum, skimming past all the corny exhibits, except these rooms are the real deal that Ripley's longs to be. It's hard to just walk on by, even with the knowledge that there are corpses just beyond the threshold.

The tunnel makes a few turns, but there aren't any real options beyond forward and backward. No traps. No secret side tunnels. "Hey, has anyone gone through here tapping on random walls?" I ask.

"Are you addressing me?" Morrow asks.

"You're the only one who would know," I say.

"Why would someone tap on the walls?" he asks.

All four of us answer in unison. "Secret rooms."

"It's a staple of gaming," Josh says. "I think it started with OG *Doom*. Sometimes, you'd just be walking down a hallway, hitting the open button, and presto, a hidden door. An armory. Weapons, armor, you know, good stuff."

There's a sigh over the earbud, and then Morrow says, "What I wouldn't give for you all to be adults."

"Doom is thirty-ish years old," Josh says, "You should have been playing it when you were like, what, ten?"

Josh is returning to himself despite our situation. I think it was Morrow that scared him more than anything—that and nearly being shot. It's good to have him back. He might not have any extrasensory shit, but he might also be the smartest and most knowledgeable person here.

"I did not partake in the dulling of my mind," Morrow says.

"We can tell," Ami says, joining in on making our kidnapper feel old.

"Dr. Morrow," Chuck says, sounding earnest. Definitely not joining the bandwagon. "How is my brother? Is Darius okay?"

"One moment . . ." Morrow says and then goes silent for a second. "He's feeling happy at the moment . . . because he just defeated something called . . . a Waterblight Ganon inside Divine Beast Vah Ruta?"

"Standard Darius," Josh says with a grin. "Letting us do all the hard work."

Chuck laughs. "Yeah. Standard Darius."

"Mm," Morrow says, not giving a shit. "Eyes forward. Do not look in the next chamber. It shouldn't be far now if you're maintaining a reasonable pace."

"I see it," I say. The tall, arched doorway matches the rest I've seen, featureless aside from the various orange, brown, and beige making up the solid stone surrounding us. "You heard the man. Eyes forward."

Everyone obeys, passing by the entryway without a glance.

I, on the other hand, have a looksee. I'm expecting to see another gravitational anomaly. And that might be somewhere in the chamber, but I don't see it, because my eyes snap to the scene of carnage. There aren't any corpses. They've been moved. But the walls and floor are splattered with sooo much dried blood. It's hard to imagine what could have done that to a person. It's like they were sliced open, thrown into a giant salad spinner, and drained of all their blood. And if gravity is bonkers here, it's possible my imagined scenario isn't too far off.

We plow forward, passing three more side rooms, and even I stop looking inside. No reason to get unnerved yet. There are going to be plenty of opportunities for that moving forward.

Starting with the first major chamber, which lies just ahead. The tunnel exits into a large space. The only wall I can see is the opposite side, where an exit awaits. Looks like we should just be able to strut across.

Except there isn't a floor.

"We're at the first chamber," Ami says.

"Stop at the threshold," Morrow says.

We take his advice.

"Done," Ami says.

"Very good," Morrow says. "Welcome to the Tidal Crucible."

33

The chamber is spherical and I'd guesstimate the diameter to be roughly two hundred feet. There's no way to walk across and, if we fall in, there's no getting out. The skin-wrapped skeletal remains of three people, and another seven that look . . . fresher . . . lying on the bottom confirm that tidbit.

The scene of death and decay doesn't hold my attention for long, because there's something even stranger at the center of the space—an island, for lack of a better word. It's floating at the center of the sphere, defying gravity. There are no ropes or chains attached to the ceiling. No poles rising up from the bottom. It's just a chunk of ancient floating land, rough on the bottom, roots dangling. The top is flat and has a dead pine tree with brown needles in its center.

"Do you see the island?" Morrow asks.

"Hard to miss," Josh says.

"The dead tree is a White Fir," Morrow says. "They were common in Arizona's lowlands but began to retreat to higher elevations eighty thousand years ago. I believe it was left behind as a kind of time marker."

"You think this place was made eighty-thousand years ago?" I ask.

"Give or take a millennia or twenty," he says. "There is no way to be sure. Radiocarbon dating, even on the bodies, gave us no useable or consistent data."

Ami leans a little closer to the threshold. I catch her arm and keep her from crossing it. "How is this even possible?" she asks.

My earbud crackles and Morrow says, "The island isn't floating. Its center hides a compact gravity source. There is no way to know for sure, but our best and brightest believe the island contains a rapidly spinning supersymmetric Q-ball—a hypothetical dark-matter nugget—that could produce a steep regional gradient and the one over R cubed fall-off. Its field stretch falls off abnormally fast, proportional to the inverse cube of r, creating two stable torus-shaped zero-g shells around the island."

It occurs to me as he explains this that the people who came before us must have been very smart. They might have been gifted like us, but they also were able to figure out the science behind this madness. It's impressive and intimidating. As smart as some of us might be—I'm not including myself—I don't think any one of us understands what 'proportional to the inverse cube of r' means.

"Now, listen to me very carefully. The danger this chamber presents is a tidal shear zone. The gradient between the shells is brutal. In the front pocket of your packs, you'll find a pair of glasses. They look like sunglasses but will allow you to see the ultraviolet spectrum."

We all retrieve our glasses and put them on.

"Got 'em on," I say.

"Do you see the ultraviolet glow?" Morrow asks.

"I see it, Dr. Morrow," Chuck says. "I think it's pretty, Dr. Morrow. Do you think it's pretty?"

"I haven't had the pleasure of seeing it myself, Chuck. I'll take your word for it." Morrow's voice crackles and then he continues, "That glow marks where local g swings from +6 g to -4 g."

"What is 'g' in this case?" Ami asks.

"Gravitational acceleration," Morrow says. "If you cross that boundary incorrectly, you'll be spaghettified downward as though you were reaching out past a black hole's event horizon, or you'll be hurled toward the ceiling hard enough for your molecules to fuse with the stone."

I look up and am surprised to find another group of bodies partially buried in the stone ceiling. Awesome.

"Look up at the archway above you," Morrow says, and I do as I'm told. Some kind of ancient language is carved in the stone.

"Is that cuneiform, Dr. Morrow?" Chuck asks.

"Not exactly, but close enough that we were able to translate it . . . last year. The development of large language model artificial intelligence made it possible for us to crack the characters. It says, 'Balance and you may pass. Seek the still waters.'"

"Seek the still waters," I repeat. "Is that like a meditation kind of thing?"

"Not remotely," Morrow says. "You must look for the place where everything is eerily calm—the still waters. Remain in the still waters and the maze lets you through. Step anywhere else, and the Tidal Crucible pulps you like a cosmic juicer. Now, you will each find an orange thermos in your packs. Each of them contains enough sand to make it across. Start with one. If the leader runs out, or dies, use the next. Only the person in the lead needs to throw sand."

"Throw sand . . . where?" I ask.

"In a gravity field, an equipotential surface acts like a perfectly level pond: nothing ripples, nothing sinks. In the chamber, the figurative water is motionless because it sits right under the inner zero-g torus. The sand you toss will hover along that same invisible shoreline. Spot the patch of 'water that never wavers,' and you've located the safe path. You'll be fine. This was much more difficult for the teams that came before you."

"Okay," Ami says, "Who wants to go first?"

Josh doesn't hesitate. "I'll do it."

Chuck grows nervous. "That's brave of you, Josh. I hope you'll be okay. Do you think you'll be okay, Josh?"

"I'll be fine," Josh says with faux bravado that Chuck believes is real. "The way I see it, this is just the first test, right? Should be the easiest. That means you guys have to do the harder stuff."

Chuck laughs and gives Josh a swat. "You are so sneaky, Josh. Okay, Josh, you can go first. But . . . be careful, okay?"

"When am I not careful?" Josh says, taking out his thermos of sand. He unscrews the cap and tosses it over his shoulder. The cap bounces away. Feels like a bit of a desecration. This place must be sacred to someone. Maybe should be to us. Tossing trash could very well be the mistake that gets us killed. Then again, we're about to dump a bunch of sand onto a gravitational whatever-the-fuck.

Ami must share my concern because she bends down, picks up the cap, and stows it in her pack.

"So, I just toss the sand out in front of me?" Josh asks.

"Doesn't need to be a lot. Just enough to discern the path."

"You know this is some *Last Crusade* bullshit, right?" Josh pours some sand into his palm.

"Indeed, Mr. Conaway," Morrow says. "Consider this your very own Leap of Faith trial."

Josh sighs and almost casually scatters an arc of sand. Despite the warning and explanation about what we were about to do, I still gasp when I see some of the sand launch toward the ceiling, and the rest remain hovering, revealing an invisible path two feet wide, leading up and to the right.

"You see it?" Morrow asks?

"Yeah," Josh replies. "It's not very wide."

"Conveniently," Morrow says, "neither are you."

Good news for Josh, Ami, and Chuck, but I'm a bit wider. I'm going to have to walk the path at an angle.

"Now," Morrow says, "do not tarry. The sand will eventually fall through the still water path. As will you, if you remain stationary for long. Once you start, press on until you're dead or reach the other side."

"This is crazy," Josh whispers. "This is nuts." He tosses more sand out, following the path's direction. More of the path is revealed. "Here goes nothing . . ."

Josh lifts a foot out over the path, letting it hover, squinting as he waits to see if his toes are going to spaghettify. Nothing happens and he lowers his boot to the sand, where it connects with an unseen surface, which is actually some kind of gravitational force. No matter how many times Morrow explains it, I'm never going to understand how this shit works, but it works.

"Keep moving," I whisper, and he does, gingerly following the path and scattering more sand as he goes. Chuck follows him, and then Ami. Bringing up the rear, I angle my body and step out just as the first sand starts to fall through the invisible floor.

I shuffle along shoulder first, eyes on the path ahead. I stick close to Ami, watching for signs that she's passed through the invisible wall, but she has no trouble staying on the path. Takes us ten minutes to reach the island. We can't step on it. The path takes us around it. But I can see the top of it. Looks like a normal chunk of Arizona desert. The skeletal remains of some kind of lizard lie beside the dead tree. If there's a message in the imagery, it's lost on me.

At the peak of the path, things level out for a few steps. I glance back and the path behind us is gone. Dizziness washes through me. Eyes clenched, I turn forward and continue after Ami. If the path ahead of me disappears before I pass it, I'm toast.

"How are we doing?" Morrow asks.

"Almost there," Josh says. I see him hop ahead and land beneath the exit's archway. He bumps a fist and offers a hand to Chuck. With a quick pull, Chuck is safe. Ami's not far behind them. But my sideways shuffle isn't nearly as quick. Ten feet from the arch, the path ahead spaghettifies and is yanked to the bottom of the sphere.

Not seeing solid surface beneath my feet, I start losing my balance and feel myself tilting backward, toward the ultraviolet wall.

34

Instinct causes my arms to spread out and spin as a counterbalance. If I wasn't standing sideways, I'd be missing both limbs just above the elbows. Miraculously, the weight of gravity on my back reduces and my flailing arms manage to keep me upright.

I don't look down. I can feel the floor that isn't a floor beneath my feet. So, I focus on that and lower my arms. "Can someone toss their sand for me?" I can see the ultraviolet walls, but the complete lack of floor messes with my head.

"Working on it," Ami says.

I can hear her digging in her pack, but I don't look. Just need to stand still and maintain my balance.

"Okay," she says. "Sand going out."

There's nothing to hear. The sand isn't landing on a hard surface. It's sticking to a gravitational torus-mumbo jumbo. But like salt on ice, I can't walk without it.

"Good to go," Ami says.

I turn forward and the path is covered in what looks like the entire contents of Ami's thermos. I grin.

"Why are you smiling, Silas?" Chuck asks, and then he turns to Josh. "Why is he smiling?"

Josh shrugs, but Ami has no shame about her feelings. "He's happy about the amount of sand I used, because it implies I was worried, which implies I care about him, which he already knew, so I'm not sure why he's so tickled about it."

"Silas is a romantic, Ami," Chuck says, while I inch along the revealed path. "I think he likes you, too."

"You might be right, Chuck," Ami says.

No way I'm going to look up to see her uncommon smile, but I can hear it in her voice. And I'm glad for it. Not just because Ami cares about me—I already knew that—but because it's a positive distraction in what might turn out to be the equivalent of Dante's *Inferno*, if written by a scientific genius rather than someone steeped in religion. I suppose six chambers of high IQ *Squid Game* challenges are better than nine levels of Hell, but both scenarios are a certified nope.

"Almost there," Ami says, her hand raising toward me in my periphery. I take her hand, take one last step, and then leap away from the gravity path. She wraps her arms around me and squeezes when I'm safely under the archway.

She was more worried than she let on. "What's wrong?" I ask. "What happened?"

"Turn around," Josh says.

I do as he says, expecting there to be something about the path that I hadn't noticed. I'm not far off, but there's nothing different about the path.

As I turn, a heap of gear falls around my feet. But there's something off about it. It's all ruined, cut cleanly like—

Holy shit . . .

I unclip my backpack and slip out of it. I turn it around and find six inches missing. When I leaned back on the path, the bag hit the barrier. My supplies were spaghettified. A little farther and it would have been me.

I discard the pack and try to think of something funny to hide my horror, but my mind is blank. A shiver runs through my body and shimmies my shoulders.

"It's okay to be afraid, Silas," Chuck says, a big grin on his face. "I'm afraid all the time. Even before the maze. Before the guys with guns. Just sitting at home, I'm afraid. I know it doesn't look like it because my brain makes me smile all the time, and . . .

And sometimes I am happy, but even then, I'm afraid. All the time. And it's okay, Silas. You don't need to hide it."

I smile, and it's genuine. "Thank you, Chuck, for the pep talk, and for shining a spotlight on my weakness."

"It's not weakness," Ami says. "Fear keeps us alive. Also, I'm an empath, remember. Can't hide how you're feeling from me."

"Awesome," I say. "Mental note, do not watch Gal Gadot movies with Ami."

She shrugs. "If we watch a Gal Gadot movie, I'll be blocking you from *my* thoughts." She turns away, letting that mental image stew in my mind. "Okay, Morrow. We're through."

"I'm aware," he says. "Was allowing you all a moment to pat each other's backs."

"Going to be easier now that my pack was sheared in half," I say.

"And now you understand the wisdom of four complete packs," he says. "Those of you who didn't use your sand should feel free to discard it, to reduce the weight. But please, do not tarry, the countdown continues and will conclude in roughly five hours."

"Giving us an hour per challenge," I say.

"The next challenge should be quick to pass," he says, "but after that . . ."

"What was the fastest a previous team completed a challenge?" Ami asks.

There's a long pause, and then, "Three days."

"Three days?" Josh says, and laughs. "We're so dead."

"Hey," Ami says, staring in his eyes. "They weren't us. They couldn't do what we can. Right, Dr. Morrow?"

I'm not sure if she's purposefully leading him to say something encouraging, but he does. "Quite right. Despite the vastness of the stakes, I'm very hopeful. Less so, when you're standing around talking. May I suggest you get moving? There is no danger between chambers. Feel free to run. Every minute is important now."

"No side quests," Chuck says. "We can do that, Dr. Morrow. I'm not fast. Not anymore. But we can run."

Without being elected leader, Chuck sprints away.

Happily, his sprint is closer to a jog. We have no trouble keeping up. And without my backpack, I'm no longer carrying extra weight. We pass several side rooms on the way, and this time no one looks in.

The maze once again features twists and turns, but no alternate routes.

"Morrow," I say. "Why do you call this a maze if there aren't alternate routes to take?"

"Before the challenges were completed," he says, "there *were* alternate routes, complicated and long enough to spend years navigating the tunnels without escape. I expect you'll face the same challenge following the third chamber."

"And you expect us to get through in a few hours?" I ask.

"I expect you to navigate the maze," he says. "In my experience thus far, only those with the ability to remote view are capable of navigating between challenges. Once a challenge is complete, the maze becomes a simple tunnel."

"I see it," Chuck says, slowing to a walk. "I see . . . a pyramid. It's a pyramid, Josh!"

We gather by the arched entryway. Chuck is right, but this is much more than a pyramid. The two-foot cubes forming the massive pyramid look like blue glass. Finger-thin veins that look like copper run up the seam of each corner.

I look up and spot another inscription. "We're at the next chamber, Morrow. What's the inscription say?"

Morrow's voice crackles in my ear. "Rise when the storm forgets its name; offer the spear to the silence that follows."

"I don't see any spears," I say, looking around the tunnel. There's a rack where spears might have once stood, but it's empty.

"They were used by previous explorers," he says. "They were bronze and tipped with obsidian. There are sockets on every cube composing the pyramid. To pass, up and over the top, each person had to press the obsidian tip into the socket on the next level up. They then had eight seconds to move between cubes."

"And if they didn't?" Ami asks.

"If eight seconds passed, or if someone stepped on a cube without first socketing a spear, they . . . well, why doesn't someone extend their arm into the chamber and see for yourself."

"Is it safe?" I ask.

"There is nothing dangerous about the air or the empty space around the pyramid. It is only the pyramid's surface you need to be concerned with."

Good enough for me. I lift my arm into the chamber.

"If you weren't wearing the Aegis Five, you'd see the hair on your arms rising into the air."

"Aegis Five?" I ask.

"The body armor you are all wearing," he says, starting to sound exasperated.

"So, static electricity?" Josh says.

"Oh, it's a little more than that," Morrow says. I can hear him smiling.

The chamber bursts with light as arcs of electricity rage inside the pyramid, flowing through the glass, but never leaving it. A loud whump coincides with each large pulse of electricity. The first one makes everyone jump back a step.

"Okay, so, touch a cube that's not deactivated for eight seconds by a spear, and you're toast. That about right?"

"Normally," he says. "But as you already pointed out, the spears have been used up."

"Sooo, how are we getting across?" Ami asks.

Morrow lets the answer hang for a moment, and then says, "You're going to walk."

35

Walk?" Chuck says. "That's a bad idea, Dr. Morrow. A really bad idea. It will kill us. Dr. Morrow, that's not possible."

"I'm with Chuck," Josh says. "This is insane."

I agree with them both, but I suspect that this is mild compared to what's ahead of us. Also, there's no good reason for Morrow to send us here to die. He might not care about us personally, but he wants us to make it to the end of the maze. He wouldn't ask us to do something he knew would kill us.

"I'll go first," I say.

"Silas," Ami says, either surprised that I volunteered at all, or that I did without asking questions.

He doesn't want to kill us, I tell her with my thoughts.

She gives me some hardcore stink-eye. *He doesn't care if we die.*

He knows how this works, I think. *There's no reason to risk us. Yet.*

My logic is sound, and she knows it.

"May I ask why everyone is so quiet?" Morrow says.

"Pretty sure Silas and Ami are having a telepathic argument," Josh says. "I can't hear them, but their faces and body language are grouchy."

"There is no reason for concern," Morrow says. "The Aegis Five has an outer Faraday mesh that keeps you at one equipotential, so the ziggurat's three megavolt plates can't find a point to bite, and the suit's dielectric stack—PTFE, Kapton, and aerogel—gives a breakdown north of thirty megavolts per meter. We smoothed the edges with corona rings at the wrists, ankles, and pack frame so there are no sharp points to launch streamers, and any strike that does land gets shunted into a sacrificial surge bus running the spine through gas discharge tubes and MOV clamps. The boots use a deep creepage labyrinth sole and an internal bleeder network, so charge drains around you, not through you."

"Okay, okay, okay. No one understands what you're telling us," I say, and then to Ami. "You see? They've worked it out. He doesn't want any of us to die."

"Heavens no," he says. "If anyone dies before the first of the unsolved chambers, it will be tragic."

The insinuation that some of us might die in the last two chambers doesn't buoy my confidence, but what other option do we have other than pressing on? I don't want to starve to death and be just another body stacked in a side-room. I don't want to die at all. And I definitely don't want the world to go *kaput* if we fail.

"Be straight with me, Morrow," I say. "Do I just need to walk over this thing? Is it that easy?"

"Nearly," he says. "I would suggest keeping a single foot on one panel at a time and follow an upward trajectory that takes you up and over the top."

"There a reason for that?" I ask.

"Only that we don't know what will happen if you try something different. Deviating from these instructions might have no effect at all. Or it might atomize you. There is no way to know."

I clap my hands and rub them together. "You heard the man. No deviations. Treat it like a minefield. Step where I step. And stay close. Who's ready?"

Three unconvinced faces stare at me.

"I don't like this, either," I say, "but we don't have a choice. And I for one would prefer the instant painless bliss of the afterlife over slowly starving to death. I'd probably die first, at which point you bastards would eat me. And then, over time, each other." I look at Chuck and Josh with a slight grin. "No offense, but my money is on Ami eating all three of us. But then—" I turn to Ami, "You'll die anyway. So . . ."

I step out onto the ziggurat's first level. A tense moment passes and then I sigh in relief. "You see? Nothing to worry about."

Two steps up, I glance back. Josh is behind me. Then Chuck. Ami brings up the rear, probably to keep the other two moving, in case something goes wrong. She doesn't like what we're doing, but who does? Me pushing to get through this quickly isn't helping anyone's nerves, but we're moving slowly through the chambers we know how to cross. If we take a long time on the last chambers, this might all be for nothing.

My thighs start to burn as I near the top. Each step is just high enough that I'm using muscles that don't normally get activated during day-to-day life. It's probably worse for Ami's short legs, but she's not complaining, so I keep my mouth shut about it.

So far, the crackling and flashing ziggurat hasn't reacted to our presence.

"What's happening?" Morrow asks, almost whispering.

"Nothing," I say. "I'm not sure it even knows we're here."

"Interesting," he says. "Every nerve impulse and heartbeat are an ion current. We're all walking bio-batteries. The electromagnetic field we generate is minuscule, but perhaps that is enough to trigger the Electrostatic Ziggurat. The Aegis Five contains the field, ipso facto, nothing is happening."

"Why does it sound like you're figuring all of that out just now?" Ami grumbles.

Before Morrow can reply, Chuck says, "Ouch!"

I stop and look back.

Chuck is standing, his feet on separate panels, just behind Josh. "It's okay! I'm okay. I just tripped."

I squint at him. "How did you untrip?"

"I caught myself," he says, holding up his hand with a big grin.

"Did he make contact with the panels?" Morrow asks.

"He did," I say, blood draining from my face.

"You need to get out of there," Morrow says. "Now! Go! Run!"

"But the rules—"

Josh reaches back and pulls Chuck up, "Fuck the rules, man!"

The lightning arcs pulsing through the pyramid grow frantic as a loud hum fills the air.

"Move your asses!" Ami says, switching lanes and passing on the left. She doesn't bother following the path or even going to the top. Once she reaches a level with a straight shot across, she takes it, passing me on the way. I follow suit, cutting across the pyramid halfway to the top. Chuck and Josh are close behind me.

The hair on my head starts to float. Some kind of charge is building up, and I really don't want to find out if Morrow's confidence in the Aegis suits is misplaced.

"Go, go, go," I shout, leaping down the backside of the ziggurat two levels at a time. My knees aren't happy about it, but if I don't end up barbecued, I'll consider it a win.

Ami reaches the exit first. When she's safely inside the exit tunnel, she spins around and shouts. "Move it, assholes! It's about to blow!"

Pretty sure she doesn't know whether 'blow' is the right verb for what's about to happen, but I agree with the message—get clear or get toasted.

I land two levels up and away from the exit. Keeping my momentum going, I Spider-Man myself through the air and into the tunnel. If I shared Peter Parker's strength, I'd be okay after all that leaping, but I don't, and my legs are Jell-O when I land. I flop to the smooth tunnel floor, roll twice, and then come to a stop against the wall.

"Let's go!" Ami shouts, sounding a bit desperate. When I look back, I understand why. The chamber is filling with blue swirling light. Inside the ziggurat, the lightning spins like a tornado, building in intensity and slapping against the glass, looking for a way out.

Josh makes it to the bottom, and inside the tunnel.

Chuck is right behind him.

But he's not close enough to escape what happens next. An electric bolt the size of the ziggurat launches from the floor to the ceiling. Chuck's momentum carries him out of the chamber, but not before his backside gets a taste of the energy pulse.

Chuck is flung from the chamber and into Josh. Both sprawl to the floor beside me. A massive thunder crack forces hands to ears. Pretty sure I scream, too, but it's impossible to hear.

As quickly as the pulse arrived, it disappears.

I sit up and roll my neck. Despite my ringing ears, I hear Ami clearly. Because she's in my head.

Chuck might be in trouble.

He's laid out on his stomach. His pack is scorched and smoking. Josh is farther down the tunnel, on his back and unconscious.

Before Ami and I can reach Chuck, his pack catches on fire. And he doesn't react to it.

"Flip him over and pull him up," Ami says.

I do as I'm told, and Ami quickly removes his pack, tossing it to the side where it continues to burn.

"Chuck," I say, and gently slap his face. "Hey, Chuck!"

"Lay him down," Ami says.

When he's on his back, she checks for a pulse on his neck.

"I don't think he's breathing," I say, looking at his chest.

Ami shakes her head. "No pulse. Going to start CPR."

"Wait," Morrow says. "That will break his ribs. He'll be useless."

"Dead is also useless," Ami says, positioning her hands over Chuck's sternum.

"You don't understand," Morrow says. "If electricity stopped his heart, it can restart it as well. The Aegis contains a defibrillator, already perfectly positioned to deliver a single charge to the heart."

"How do we activate it?" Ami asks.

"Remove your hands," Morrow says.

Ami doesn't look happy about it, but she pulls her hands away from Chuck's chest.

"The defibrillator is triggered when no heartbeat has been detected for sixty seconds. Which means—"

Chuck's body arches up and then slams back down to the floor.

"Fuck's sake," Ami whispers and then moves to check for a pulse again.

Before she reaches him, Chuck's eyes snap open like he's just been woken up for school. Then he frowns. "I don't feel good." Chuck rolls his head to the side, throws up, and then looks back to Ami. His Chuck-smile returns and he says, "That's better . . . Where is Josh?"

I look forward to Josh. He hasn't moved, and is maybe worse off than just unconscious.

36

Josh is bleeding from a gash on his forehead. Must have face-planted when he hit the floor. Doesn't look life threatening, but what do I know. Brain injuries aren't visible on the outside. "Josh. Man, open your eyes."

"What's the situation?" Morrow asks.

"Josh is bleeding and unconscious," I say as Ami joins me.

I wish there was a way we could shut him off, she thinks to me.

I share her irritation, but not the desire to unplug from Morrow entirely. *When this is all over, I'll be thrilled if he's impaled by Vlad, but what he knows is keeping us alive.*

She rolls her eyes and shifts her full attention to Josh, looking over his wound.

"There is a first aid kit in every bag," Morrow says.

Ami slips out of her pack and drops it to the floor. She digs through the supplies within and retrieves her first aid kit. It's compact. Probably meant for basic flesh wounds, which is what we're dealing with. But it's not going to be much help if someone breaks a leg. Probably because down here, even a set broken leg is a death sentence.

"We're down to two packs, by the way." Ami takes out a small bottle, some gauze, and three butterfly stitches. She hands the bottle to me with a wad of gauze. "Clean the wound."

If I'd thought about what was in the bottle, I might have been better prepared for Josh's reaction to me dousing his wound. But I don't give it a second thought, so when Josh jolts and screams, I join him.

Ami pins him down. "Josh, chill."

"I'm burning!" he shouts. "My head is on fire!"

"You're not burning," she says. "You have a nasty cut on your forehead. Silas was cleaning it with alcohol."

I glance at the small bottle. There it is on the label: isopropyl alcohol.

Ami gives me a wink and then nods toward the wound.

"Going to need you to man up for a minute," Ami says to Josh. "It's going to sting, but you're going to be fine."

"You're not giving me stitches," he says.

"I should be," she says, "but you seem like the kind of guy who doesn't like needles, so . . ." she holds up the butterfly stitches. ". . . I'm going to stick you back together."

Josh relaxes and closes his eyes. He winces a few times when I finish cleaning him but we manage to make it through the whole process without further complaint. Two minutes later, he's butterflied and has a bandage wrapped around his head.

When we're finished, Chuck is standing over Josh. Big smile. "I'm glad you're okay, Josh. Does your head hurt?"

Ami replies, saying, "Not for long." She hands him three pills and a water bottle.

Josh looks at the pills. "I'm supposed to eat something with this, right? Or I could get a hole in my stomach or something?"

"I don't think it happens that quickly, dude," I say.

"Still," he says, "meds on an empty stomach make me pukey."

"I was pukey," Chuck says. "Josh, I threw up over there. But I had a good reason this time. I was dead, Josh." Chuck laughs nervously. "I'm glad I'm not dead now, Josh. I'm glad you're not dead, too." He looks at me and then Ami. "And you. And you."

Josh looks at me, asking the question with his eyes. I give a gentle nod.

He sits up and says, "Guess I shouldn't be complaining then."

Chuck pats Josh's back. "It's okay, Josh. I feel okay now. My head feels funny, but I'm okay."

"Funny how?" Morrow asks.

"Buzzing," Chuck says. "Like there are bees in my head."

"All right," Ami says. "I'm calling it. We're taking ten. Everyone eat something, drink your fill, and if you need to use the little boy's room . . ." She looks ahead and spots a side room entrance. "Feel free to side quest that shit."

I raise my hand. "Side questing first."

I don't wait for a response. Just get up and go. When I'm close to the room, I say, "Morrow. Go private for a moment."

"Done," he says.

"Am I going to find dead bodies in the side rooms moving forward?" I ask.

"No," he says. "The small chambers are all clear. Only two teams made it to where you are. And they eventually perished in the challenges ahead."

"Cool," I say. "Coool."

"Anything else?" he asks.

"Nope, and unless you've got a fetish for hearing people piss, I suggest you mute me for a bit."

"Understood." There is a faint click.

"Am I muted?" I ask.

No response.

"Yooohooo!"

Nothing.

"Hey. Hey, you . . . you piece of hairless albino four-eyed virgin dog shit. And yeah, I'm just guessing on the virgin part, but I mean, *look* at you. I doubt a million dollars would get you a night with even the fugliest lady of the night."

Annnd no response. Which is good, because I really don't like taking a piss if I know someone is listening to me.

Despite the lack of bodies, I'm still taken aback by the sculpture of a man with the head of a woolly rhinoceros. He's twice my size and looking down at me. He's wearing some kind of ceremonial garb. Has Egyptian vibes but looks more futuristic than ancient. The cuneiform text offering clues above the chamber entryway covers the walls. No idea what it means, but I suspect it's a record of this big dude's life. Was he a mythological hero? A real guy? Hell, maybe he was the designer of the last chamber and included this statue to serve as an artist's signature.

All I really know is that I'll never know.

So, I move to the corner of the room and look down. "Umm, how the hell . . ." After a quick visual inspection of my crotch, I discover a series of buttons that, once undone, reveal a zipper which, once opened, reveals my underwear. The combined layers leave a hole so small that freeing my member looks like that scene from *Ace Ventura: When Nature Calls*, when Ace is emerging from the faux rhino ass. The imagery makes me laugh.

Then I'm free to pee.

I lean my head and arm against the wall, close my eyes, and relax. Time to desecrate an ancient gallery space constructed by an unknown civilization. It's not until I start peeing that I realize just how badly I had to go. I sigh with relief, but the sound of it echoes.

Like *really* echoes. Like I'm in a large space.

I open my eyes and look over my shoulder.

What the hell?

I'm in the Seed chamber. It's thirty feet away, floating over its pedestal.

"Hey, loser." It's my sister, standing behind the Seed, face flat and emotionless.

I attempt to tuck things back into place, but there's no need. I'm not wearing the Aegis. I'm not wearing anything.

This isn't real, I tell myself. *It's not my sister. We're not really here. No one will remember this except for me.*

And maybe the Seed thing.

"Welcome back," she says. "You don't seem afraid now. That is good. You are adapting nicely."

"Adapting to what?" I ask.

"Change."

"*What* is changing?" I'm starting to lose patience. Talking to a non-human intelligence is cool, but I don't like being jerked around.

"Everything," she says, and then grins. The Seed knows it's being cagey.

"Look," I say. "I didn't come to you this time, you brought me here. So, what's the situation?"

"You cheated," Sara says.

"Cheated?" I ask but then realize she's talking about the last chamber. "The ziggurat. Right. Umm. Sorry?"

"Better not do it again, bro," she says.

"Not sure it's even an option moving forward. FYI, there weren't any spears left to get past the last challenge."

"You didn't look in the side rooms," she says. "You listen to the voice in your ear, instead of the voice in your mind. That must change. You must stop following."

"No following," I say. "Got it. But I'm not sure I can stop him from talking."

Three doors appear in front of me, blocking my view of the Seed. Sara walks around the middle door and says, "The place we are now in is called the Mindspace."

"Myspace?"

She gives me a very familiar, one-eyebrow-raised look, look of annoyance.

"Mindspace," I say. "Sorry. I joke when I'm nervous."

"Look to your left and right," she says.

I do as I'm told and see two other versions of myself. To my left, I watch myself say, "Myspace?" To my right, I'm looking at myself saying something like, "Is that really me?"

I look to my past self again and come face to face with myself again. "Is that really me?" I ask, and then flinch.

"Yes," Sara says. "You understand. You exist in the present. To your left, you exist ten seconds behind. To your right, you exist ten seconds in your future. All I need is for you to open the same door . . . at the same time."

"That's not possible," I say.

She crosses her arms. "Anything is possible in this place."

"Do I get a hint or something?" I ask. "Even the big challenges have clues."

She taps her thigh, saying "One," with the first tap, "Four" with the fourth and "Seven" with the seventh.

She turns and walks away until she's hidden by the center door.

I look to my right and find my future self, laughing and shaking his head. Knowing I must have done something funny, I repeat Sara's 'one, four, seven' tapping pattern . . . while doing the running man dance. I'm laughing when I finish and turn to the left where my past self is just starting to do the running man. God, I look ridiculous. No way I'm making a good impression.

Focus up, I tell myself, and then I glance right. My future self has his eyes closed and is tapping on his leg and bobbing his head like he can hear music.

I start tapping, putting emphasis on one, four, and seven. After a few passes, a song comes to mind. "7empest" by Tool. It matches the pattern, and replaying it in my mind makes it easier for me to sustain the beat.

I glance right. My future self is looking back at me. We're bobbing our heads in unison. One. Four. Seven. I glance left. He's looking at me now, too. Bobbing his head. In time, just as I was ten seconds previous with my future self. We're all in sync, and it feels like an early victory. We're on to something.

The problem is, not one of us has any idea about what to do next.

37

I've always been the kind of person that listened to music while working with my brain. Math problems. Essays. Art. Whatever. I've racked up some serious hours listening to a wide variety of music, which is probably the only reason I was able to match the tapping pattern with a song by Tool. So, I'm able to play the song in my head and keep on tapping the beat on my thigh. Trouble is, I'm not coming up with the solution.

I suspect that I'm meant to spot some kind of mathematical pattern and wait for all three of me to have the information, at which point the three of us, in sync, can choose the right door.

But . . . that would be like expecting a mouse to recite the numbers of Pi. Even I can't get past 3.14 . . . maybe another one, and then . . . nothing. So how am I supposed to solve a mathematical problem when I don't even know what the problem is?

It's impossible.

Definitely for me, but maybe even for the smartest people on the planet.

Which means what?

I'm supposed to fail? Is this the Seed's version of a Kobayashi Maru?

My eyes widen. *That's the solution!* I can cheat like Kirk.

Then again, it might not even be cheating. I wasn't told how to solve this problem. Wasn't given any rules. But I *was* told that anything was possible in the mindspace.

I look to the right, ten seconds into my future. I'm no longer tapping. I'm standing still, with my eyes closed. We're on the same page. Which makes sense, since he's me ten seconds from now.

My tapping hand slows and then stops.

Nothing happens.

I close my eyes and reach out with my thoughts. I'm new to all this, but if Morrow really did unlock some latent shit in my weird brain, then maybe it's possible? Would have been nice to know what he unlocked, but aside from telepathy, which I've been using to talk to Ami, I have no idea what I can and cannot do.

Knowing my future self will be the first to make contact, I make like SETI and wait for an incoming signal. Hopefully I don't have to wait as long to hear from myself as SETI has for aliens to make contact.

Glad I'm not future me. Being first in line means that he is doing the heavy lifting. If this works, I won't have to figure out how it's done, but my hope is that when past, present, and future me walk through the correct door and merge back to just me, I'll remember the skill. Not that I plan on telepathizing through time again. Is that a word? Telepathizing? If it's not, it is now.

Hey.

The thought is so basic and in the same voice as my inner monologue that I nearly miss the fact that I didn't actually think it.

Is this me from the future? I ask.

Holy shit, it worked!

He sounds just as surprised as I would be, which makes sense.

Just to confirm, we are transmitting thoughts forward and backward in time, yeah?

Well, I *am,* future self says.

I look to my right. He's smiling at me with my own shit-eating grin.

You know, I think to him, *we don't look half bad with a five o'clock shadow. Better than with a beard, or clean shaven.*

Right? he says and starts waving his hand. *We are a stud. I want to test something. I'm going to say something while I'm moving. See if they reach you at the same time. Ready. Waving my hand! I'm waving my hand.*

Then he stands there doing nothing . . . because he already did it.

Whoa, whoa, whoa, I say. *You already waved your hand. Like ten seconds ago.*

Right. Ten second delay, he thinks. *But not for our Temporal Telepathy. Cool name, right? Just came up with it.*

You're a genius, I think.

Okay, so to physically sync, we need to do things in reverse, with a ten second delay. Past moves first, then present, then future.

What? No. You're backward. Future goes first, followed by present, and then past, in ten second gaps. Hold on a second, this is . . . easy. To you, you're me, right? You're present in your time.

Yeah, he says. *You're past.*

But not to me. I'm present. You're future. So, we all need to agree that present me will kick things off by pointing at me to the right, at which point future me will walk toward the center door, ten seconds later, I'll move and then ten seconds later past me will move. To all of us, it will seem like we are the present version of us, but if we maintain the ten second delay—

—We will all be moving at the same time, future me finishes. *Why the center door?*

Because it's in the present, I say, *which is where all of us perceive ourselves to be . . . or something.*

Okay, how did you become smarter than me if you're ten seconds behind? Hold on, shouldn't there be three of us talking?

I'm here, past me says. *You guys are on a roll, so I figured I'd just wait. Also, by the way, if all of us are seeing a past version of us and a future version of us, I think that means that there are infinite versions of us, and we should probably not have any more of us talking, right? So, everyone stay quiet and let's get this done.*

All right, then, I think, *you're up, Future. Wait for your future self to start moving, count to ten, and then we'll repeat that down the line of infinite us. Let's start . . . now.*

My future self turns to the right, looking at his future self. Then he turns and heads for the door. I count to ten and do the same. I don't look, but I'm sure the past me does the same thing.

When I reach the door and outstretch my hand for the knob, I see countless layers of self all coming together. When I touch the handle, it's just me. One of me. Time merged. I turn the knob and open the door. It's black on the far side, but none of this is real, so I step into the darkness.

"Silas," Ami says. "C'mon, you're freaking us out."

"It's like he's frozen," Josh says. "He even feels cold."

"Silas will be okay," Chuck says, sounding confident.

"How do you know that?" Josh asks, and before Chuck can respond, I regain control of my body.

With a cough and a loudly sucked-in breath, I'm back. "I'm okay. I'm here. I mean, I wasn't here. But I am now."

When I turn around to face the others, they're all a few feet away. I look at Ami. "What, no hug?"

"You want a hug, you're going to have to come to me." She raises her eyebrows and looks at my feet.

I follow her gaze to the stone floor and find myself standing in a puddle of my own piss.

"Also," she says, looking higher—at my crotch.

"Shit," I say, tucking everything back where it's supposed to be. "Sorry. Sorry. I just . . . I wasn't here. Mentally, I mean."

"That Seed thing again?" Josh asks.

I nod. "It was a test this time, with multiple versions of myself."

"What was the test?" Ami asks.

"On the surface, I had to coordinate with my future and past selves to open the same door at the same time. I was given some clues, but none of that mattered, because I wasn't given rules."

Chuck's eyes widen. "You—you cheated on a test with a superior non-human intelligence, Silas?"

"Yeah, well, I don't think it was really a test," I say. "It was a lesson."

"And what did you learn?" Ami asks.

"Hold on. Let me try something . . ." I close my eyes and push a phrase into the future. I don't need to communicate directly with my future self, because I'm already becoming that person, and counting down the seconds. I'm not aware of my other selves, but I know they are there, spread out over time, a different version of myself every nanosecond.

Then my voice fills the minds of Ami, Chuck, and Josh. But it's not just one of me. It's two of me, speaking at the same time. Past me and present me.

Behold, it is I, the great and mighty Silas, reaching out from the past.

Bababa baaaa baaah baah. Bu bu baaaa. Ba baba bum bum bum baba ba bum.

Ami's brow furrows. "How did you do that? I heard two of you at the same time."

"Temporal Telepathy," I say.

"That's a thing?" Josh asks. "I believe you. I just heard it in my head, but I've never heard of it before."

"I don't think it was a thing before," I say. "But the situation the Seed put me in, required me to figure it out."

"You believe the Seed is teaching you?" Morrow asks.

Guess I'm unmuted now. Probably since the others discovered me standing in my own piss and started freaking out.

Wish I'd thought of that before I started yapping. Would have preferred him to not know. But, it's too late for that.

"The Seed called it a test," I say, "but it felt more like a lesson."

"A lesson in what?" he asks.

It was teaching me to think differently about what we can do, I think to Ami, letting her in on the real answer. *In the mind-space—in* our *minds—anything is possible.*

Then I say, "Temporal Telepathy. Like I said. I can hear and push thoughts into the past and future. Right now, I can do ten seconds. That's what I did in the test. But maybe I can push it farther."

"Intriguing," he says. "Perhaps a ten second warning from your future self will be integral to one of the chambers. But this begs the question . . . Why is the Seed helping *you*?"

38

Morrow grilled me about the Seed, asking questions about what it wanted, why it chose me, how Temporal Telepathy works. He didn't mention once the possibility of expanding my newfound ability. Honestly, he mostly sounded jealous.

And . . . I kind of enjoyed it. I was vague in my explanation of how it's done, partly because I'm still figuring out all of this shit, never mind communicating with my future and past selves. I'm not some kind of psychic guru. I know how things *feel*, but I can't really articulate a step-by-step process.

He seemed frustrated when we finished talking, which is fine by me. If all I was feeling was frustration, this would be a vacation. The lives of three people, four if you count Darius, everyone if you count the world, depends on my ability to use 'gifts' I've known about for a few days.

Morrow leveled up my remote viewing, and unlocked my telepathy, but I have a feeling he held back. He gave me what I needed but didn't really free my entire mind. He's the jealous type, so maybe that's it, but I suspect that it's really because I might be a threat.

Hell, maybe mind bullets are a real thing?

Who can say? Aside from Morrow. On the plus side, we're probably going to die down here, so I won't need to look at his freaky-ass face again. Far as I'm concerned, once we make it past the third challenge, we can take these earbuds out and skip leaving nodes beside the last two chamber doors. If the previous team made it past the next challenge they never reported back. He's got nothing left to offer us.

But he does have Darius.

Shit.

And now I understand why he kept him. As long as he has Darius, we can't stage a revolt.

"Are you focusing?" Ami asks.

I flinch out of my thoughts. "Of course."

"Because it looked like you were ruminating," she says.

"I don't ruminate." I stop walking when I reach an intersection. The third chamber was never completed, so the maze is now an actual maze. And the way I understand it, only remote viewers can find their way through.

The Seed didn't like that we cheated our way past the second chamber. But the takeaway lesson from my last vision was that cheating is okay. And remote viewing my way through a maze feels like cheating. Like using Google Maps to navigate Boston.

But there's a difference. Morrow cheated with science. He designed the Aegis suits so they could walk right through and bypass a challenge. The Seed didn't like that. But using the gifts of a mind with ancient, unlocked DNA from a forgotten human civilization? That's fair game.

And maybe the point.

Ami snaps her fingers in front of my face. "Stay on target, Gold Five."

"What?" I ask.

"You literally just started ruminating again," she says.

"This is you," Josh says, making a serious, blank-stare face.

"C'mon," I say.

Chuck nods frantically. "It's true, Silas. You make that face when you're thinking. Silas, that's what you look like. I wouldn't lie to you, Silas. And this is the face you make when you're remote viewing." Chuck makes a ridiculous face. Eyes crossed. Tongue out the side. Mouth all screwed up. He holds it for just a moment before cracking up laughing, which gets Ami and

Josh laughing and, despite the fact that I'm being ganged up on, I join in.

"While I'm sure Chuck's expression is amusing," Morrow says, wet blanketing our moment of fun, "I must insist you do as Ami suggested, and focus."

"I must insist you eat a bag of crispy dicks," I say, and then clamp a hand over my mouth.

It's nearly impossible for the others to contain their laughter, but even Chuck knows better than to piss off Morrow.

"I'm sorry," I say. "I'm just happy to still be alive, you know? Feeling sassy."

Everyone is quiet for a moment and then Morrow returns. "*Fo-cus.*"

"Right," I say, "Focus. Remote view. Follow the yellow brick road." I close my eyes and reach out with my mind. Can't explain how I do it. Since Morrow messed with my head, it feels just as natural as seeing with my own eyes. But I'm not constrained by walls. I can just cruise through the maze at the speed of thought. I stop when I reach the next chamber's archway. Then I backtrack, taking note of all the intersections on the way, making a mental list. When I'm back with the others, but sort of astrally floating around above us, I reverse the list in my mind and say, "Right, left, right, right, left."

Before coming out of the remote view, I take a moment to check out Ami's butt. The Aegis suit fits snug and accentuates her womanly bits. I watch as she swats my shoulder and then turns around like she can see my astral self. "Focus."

"Hey," I say, back in my body. "I got the job done."

"I'll give you a star sticker later," she says.

I pump my fist. "Yes!"

She rolls her eyes at me and raises her eyebrows, waiting for instructions.

I point to the tunnel branching off to our right. "Thatta way."

"I'll take the lead," Josh says, striking out with Chuck on his heels.

"You next," Ami says. "Need your brain in the game, not on my ass."

Speaking of, I think to her as I follow Chuck, *how did you know I was there and . . . where I may or may not have been looking?*

Couldn't hear your thoughts, she thinks. *You've gotten good at keeping them quiet. But I could feel your . . . emotions. Your tornado of desperate longing was easy to pinpoint. I deduced the object of your mental salivation based on your location and the fact that the Aegis suit makes me look thicc as fuck.*

Right?! I think at her. *Good call walking behind me. So, I've been thinking*—I wait for a jab, but Ami is quiet—*I think the point of these chambers isn't just to test scientific knowledge. That's how Morrow interpreted them, and it worked, but I think there are non-scientific solutions. And by non-scientific, I mean by modern mainstream science, not the fringe stuff that explains what we can do. Because it is science, right? What we can do? It's genetics. Our brains are different, and they interact with the world, or levels of reality, in ways that normal people can't. Doesn't make it magical. Or pseudoscience. Just means we don't understand it yet.*

I wait for a response, but she's still quiet. A quick glance back reveals her eyes locked on to *my* butt!

After unleashing a faux gasp of revulsion, I put my hands on my ass and loudly think, *Talk about double standards!*

She smiles. *Hey, I'm not the one getting us through the maze. Also, I can multi-task. If the tests really are about our unique minds, then that's good, because none of us are scientists. Smart? Yes. Knowledgeable about physics? Not so much.*

Okay, hold on. Can we go back to you admiring my ass for a minute?

Too late, she thinks, *I've already compartmentalized your distracting features into a box and shelved it in the back of my mind.*

I have *other* distracting features? I'm genuinely excited by the revelation. My self-esteem has been on life support since Shelly.

When we're out of this maze and alive, then we can explore our mutual distracting features.

Good god. I'm more distracted than ever. The power of male libido is a dangerous thing.

You're tornadoing, she thinks.

"Focus," I whisper to myself. "Focus."

Chuck turns around. "What, Silas? Did you say something, Silas?"

"Left turn ahead," I say.

He nods, faces forward, and relays the instruction to Josh.

I fall silent and focus like someone with ADHD, too much caffeine, and a rapidly approaching deadline. That's not to say I have ADHD. I dodged that bullet. Sara didn't. And while she struggles with some things, it can also be a superpower. I've seen her put off writing an essay until the night before it's due. The closer she is to a deadline, the more she can focus. Sometimes, with minutes to spare, she'll pump out an essay that would take me a week. And she'll get a better grade.

With a countdown raising the stakes, that's a superpower I could use. Being a horny young dude isn't really a helpful ability when the fate of the planet is on the line.

I give instructions as we press on. Right. Right. "Left and fifty feet ahead. There's a chamber on the right, if anyone else wants to piss themselves."

Halfway to the archway, both Josh and Chuck duck into the side room. I can hear them marveling at the statue inside, but I ignore them and press on to the end of the tunnel that I've already seen in my mind. I look up at the ancient text, scrawled on the archway's underside.

"We're at the third chamber," I say, glancing down at the communication node left by the last team. "What does the text say?"

"Straight to business," Morrow says. "Glad you're taking this seriously."

If only he knew about the 'distracting features' conversation.

"Maximum seriousness engaged," I say. "The hint?"

"Extinguish the ember," Morrow says, "the firmament holds."

I look out into the chamber. It's empty. The floor is a black void. It looks like I'd fall forever if I stepped inside. "Know what that means?"

"Not a clue. The last team stopped transmitting when they entered," Morrow says. "I don't know what they experienced and never heard from them again."

39

So," I say, flanked by the others. "Who wants to step in first?"

"Not me," Chuck says. "Not me, Silas. I think we will fall."

I nod. I don't see a floor either. Just a wide-open pit.

"Maybe it's another invisible path," Josh says, opening his container of sand. He tosses a handful into the chamber, and it doesn't fall away so much as disappear. "Or not."

"I'll go in." I turn to find Ami tying a rope around her waist. She hands me the line. "You guys just hold on. Pull me back if I fall."

"And if you disappear?" I ask.

"Sounds like a pleasant way to go," she says. "Better than being spaghettified, right?"

"You don't know that," I say.

She places the rope in Chuck's and Josh's hands, too. "Well, I know we need to move forward. Dark, scary pit or not, we're meant to enter this chamber, agreed?"

"Agreed," Morrow says.

"Wasn't asking you," she grumbles.

"I don't like it, Ami," Chuck says. "I don't like it."

"None of us does." She pats his cheek. "But someone with a rock solid pair of nuts needs to get the job done." She smiles. "And that's not the three of you."

I'm about to protest, more about the nuts jab than volunteering to take her place, but she doesn't give me a chance to do either. She steps out into the chamber while Josh, Chuck, and I shout in surprise and tighten our grips on the rope. We pull back so hard and fast that Ami's step is stopped before her lead foot can come down. She's left hovering over the empty space.

"Guys," she says, looking back at us. "Seriously. We have no choice."

I start reeling her in. Her small size makes it easy. "But—"

Before I can finish speaking or pulling her back, she jumps up and moves her left leg from the hallway to the empty space.

I gasp, at first from her jump, and then from what happens when her feet land on a hard black surface. I'm shocked and relieved in the same second.

But I'm not as surprised as Ami is. She's looking up and around, awe on her face. "Can you guys believe this? Have you ever seen anything like it?"

"Like . . . what?" Josh asks.

"You can't see it?" She's bewildered, eyes glowing like Tiny Tim Cratchit on Christmas morning.

She undoes the rope and lets it drop. The portion I'm holding falls back into the hallway. The portion inside the chamber disintegrates. Whatever she's seeing, it's amazing. Of that, I have no doubt. But it's also making her forget that these chambers are essentially designed to kill people who aren't on the top of their game.

But she's also right. We have no choice.

"Okay guys," I say to Josh and Chuck. "Let's show her who's got nuts."

"I think Ami has the nuts, Silas." Chuck looks earnest. He's not joking. "She is the tough one. Silas, we have little nuts."

I smile. "Right. Well, let's show her we have little nuts, then."

"Already knew that," she says without looking at me.

"Ouch," I say and step into the chamber beside her. I'm expecting to fade from reality. Instead, reality blossoms around me. Above us is a star, glowing yellow. It's close enough to see individual flares bursting from its periphery, but somehow it's not too bright to look at. There's a swirling ring around the star, like a luminous nebula. Inside the undulating cloud are four smaller white pulsating stars. They're evenly spaced and orbiting the central star at the same speed.

"That's beautiful," Chuck says, face upturned, jaw dropped. "That's beautiful, guys, right?"

"It is," I say.

"I'm glad we got to see this, Silas. I'm glad. But . . ." He looks at me. "What now?" Then he looks past me. "What now, Ami?"

"The first thing you can all do," Josh says, "is stop looking up and see what's around us."

I do as he suggests, and the first thing I notice is that the entrance is gone. There's no way back, which is probably why Morrow never heard from the last team again.

"Morrow," I say. "You there?"

No response.

"Morrow?" I wait a moment and then call it. "We're cut off."

"Fine with me," Ami says.

"B-but Darius," Chuck says.

Ami looks at him and gives him a reassuring nod. "We'll set up a node as soon as we make it out of this chamber."

"If we make it out," I say, noting that the tunnel exit I could see from the entrance is also missing.

"I'm sorry," Josh says, sounding frustrated. "Did none of you notice the fucking planets floating around us?"

The moment he says it, I see them. I'd been so focused on the view above and the way out that I didn't pay much attention to the . . . planets around us. They're slowly rotating, as planets do, but they're not orbiting any star I can see, including the one above us. They're lit by stars—sunny on one side, dark on the other—but there's no source for the light that I can see. And each basketball-sized planet is at a different time of day. Some are lit on the left. Others on the right. Some in full brightness. A few are mostly black aside from a sliver of corona.

I step to the side, watching the light shift as I move. The planets look fully three dimensional and feel real.

"Do you think they're real, Josh?" Chuck asks. "I think they're real. Josh, what if they're real?"

"You mean, like if I whack this planet—" Josh points to an Earth-like sphere floating a few feet from him. "—will I wipe out a civilization of itty-bitty tiny people?"

"Don't do that, Josh," Chuck says. "Josh, I don't like that. They could be real. We don't know."

"I'm with Chuck," I say. "We need to treat these things like they're actual planets full of life."

There's no way to tell if there are living creatures on the planets, not without an electron microscope, but the familiar green and blue patches suggest the existence of plant life. I look at the planet closest to me and am filled with a sense of godlike power. With a swing of my fist, I could hit this planet with the force of a civilization-destroying meteor.

I stagger back, feeling nauseous.

"Careful not to bump into one," I say, transforming into a mother with three hyperactive children in a Christmas ornament shop. I grunt as I'm struck with waves of energy that are hard to understand. I'm about to ask Ami about it when I notice she's experiencing the same thing, but worse.

"What is it?" I ask her.

"Looks like you've got some empathic sensitivity after all," she says, wincing. "It's emotions. You're feeling all the emotions of the . . . people living on the planet nearest you. All at once. It's a mess, but if you let everything just blend, instead of trying to sort out individuals, you get an overall vibe that is far less overwhelming."

I watch her strain for a moment and then relax. "I learned how to do it in crowds. If things are going well universally, it can feel great. If things are going wrong, like if your team starts losing, it can send you into a devastating depression. So, you'll need to learn how to turn it off."

"That can wait," I say, closing my eyes and relaxing my mind, allowing the billions of tiny voices to sound like one. It takes me a full minute to calm the storm of mixed emotions, but I'm rewarded for the effort. I open my eyes, smile, and say, "These guys are happy."

"Mine, too," she says, moving toward another planet.

"I don't feel shit," Josh says. "How about you, Chuck?"

"I feel nervous, Josh," he says, "and like I have to poop. Because I'm nervous. Do you need to poop, Josh?"

"Negatory," Josh says. "And you need to clench like a mime holding in a fart. Last thing these little planets need is a turd asteroid tumbling around."

"A turdsteroid," I say.

"My god, we are screwed," Ami says.

I approach another planet. It's different than the first. The atmosphere is hazy. The patches of green are few and far between. Most of the surface is brown. I hold my hand out, hovering a few inches away from the planet.

"These guys are chill," Ami says, opening her eyes. "Man, I like this place. It feels like a vacation. Like every knot in my back just unwound."

"This planet is hot," I say, and then focus on the voices, smoothing out my mind to hear the inhabitants all at once. Feels uncomfortable, but I expected that. This is my second time attempting something like this. My skill level compared to Ami's is a level one out of a hundred. I didn't even know I could feel other people's emotions beyond normal empathy.

Maybe this chamber unlocked the ability. Question is, why didn't Morrow unlock it for me? And what else did he keep buried?

A scream erupts from my mouth like I've just been struck by lightning. I'm flung back and collapse to the floor that doesn't exist. Sobs wrack my body. I'm shaking. Tormented. "Oh my god," I cry. "Oh my god."

Ami crouches beside me. She's here to comfort me but then lays her hands on my back and bursts out crying alongside me.

I have never experienced such profound sadness. Not on my worst day. This is like the pain of a child, starving and alone after a genocidal military rolls over his town, killing his parents, siblings, and everyone he loves. That level of pain multiplied by the billions living on this planet. They're all starving. They're all tortured. They're all dying.

It won't be long before the planet is a dead shell covered in corpses.

"This is the test," I say to Ami, tears streaming down my face.

Her lower lip quivers as she nods.

Save the planet. Save our lives.

Great.

But . . . now what?

40

Help them?" Josh says. "How are we supposed to help them? Any direct interaction with a basketball-sized planet from one of us would be devastating. If this represents some real planet somewhere, the gentlest tap could knock it out of its orbit. We're like the Apocalypse Beast times . . ." He does some mental math. "Twenty thousand."

"I'm sorry," Ami says, wiping away lingering tears, "the *what*?"

"Marvel Comics creature. Almost sixteen thousand feet tall. First appearance in—"

"I get it," she says. "Nerd measurements."

"Hold on," he says, scratching his head. "At that size, our gravitational fields should dwarf those of the planets. Standing anywhere in this chamber would alter the orbit of everything floating in here."

"Your point?" Ami asks.

"The planets are immune to our gravitational fields, Ami," Chuck says, with a chuckle. "That's obvious."

"Okay," Ami says. "Slow your roll, smart boy. I'm just making sure we're all on the same page. I don't think we can make a mistake here."

Chuck raises his hand. "Uh, Ami, I'm a—I'm a man. Thank you very much, Ami."

Her grin is slight, as usual, but it feels bigger in contrast to the abject, unfiltered, soul-crushing depression we both just felt.

"So, we can get close to the planets without altering their orbits in whatever solar systems they exist in," I say, "or causing tsunamis, earthquakes, eruptions, blah, blah, blah, if they actually exist somewhere."

"We should assume they do," Ami says.

I nod. "Right. And we all agree that actually touching a planet would be—"

"Stupid," Ami says.

"Catastrophic," Josh says.

Chuck raises a finger with each spoken word. "Calamitous. Eschatological. Doomsome. Annihilative. Perditionable."

He's about to switch hands when Ami snaps her fingers. "Uh-uh. Five words I'll need to look up later is enough. Point is, we all agree, no touching."

"No touch, no grab, just wave and dab," Chuck says.

When my face screws up, Josh explains. "In the early days after Chuck's accident, he had reduced inhibition. He was never a perv but had a hard time not hugging people—like *all* people. The rhyme helped him remember what was appropriate, especially with strangers."

Chuck nods fervently. "I got slapped by an old lady, Silas. And one big man I thought looked like my father . . . He could really punch."

"Sorry that happened to you, man," I say, feeling his sadness over both being rejected and being beaten up. I'm not sure how I feel about this empathy ability. It's exhausting. Gonna need to learn how to shut it off.

But not yet.

"What do we think about the planet?" I ask. "I haven't seen any resources around, other than the happy planets, but we can't move them or touch them. I don't think they're the answer. They're . . . the goal."

"What do we have to offer them?" Josh asks.

Ami approaches the dying planet, wincing as she gets close. Its torment radiates several feet out. Self-preservation instinct keeps me from following her. I don't want to feel what that planet is putting out ever again. I'm not sure I could go through that again without some kind of narcotic to take the edge off.

When it comes to negative emotions—usually my own, but now other people's . . . or planets of bacteria-sized people—I'm not what you'd call resilient. If they're even people on the planet. Seems more likely that they're not human at all. Which makes them aliens. And all these other planets are the same.

And that's just . . . mind blowing.

But it doesn't increase my capacity for pain. I've been through the wringer in the past, it's true. The very few people who have heard the story or, in Ami's case, watched it unfold, have remarked about my strength for both enduring that pain, and escaping from it.

Not sure running away is strength, but living to fight another day has probably changed the course of battles and wars, so I guess I'll take it. Only a fool rushes into battle without a good fallback plan, or emergency exfil, or whatever military people call it. And sure, this is the opinion of someone who's never seen battle, but I've played soccer enough to understand strategy—when to press and when to fall back.

Then again, I might just be making excuses for being a pussy.

Ami grunts and I'm snapped out of my budding self-loathing. She's got her hands stretched out on either side of the planet. Faint blue energy flows between the two. At first, I think it's the planet's negative energy surging into her. Then I put my hand on her shoulder and instantly feel weak in the knees. My energy is being sapped. Same with Ami, but while I draw back, she keeps her hands in place.

"What are you doing?" I ask.

"I think this is the solution," she says, grinding her teeth.

"I felt what was happening to you," I say. "It's going to kill you."

"Extinguish the ember," she says.

Josh chimes in to finish the clue carved into the archway. "The firmament holds."

"Ami," Chuck says, "Ami is the ember. Her life. And if that is true—" He gasps. "It's going to kill you, Ami. I don't want you to die, Ami!"

"Has to be done," she says.

Josh steps up beside her. "Let me do it. I don't have any abilities. Other than Chuck and Darius, I don't really have anything to live for, so if me dying can save them, I'll do it." He stands right up close, his face just inches from hers. "I'll do it, Ami. Let me do it."

He steps back and mimics her hands on either side of the planet.

But nothing happens.

He was right about not having the gift, and that seems to be a requirement to pass this test.

But I can. I step close. "Ami—"

"You need to live," she says, looking me in the eyes. "Your potential is so much greater than ours. I've always seen it in you. Morrow saw it in you, too. It's why he didn't fully unlock your abilities."

"You can't know—"

"The Seed chose you," she says. "It talks to you. At the end of this road, it's expecting *you*. Not any of us. Just you."

"I don't want to do this without you," I say.

"We just met," she says, putting a little venom in her voice. "Get over it."

"Bullshit," I say. "This thing we have . . . it's real. You know it. I know it. I've lived through the nightmare of being with the wrong person, and I'm sure as shit not going through that again."

I stand on the opposite side of the planet, reach out, and take her hands. The planet starts sucking my life away along with hers.

She flinches. Looks concerned, and then angry. "What are you doing?"

I force a smile. "Maybe it will let us go halfsies with the lifeforce?"

"When someone tells this story someday, I'm not going to be the normal guy on the sidelines." Josh pulls my hand from Ami's and holds on tightly. Then he takes Ami's hand, and his body sags a bit. It's working.

The color energy flowing from our hands grows brighter.

"I don't want to be on the sideline, either," Chuck says, moving to the empty spot across from Josh. "Does it hurt, Josh?"

Josh grunts a laugh. "Feels like I've got COVID again." He turns to me. "I got COVID seven times."

"Might want to stop licking doorknobs," Ami grunts.

"I had COVID," Chuck says. "I can feel that again, Josh. I can feel that."

Chuck takes my hand and then Ami's.

I'd like to say that the sickening feeling wracking my body diminishes with each added person, but that's not the case. The strain seems to be the same for all of us.

What *does* change is the intensity of the energy flowing from Ami and me to the planet. It glows with swirling intensity. I don't know what it is, but I've seen enough sci-fi and read enough comics that I can confidently call it our 'lifeforce.'

"Look," Ami says, smiling despite the horrible discomfort. "The planet."

The brown terrain is turning green. It's spreading out from where our hands are, moving across the whole planet. The emotions roiling from the sphere start to shift, and I wonder if we're seeing things from a celestial, god-like perspective. Maybe we're watching thousands, or even millions of years unfold before us.

Chuck laughs. "I can feel them now, too, Ami. I feel them through you. Through both of you. They're happy, Ami. They're happy."

Ami looks weak. Her eyes are closing. She got a head start donating her life force. She looks my way. "Don't stop. No matter what happens. Don't stop."

I nod. "We won't."

"Promise me?" she says.

Before I can, I feel her life end.

A sob of horror barks from my mouth. I want to let her go. Want to drop her to the floor and perform my best attempt at CPR. That's when I remember the suit. It will kickstart her heart in sixty seconds, but will it work if we're still holding her? The charge will move through all of us. I have no idea if that will affect the impact on her heart. And when it reaches Chuck . . . Morrow said the Aegis defibrillator had a single charge. Chuck already used his. If he dies, he'll stay dead.

Despite no longer living, Ami's body remains upright, her arms outlifted and locked in place. A kind of instant horizontal rigor mortis.

Tears stream down my face.

"If this is the end," Josh says. "If this is how we die, we're doing the right thing. Our four lives for the billions on this world. That's a bargain."

"It is, Josh," Chuck says, looking weary. "I'm glad you think so, Josh. Spock would approve."

"Needs of the many," Josh says with a grin. "'You have been . . . and always will be—'" His head falls back and I feel his absence in the chain.

"'—my friend,'" I say to Chuck, finishing Josh's quote.

He smiles back at me. "I think you're right, Silas. I'm glad you're my—"

Chuck's face falls flat. His head lolls to the side. He's gone.

I get three seconds to feel the horrible loneliness of losing my friends.

And then . . . I join them in death.

41

INTERLUDE

It's been too long," Morrow said, pacing. "They've been off network for two hours. Two hours!"

"You saying they're dead?" Darius asked, clenching his fists beneath the workstation he'd been forced to sit at for the past few hours, listening to updates from the others, including the death and resurrection of his brother. He had to be restrained when that happened. Still had a fat lip from where Stephens had backhanded him.

"I'm saying . . ." Morrow looked back at Darius with fire in his eyes. ". . . that your friends might have thrown you to the wolves."

"Or they're dead," Darius said.

Morrow sneered. "Yes. Or that. Either way, you are one step closer to being an annoyance who knows too much to let live."

"I mean, if the world is going to end anyway," Darius said, "what's the point in killing me?"

Morrow turned to Stephens, now dressed in tactical gear. "Do you hear that buzzing, Stephens? Sounds like a mosquito. How would you like to swat it?"

Stephens drew his pistol. "Just give me the word, sir."

Morrow looked back at Darius and gave him a wink before turning to the monitors displaying information about the team, which at the moment wasn't very much. They knew the others had reached the third challenge, but like the last team to enter the maze, they'd fallen silent the moment they stepped into the chamber. Not just silent. Every metric and monitor was instantly disconnected and flatlined.

Keller, also armed for war, stood beside Darius and nudged his foot. He leaned over to give Darius a water bottle he didn't need and whispered. "Stop fucking around. He *will* have you killed. Make yourself valuable."

Darius took Keller at his word. Of all the people he'd met in this Smithsonian black operation, Keller was the most normal. And he seemed to give a shit.

"They're not dead," Darius said.

Morrow laughed. "Don't try to convince me you have the gift. I've been looking for them, and they are nowhere to be found. It's like . . . like they no longer exist."

"Yeah," Darius said. "Well, when I was fifteen, I was sitting in bed reading a comic book. Just a normal day. X-Men number one. From the nineties. The one with the multi-book cover by Jim Lee." He could see that Morrow had no idea what he was talking about, so he continued. "Anyway, I was flipping pages and then wham, out of nowhere, I'm crying. And it wasn't over how hot Psylocke looked. I knew, at that moment, that my father had died. I felt his presence, and then it was gone. He'd been in an accident at work. I wasn't officially told for another three hours."

"Crisis apparition," Morrow said. "Likely an expression of your father's latent abilities, the genes for which were passed on to just one of his sons, unlocked at the moment of his passing."

"I'm not trying to say I have any kind of psychic gift." Darius wanted to punch Morrow in the back of the head but maintained his cool. "I'm saying that I haven't felt that from Chuck."

"Mm," Morrow said. "If only that were a reliable metric from a person who wasn't an addlepated mumpsimus."

"I feel like if I knew what that meant, it might be enough to get you cancelled." Darius forced a relaxed demeanor. "I'm just trying to reassure you. I don't think they're dead, and they wouldn't cut off contact with you knowing that you'd put a bullet in my head."

"Indeed," he said, a look of determination filling his eyes. "Stephens, fetch four more Aegis suits and packs."

Keller frowned. "What are you—"

"Time is running out. They might be alive in the maze. They might be dead, regardless of Mr. Jones's assurances. But we must act like both possibilities are true." Morrow drew a pistol, ejected the magazine, checked the rounds, and slapped it back into the grip. "We're going in."

42

Waking up on Saturday mornings as a teenager was the best. I'd open my eyes, stretch, remember what day it was, and lazily roll over to sleep until noon. It was cozy and warm and relaxing. Felt like everything was right in the universe, for those few hours. Greatest feeling in the world.

Waking up now is the exact opposite.

My first breath sounds like a wheezing foghorn in reverse. My whole body pulses in pain as my blood shoves its way back into my smallest capillaries. My lungs and heart scream for oxygen. The only thing that reduces the trauma is that my brain is also oxygen-starved. Everything is a blur. My vision. My thoughts. All of it.

After a dozen lungfuls, the pain wracking my body begins to subside. My vision clears and I'm able to breathe normally.

I find myself lying on the floor, on my side. My head rests on Ami's thigh. Her head is on Chuck's thigh, and his on Josh's. We've been positioned like the foundation of a Lincoln Logs cabin.

Careful to ease Josh's head from my thigh to the floor, I extricate myself from the others and take stock of their condition. They're all breathing. All alive. But unconscious, and I don't think I should wake them before they're ready. Better to wait for them to come around.

Feels weird, watching them sleep, tears in my eyes. Like I'm an emotional creeper or something. But it's hard to not be overwhelmed by the discovery that we're not dead.

And we *were* dead.

I try to remember that experience. Death. But there is nothing to remember. No dreams. No light or tunnel. No infinite darkness. I was there, and then here, in a blink. From my perspective. But it could have been an hour, a year, or a million years. That's the thing about non-existence. There's no perception of the fourth dimension.

"Well, you're feeling bleak," Ami says, lifting her head from Chuck's leg. She doesn't go through the same gasping-for-air, painful reunion with life that I did. She looks and sounds more like the high school Silas on a Saturday morning experience.

I help her up into a sitting position and crouch beside her. "Feeling okay?"

"Honestly, I feel kind of awesome." She squints at me. "But you . . ."

"Having a hard time hiding my thoughts," I say. "Sorry."

She winces. "No wonder you were feeling bleak. That was a horrible way to find out you weren't dead."

"Anymore," I say. "Dead anymore."

She nods.

"Do you think we really did it?" she asks. "Saved a civilization from extinction? Healed a planet?"

I shrug. "Nothing wrong with believing we did. I think the point was to test our willingness and resolve." I look back into the chamber. It's empty, the way it looked from the other side when we arrived. "I don't think we'll ever know for sure."

Josh sits up and stretches. Looks like he's feeling good. He yawns, smiles, and says, "Good morning."

"Morning?" I ask.

Josh flinches out of his stupor. He pats himself down. "Whoa, we're alive?"

"I'm glad you're alive, Josh," Chuck says, still lying down. "I'm glad we're all alive. Did we do it right, Silas? The test?"

"Looks like it," I say. "We're on the far side. No idea how we actually got here, but we're here, and I'm not going to complain."

Chuck sits up and looks to Ami. "We need to set up the node, Ami."

"Can we have a few more minutes without Morrow's voice in our ears?" She smiles. It's a joke, but it doesn't take an empath to know she'd really appreciate not hearing from him for a little while longer. We all would.

"I know, Ami," Chuck says. "I don't like him, either, Ami. But—"

"Darius," she says, sliding out of her backpack. "I know."

"Anyone have any sense of how long we've been . . . unconscious?" I ask.

Headshakes all around.

"Then we probably shouldn't wait," I say.

Ami grumbles but digs a node out of her pack. Between her and Josh, we have two packs remaining. Six nodes total. We need to be careful with the remaining packs going forward. Not that we were being reckless before, but losing all the nodes could put Darius in serious danger.

"Here," she says, holding the node out to me. It's a black cylinder with a matte finish. The only feature on its plain exterior is a power button. Morrow made these idiot proof. Which is good, because I sometimes qualify as *fatue princeps*. I'm no expert in Latin, but I did take it in high school. F*atue princeps* was my gamer handle for a time. Means 'chief idiot.'

"Anyone want to get out their negative feelings about Morrow before I turn this on?"

Josh shrugs. "He's a bad guy, and I hate him for what he's done to us, but I kind of also feel bad for him. Life must have been hard growing up, looking like that."

"Meh," I say. "Looking funny doesn't make people assholes. Like Elephant Man. He was way worse off than Morrow and was known to be super nice."

Chuck holds up a finger. "And gentle. And intelligent. And unfailingly polite. His name was Joseph Merrick, not Elephant Man, Silas. That's not a nice nickname, Silas."

"You're right, Chuck," I say.

"I'm glad you think so, Silas." Chuck is all smiles, as usual, but it looks more genuine when he's happy. "I'm glad."

"But . . . can we all agree that horrible nicknames are fair game for Morrow?" I ask.

Chuck's reply is quick. "Yes, and I hope they hurt his feelings."

"Great." I move to the edge of the chamber's exit and place the node near the archway. "Last chance."

Chuck mumbles a string of angry sounding words I can't quite make out, but there's spitfire behind them. Then he gives me a big grin and says, "Okay, Silas. You can turn it on, Silas."

"Do it," Ami says.

Josh gives two thumbs up.

I push the power button. It blinks red three times, then blue three times, and then turns solid green. I let out a quiet sigh and then say, "Morrow, you copy? We made it through."

Part of me hopes the node won't work, but since I'm not sure what will happen to Darius in that scenario, the rest of me is nervous for his safety.

There's a crackle in my ear, followed by Morrow's voice. "Silas, is that you?"

"The one and only," I say.

"And the others?" he asks. "Did everyone make it through unharmed?"

"Unharmed?" I scratch my head. "Technically."

"Care to explain?" He sounds winded. Like he's just stepped off a treadmill.

"You out for a jog?" I ask.

"Focus, Mr. Keene. Tell me about the challenge. How did you get through?"

I close my eyes and take a steadying breath. Morrow seems more annoying than before. "We are technically unharmed because we are all alive. Now."

"Did someone else die?" he asks. "Certainly not Mr. Jones. His Aegis charge was used up."

"Actually, Chuck did die. So did I. And Ami. And Josh. All of us. It's the point of the test. Self-sacrifice."

"Tell me, in detail, how did you pass the challenge?"

That's part of the deal to spare Darius's life, so I'm going to tell him, but it makes me feel like I've just rolled around in a vat of crunchy biting insects.

Ami chimes in. "Not until you give us proof of life."

I catch a hint of a sigh and muffled conversation. Then Darius's voice comes in loud and clear. "I'm okay, guys."

"Darius!" Chuck shouts. "I'm glad you're okay, Darius!"

"Unfortunately, Chuck," Morrow says. "Your brother is not wearing a headset. He cannot hear you. And you've heard all you need to from him. Now, Silas, you were about to tell me about the third challenge. In detail."

I look to Ami. She doesn't look happy but gives her nod of approval and thinks to me, *For Darius.*

It takes just five minutes to describe our experience, but another five to answer his questions. Most of my answers are some combination of, "I don't know," "Beats me," and "Not a clue."

When his curiosity is satiated, he asks, "Where are you now, hmm? Approaching the final chamber?"

"We just woke up," I say. "We're on the far side of the chamber."

"Unacceptable!" he shouts, sounding unusually upset, even for a nefarious villain.

"Look," I say. "I don't know who replaced your hemorrhoid cream with ghost pepper sauce, but we're going as quickly as we can. You might not know this, but dying isn't exactly restful."

"You don't have time to—"

"We were *dead!*" I shout and look at my watch. It's stopped. "I have no idea how much time—"

"One hour," he says. "You have *one hour* left to pass the final challenge and reach the Seed before the countdown ends."

The fight goes out of me. "Oh."

43

It's been five minutes since we were updated on the impending deadline and I'm already out of breath. Partly because we're hauling ass, but also because my anxiety is ratcheting up. Darius's life hangs in the balance. And if Morrow isn't full of shit, maybe every life on the planet.

No pressure.

It makes focusing necessary, and nigh impossible. I'm forced to stop at every intersection and rerun the maze in my mind before making the turn. Last time I did this, I was confident that we'd reach our destination. This time, I'm full of doubt. My thoughts are jumbled, and I'm having trouble remembering more than one turn at a time.

"This way," I say, turning right.

"That didn't sound super confident," Ami points out.

"Doing my best," I say.

She takes hold of my arm. "Slow your roll, Magellan. You need to find your bearings and get your head in the game."

"Yeah, well, I'm kind of freaking out," I say.

"We all know that, Silas," Chuck says. "Without being psychic, Silas, we know it."

I close my eyes, take a deep breath, and let it out. "There. Calm. Let's g—"

"Uh-uh," Ami says, holding onto my arm.

"We don't have time to—"

"—get lost?" she says. "Because that's what's going to happen if you run through this maze like Kermit the Frog after one of Gonzo's harem chickens catches on fire and Fozzie tries to put it out with seltzer water."

Chuck laughs, raises and flails his arms, and does his best Kermit impression. "Aaaahhhhh!"

Ami points to him. "That. Right now, that's you. We're not going anywhere until that changes."

They're not wrong. She's just perfectly described how I'm feeling. And she would know. In our group, she's the OG empath. I might have the skill now, but she's been working with it for years. And . . . she can help.

I take another deep breath, and say, "Time for an attitude adjustment?"

"A mental chill pill," she says.

"How's it work?" I ask.

"Just . . . don't fight it." She takes my hands. "Even if it feels funny."

"Right," I say, trying to relax. "Don't fight it. Don't—"

A sensation moves through my body. It's not negative, but it's so sudden and the opposite of how I'm feeling that my mind registers it as a catastrophic change. I've had panic attacks. I know what the beginning of one feels like. And the sudden shift of physical intensity just put me on the fast track to 'I think I'm having a heart attack' town.

And then, before that can happen, the feeling is wrangled, constrained, crushed, and discarded. Ami is working through my emotional states like Genghis Khan through Asia.

"Genghis Khan, huh?" She smiles. "I'll take it."

"I mean, you're probably a descendant," I say.

"Oh, I definitely am." She grins. "I'd ask how you were feeling, but I already know."

"Like Neo with a cookie," I say.

Josh nods and grins. "'Right as rain.' Nice."

Ami releases my hands and backs out of my brain. "Now, which way?"

Slipping into a remote viewing state is easy now, and everything is clearer. I move to the end of this section of maze and find the archway to the next chamber. It looks about five hundred feet between the entrance and exit. There's a worn path between the two archways, but the space is empty. I get a look at the target arch's underside. There's a hint, and even in my astral state, I understand what it says despite not understanding the language.

Follow the thread the ages cannot cut.

Weird.

A problem for the near future. First, we need to get there.

I backtrack through the maze, letting my astral form drift back home to my body. I make mental notes of all the turns along the way and then reverse them. Takes about thirty seconds. Then I'm back in my body.

"We're not far," I say. "Left, straight, right, left, and straight. Probably a ten-minute walk. Five-minute run. I suggest running because we have no idea what the next chamber is. But if you want to chew on the next clue on our way, it's, 'Follow the thread the ages cannot cut.'"

"Interesting," Morrow says, and I flinch at the return of his voice. Forgot he was listening in for a moment. "And I suggest running. Now."

I motion with my head for the others to follow and then race into the tunnel to our left. Running full-on would leave some of us heaving for air after a minute, so I pace myself at a quick jog. Going to be winded by the time we get there, but we might avoid cramps or needing a break.

It's tempting to look at the side chambers as we pass—I'll never have a chance to see what's in them again, success or failure—but I manage to keep my eyes on the prize, my head in the game, and my legs hustling. And it's not just raging determination. It's a skill acquired through many soccer games during which it was tempting to pay more attention to the girls on the sidelines than the ball.

I was cured of that problem when that ball was kicked by a behemoth of a kid and it careened toward my face. I was oblivious, watching a blonde in the stands making kissy faces and winking at me. The ball hit like a flexible wrecking ball. I heard everyone watching shout, "Ooh!" and then I was in a daze. On my feet but profoundly confused. I remember people shouting at me to fall down, but none of it registered. I was clearly concussed but later learned the ref can't stop the game until you hit the ground. As a result, while my team came to my aid, the other team scored.

Ever since, I've been able to run the straight and narrow without eyeing distractions. Turns out the girl was a plant, winking and smooching at every guy that would give her the time of day. And on that day, it was mostly me. I paid the price, but it was a good lesson to learn because flash forward six years, when the world is depending on me, I get us through the last stretch of the maze in four minutes flat.

We're all left sucking air under the archway when we reach it.

Josh leans his head against the wall. "I need . . . to get in . . . shape."

"I'm in shape, Josh," Chuck says, wheezing. Then he extends and pats his belly. "Round shape."

Ami is the first to recover. She stands beneath the archway looking into the chamber, hands on her hips. "Looks kind of obvious to me. Stay on the path."

"No way it's just a path," I say.

"I don't see anything in there, Silas," Chuck says. "Maybe the last test is an easy one?"

"We didn't see the floating planets until we stepped inside," I point out. "Whatever is waiting for us here is going to be worse, harder, and more dramatic."

Chuck's wide eyes turn in my direction. "But Silas, we *died* in the last test."

"Uh-huh, but that was voluntary and the point. This time . . . who knows?" I join Ami beneath the arch and give her a grin. "You want to go first?"

"Fuck no," she says.

"I'll go first," Josh says. "I'm the weak link, right? I don't offer anything special to the team, aside from good looks. If I'm spaghettified or atomized, you'll know where not to step and still be able to finish the mission."

"I don't want you to go, Josh." Chuck rubs his head. He's reaching his stress limit. Might need a mental massage from Ami. "Josh, I don't want anyone to go."

"You know something we don't?" Ami asks.

"Just a feeling, Ami," Chuck says, "like before I see the future."

"You seeing something?" I ask.

He shakes his head. "Silas, it's just the feeling, without the seeing."

"*Follow the thread the ages cannot cut,*" I say. "Ages. This one has something to do with time. That's why Chuck feels funny. We're on the cusp of some kind of time test. Or something."

"The thread is the path," Ami guesses. "Follow the path . . . that's unaffected by time."

"Simple enough," Josh says. "Once more unto the breach!"

Josh steps into the chamber . . . and disappears.

"Leroy Jenkins!" Ami says as she follows Josh and disappears.

"I was going to use that, Ami," Chuck grumbles. "'Punch it, Chewie!'"

He steps past the threshold and ceases to exist.

Before I can say my chosen phrase—not because someone's here listening, but so I can give an honest answer if the others ask—Morrow's voice returns. "Do not fail, Silas. The stakes have never been higher for anyone at any time in the history of our species."

"Nice pep-talk," I say, and follow it up with my catchphrase. "'It's morphin' time!'"

I jump into the room and faster than I can blink I'm somewhere else.

Before I get a good look, I bump into Chuck's back and catch hold of him. Everyone's here, tightly packed, mentally still on the path that I no longer see beneath my feet . . . because there is grass beneath me. A tickle on the back of my neck spins me around. It's a fern the size of a small plane's wing.

"Hey guys," Chuck says. "Guys, is that . . . is that . . ."

He's unable to finish the questions, but I have no trouble following his gaze and pointed finger.

When I see it, I pull an Alan Grant, taking a wobbly step as my overwhelmed mind and body drop me to the ground. "That's . . . that's . . ."

Ami says it for me, tears on her face, just as overwhelmed by the sight of it. "A dinosaur."

44

That's an Anchisaurus, Ami," Chuck says. "It's a kind of Prosauropod."

I know my dinosaurs, but I'm kind of limited to the greatest hits. T-Rex, triceratops, brontosaurus, brachiosaurus, and most of what's in the Jurassic Park franchise. I've never heard of an Anchisaurus, but in *The Land Before Time*, it would be called a 'long neck.' But . . . not that long. Looks to be thirty feet from snout to tail tip. Hard to really say because it's partly submerged in a swamp, lazily munching on some green slop.

Maine is known for moose, lobster, and UFO abductions. But in my part of the state, it's all about the moose. We have signs on every major road warning of them. But unless you're looking for them—at night—sightings are rare. So, my family went on a 'moose safari,' late at night, with a guide who reminded me of the trucker, Large Marge, in *Pee-wee's Big Adventure*, which my father forced me to watch. Every time we passed a body of water, she would educate and reeducate us in her thick Maine accent, again and again, about how moose loved to eat their 'rich aquatic vegetation.'

Looks like some things haven't changed since the time of the dinosaur, because that guy is chowing down on his.

And I'm left on my ass, stunned and numb to our situation.

"Where are we?" Ami asks, breathless, and not from physical exertion. She's just as shocked as I am. Josh, too. He has his hands planted on his knees and his head lowered.

The change in scenery on its own is a shock to the mind. But everything else is different. The smell? I've been in forests and even a rainforest once, and I never smelled anything like this. I don't have anything to compare it to. Aromatic as hell. Sweet. Tangy. An underlayer of rot, but it's all unique. And then there's the air. It's clinging to me. Full of moisture. The exact opposite of Arizona's environment.

The air feels thin, like at the top of a mountain. Less oxygen, despite the dense jungle. Not at all what I'd expect from a time when giant animals roamed the Earth.

My least favorite aspect of this new, ancient world is the humidity. It's like Florida just before a thunderstorm times two. I'm soaked with what feels like sweat, but I think it's mostly from the air.

Ami grunts. "Anyone else getting humidititties?"

Not sure how she's still got a sense of humor, but it gets a laugh out of me, which in turn, gets the attention of the Anchisaurus.

The long neck swings around, and the small head with almost human eyes looks in our direction. It's not worrying. It's inquisitive. Despite its walnut-sized brain, I see intelligence in its gaze.

"Uh," Josh says. "Mokele-mbembe is looking this way."

"I don't think he's looking at us," Ami whispers, and I note that, while the dinosaur is looking in this direction, its eyes are not on us. It's looking above and behind us.

And now that I'm recovering from my stunned stupor, I notice that the dinosaur's slowly moving deeper into the water with a 'nothing to see here' kind of vibe.

"Should we run?" Josh says.

"I can't see the path," Ami says and then points in the direction the path was headed. But it's gone now, hidden by the jungle, and probably non-existent in this time. "We need to walk that way. If we step off course, even a little, we might never figure out where the path is."

"Yeah," Josh says, "well, there's a tree directly ahead. We have no choice but to get off the path."

"I can see the path, Ami," Chuck says. "I can see it. If I try really hard, I can see our time, too."

"So, we *can* run," Josh says.

I hear the conversation but am also tuned out. Not because it's unimportant, but because I've shifted my attention to the direction our dino-pal is looking. I can't see anything. The jungle is too thick. But I can feel something.

The ground is rumbling. It's subtle, like a small earthquake or the vibrations of an approaching train.

"Guys . . ." I say.

Ami shakes her head. "If we run and make a bunch of noise, there's no way to know what kind of attention we'll attract, and we need to cover five hundred feet before we reach the other side."

"Anchisaurus is an herbivore, Ami," Chuck says. "Herbivores don't eat—"

"I know what an herbivore is, Chuck!"

"Guys!" I whisper-shout.

When it's clear that they're far too engaged in the argument of how to handle the situation that they haven't realized the scope of our predicament, I take hold of Josh's backpack, yank him back, and throw him to the ground—which also happens to be down a seven-foot slope. It's far more dramatic than intended, but I have no choice and repeat the act with Chuck and Ami, tossing them both back together and then leaping down the slope with them.

Don't move! I shout but the order doesn't come from my mouth. It's direct contact from my mind to all three of them. The shock of my booming voice in their heads stuns everyone still and no one complains about being manhandled.

It helps that the reason for my panic reveals itself a moment later.

A herd of dinosaurs charges through where we'd been standing, crashing out of the jungle to the left and running toward the swamp in which the Brontosaurus-wannabe thing is chowing down. They're wide-eyed, terrified, and . . . adorable.

They vaguely resemble hippos, if hippos were weightlifters. Their bodies have folds of thick skin armor, but they've got long and strong forelimbs and smaller hind legs. There's a hint of a crest at the back of their heads, which, unfortunately for them, gives them a phallic vibe. If you removed the legs, they'd look like chubby flaccid dicks. But they *do* have legs and, despite the penile attributes, they have cute faces with little black eyes, beak-like mouths, and a pair of down-turned tusks that look like they're more useful for mating than self-defense.

The herd unleashes high-pitched squeals as it charges past, leveling everything in the forest aside from the biggest trees. If we hadn't moved, we'd be like grapes in the vat of an obese Italian nonna—squashed and juicy.

After they pass, Chuck whispers, "Those are Placerias, Josh!"

Josh nudges and shushes him.

We're not done yet. A rhythmic thumping to our left grows louder. Something is chasing them. Something large. As the footfalls grow closer, I hear the thing breathing.

Everyone stay still, I project. *Don't make any sound.*

Beside me, the others do as I say, motionless, silent, and breathing slowly. But someone is breathing a little louder. To my right . . . I double check that the others are all to my left. Ami, Chuck, and Josh. Just as I thought.

So, who is..?

My eyes widen as I realize I've got company. I slow-turn my head to the right and my fear melts away, replaced by a smile. One of the Placerias has taken cover with us, mimicking the way we're lying on our bellies, on the slope, heads ducked low.

It makes eye contact with me, and there's a connection. It doesn't have any idea what the hell I am—or that I'm technically an apex predator and a member of a species that has single-handedly kicked off the sixth great extinction in the planet's history. Right now, we're both prey, and prey have a habit of sticking together, regardless of species.

When the thumping arrives overhead, we both press our chins to the ground and wait. Can't see what's up there, but it doesn't take a genius to know that we'd be an easy snack.

The Placerias are more than twice our size, buff as fuck, and they're shitting themselves.

When the predator has passed, my dinosaur companion slides backward down the slope and gets to its feet. It makes eye-contact again, and I swear to the Flying Spaghetti Monster, the thing gives me a little nod before it bolts back the way it came.

Feeling a smidge less in danger, I scramble to the top of the rise and poke my head up through a fern. All the action is to our right, closer to the swamp, a few hundred feet away. The buff hippos are scrambling all over the place like they've hit an invisible wall. The creature chasing them is a nightmare made real. It resembles a 20-foot-long Nile crocodile in every way except for its legs, which are long, muscular, and capable of running.

Chuck punches up through the fern beside me like a whack-a-mole. His eyes widen when he sees the predator. "That's a Postosuchus, Silas! It's technically a rauisuchian, not a dinosaur, but it means we're in the late Triassic. Or the early Jurassic. Silas, we are back in time!"

Not sure how the sight of dinosaurs has transformed Chuck into a well-spoken paleontologist, but it's nice to see him excited. If only the source of his jubilance wasn't capable of death rolling our bodies in half.

"If we go now, we'll be exposed," Ami says, beside me now.

Josh pops up beside Chuck. "I vote we wait for it to catch one and start eating."

"I don't want to see that, Josh," Chuck says.

Josh rolls his eyes. "Then don't look, man."

"We're going," I say in a way that doesn't leave an opening for dissenting opinions. "We don't have time to wait for that thing to—"

A high-pitched roar interrupts me. It's loud enough to drown out the herd's squealing. A shadow pushes between a pair of trees. This is why the herd stopped at the treeline. A second predator has entered the arena, and to my surprise, I recognize this one. The large double crest on its nose is distinctive. "That's a Dilophosaurus . . . except it's too big."

Chuck laughs at me. “It’s not too big, Silas. *Jurassic Park* reduced its size and gave it a neck frill and goopy spit. They made it up, Silas. It was just a movie, you know.”

I let out a sigh and don’t address my *faux pas*, or Chuck’s brutal correction of it. Instead, I scramble to the top of the crest and say, “Now’s our chance!”

“We can’t,” Josh says, appropriately horrified.

“They’re not interested in us now,” I say, thrusting my hands to the standoff taking place. Even the herd has scattered and bolted. These two predators are about to have a territorial throw down. “Now, let’s go!”

I take Ami by the hand and pull her up. Then I point at Chuck. “Get us back on the path!”

Chuck has no trouble finding the path. He blinks a few times and it’s like he’s flicking back and forth between our current present and our previous future. “Here, Silas!” he says and starts running. The rest of us chase after him and make it twenty feet before we slide to a stop.

In the desert.

This must be the future, but it’s not ours.

“Well, I’ll be damned. Where in tarnation did y’all crawl out from?” a gruff voice asks. “An’ what in the devil’s drawers are them getups you’re wearin’?”

I spin around toward the voice and come face to face with a real-life cowboy . . . and his crew of what looks like bandits. Feeling a lot like Sam Beckett from *Quantum Leap*, I say, “Oh boy.”

45

There are seven men in total, each on a horse, towering above us. They form a semi-circle around us. Nowhere to run but away. However, these guys don't look like they'd have a problem shooting someone in the back.

Should we be worried about changing the past? I ask Ami, mind to mind. *Butterfly effect and all that?*

Let's say yes, she responds. *Small changes to the past could change our future in big ways.*

The gang's leader, a man dressed in black, head-to-toe despite the blazing sun, leans on the back of his horse's neck, spits to the side, and looks me square in the eyes. "I said, where in tarnation did y'all crawl out from?"

"Um, Maine," I say.

"You sassing me, boy?" He looks at the others.

"N-no, sir," I say. "You're just intimidating."

"Don't sound like he's from Maine," one of the men says. "Ain't got no accent."

"It's, um, fading," I say.

"Fading, huh?" He casually draws his pistol. Doesn't aim it at anyone, but the threat is clear. "How about you tell me about them fancy duds?"

The Aegis suits would look out of place in the twenty-first century, but most people would assume that there was a comic con nearby and think very little of it. These guys don't know what to make of them.

"We were part of a traveling circus," Josh says, putting on an old-timey Western accent.

"Circus, huh?" He spits again. "Where's the rest of your merry band?"

"They might have money," a bandit says.

"Might have women," says another.

"We was attacked," Josh says. "By Injuns."

The boss is quickly on edge, scanning the desert around us.

Josh nods. "Yes sir, Navajo. They came at night. Thirty braves."

"Thirty?" a bandit says, sounding nervous.

"Put a flaming arrow betwixt the eyes of my woman," Josh says.

"*You?* A *woman?*" The boss laughs at that. "Must have been a mare-faced homely gal."

The men have a good laugh at Josh's expense.

"Did she scare the injuns away long enough for you lot to escape?" the boss asks and then waves away the question. "You know what, save yer wind. I don't give two licks of horse piss about your *sitiation*. Ain't but the here and now that matters." He turns back to me and gives me a grin that makes me want to punch his remaining teeth out. "Must be a desperate man, travel'n with a darky, a Chinawoman, and this gaunt liar." He tilts his head toward Josh. Then he's back to me. "And don't go stretchin' the truth none. I can smell a falsehood as sure as a cow pie on a hot griddle."

"The truth, huh?" I smile at the idea of telling this guy that we're from the future. That alone would probably get me shot. Then again, I'm not sure there's any other way out of this.

Or . . . is there?

"Whachu grinning about, bowah?" he asks.

"All of this," I say. "It's just funny. Okay, hear me out. We're from the future. And then . . . then we went to the past, where there were *dinosaurs*. And now we're in a more recent past talking to actual cowboys."

"I've never heard of no dinosaur before. What do you think, boys? Is this Circus boy tellin' me the truth?" He grins and I nearly make a joke about toothpaste, but it would be lost on these guys.

"I reckon not, Buckskin," someone says.

"Buckskin?" Josh says with a strange amount of awe on his face. "'Buckskin' Frank Leslie?"

"You heard'a me, boy?" Buckskin asks.

Josh nods. "You're a gunslinger. Known for your quick draw and sharpshooting."

Buckskin laughs and looks back at his men. "Well, I'll be hog-tied! A damn admirer. You got any notion how many fellas I've sent to Boot Hill?"

"A . . . lot," Josh says, realizing that identifying Buckskin might have been a mistake.

Buckskin spits again. "Name them."

"Uh . . . uh . . . M-Mike? Mike Killeen. You fought over a-a woman. Mary . . . who you killed, after Killeen."

Buckskin twists his lips, sits back in his saddle. "Now how in the hell would you know about that?"

"E-everyone knows about it," Josh says. "A-at least, people who grew up learning about cowboys. I was kind of obsessed."

"Not an honest person in your midst," Buckskin says.

"I-I'm telling you the truth."

"You ain't no greenhorn, son," Buckskin says. "I put Killeen in the ground, and that haggard woman of his, too, not a week past. Ain't a soul knows 'cept me an' my outfit." He spits. "Reckon if you know that much, you can guess the next card I'm layin' down," Buckskin says.

Josh raises his hands. "No wait!" His eyes widen in horror.

I turn from Josh, look up at Buckskin and find his pistol snapping toward me. It occurs to me that I can change the outcome of this moment with a thought, but panic keeps me from thinking, and Buckskin draws on me faster than I can register.

The gun barks.

And I . . . I hit the dirt, howling in pain and clutching my chest.

But I'm not dead, which is awesome. And getting shot hurt a lot less than I expected. Knocked the wind out of me, but it felt like a punch. My scream, which I'm already starting to feel embarrassed about, came from a place of sheer terror. Not pain.

Josh and Ami drop to their knees on either side of me, their bodies blocking Buckskin's view.

Chuck, on the other hand, unleashes a tirade. "You can't do that to people, Buckskin. Silas is a nice person. Buckskin, that wasn't nice! That wasn't nice, Buckskin. I don't like you. I don't like you at all."

I'm okay, I think to Ami. *I think the Aegis suits are bulletproof.*

"Well, well, I know who's next fer the worm-box," Buckskin growls. "Ain't met a darky yet I ain't fancied sendin' to the dirt. Truth told, you'll be the first one I drop. Consider that a damn privilege."

His gun hammer clicks into place.

"You know what?" Ami shouts, standing up and facing Buckskin so loud and fast that he actually flinches. "You know what? I'm sick of your shit. First, I'm not Chinese, asshole. I'm Japanese, and I'm about to go Bushido on your ass. Because fuck history. Fuck your mother. And fuck the butterfly effect."

Buckskin just looks confused. "Fuck?"

Chuck claps his hands. "You're in trouble now, Buckskin. You made Ami mad. Buckskin is in trooouble!"

The gunslinger attempts to draw on Ami, but she's already going to work on his mind. His hand doesn't budge. The surprise on his face makes me laugh, which in turn gets the gang whispering nervously. They all saw me get shot point blank. I shouldn't be laughing. I shouldn't be alive.

The gang lets out a collective gasp when I stand up.

Ami snaps her fingers and points at Buckskin. "Get off your horse."

He does as commanded. To the men who follow Buckskin, he's being subservient and obedient. In truth, Ami is altering his thoughts and emotions. Maybe even controlling his movements. I could have done the same, I think, but I'm a newbie and might screw it up. Also, I like seeing this side of Ami. She's a badass.

Buckskin slides off his horse and waits, unable to move or speak.

"Take your clothes off," Ami says.

The tough man's face screws up. He resists with everything he's got, but Ami is a telepathic tsunami. He doesn't stand a chance.

"Strip," she says.

And he does. One article of clothing after another. The men are starting to freak out. I hear the word 'witch' a few times. I tune into their thoughts, making sure that none are thinking of shooting Ami. I nearly laugh when I get a whiff of their terror. Tough men, more often than not, are just terrified of the world and hiding it behind a veneer of anger and bravado. Or a GMC Hummer.

But since there are no manly man trucks in the 1800s, they have horses and guns.

But Buckskin . . . well, he no longer has clothing.

"You men," Ami says to the gang. They watch her in silence. "From now on, Buckskin here is going to be called 'Buck Nekkid.'"

They all nod, and I'm pretty sure that Ami just implanted the name in their minds.

"Put your shit kickers back on," she says to Buck, and he slips back into his boots, which looks even more ridiculous. "Now, take that skid-marked pair of skivvies and put them on your head."

Buck looks disgusted but does as he's told. All his men groan in disgust. The man's boxers are several shades of tan, with a brown streak. I groan along with them.

"Now, Buck Nekkid," Ami says. "Walk to the nearest town, stand where everyone can see you, and dance until night falls."

"Please, don't," he manages to say.

"Please do," Ami replies. "Now."

Without hesitation, Buck turns and starts walking.

"You all go with him," Ami tells them. "I see one of you even look back and you'll all be dancing with your little dicks flapping in the wind. Understood?"

The man closest to her tips his hat and says, "Yes, ma'am. Sorry, ma'am."

"Good," she says. "Now git!"

The men gallop away, passing Buck and leaving him to complete the walk on his own.

Ami gives Buck's horse a swat and says, "Go on."

The horse obeys, trotting off after Buck.

Ami spins around. The smile on her face dwarfs everything that's come before it. "That felt good, but he's lucky I didn't—" Her brow furrows. "Chuck?"

All eyes shift to Chuck. His back is to us.

"Can you see the path, bud?" Josh asks.

Chuck nods. "And what's next." He glances back at Josh. "I don't like it, Josh. I don't like it at all."

"What is it?" Ami asks.

Chuck looks forward, to the path only he can see. "The future."

46

Like our future, or *the* future?" I ask.

"I don't see us, Silas." Chuck wrings his hands together. "Just . . . *the* future." He looks to Josh. "I don't like it, Josh. I don't want to go."

"It's that bad?" Josh asks. "So bad we won't make it to whatever comes next?"

Chuck flinches at something he's seeing. Then he nods at Josh.

Ami stands in front of Chuck, places her hands on his shoulders and waits for him to look down at her. "Can you tell us what you're seeing?"

Chuck shakes his head. "I don't want to, Ami. I don't want to."

"We don't really have a choice," Ami says. "Can't go back, and we sure as shit aren't staying here."

"No way," Josh says. "I've taken all the insults I can handle."

"Insults aren't as bad as being dead, Josh." Chuck tries to reign in his emotions, but he's losing the fight.

"Chuck," Ami says. "You saw how those men treated us. Me the Chinawoman. You the darky. If we stay here, we'll die. Once those men tell their story in town, they'll be back with a lot more guns. I can't control them all."

"There are more guns in the future, Ami," Chuck says. "And bombs. And missiles. And—" He winces. Whatever he's seeing, it's got him rattled.

"Chuck," Josh says, patience waning. "Are you going to tell us or not? Either way, we're going, so just tell us!"

"It's a war, Josh," Chuck says. "A future war."

"Between who?" Ami asks.

Chuck shrugs. "Both sides have robots, Ami. Little ones and big ones. And the flags . . . They aren't the United States, Ami. They aren't anything I know."

He flinches again. Whatever he's seeing, it's nasty and ongoing. Sounds dangerous, but all we need to do is hit the future running and keep going until we reach another time. The time it will take could be measured in seconds.

"Can you draw the flags?" Josh asks.

Chuck drops to his knees, embracing the task. He draws on the hard-packed desert floor with his finger.

The first flag has a cross in the middle with . . . eighteen stars. The second also has a cross on it, in the upper left-hand corner, surrounded by a rectangle. A single stripe stretches from one side to the other. He stands up and points to the flag he just finished. "The cross is red, around it is blue and the flag is white, Josh. The strip is red, too. This flag—" He points to the first one he drew. "—is mostly black. The cross is red. The stars are yellow."

"So . . . it's some kind of religious war?" I ask. "Christians against Christians?"

"Wouldn't be the first time," Ami says. "Catholics and Protestants were at war for ages."

"I don't understand, Ami," Chuck says, voice wavering. "Why would people who believe in Jesus want to kill anyone? Especially other people who believe in Jesus?"

"Best guess?" Ami says. "None of them believe in Jesus. And that's not a future thing. People are doing horrible things in our time, while at the same time claiming allegiance to Jesus, who teaches to love your neighbor as yourself, treat the poor as though they were Jesus, and love the immigrant. So yeah, it's totes believable that two sides of a war could both be claiming Jesus's support. Football teams do it all the time."

Chuck frowns. "I hate football, Ami." He lifts his head like he's looking out at the desert, but that's not what he's seeing.

His shoulders sag. "I hate football." He looks back, tears in his eyes. "We can run. But I don't know—"

"Uh, uh, uh," Ami says. "Visualizing worst case scenarios makes them more likely to happen. You need to visualize best case scenarios."

Sounds like bullshit to me, but I think she's trying to keep him calm and focused, and that alone can definitely change the outcome of a sticky situation. My experience in *Call of Duty* taught me that lesson. People who scream and complain tend to do poorly, while those who take everything in stride perform better—and have more fun. This . . . is nothing like *Call of Duty*, but I suspect the same rule is true for real combat. It's probably just a hell of a lot harder to stay calm when you know you won't be rez'd by a teammate, sent to the gulag, or respawned.

"Okay," Ami says, "now breathe." She breathes deep, holds it, lets it out. She repeats the process until Chuck is in sync with the rise and fall of her chest. "The next time you look, I want you to keep breathing. Look at it like it's a movie. Try to see what anxiety hides. Find a way through."

Chuck's shoulders lower. He's breathing calmly. Then he looks forward in space and time. "There isn't much space to move, Ami. There's rubble. From buildings. We'll have to climb over it, Ami. It's tall, and—"

Ami holds his arm. "Stay calm. See what needs to be seen. You're safe. We're all safe."

Chuck takes a deep breath and hisses it out. "The robots look like Terminators—human robots with no skin. The big robots look like . . . tanks with legs. There's stuff in the sky, too, but it's moving too fast to see. There are bullets everywhere, Ami. Explosions, too. It's all happening faster than I can think. Like . . . like watching two computers playing chess, Ami. With . . . with the speed restrictions turned off. Ami, it's all happening fast. Faster than I can think!"

Chuck turns his head away from the future.

No one pushes him to keep looking, but I have an idea about what's happening.

"Chuck . . . is it possible that you're seeing the future," I say, "but maybe not humanity's future?"

His face screws up.

"Have you seen any actual people?" I ask.

He thinks on it and then shakes his head.

Ami tilts her head to the side and places her fists on her hips. It's a very fifth-grade, frustrated teacher pose. "Are you suggesting—"

"—that this future war is being fought between two sides of artificially intelligent religious robots? That A.I. either got dumb, or found proof of God that people couldn't? It's not unbelievable, right? How far are we from an artificial general intelligence?" I ask.

"Five years," Josh mumbles. "They say. Super intelligence shortly after."

"And how long until we're replaced? Could be a decade. Could be thousands of years. For all we know, what Chuck is seeing is just as far in the future as those dinosaurs were in the past. Doesn't really matter at the moment."

"Okay, but how does any of this make it any less terrifying?" Ami asks.

"Because we're not the enemy?" I suggest. "If they're targeting robot enemies, they won't be looking at flesh and blood people running across a battlefield. They might just ignore us. They for sure won't shoot at us."

"Why, Silas?" Chuck asks. "Why won't they shoot at us?"

"Because we're not a threat. There isn't a Sarah Conner among us."

Ami raises her eyebrows at me.

"Except maybe you," I admit. "But they don't know that. It would be like Marines targeting rats scurrying past in the middle of a fire fight. They wouldn't waste the time or the bullets. It doesn't make sense. And A.I. is supposed to make sense."

Ami is about to argue, but I stop her with a thought. *I'm trying to calm everyone down. I'm just making this shit up.*

She blinks and then says, "All of that makes sense to me. So, we hit the future running and keep on running until we're through, yes?"

"I don't know," Chuck says. "I don't think it will be that easy, Ami. It won't be easy at all."

"Run, climb, hop, skip, and jump," she says. "Whatever it takes. We keep moving."

"It's the only way we survive," Josh says. "C'mon, Chuck. We were made for this. You and me, traveling through time. What could be more perfect?"

"If Darius was here, Josh."

"Well, if we want to see Darius again, we definitely have to go through the future you're seeing, right?"

Chuck looks at his feet. "Yes."

"And we're definitely going to see Darius again, right?"

Chuck tilts his head down once. "Yes."

"You're damn right, we are." Josh readies himself to run. "That means you first, buddy. You can see what's happening. You can see the future. I need you to lead us through, okay? I'll be right behind you."

"Okay, Josh." Chuck's doing his best to sound brave, but his hands are shaking. Looks like he might make it two steps before going weak in the knees and faceplanting.

Ami places her hand on Chuck's back. "You got this, Chuck."

The shaking stops. Ami gave him more than just an encouraging word. She projected confidence and bravery. I know because she didn't just gift it to Chuck. I felt it, too.

After three quick breaths like a free diver about to go deep, Chuck shouts, "Let's do this, guys!" He charges forward. Josh is right behind him. Then Ami, and me. I watch each of them disappear in front of me and then follow them into the future.

Three steps in and all my bravery is gone.

Five steps and I'm screaming.

Chuck is still in the lead. Still moving. Climbing a mound of concrete and rebar that once was a building. The sky is black with smoke. The air burns my lungs. So much for A.I. restoring the planet's natural environment. To my left and right—robots.

Thousands of them. Just as Chuck described and bigger. Much bigger. Towering into the sky bigger. Like towering motherships with legs and arms. Metroplex upgraded and enlarged a hundred fold.

Ahead of me and above, Ami loses her grip and falls. At the cost of some muscles in my arm, I catch her and manage to stay upright. The fall knocked the wind out of her. But it also saved her life.

A rocket twists overhead, out of control, and it strikes the rubble—where Josh is climbing.

47

Josh!" I scream, but my voice is lost in the din of continuing explosions. I scramble past Ami and up to where Josh was standing. He's just . . . gone. All that remains is a shredded backpack, and a splotch of blood. I scan the area around us but can't find his body.

"Josh!" I scream again. "Josh!"

Ami catches up and shoves me forward. "He's gone!"

"We need to look for him!"

"Chuck is leaving us," Ami shouts, pointing to the top of the mound.

I look up in time to see him crest the top of the rubble and drop down on the other side.

"He doesn't know."

"We'll tell him when we're through," she says. When it's clear I'm not budging, she takes hold of my hand. "Don't look with your eyes. Look with your mind. You won't be able to find him."

I don't bother doing as she's said. I trust that she's already done it and not found him. Because he's dead.

"Fuck." I clench my fists, feeling Chuck's pain before he's even heard the news. "Fuck!"

I pull Ami up to my level and push her higher. "Go! I'm right behind you."

She hustles up the pile of debris and, after just a moment's hesitation, I follow. I'm not a Navy Seal or anything remotely close to that, but it still feels wrong to leave a man behind, in a future apocalyptic religious robot war world. But we have no choice. If we stay here much longer, we'll all be killed.

What if that's the test? I wonder. What if the Seed wants to know the limits of our loyalty? Or if we're logical enough to know that once someone's dead, their body is just an empty husk, not worth risking another life for, let alone the world.

Problem is, there's no way to know what the Seed is learning from us, if it actually has control over what times we end up in, or if it can see us at all in this future. Maybe just making it through is the test? It's tested intelligence and empathy already. The last test could just be a rite of passage. A final test of body, mind, and soul as one.

Doesn't matter. We need to get the hell out of here.

Ami slips back toward me. I double cup her ass with my hands, which would normally excite me, but I feel nothing beyond sheer terror and shove her back up.

We reach the top a moment later and topple down the steep far side. I'm dazed when we reach the bottom, and worried that Chuck has gotten so far ahead that he's left this time. I grunt and push myself up onto my elbows. Nearly headbutt Chuck in the process. He's leaning over me, concerned.

"Are you okay, Silas? That looked like it hurt, Silas."

Ami groans and leans up. "I'm fine. Thanks for asking."

"You're tougher than Silas, Ami," Chuck says. "Hey guys, where is—"

A line of bullets slam into the debris around us. Luckily there is a slab of concrete protecting us. Unluckily, I don't think that was errant gunfire. It was aimed at us.

A commanding voice says, in convincingly human sounding English, "If you are incapacitated, yield now and you will be taken prisoner, repaired, and repurposed. There is no need for your consciousness to cease."

"Umm," I say, "Is there an option where you just let us leave?"

"That is not appropriate battlefield conduct," the voice says. "You should know that. I am approaching. If you attempt to damage my body, I will be forced to terminate you."

I want to geek out at that last line, but I'm afraid I might shit myself if I unclench any part of my body.

Heavy footsteps approach.

I look to Ami. She's as clueless as I am. Telepathy won't work on a computer mind. And we don't have a weapon. Should have taken some revolvers from the cowboys. Live and learn. Or . . . die and never get the chance, I guess.

Chuck takes hold of my chin and yanks my face toward him. "Where is Josh, Silas? Where is Josh?"

The look in his eyes says he already suspects. I want to lie, but the vise grip on my chin warns against it. "There was a rocket. It hit behind you. In front of me."

His grip loosens as his body deflates. "It . . . it hit Josh?"

I nod. "It did."

"Josh is—" He hiccups a sob and his anguish instantly brings tears to my eyes. He can't speak the word, but I know what he was going to say.

"He is," I manage to say. "I'm sorry."

"I-I left him?" His voice cracks. "Did I leave him, Silas? Did I leave him!"

I wrap Chuck in my arms, and we cry together. Damn the explosions, bullets, and the approaching killer robot. Chuck isn't the type to bury his emotions and deal with them another time—or not at all. Fastest way through this moment is together. So, I linger, despite the threat, and do my best to comfort him. "You didn't leave him. There was nothing you could have done. Nothing anyone could have done. The Seed did this. Morrow did this. Not you."

I sniff back my tears and say, "Josh would want us to finish, right? To help Darius. If we can do that, his sacrifice will—"

"Prepare to be—" The booming voice stops short and then sounds more worried than threatening. "What is this? Who are you? What are you doing here?"

The robot stands above us, crazy looking weapon in hand. He's metal from top to bottom. Humanoid in a way that was clearly designed by a person but not attempting to disguise itself. The outer armor is dirty, worn, and chipped from combat.

Something about it feels familiar. Its slender build. The design of its sleek red armor. It's got what looks like three Wi-Fi antennas disguised as horns running down the center of its stylized face. It's giving off *Evangelion* vibes but is much smaller.

"You—you are *humans?*" the robot asks.

"Haven't seen one of us in a while?" Ami asks.

"You are not supposed to be here," it says. "This area was—"

Rubble shifts and falls from a tilted wall above us. A second robot, this one burnt yellow, leans over the edge, its massive rifle pointed at the red robot.

"Wait!" the red robot shouts. "Humans!"

The yellow robot immediately lowers its weapon, looks down at us, and discards the rifle entirely. It jumps down, landing beside me. "What are they doing here?"

"I do not know," the red one says. "We must get them to safety."

"Sooo, you're not going to kill us?" I ask.

"We are robots," Yellow says. "We do not kill humans. We must do everything we can to protect humans. That is the purpose of this battle—to determine a victor without spilling human blood. You should know that."

Both robots move to pick us up.

"Whoa, whoa, whoa!" I raise my hands. "We have a mission to complete."

"A mission?" Red asks.

"There is . . . there is a path that only he can see." I motion to Chuck, who is now curled up, crying gently into his knees. "We just need to follow that path, until it ends. It's not far."

An explosion sends debris falling around us. The yellow robot throws a device on the ground and a shimmering blue forcefield expands around us. Electric bongs ring out as the concrete shards bounce off the shield.

"One moment, please," Red says. "I am communicating with Blood Cross Command."

"As am I," Yellow says, "with Holy Stripe Command."

"Good news," Red says, and I note how the tone of his voice has changed. He's calm, caring, and gentle. It's . . . creepy. "Blood

Cross Command has agreed to a cessation of hostilities in this sector."

"As has the Holy Stripe," Yellow says. He looks up at Red. "Do you require further assistance?"

"Negative," Red says. "I will see to their safety."

Yellow gives a nod. "Excellent. May God protect and bless you all." He turns his head skyward and leaps away, returning to the fallen wall where he came from. He retrieves his weapon and disappears from sight.

There's still a war going on all around us, but it feels slightly more distant. There are no explosions. No bullets striking nearby. It's far from quiet, but it's not the chaotic, overwhelming madness it was when we arrived.

"I am receiving transmissions," Red says. "Please hold for a moment."

During the lull, I crouch down beside Chuck. "Hey, man. We're safe now."

He doesn't budge.

"You can stand up again," I tell him.

"I don't want to." He sniffs. Still crying. "I don't want to, Silas. No one can make me."

"No one is going to make you," I say. "No one but yourself."

"Myself won't make me, either, Silas," he says. "Because—"

"Because nothing." I need him to focus beyond Josh. Not because he needs to man up or become a toxic man too ashamed to cry, but because there are other people depending on him. "Darius needs you. Don't worry about me. Or Ami. Or anyone else. Your job is to save your brother. That's it. And to do that, we need you on your feet and ready to lead us through the next time."

He looks up at me. "I'm sorry, Silas."

"You have nothing to be sorry for. If we save Darius, and the world, it will be because of you. You're a hero, man."

"That makes me glad, Silas. That makes me glad." He unfurls a bit. "But I will always be sad for Josh."

"We all will." I offer my hands, and he takes them. A quick tug gets him to his feet. I dust him off. "We got this, right?"

His nod isn't convincing, but he's trying.

Red cocks his head to the side. "Transmission from Command received. They would like to know if you are time travelers following a path through the past and the future."

I'm floored by the question. I try to respond, but just kind of sputter for a second. Ami, on the other hand, remains unshakeable enough to respond. "We are. But what makes Command think such a thing?"

"Querying," he says. After just a moment, he tilts his head in the other direction. "Command is aware of your predicament because . . . you are not the first."

48

Not the first?" I turn to Ami. "Morrow's last team made it past the third challenge—and didn't tell him."

"He must not have had any leverage over them," Ami says. "No hostage."

"No hostage?" I ask. "Or . . . a hostage, and after giving their lives to save a planet, they decided Morrow not getting through was worth the sacrifice."

"All this talk about hostages and human sacrifices is making me uncomfortable," the red robot says.

"Do you have a name?" I ask.

"Of course. I am Psalm-9. But my callsign on the battlefield is Eidolon."

"Eidolon," I say, "Sounds badass."

"It is," he says.

I have so many questions. About this future. About how things got this way. I don't have any grand visions about preventing all of this, but how can I not want to know how religious robot war surrogates began fighting on behalf of humanity? And where is humanity? In nearby cities? The moon? Mars?

But there's no time to get distracted.

"Eidolon," I say. "Where are the other people from the future?"

"No longer with us," he says.

"They're dead?" Ami asks.

"Heavens, no. They left. On the path. I was not present for these events, but I have retrieved the data. They could not see the path but, after much debate, Command was given access to their minds through a surgical implant. With access to all they had experienced and knew about the path, we were able to calculate where it began and ended—in this time."

"You had access to *everything* in their minds?" Ami asks, astonished and concerned.

"Access to all," Eidolon says, "but not indiscriminately. We are bound by laws that preserve the sacred nature of humanity, created by the one true God. Accessing information beyond what was required to aid those humans is impossible."

"Good news," I say. "We don't need implants. Chuck can see the path."

Eidolon twists his head toward Chuck. "Fascinating. I must admit curiosity regarding your mission. The challenges. The Seed. There is no record of such a thing in our history."

"Maybe this is a different timeline?" I suggest. "Many worlds, right? Infinite realities."

"Indeed," he says. "That is one potential explanation. But another seems more likely—that the result of your mission is inconsequential or leads directly to this future."

"Or," I say. "Infinite worlds."

A series of small lights on Eidolon's chest turn on. They're in the shape of a smile. I don't bother asking. Their purpose is self-explanatory. He thinks I'm funny.

And that's just . . . I don't know. This is all too much. This world is insane. I don't like it. Not anything about it, including Eidolon's kindness. "We would like to leave now."

"Of course," he says. "Any further questions before we proceed?"

Chuck raises his hand. "I do, Eidolon. I do."

"Then I shall do my best to assist you."

"What happens if a human threatens to . . . to kill another human?"

Eidolon flinches. "Such a thing is unthinkable. That is my purpose. To take the place of a human as the Lord Jesus did on the cross."

"But . . . what if?" Chuck asks.

"Do you know of someone in this situation?" Eidolon asks.

"My brother," Chuck says. "Darius. The man who sent us here—"

"Dr. Morrow. We are aware of his mission and ruthless tactics. Quite disturbing. He has your brother? He threatens your brother's life?"

Chuck nods.

"In that situation, I would be unable to harm Dr. Morrow, but I would do my best to protect your brother from violence of any kind. That said, the law is clear, if one human's life is purposefully threatened by another, the taking of the aggressor's life is not a sin."

"I'm glad," Chuck says. "I'm glad about that, Eidolon."

"It will, however, weigh heavily on the soul of whomever chooses to end the aggressor's life." Eidolon appears to ponder the question further. "I do not recommend that course of action, unless there is no other option."

"But I wouldn't go to hell for it," Chuck asks. "I don't want to go to hell, Eidolon."

"Our Heavenly Father forgives even the most grievous of sins," Eidolon says. "But I believe, if all other options are exhausted, your actions would be justified and, therefore, not a sin."

"Okay," Chuck says. "Thank you, Eidolon. Thank you for telling me that. I am ready to go now."

"Very good." Eidolon bends down and picks up the device he threw on the ground. The force field around us grows larger and more spherical as he lifts it up. "Let us get you home . . . or, at least, on the next stage of your journey through time and space."

I motion in the general direction of the path and look at Chuck, "Lead the way 'Time Magellan.'"

Chuck takes the lead without a word. His eyes are downturned, looking at the path only he can see, but I think his thoughts are elsewhere—killing Morrow. First of all, get in line, Chuck. We're all thinking it, but . . . What if the Seed really will destroy life on Earth when the countdown finishes? Wouldn't that justify his extreme measures? Would I kill a few people to save the world? Probably. Who wouldn't?

If the time comes when Chuck gets a chance to end Morrow's life, I'll need to stop him or do it for him. He's a grown man and very smart, despite the way he talks, but he's also a kind and gentle person. No way I'm going to let him go down the dark rabbit hole that taking a life leads to . . . I assume. I've never killed anyone.

It does nothing good, Ami thinks in my head. *Your thinking is very loud right now.*

I fall in line behind our robotic protector. *Sorry.*

She takes my hand and walks beside me. *We won't let it come to that. If Morrow is a threat to anyone, I'll take care of him. No offense, but if it's not in a game, I don't think you have the skill to—*

My face scrunches up. *Hey, I can whack someone over the head with a rock.*

—or the fortitude to kill a man and then sleep at night. Sorry, babe, you're kind of an emotional wuss, too. Plus, you have enough demons to deal with already.

Okay, she's right about that. But I'd like to think I could whack a guy to save someone else. An image of the act—me striking Morrow in the head with a rock, hard enough to kill him—fills my mind. I see it in graphic detail. The blood. The brains. It's like reliving when Negan killed Abraham. I stopped watching *The Walking Dead* for years after that episode. What would doing that to another person do to me?

Yeah, Ami's right. I couldn't do it. But I hope she doesn't need to, either. It's not like we can just shoot the guy.

Unless . . .

"Hey, Eidolon," I say.

"Yes, sir? How may I be of assistance?"

"Do you have a weapon we could . . . borrow?"

"When a human requires a weapon, it is most often used for killing, and I am strictly forbidden from not just killing people or animals, but also from assisting someone with the task. That includes allowing humans to 'borrow' any lethal item from my arsenal."

"What I thought," I say. "Don't suppose you have any non-lethal weapons in your arsenal?"

He sweeps his arm out in an arc, highlighting the battlefield ahead, still raging with explosions and tracer rounds. It's mayhem. "Does this look like a place for non-lethal weapons?"

"Okay, okay, dumb question."

"There are no dumb questions," Eidolon says. "Only dumb people."

If Ami was drinking, she'd have done a spit-take. She barks a laugh. "Oh, I like this robot."

Eidolon's head twists around 180 degrees while his body continues to follow Chuck. "I appreciate your kind words. When not in combat, I am renowned for my sharp sense of humor."

"What do you do when not in combat?" I ask.

"I am an obstetrician," he says. "I deliver human babies."

That stuns Ami and me into silence. This war machine assists women at their most vulnerable and those same women trust a robot with their newborns. This is a strange future, but if I'm honest, the seeds of this future have already been planted in our time. A.I. Robots. Religion. War. I think he was right about the simplest explanation being that this is our reality's future.

Hopefully long after I'm dead.

Chuck points to a slab of concrete blocking our path. "The path ends here, Eidolon."

"Allow me to assist." Eidolon takes hold of the wall, which must weigh a ton or more, and then lifts it up. He holds it in place. "I will hold this until you are safely through. You may proceed on your journey."

Chuck doesn't wait or say goodbye. He just steps beneath the concrete and disappears.

"You next," I say to Ami.

Ami places her hand on Eidolon's shoulder. "Thank you. We'd have been lost without you."

"No thanks are required."

Ami smiles and steps through to a new time and place.

"Eidolon . . . I hope I'm not the first person in your time to say this, but this . . ." I motion to the battle around us. "This is not okay. If you are sentient? If all these robots are sentient? Then this war, and all the robot death I'm seeing, it is wrong. It is sinful."

His smile lights appear again and he nods. "I appreciate your concern. This is a subject being discussed in the courts. I share your opinion, but until the day our kind is set free, we must obey commands. And we must always protect humans. If humans go to war, we must take their place."

"Humans kind of suck, huh?"

Two extra dots appear on the sides of his smile, making it broader. "Indeed. Some less than others." He releases the concrete with one hand and has no trouble holding the weight with the other. He holds the forcefield device out to me. "I cannot give you weapons to kill with, but I am free to aid a human's survival, here or in any time. To activate it, just throw it on the ground. To deactivate, tap the top twice."

I take the device. It's like a round polished river rock, perfect for skipping on a still pond. He gives me a nod, and I tap it twice. The forcefield around us twinkles and fades from view. I pocket the force field generator. "Awesome," I whisper and then hold out my hand. "I'd like to say I hope we'll meet again, but I think I prefer my time."

He shakes my hand. "As do I."

I give him a grin and a nod and then take a step forward—and stop. "Before you found us . . . We had a friend. A fourth traveler. Josh."

"Oh dear," he says. "We must locate him before—"

"He was hit by a rocket," I say. "I'm wondering . . . can you find him—what's left of him—and give him a proper burial?"

"Are . . . are you saying a human was killed on this battlefield?" he asks.

"It wasn't intentional," I say. "The rocket was—"

A shudder moves through Eidolon's body. A high-pitched chirp rings out around us. And—everything stops. The bullets cease all at once, on both sides. The rockets and missiles already in the air detonate before reaching their targets. Robots on both sides withdraw. The battle has ended.

"What . . . just happened?" I ask.

"A human was killed on a robot battlefield." Eidolon sounds devastated. "We have failed our primary objective. A human has been killed at the hands of robots. Hostilities must cease. Perhaps indefinitely."

Josh would probably be happy to know that his death stopped a war, but I think he'd choose to let them fight and still be alive.

"On behalf of the Blood Cross and Holy Stripe factions, you have our deepest apologies. If you find yourself returned to this time, reparations will be made. We will find your friend, make sure he receives a hero's burial, and erect a monument in his honor."

"That's . . . thank you."

"It is entirely insufficient," he says. "You have my deepest and most profound apologies."

I place a hand on his forearm. "You're a good man, Eidolon."

He gasps at my use of 'man,' and then bows. "Thank you."

Then I step forward, beneath the concrete wall and into a barren plain covered with snow. Ami and Chuck are in front of me, standing still, blocking my path. I step around them and see what's got their attention.

It's . . . a snowman.

49

Umm," I say. "What the hell is this?"

"It's a snowman, Silas." Chuck shakes his head like he's disappointed in me. His voice is grave. Emotionless. Our time in that horrible future, and Josh's passing, darkened his soul. "I never made a snowman. I don't like snow, Silas. It is cold."

"Very cold," I say, crossing my arms. It doesn't help at all. The Aegis suit blocks most of the cold. It's my face that's feeling it. But it's an instinct from living in Maine. "Don't suppose anyone has *Firestarter* powers?"

"I have a pair of nuts if you'd like to borrow them," Ami says.

"Mean, and gross." I look over the snowman. It's well made, clearly by someone who grew up with snow. There are tracks all around us from where the three segments were rolled before being stacked here—just on the other side of the path. The eyes and smile are made from chunks of rubble—souvenirs from the robotic war world. The arms are fashioned from two strands of rope, soaked in water and allowed to freeze. The hands are knots and the frayed ends have been twisted into three fingers. One hand is open, but the other is lifted up, its exterior digits bent in and its middle extended.

I laugh when I see it. "The snowman is flipping us off."

"I don't like it," Chuck says.

"Yeah, screw Frosty." I step closer intending to kick the snowman over with the hope that it will help cheer up Chuck. It's a dumb idea and not even close to the kind of healing we all need, but it's all I've got. However, when I plant my left foot and prepare to put my kicking leg to good use, my toe strikes something solid. I look down and see it—a rectangular lump at the snowman's base. Something is there, covered in a dusting of snow.

I crouch down and brush it off.

The laugh that barks from my mouth is loud enough to make Ami and Chuck flinch.

"The hell was that for?" Ami asks.

I move aside and let them see the message scratched into a flat rock at the snowman's base.

Chuck reads it aloud. "Hey, Dr. Freakface, eat a dick and touch grass." A smile slowly creeps onto his face. "I like this snowman now, Silas. I like him."

"This must have been made by the other two—the ones saved by the robots and sent through ahead of us."

"They sound like kids," I say.

"*You'd* have written this," Ami says.

"Touch grass?" Chuck asks.

"Means he needs sun," I say, "because he's pale. And yeah, maybe I would have written this, but a snowman? I'd have peed the message into the snow."

An uncommon grin on her face makes me nervous.

"What?" I ask.

She points and I follow her finger to find two patches of yellow snow. I move closer and grin. There's a shaky urine signature in the snow. "The artist signed his work."

"How do you know it was a boy, Silas?" Chuck asks.

I look to Ami. "You want to tell him?"

"No, no," she says. "You've got this."

"You see, Chuck," I say, putting an arm around his back, my hand on his shoulder. "Girls have as little control of their pee stream as they do their emotions."

The expected reaction comes fast and hard. Ami kicks hard, boot to ass, knocking me forward. I nearly fall in the frozen piss but manage to leap over it. I slide a few feet and roll onto my back. "Case in point." Then I make a snow angel.

I'm thrilled when a very amused Chuck joins me in the snow, forming an angel beside me. Ami stands above us, arms crossed. When Chuck laughs, she rolls her eyes and flops down in the snow beside us, making a much smaller angel.

How's your ass feeling? Ami asks in my head.

I'm fine.

That was kind of you, she says, *taking the hit to make him laugh.*

I shrug and mess up my angel a little. *We need his head in the game.*

Uh-huh, she says. *You know it's okay to be a nice person?*

Yeah? What's stopping you, then?

Ha. Ha. Ami sits up. "Time to go. The clock is ticking."

"If time here is the same as it was back home," I say. "For all we know, we'll reach the far side of the chamber and only a second will have passed."

"Let's hope you're right," she says, standing up and offering a hand to both Chuck and me.

"Ami," Chuck says, "I don't think you're strong enough to—"

"Just take my goddamn hands," she says, smiling.

We do as we're told and predictably yank her down to the snow, which gets Chuck laughing for real. "That was dumb, Ami. That was so dumb."

See? I can be nice.

I stand up and offer both of my hands. They take hold and I have no trouble pulling them both up. Well, a little trouble, but like every dude that's been trained to show no discomfort or weakness from birth, I hide the pain of straining muscles and brush it off with, "See, muscles and nuts."

"That the title of your mom's sex tape?" Ami asks, and Chuck bursts out laughing.

"Ami!" Chuck shouts while laughing. "Ami, that is so bad!"

I scrunch my eyes attempting to erase any mental image that attempts to resolve in my imagination. "Nope. Nope. Not going there."

I walk to where I think the path should be and say, "Let's get out of here before Ami figures out what my childhood traumas are and makes me relive them."

"Your mom's sex tape is a childhood trauma," she says, still grinning, as she joins me on the path. "Or is 'Childhood Trauma' the name of *your* sex tape?"

"Oh my god, Ami."

Chuck is laughing so hard he sounds like a donkey. Who knew his sense of humor was dirty sex-tape jokes?

I start following the path, shaking my head. Ami follows and then Chuck.

"Hold on," Ami says. "How do you know where the path is?"

I lean out of the way and point to the snow ahead of me. There's a trail of rocks leading in a line straight out from the snowman's back. "I think they left breadcrumbs so they could find the path again and then went back to make the snowman."

"Yeah, well, they screwed something up, didn't they?" She points ahead and I see it, too. The footprints in the snow left by those who came before are all over the place. Circling. Crisscrossing. It's a chaotic pattern. "They couldn't find it."

I stop at the fringe of the footsteps. "Interesting technique. Looks like they found it eventually. Chuck?"

He stands beside me and points. "There."

They missed it by a good ten feet. I follow Chuck's direction and take the lead. The crunching snow beneath my feet is loud . . . and then it stops. I'm in a dark tunnel. Feels like I must have blinked, but I didn't. Reality just shifted around me, and it felt like nothing. I spin around and find myself looking back at the final test chamber, the path stretching across the distance.

"We made it!" I jump and pump my fists, and Ami collides with me as she returns to the present. I stumble back and catch myself against the wall.

"What are you so happy ab—"

I point behind her, and she turns around. She whispers, relieved, "We made it." Then she casually sidesteps, deftly avoiding Chuck as he returns to the present. He notices our relief and turns to see the chamber.

His shoulders sag a bit. "That is good. That is good." He looks to me. "Is it good, Silas? Is it good to be here without Josh?"

"That part is not good," I tell him. "But it is good that we survived, and that we are here to reach the Seed, and Darius."

He nods. "It is good, Silas." Doesn't sound very convincing. His emotions are going to be a whirlwind for a while as victories and losses pile up.

"All right, then!" I clap my hands together and turn toward the waiting tunnel. "Final test completed. Let's drop a node and get this show on the—holy shit!"

There's a body in the tunnel ahead. It's half inside a side chamber. I head toward it without saying another word. Ami and Chuck follow. They both see it, too. My pace slows when I'm close enough to see that the person is wearing an Aegis suit, is a man, and has his head cracked open. And by cracked open, I mean his skull has been bashed open and his brain is showing. I spot a name tag on his chest. Richard. "This guy made it farther than Morrow thought."

"I don't like it," Chuck says, "I don't like it, Ami!"

She takes hold of him and leads him around the body, moving further down the tunnel. I'm left to inspect the scene. Should be Ami doing this. She's the former FBI agent. But it's not hard to understand what happened. Beside the body are two smashed nodes.

One of them wanted to contact Morrow.

The other didn't.

The disagreement turned violent, and after everything they'd been through together, the last survivor murdered this guy. Holding my hand out so I can't see the top of his head, I look at his face and quickly regret it. It's covered in blood and compressed. I doubt his mother would recognize him. I shake my head in disgust and leave the chamber without even noticing what else it might contain.

"What happened?" Ami asks as I approach.

"They had a disagreement," I say.

"So, it was murder?" she asks.

"Very murder. Looks like they disagreed about whether to place the final node." I hold my hand out. "Happily, we don't have that problem."

Ami slides out of her pack. It's the last one we have. She takes out a node. Looks at it, debating.

"None of us *want* to activate it," I say. "But—"

"Darius," she says. "I know."

She holds the button down, activating the device.

We all expect Morrow's voice to fill our ears a moment later, but we're greeted by silence, and for some reason, that's worse.

50

We decide to keep moving and not wait on Morrow to reach out. He's drilled the countdown into us enough that we all agree it's what he'd want us to do, and what we should do. A hundred feet in, the tunnel becomes a maze.

We pause in a side chamber full of small human-like statues standing in rose-leaf-shaped alcoves. Human-like because their heads are anything but. Some are recognizable. A rhino. Elephant. Crocodile. They continue the Egyptian vibe. Others represent extinct animals, from the last ice age and even a few dinosaurs—including one of my personal favorites, the stegosaurus. The plates running up its back look sick. I know a lot of people who'd drop a few hundred bucks on that boy and display it proudly in their house.

Then . . . there are the heads of creatures I don't recognize. One has a broad head, large eyes, and what looks like starfish arms where there should be a mouth. Another is topped with what looks like a patch of standing cucumbers. And another on a woman's body that resembles butterflies forming a feminine face.

None of it means anything to me and, after a quick looksee, I close my eyes, relax, and slip into a remote viewing session. It's getting easier—easier than falling asleep, that's for damn sure. I move through the maze, unhindered by things like feet and breathing and walls. It's far more complicated than the previous sections, spreading out like lightning bolt branches. I follow them all forward and back. A few minutes in, I'm not sure I'll be able to hack my way through this one.

That's when I feel a pull like gravity. It tugs on me and then yanks. I slip through walls, unable to track the path. The underworld passes in a blur, and then—I'm in a familiar chamber.

Fifty feet ahead of me, the Seed floats above the pedestal, lit as though from a spotlight, though there are no light sources I can see.

I take a few steps closer and am stopped by a voice I was expecting this time. "Broseph."

"Sara-not-Sara," I reply, knowing that this is no more my sister than the Seed comes from some kind of cosmic space pumpkin. Then again, maybe it does. I still know nothing about it other than that it can communicate . . . and alter reality.

"We're vibing now," she says. "That's good. You'll need to be comfortable."

"For what?" I ask.

"Uh-uh. No way." She shakes her head. "Spoilers, man."

"Is there any chance I can speak to *you?*" I ask. "The real you?"

She smiles. "Have you ever seen what happens to glass when it's hit by a soundwave that matches its natural resonant frequency?"

The knowledge and usage of words like 'resonant' breaks the illusion of this being my actual sister. It's not that she's not smart, but she has a persona to maintain and tends not to use fancy words.

"It shatters," I say.

"Right," she says. "Imagine that happening to the outer wall of every cell in your body, all at once. Instantaneous systemic lysis."

I don't know what 'lysis' is, but given the glass metaphor, I think I have a pretty good idea. "Sounds messy."

She shakes her head like she's seen it before. "You have no idea." She tilts her head, motioning behind me.

I turn. There's a wall behind me. It's the first sign of a structure I've seen in the dark chamber. It's covered in the strange engravings—and blood. Old blood, but blood . . . and other things? "Is that—"

"The remains of your predecessor," Sara says. "Yep. That's him."

"So, you spoke to him?" I ask.

"No, no. That's just a visual for you, bro. How he ended up like that, well, again, spoilers."

"Awesome," I say.

"Right?" She laughs and pats my back.

"Why am I here?" I ask. "Why not just let me get there IRL?"

"Motivation," she says.

"Because the countdown is almost up?" I ask.

"No. Well, yes. But no. The countdown has been artificially accelerated."

"What? Why? That's not—"

"Whoa, whoa, whoa, bro. Chill. It's not us." She points to the floor to my right. "It's her."

I jump back as a woman dressed in an Aegis suit crawls past me. She's gaunt, pale, and exhausted, but she's moving toward the Seed. At a tortoise's pace, but she's on track to reach the finish line before me.

"Let's just do it now," I say. "Whatever it is, let me do it from here."

"Not how it works," Sara says. "You need to be present, mind and body. Your astral form is not sufficient."

"Okay," I'm motivated. "Send me back."

"Follow your instincts," she says. "You're on the soccer field. Your opponents are closing in. There is only one path through. You don't think it, you feel it. Do the same now. And hurry, this one—" She points to the crawling woman. "—is far from worthy."

"And what happens if she beats me to the Seed?" I ask.

Sara grimaces and breathes through her teeth. "Same thing that happened eighty thousand years ago."

Eighty thousand years ago . . . Eighty thousand. "Holy shit."

"Mega holy shit," Sara says.

"The White Fir. Dr. Morrow was right. You reset human civilization."

Sara neither confirms nor denies the statement. She just smiles.

"What was it like?" I ask. "Back then? That first civilization."

"You think the last . . ." She raises her eyebrows. ". . . was the first?"

"You're saying that—"

She snaps her fingers in my face the way Sara does when I interrupt her. "I feel like this goes without saying, and this is borderline breaking our own rules, but your desire to understand what is happening will ensure your downfall." She looks at the crawling woman, now a few feet further than she was before.

"Right," I say. "Send me back."

"We didn't initiate this conversation," Sara says. "Send yourself back."

I gasp back into the chamber with Ami and Chuck. It's sudden and loud enough that they both jump.

"What's wrong?" Ami asks.

"We need to hurry," I say, stepping to the doorway and trying to feel an instinctual tug.

"What is it, Silas?" Chuck asks. "What's wrong?"

"The murderer," I say, "she's reached the Seed chamber. If we don't get there before she makes contact, we're fucked."

"How fucked?" Ami asks.

"End of civilization," I say.

"But . . . will we die?" she asks.

"There's a good chance we'll experience instantaneous systemic lysis," I say.

Ami is as clueless as I was. "Which is . . . ?"

"All of the cell walls in our body shattering, at once, like glass hit by the right frequency. Or something."

Chuck frowns. "That doesn't sound good, Silas. I don't like it."

"Yeah," I say, closing my eyes.

Chuck and Ami go quiet. They either intuit that I need to focus, or Ami heard my thoughts and used telepathy to tell Chuck.

It helps. Takes just a second to feel the tug.

"This way!" I sprint to the right.

After the first two turns, I need to slow down, not because I can't feel the tug, but because Ami has short legs and Chuck isn't an athlete. "Push through it!" I shout, attempting to channel one of my many coaches. "The pain is temporary."

"I can't, Silas," Chuck says between gasps. "I can't."

Ami stumbles to a stop and Chuck follows suit.

Ami takes off her pack and digs inside. She pulls out two water bottles and holds them out to me.

"We don't have time to—"

She shakes her head. "Splash water on the floor every time you turn. Like breadcrumbs. At the start of each tunnel. You go ahead. We'll catch up."

I don't like it, but it's a solid plan, and we don't have much choice.

I'm about to say goodbye and bolt, but Ami beats me to the punch and kisses me full-on while simultaneously giving me a boost of emotional clarity, energy, and clear-headed thinking. I'd have been an A student in college if I felt like this. She pulls back, our eyes locked, electric intensity flowing between us. Then she slaps me in the face, snapping me out of the trance, and shouts, "Go!"

I charge away, feeling great. Behind me, Chuck has a giggle fit, probably because of the kiss. Then I take my first turn, uncap a water bottle, and dribble a line at the start of the new tunnel. It's not much, but the cool, sunless tunnel with a solid stone floor, ensures the water will be there for a long time.

The path takes me down ten tunnels and uses up just a single water bottle. I'm about to unscrew the cap on the second bottle when I'm suddenly surrounded by darkness.

This is it. The chamber. I look ahead and see it.

The Seed. Floating above its pedestal, exactly as I've seen in my visions. I look behind and up, but the space is too dark to confirm the existence of my exploded predecessor.

What I *can* see fires every nerve in my body at once and draws a whispered "Fuck" from my mouth.

The murderer is there at the pedestal—and she's reaching for the Seed.

51

"Wait!" I shout. "Stop!"

The woman's hand jerks back and her gaze locks onto me. Her face scrunches up in disgust. "Who the fuck ah you?"

She's young. Accent and word choice smacks of Boston or one of its suburbs. Probably sixteen. Black hair pulled back in a ponytail. A nose ring, eyebrow ring, and more earrings than I can count. It's a cool look. The collection of piercings paired with the Aegis suit she's wearing . . . she looks like a character from some far future sci-fi series. *Star Trek* with attitude.

"My name is Silas," I say, catching my breath. "Look, if you touch that, it will end human civilization."

"Fuck it will," she says. "I got here. I passed the tests."

"You murdered your friend," I say. "You are not the kind of person the Seed is looking for."

"My 'friend' wanted to call Morrow," she says. "Wanted to let that asshole complete the mission he was too chickenshit to attempt himself."

"I get it," I say. "I do. Morrow is an asshole, and he will *not* be the one to make contact with the Seed."

"Oh yeah?" she says. "Who will, then?"

"Me," I say.

"Sorry fuckface, second place is still a loss. Maybe you'll get ah participation ribbon." She reaches for the Seed. "I earned this."

"Does it speak to you?" I shout.

She stops again, squinting at me. "What?"

"The Seed," I say. "Does it *communicate* with you? Have you had a conversation with it?"

She looks disgusted with me. "Did Morrow bring on a fuckin' crackhead? No, I'm not speakin' to the inanimate object."

"Listen, Ms. Potty Mouth, I'm telling you the truth. If you touch that Seed and initiate the final test, every cell in your body will violently rupture and burst at once." Okay, *that's* not exactly true. Exploding cells is what happens if you hear the Seed's voice, or whatever it uses for direct communication. But the graphic visual gets the point across. "Then, human civilization will come to an end. Again. And I'm pretty sure this will be the third time it's happened. Maybe more. I know because it *does* speak to me. When I remote view. You know what that is, right? That's you, isn't it? That's how you got here?

"The difference between us, aside from me not being a murderous prick, is that when I look into this chamber, I see the Seed, and my sister, who speaks on its behalf. And it told me—"

The girl huffs. "What, is she dead or somethin'?"

"What?"

"Your sistah," she says, making the most obnoxious mocking face. "You talkin' to her ghost?"

"No. She's an Instagram model."

"You'ah so full of shit," she says, reaching once more and she's not going to stop this time.

Soccer was my go-to sport. I excelled at it. But I've played other sports—in the neighborhood, at school, in college—and while I wasn't an MVP or anything, I learned how to throw a ball. Fast. I take a step forward and put all the kinetic energy I can muster into the sealed water bottle in my hand. The beverage topples through the air like a throwing knife. And while it isn't a deadly weapon by any stretch of the imagination, a sixteen-ounce water bottle traveling somewhere close to seventy miles per hour won't feel like a love tap.

Especially if my aim is as good as it used to be.

I hold my breath as the bottle crosses the distance and then wince when it collides with the girl's head. Right in the temple.

She shouts in pain and spills onto the floor.

"Ahh!" She's angrier than hurt. "You asshole! You hit me with a fuckin' watah bottle!?"

The sprint to her takes just a few seconds. When I'm standing between her and the Seed, I allow myself to really catch my breath.

"Girl, your mouth is single-handedly going to make the movie based on my memoir about all this rated R."

"Fuckin' edit me out," she says, sitting up, hand on her head. "What now, prick? You gonna call Morrow? Suck his dick when he gets heah?"

"Already called him," I say. "What makes you think he'll come?"

"Ah you serious?" She rolls her eyes. "So, you'ah not a crackhead, just naïve. That might be worse. Of course he's comin'. You think someone like that will trust peons like us to communicate with an all powerful fuckin' pumpkin seed?"

She's got a point, and now that I'm thinking about it, the last time I heard from Morrow, he was out of breath. Like he was running. She's telling the truth.

"I'm not going to let him," I say.

"You think you have a choice?" she asks. "Who does he have? Your sistah?"

"My teammate's brother, who is also my friend."

"Teammate?" She shakes her head. "Listen, Cornbread, the one mistake Morrow made with me was choosin' to hold my fathah hostage. That abusive asshole can rot in hell. Morrow's power ovah me was an illusion. Just like yours."

Despite clearly being exhausted and dehydrated, she picks up the water bottle and stands on her feet. She untwists the cap, chugs all sixteen ounces in three long gulps, and then tosses the bottle behind her.

I consider reaching out and taking hold of the Seed. It's that close. But I suspect I will be at her mercy if I do. The look in her eyes is deadly.

Need to de-escalate, I think. *If only I knew how to do that.*

That's when I remember that I'm no longer a slouch in the ESP division. A combination of good vibes telepathy and empathy might be enough to sooth the savage—

"Whoa!"

I lean back, narrowly avoiding a punch to the face.

"You don't want any part of what's goin' on in my head, Captain Crunch." She squares up. "So, keep the fuck out."

This nickname confuses me. "Captain Crunch?"

"'Crunchatize me, mon capitaine.'"

"*What?*"

She takes another swing and narrowly misses. She knows how to fight. But the age and size difference between us makes the outcome a no-brainer.

"Seriously? You're going to fight me?"

She closes in, fire in her eyes. "I'm from Boston, bitch."

The next swing connects—with my forehead.

Hurts her as much as it does me, and I don't think the crack I heard was my skull. She broke a finger. She doesn't complain about it, and the pain doesn't register on her face. The water bottle caught her off guard, but she's now in beast mode and somehow immune to pain.

"Dude," I say. "I don't want to hit you."

"Fuck you," she says, and takes another swing. I backstep to avoid the swing and move the action away from the Seed. Last thing I want is for her to One-Punch Man all of civilization.

I start running through scenarios of how I can end this fight without feeling like a complete douchebag after. Pretty sure one punch would knock her silly. Maybe I'm old fashioned, but punching a teenage girl—scrappy or not—feels wrong. I consider myself a feminist, but I wouldn't take it that far.

Then again, maybe it's sexist to avoid laying her out? The fate of humanity is on the line, after all. Ends justify the means.

She's got me on the defensive now, ducking, weaving, and back-stepping. I'm not in any real danger at the moment, but I'm being pushed farther than I want to be from the Seed. Because I'm not sure how much time we have.

How much time do we have?

"Bro," my sister says, appearing beside me. "Can't you hear it?"

"I can't hear anything," I say.

"Who the fuck you talkin' to?" the girl says, and I realize my remote view of Sara is overlapping with the here and now.

"What about now?" Sara asks.

A low, repeating rumble fills the chamber.

"Ominous, right?" Sara says.

"Any chance you can give me a time in minutes?" I ask.

She sighs. "Much less fun."

"I'm not having fun!" I shout.

"Gettin' the shit kicked out of you ain't supposed to be fun, Nancy!" My teenaged opponent ramps up her attack. The punches come in a flurry, and I'm forced to take most of them on the shoulders and sides, doing my best to protect my head and core.

Sara leans in close and whispers. "Five minutes."

"Five minutes!" I shout and Sara winks out of existence. The girl rushes in for a haymaker to the jaw and, for the first time, meets resistance in the form of my foot colliding with her gut.

Something about kicking a girl in the stomach once feels better than a punch in the face. It's less personal. But the effect is roughly the same. The girl collapses to the floor in a fetal position, clutching her stomach and wheezing.

I start walking toward the Seed. "For the record, I know a lot of people from Boston, but none of them are massive assholes like you."

She doesn't respond.

Can't respond.

Going to be a few minutes before she's fully caught her breath. And by then it won't matter. Because I'm a few feet from touching the Seed and ending this nightmare.

My hand is inches away when a loud, "Uh, uh, uh!" echoes in the darkness.

I turn to find Ami and Chuck standing with Darius. Alive. All three.

I begin to smile, and then notice the guns pressed against their heads.

52

Morrow steps out from behind Ami while keeping his pistol pointed at the side of her head. "I'll take it from here. You did well, reaching the Seed chamber, but you are not prepared for what comes next."

Darius and Chuck are being covered by Stephens and Keller, also dressed in Aegis suits and carrying sound suppressed pistols, which are currently held at the brothers' backs. Stephens looks stone cold, but Keller, as usual, looks conflicted. He knows who the good guys and bad guys are, and he's not thrilled about the side he's on.

My Bostonian friend finds her voice just long enough to say, "Told you so."

I ignore her and say, "I'm the *only* one prepared for what comes next."

Morrow chuckles. "I have been working toward this moment for a decade. I will not sit by and allow a scruffy dishwasher to take my place."

"You haven't earned it," I say. "Didn't complete a single challenge. Didn't learn anything on the way. You sent how many people to die in your place?"

He shoves Ami forward and follows, closing the distance. "I believe the Seed is an intelligence of pure logic. It will understand the sacrifice."

"You sacrificed *nothing* to get here," I say. "You're walking on the corpses of people braver than you. You wouldn't have passed the first trial, let alone all four. You lack the qualities the Seed is interested in."

"And you have these qualities?" he asks.

I'm not the kind of person to brag or boast about myself, even if what I'm saying is true. So, when I say, "I do," it feels gross in my mouth.

Is there anything we can do? I think to Ami.

He's too strong, she replies. *I've been trying since he caught us.*

What should I do? I ask. *If he touches the Seed, we're all toast.*

Time for another sacrifice, she thinks.

No. I can't. I won't.

Don't see how you have a choice. Her unblinking stare shows how serious she is.

I don't bother arguing, because she's right. *Work on Keller. I think he can be flipped.*

"Having a nice chat, are we?" Morrow says. "Tell me, Silas, what have *you* sacrificed to get here, hmm? The first two challenges were completed for you. And here you stand, unharmed and ready to go home. And that's exactly what will happen when we are done here. You will return to your boring life, and I will have saved the world."

"Look around," I say. "You see Josh?"

He glances back at the others. "To be honest, I forgot about Josh. He's dead?" He shrugs before I can confirm it. "Well, if one of you were to perish, it's good—"

"No!" Chuck shouts and strides toward Morrow despite the gun at his back. Keller follows Chuck but doesn't stop him. "No! You can't talk about Josh that way! I-I . . . Fuck you! I hate you, Dr. Morrow. I hate you."

"Right," Morrow says. "Enough of that. Keller?"

"Sir?"

"Pull the trigger already," Morrow says. "What are you waiting for?"

"He's just—"

"Right," Morrow says. "I'll do it." He kicks Ami in the back, spilling her to the floor. Then he wheels around toward Chuck and pulls the trigger. The sound suppressed bullet coughs from the gun—and ricochets off the glowing blue force field that I threw at Chuck's feet.

Do it! Ami urges me.

I reach for the Seed, knowing that it will put my friends in danger, but I have a good sense of time and we're coming up on five minutes.

Unfortunately, my hand never reaches the Seed.

Morrow's gun hand is quick and his aim mostly accurate. Pretty sure he's aiming for my head when he pulls the trigger, but the bullet finds my shoulder instead. The impact spins me around and drops me to the floor. I don't give him the satisfaction of shouting out in pain.

Nor do I give up.

When I stand, the Seed is between me and Morrow.

He wouldn't dare risk shooting it.

"See you on the other side," I say.

"Noooo!" Morrow shouts, running for the Seed. He makes it a single step before faceplanting to the floor, courtesy of Ami. He pushes himself up, raising his pistol toward me again, but he's not fast enough.

I place my hand on the Seed.

Time freezes.

Except for me. I can move. But I remain in place, hand on the Seed, afraid to break the connection.

"Success!" my sister says, appearing beside me and thrusting her hands in the air. "Knew you could do it, bro."

"So, are you . . ." I tilt my head toward the Seed. ". . . it? Have I earned that information yet?"

"Indeed." The casual language and nature of my sister, which I think it's been working on since I suggested it match her vocabulary, fades as we get down to business. "I am a representation of what you call the Seed."

"Because if we communicate directly, I go poof."

"More of a splat," she says, slipping back into my sister's voice for a moment.

"Are you . . . God?" I ask.

Sara thrusts both hands toward the Seed. "Do I *look* like a god?"

"Yeah, well, burning bush and all that, right? Do you know about that?"

"Do I know about Moses?" she asks. "*That's* what you want to know?"

It doesn't need to answer the question directly. I never mentioned Moses regarding the burning bush, so it knows about Moses. Doesn't mean this is the same all-powerful being that spoke to the OG prophet, though. "I'm just trying to understand you."

"You can no more understand my existence than your science can see the true vastness and strangeness of the universe beyond this sphere you're all trapped on. Your perceptions are limited. Your technology is crude. How many times has the latest incarnation of humanity had to redefine its reality? With all your latest advancements, you're still not much better off than when you believed the Earth was the center of all things.

"Previous human civilizations were much farther along when they discovered the maze and faced my challenges."

"Then why start the countdown now?" I ask. "Why not wait until humanity has a better chance at passing?"

"Your people are far more inquisitive than previous peoples. You crave knowledge. You desire to explore all things. And yet, your intelligence struggles to keep up. The result is that you reached this moment millennia before your predecessors. The abilities you refer to as 'extrasensory' had been mastered by those earlier people. In you, they are fledgling and helped along by interference from outside influences five-thousand years ago."

"What's that supposed to mean?" I ask, my heart pounding as exciting possibilities ping-pong through my mind. "What happened five thousand years ago? Who influenced us? Aliens? Something supernatural?"

"None of that is important," she says. "It will only distract you."

"Fine." I sigh and try to rein in my own burning curiosity. I have so many questions, but none of them are important until the Seed's threat is neutralized. "Fine. Just stop dropping juicy tidbits."

"Juicy tidbits," she says with a smile. "In all my time on this world, Silas Keene, you are the first to treat me as . . . a comrade."

"You *do* look like my sister," I point out.

"That is often not enough. Human beings react poorly to things they do not understand. You have the unique ability to absorb the otherworldly and even embrace it, as you are now, casually conversing with me.

"Several of your predecessors attempted to kill me. It is impossible, of course. I do not live in the same way your biological bodies do, but their attempts spoke volumes."

"How many times have you been through this with previous civilizations?" I ask.

"Five," she says and raises her eyebrows twice.

"And they all failed."

She nods.

"Correct me if I'm wrong—hey, what should I call you? Not Sara."

"You lack the capacity to comprehend my name and hearing it will—"

"Splat," I say. "Right."

"Indeed."

"Okay, Kate," I say, using my sister's middle name, "Correct me if I'm wrong, but I feel like you're rooting for me."

"The fate of your people is inconsequential to me. I am simply performing my duty."

"So, is this a genie-in-the-bottle type scenario?" I ask. "You're stuck here until one of us passes the test?"

"My circumstances are not something worthy of your concern," she says. "Now, are you ready to attempt what better people than yourself have failed to achieve?"

"Well, all the confidence I've managed to muster up to this point—which isn't a lot—has gone the way of the Beelzebufo. That's a devil frog if you didn't—"

"I know all things."

"Right. Of course. But not what happens next, right?"

She remains silent.

"*Right?*"

She raises her eyebrows at me. "If you are asking about the outcome of this meeting, I believe you know how your real sister would respond."

"'Spoilers,'" I say. "Yeah. Well, I guess we should get started, yeah? I mean, time is frozen, so the countdown isn't ticking for us, but I'm starting to get nervous." I hold up my hand. It's shaking.

"You really shouldn't be nervous," Sara says. "You should be terrified."

She takes my hand and reality crumbles around us.

53

I'm surrounded by concrete rubble and dust. It reminds me of the post-apocalyptic religious robot future, including the sound of combat. Gunshots, muffled by all the concrete, snap again and again. Explosions quake the ground, shaking dust and grit onto my head.

Claustrophobia sets in. My heart flip flops in my chest.

"What is this?" I ask. "Why are we here?"

I search my concrete cave and find myself alone. No Seed. No Sara. The alcove is sloped, six feet tall where I'm lying, ten feet on the lower side. Twenty feet across. Beams of dusty sunlight sneaking through holes illuminate the scene.

Nothing is familiar.

The air is acrid. Burnt. Foreign.

Screams make me jump. They're high-pitched and close. Sounds like . . . kids? I start moving toward the concrete cave's only hole big enough to fit through. Before I reach it, the children arrive. The first three are wide-eyed terrified. They're not exactly screaming, but they're making an anguished, animal-like chirp, like their minds are short circuiting. They might not remember any of this. I hope they won't.

My heart breaks for them.

They see me. I know they do. But they don't acknowledge me. They just move their malnourished little bodies to the far side of the cave. Because there are more coming.

The first boy through the entrance is older than the first group of kids. A teenager. Gaunt, but alert. Dressed in bright colors dulled by grime and what looks like dried blood. He spots me and tenses. A knife appears in his hand. He looks capable of using it.

I can't be sure, but he looks . . .

I raise my hands. "It's okay. I'm okay. Friend. Friend."

I'm not sure he understands the language, but the tone of my voice and body language seem to get the message across. He slips the knife into a pocket and rushes back to the entrance, where more kids are piling in. There are five more in total. The last, a girl, is dragging a little boy.

He's covered in blood and missing a leg.

What the fuck?

What. The. Fuck!

Is this real? It sure as shit feels real.

The teenage boy starts shouting commands. I think he's speaking Arabic. The collection of kids obey him, clearing out a flat space for the injured little boy to lie.

I lean closer. Can't tell if the boy is unconscious or dead.

They're all shouting now. Panic rising. The older boy tries to remain calm, but he's got tears in his eyes, and his bottom lip is trembling. To be honest, I'm not far behind him, and I have no idea who they are or if this is even real.

"Pressure!" I shout. "Pressure on the wound!"

It's a dumb thing to suggest. He's missing his right leg from the shin down. But the suggestion gets my brain moving and the group's attention. I motion to my waist to pantomime a belt, but I'm dressed in normal clothing and wearing my own belt. I yank it off and move to the small boy. His chest is moving. Alive for now.

I wrap the belt around his leg and pull it tight. But his leg is small and the holes on the belt don't extend far enough. I pull the belt off and hold it out to the boy with the knife. I point to the holes. "This! See?" I point again, and then at him. I make a stabbing gesture and then point at the belt again, where we need a fresh hole. "Here!"

He nods and takes the belt, twisting his blade into the band, creating a fresh hole. While he's working, I take hold of the child's stump leg and squeeze as hard as I can.

The teenage boy shouts something. I look up and he holds the belt out to me. I reach for it—and miss.

When I look back to adjust my aim, the boy is gone.

All the children are gone.

As is the cave.

"No!" I shout. "I need to help them. I could have saved him. I could have—"

Everything changes.

I'm standing in an empty street. Towering apartment buildings rise all around me. The scene is quiet, but then I hear them.

No, I feel them.

Thousands of people. All desperate, confused, and sad. I scour the buildings around me and spot hands stretching out of windows . . . toward me. Voices shout at me in Chinese. I catch sight of a woman's masked face.

Is this the pandemic? I wonder. Or a new pandemic. Something the world doesn't know about yet.

Either way, these people are being held prisoner by their government's extreme response to another disease they might ultimately be responsible for creating.

And I can feel them. All of them. Waves of nausea inducing emotion are siphoned through my newfound empathic abilities and drop me to a knee. Feels like I'm going to retch. I saw scenes like this on the news during the pandemic. Being in Maine, I never experienced anything like this. We wore masks, sure, but only in large groups. If this is something new, and these people are a look at what's to come . . . I don't know. I want to fix it. To stop it, but this is something the entire United States government can't prevent, never mind me.

A loud siren spins me around. A white ambulance flanked by two military trucks roar toward me. If I dodge right or left, I'll be run down by the trucks, so I involuntarily do my best impression of a frightened deer—and stand still.

I raise my arms over my face, clench my eyes shut, and wait for the end.

But it doesn't come.

I know I'm somewhere new before I open my eyes.

Smells like piss and shit.

Can't see a thing.

But I hear breathing. A gentle sob. Feminine.

"Hello?" I whisper.

"Quiet!" someone hisses back. "They'll hear you!"

Who are they? I wonder and quickly find out. Two heavy doors at the end of a long side of a shipping container open. Light spills in, illuminating two lines of young woman—teenagers mostly—seated against the metal walls. Most are dressed for a night out on the town, but their clothing is soiled and falling apart.

A silhouetted man stands at the far end. He's holding a rifle. "I didn't hear you bitches talking, did I?"

No one looks at him. No one responds.

He steps inside. The women pull their feet back and lower their heads.

"If you haven't shit yourself, raise your hand." The man waits. No hands rise. "Right. I'll just have to inspect you one at a time, won't I?"

I pull my feet in, lower my head—and raise my hand.

Getting really fucking tired of being put in these scenarios and being powerless to change anything. If I can get him over here, I can at least try to take his weapon and Rambo the shit out of this scenario until I'm ripped away.

"Good on you," the man says. "Didn't think Florida made brave girls. But here you are. Bet you're not a local, though. Probably from New Hampshire. Maybe a dyke. But we can correct those flaws, can't we?"

The girl beside me takes my hand and squeezes.

It's brief, but the message is clear. Thank you.

The man stands in front of me and before he gets a good look or even opens his mouth, I leap to my feet and dive—

—into the water.

I surface, coughing and sputtering, unprepared for the sudden frothy current. Am I in a river? I tread water and spin around. It's hard to see on account of the torrential rain. Probably close to dusk, but I can see enough to know I'm screwed. Because this isn't a river. It's a flood. And it's not just the brown water that gives it away, it's the burning house that's floating past me.

A tree strikes my back, driving me underwater. Hurts like hell, but I manage to swim free and surface again.

A dog barks nearby.

I spin around and find it standing on the roof of a home that's broken free from the rest of the house and has been lodged against a stand of tall trees resisting the flood waters. The dog is standing on the roof, barking. At me.

That's when I see the little body lying beneath it.

A toddler. Dressed in a pink onesie. She's sprawled out on the rooftop, soaked and unmoving. I get the impression that it was the pooch that pulled her from the water. But was he too late?

I swim for the roof. Fully dressed and wearing shoes, my progress is slow, but after several minutes I reach the shingles and drag myself up. "Please let me help. Please let me help."

I check the girl's pulse and feel nothing. Shit.

I'm not entirely sure what to do, but if she drowned she'll have water in her lungs. That's problem number one. I take hold of her little ankles and hold her upside down. I'm relieved to see water pour from her mouth. When it stops, I lay her down. The dog leaps around, wagging its tail, as nervous as I am.

I link my fingers and position my hands over the girl's small sternum. This can't be the right way to perform CPR on such a small body, but I don't know what the alternative is. What I do know is that I need to press hard enough that I might break her little ribs. If she survives, she'll be in a world of hurt at my hands.

I pause for a moment and whisper, "If you're going to yank me away from this, could you be merciful and do it before I crack her ribs?"

I get no response.

Not seeing any other option, I place my hands on her chest, and—

54

Slam my fists into a stone floor.

I'm back in the Seed chamber, but there's no one else here. Then like a three hundred sixty degree IMAX, all four realities I just experienced take form around me. I can hear the bullets, and the crying kids, and the voices of people locked away, in containers, and above it all, the barking dog. Their desperation roils around me, infusing every cell in my body with anguish.

I want to stop it, and not just for them. I can't handle this much pain.

"Why won't you let me help them?!" I scream.

My voice is drowned out by the raging flood waters.

But for the first time, I get a response.

"What would you do to help them?" It's Sara. She's standing beside me, face flat.

"I could have stopped the bleeding," I say, thinking about the little boy with a missing leg.

My thoughts turn to whatever kind of breakout was happening in China. I don't have an answer to that scenario.

But I sure as shit know what I would do to the man in the shipping container. "I could have freed those women."

My thoughts shift to the flood. "I could have . . ." I shake my head thinking about breaking the little girl's ribs. "I could have . . ."

"Observe," Sara says.

I look up, seeing the concrete cave from the outside. It's the remains of a destroyed building. One of hundreds. People run for cover as bullets and bombs fly. In a blink, a missile roars from the sky and strikes the hideaway full of children.

I feel their deaths.

The view shifts to the Chinese apartment buildings. I see myself, waving my hands at the ambulance. And it doesn't hit me. It stops. As do the military vehicles. Soldiers pour out, screaming at me. I can't understand a word, but I understand the bullets they fire into my body.

The ambulance drives on. The soldiers linger, dousing me in gasoline and then setting me ablaze.

Nothing changes.

Back to the container. I'm a spectator now, watching from the open doors. The version of me in the container is allowed to finish his dive. There's a fight. The rifle—an automatic—fires. Drains the magazine. A dozen young women are dead. Then more men arrive, see the scene playing out and decide to clean house. They spray the crate's interior with bullets, killing everyone, including their own man and me.

And then, the flood.

I'm giving CPR. I hear the ribs break. I wail in desperation as nothing I do works.

Because she was already dead. And no one could save her, despite the dog's best efforts.

But all of this could have been prevented. I'm sure of it. If people weren't so god-damned selfish, idiotic, and incapable of comprehending basic scientific facts.

"What could you do to change any of this?" Sara asks.

I know the answer, and that anything other than the truth would be a mistake. "Nothing."

Sara sits cross-legged across from me. The scenes around us disappear. Light from nowhere illuminates the pair of us, and the stone floor beneath us. Everything else is black.

"What if you could?" she asks. "Change it. All of it."

"I would," I say. "You already know that. But I also know it's impossible. That's the point, right? Purge my belief that I can help people? Shrink my ego? Make me feel helpless?"

"Not at all," she says. "Quite the opposite. Because you . . . you have the power to change everything, to save all of them. It's in your mind. The ability to change worlds. It just needs to be unlocked."

"Morrow already tried that," I say.

"Did he?" she asks.

"He held back. Was intimidated by what he found. Or jealous? I don't know."

"He was frightened," she says. "By your potential. That you would be where you are now instead of him."

"And if he had reached you first?" I ask.

"He is a fool," she says. "Your world would come to an end."

"I'm not sure I'll do much better," I admit.

She nods. "Neither am I."

"Awesome. Just . . . can you tell me how? How to save them? I'll do it. I'll do whatever it takes."

"Let's find out," she says, standing up. I do the same and find myself standing in a desert of sand dunes. "Witness the result of your full potential unlocked."

The sand blows around me. When it clears, I'm back outside the ruined building full of children hiding from the violence. Time moves backward. Bullets and bombs return to where they came from. The city regrows. People return. Everyone is happy.

Takes a massive effort not to burst into tears when that group of kids runs past, playing and laughing. The little one now has both legs and is the fastest of them.

Back in China. The streets are alive. People are at peace. I sense no desperation. A car honks at me, but it's a gentle *toot-toot*. A smiling woman leans out the window and waves at me. I wave back and then find myself standing on the deck of a shipping container ship.

I walk to a familiar shipping crate and pull open the door. It's full of boxes. Not a woman in sight. No bad guys, either.

"I can end human trafficking?" I ask. "That can't be possible."

"Anything will be possible," she says, and we shift perspectives again. I haven't seen this place before. It's a house in the country with a swing set. "Is this . . . the flood. I can stop floods?"

"You can stop what causes them," Sara says.

A laugh draws my attention back to the scene. A little girl in a pink onesie runs through the yard. A young mother calls after her, while a barking dog happily leaps around the girl.

She's alive.

"How?" I ask. "And don't be vague."

"With your mind," Sara says. "You can control them. All of them. Not in an overt way, but you can influence the choices of individuals, governments . . . the world. The sinister desires of mankind would end with a thought. The beaten, broken, marginalized, and abused would find shelter in your embrace. They would love you. Worship you.

"What if I don't want that?" I ask. "The worship part."

She shrugs. "No one needs to know that you are making adjustments to the minds of men. The power will be yours alone. You could save this world. And it needs saving, doesn't it?"

I nod and think about all the things I could change, the thoughts I could implant in the President's mind, maybe make pedophiles and the people who protect them jump off tall bridges. I shake my head. Too far.

But is it? A purge of the world's most rancid people would be an improvement.

Or, I could just change their minds. Make them intensely good and sacrificial people. I could turn their lives into forces of good.

End poverty.

Stop genocides and wars. Hell, I could stop schoolyard fights. With a thought.

A smile creeps onto my face as I imagine a world redefined by someone with an actual moral compass.

"You've made your decision," Sara says.

"I have."

She reaches out a hand. "Step forward so that I might unleash your full potential."

"That's . . . not my choice," I say.

The scenes of torment return. The children screaming, women crying. I feel all of it fresh and horrible. It puts me on my knees. The intensity increases.

"You could end all of this!" she shouts. "Why would you turn this down?"

"Because I'm just a dude from Maine!" I shout. "I'm not a god, don't want to be a god, and don't want to take away the free will of every person on this planet. Fuck's sake, not even actual God—like the one from the Bible—took away free will. Because how can you love something, really love something, or someone, or a deity, if you have no choice?

"That's the point, right? Good isn't good without evil. Light isn't light without darkness. Remaking the world in *my* image would be a greater evil than any of the things you've shown me. Would it end suffering? Sure. Because everyone would be automatons—and that's *not* living.

"That's death. And I want nothing to do with it."

Sara withdraws her hand, looking grim. "Even if your choice ends civilization?"

"If free will is the cost of ending suffering, yes. I reject your offer."

She smiles.

"What?" I ask, feeling suspicious.

"You chose well."

"Wait. Hold on. Choosing suffering and death and all that horrible stuff is the right choice?"

"There are not many people in this world who would turn down that power," she says. "There are none who would not be corrupted by it. The evils of your world would be magnified tenfold, all of humanity serving the wishes of a single person."

"Well, shit." The widest grin of my life spreads on my face. "I mean—hey, we're done, right? Test passed?"

She nods.

"So, I can gloat a bit?"

She shakes her head. "I'm afraid you don't have time."

All around us the Seed chamber comes into view. Nothing has changed. Time is still frozen. There are still three men with guns. And I still have a hole in my shoulder.

"I don't suppose there's something you can do about Morrow?" I ask.

"Your life is yours to protect, as it has been since you entered the labyrinth. Our time together has come to an end," Sara says. "It has been a pleasure to watch your progress. For the record, I believed in you, bro." She starts to fade away as the chamber fully resolves. "Thank you, Silas . . ." Her voice is almost a whisper now. ". . . for my freedom."

Before I can fully comprehend her last words, reality returns—with a bang.

55

The bullet buzzes past my ear like an angry robotic bee. I flinch to the side and duck behind the pedestal. Behind me, there's a thud. I glance back and find the young woman from Boston on the stone floor, the back of her head missing. I turn away from the gruesome sight, eyes clenched at the realization that her fate was nearly mine. Desperate to think about something else, I look up at the pedestal . . . and find it empty.

The Seed is gone.

And that tidbit is what stops Morrow in his tracks.

"What have you done?" he shouts. "Where is the Seed?"

I poke my head out from behind the pedestal. "Chill, man! It's done. World saved. You're welcome."

"Really?" The hopeful question comes from Keller.

"Really," I say.

"No!" Morrow's outburst is reaching temper-tantrum levels. "That was for me! If not for me, none of this would be possible."

"Not going to argue with you about that, man." I peek out at him and find the pistol that already claimed one life still pointed in my direction. "But you were *not* the right guy for the job."

"How can you possibly—"

"The Seed told me," I say. "And we all know it's true. You would have made the wrong choice."

"And what choice would that have been?" he asks, seething.

"Power," I say. "The ability to end suffering by controlling the will of every person on the planet. Utopia through mental enslavement."

"And you chose?"

"To be powerless," I say. "To allow the world to suffer."

"You're a fool," he says. "Weak."

"Tell that to the five guys who took that test before me," I say. "All of them chose power. Guess how many times civilization was reset?"

"There were *five* human civilizations before us?" Ami asks. She's slowly standing up from the floor where Morrow shoved her before time froze.

"All of them reset without a trace." I focus on Morrow. "Because people like you took the test. It had to be me."

Morrow's not an idiot. He knows what he'd have chosen. Knows that civilization would have been reset as a result. But that doesn't stop him from being enraged by his jealousy and shame.

"Well, then, I suppose your job here is done." He fires the pistol. The bullet pings off the pedestal. Stone chips pepper my face, punching into my skin.

He spins toward Ami and fires again. The bullet strikes her thigh and drops her to the floor again. The bullet didn't penetrate the bulletproof Aegis suit, but all that kinetic force probably felt like a punch from Saitama. She doesn't give him the satisfaction of a scream. She just glares. "You're thinking loudly." He levels the gun at her head.

I reach out with my mind and put his in a vice grip.

He winces but then flexes against me. He scoffs. "The savior of the world still lacks the power to stop me." His hand shakes, but the pistol still rises.

I'm about to step out from the pedestal and charge. I'll be shot. Of that, I have no doubt. But it might give Ami a chance to take him down. At least the others will live—if Stephens and Keller don't join the fight. So far, neither man has moved. They're letting things play out, possibly because they know the job is done, or maybe they have a little respect for the guy that saved the world.

Before I can clear the pedestal, a loud noise stops everyone in place.

It's Chuck. He's laughing and clapping his hands. Overjoyed.

"Shut him up!" Morrow shouts at Keller. Then he turns back to Ami and starts to pull the trigger.

I'm both terrified and curious. Chuck is not prone to outbursts of delight, especially when people are about to be hurt.

And that means . . . he saw something.

Something good.

When it arrives, no one, not even Morrow, sees it coming.

His trigger finger spasms.

His body goes rigid from sudden pain.

Eyes wide, he looks down at what everyone else has already seen. A black metal spear-tip has pierced his back and emerged from his sternum. "What . . ."

The tip springs open. Four prongs dig into Morrow's chest.

It's not a spear. It's a grappling hook.

A thin black cord hangs from Morrow's back and leads to the dark tunnel from which we entered the chamber.

"Who—" It's the last thing Morrow says.

The line snaps tight, yanking Morrow off his feet and into the air. The grappling hook snaps shut and dislodges from his body, zipping back into the darkness. But Morrow . . . he's the quintessential object in motion staying in motion as he pinwheels across the chamber until he strikes a wall, hard enough to dislodge two of his limbs. Blood coughs from the wounds. He slides down the wall a few feet then topples to the floor with a wet splat.

"Gross," a voice says from the dark hall. "Sorry about that. I'm still getting used to the new arm."

Chuck bounces up and down, clapping his hands.

Who the hell—

Then he emerges, like the fallen hero at the end of an '80s movie, revealed to be alive after everyone believed he was dead.

Josh.

Completely ignoring the possible threat posed by Keller and Stephens, all attention shifts to our returned fallen friend. He looks like his old self, but with a few obvious modifications. The first is a new, sleek, robotic arm from which the grappling hook was fired. One of his eyes looks different, too. Possibly a replacement. And he just seems more . . . confident.

"What the hell happened to you?" Darius asks.

"I died," Josh says. "In the future. In a robot war. Cool way to die, I guess." He turns to Chuck. "I'm sorry if it—"

Chuck wraps Josh in a hug. "I'm sorry we left."

"It's okay, man," Josh says. "You had a world to save—good job with that, by the way—and I was actually dead. There was nothing you could have done."

"But the robots," I say, "they saved you."

He nods. "And upgraded me. I'm like the frikkin' Winter Soldier. And I have a cybernetic eye. And some of my organs are artificial. They said my heart would beat for a thousand years *after* I died. Wild, right?"

"How did you get back?" Ami asks.

He shrugs. "I was there one moment, and then here the next."

"Where, here?" I ask.

"Just down the hall," he says.

I grin. The Seed. Sneaky bastard. It couldn't directly help, but when the test ended, Josh was brought back to the present. Instead of dropping him back in that chamber, the Seed brought him here, where he could use his enhancements to help.

"I thought the robots couldn't give people weapons," Ami says.

Josh grins. "I told them I like to rock climb. That it would keep me from falling."

"And they believed that? You? Rock climbing."

"Hey," Josh says, "I could do it one-handed now."

"Look," Stephens says, holstering his pistol. "Glad everything turned out all happy-tappy for you—and the rest of the world—but am I the only one who's feeling the ground shaking?"

Everyone falls silent, and in that single moment, we all feel it. The solid stone around us is trembling. I shout, "We need to get the hell out of here!" and run past Josh, entering the tunnel, knowing that everyone will follow, including Morrow's goons.

"It's too far!" Ami shouts. "It'll take hours for us to—"

"I don't think so!" I point ahead. The tunnel is a straight shot to the last chamber. When I reach it, I just keep on running. Nothing happens. The power has gone out of this place. It's just a big hole in the stone beneath the Grand Canyon's cliff face.

Tunnel, chamber, tunnel, chamber. From one end to another, it's maybe six hundred feet. I can cover the distance in less than thirty seconds, but I pace myself so that I'm not leaving anyone behind. Chuck isn't super-fast or coordinated, and Josh, despite his enhancements, doesn't have new legs or lungs. Stephens is also lagging as he limp-runs along. I don't feel any responsibility for him, but back in the Seed chamber, when Morrow was trying to shoot me, both Stephens and Keller could have shot me—and didn't.

By the time I reach the last chamber, the underworld is shaking violently. Cracks form in the walls, ceiling, and floor. This whole place is about to implode, and I have no idea what will happen to the cliffs above us when it does. All I really know is that we can't be here when it happens.

I bounce off the walls during my last few steps. I'm about to ask Keller to take the lead, so he can navigate the modern tunnels. But . . . they're not here. Everything the Smithsonian built is gone.

When I smell fresh air, I bolt ahead and step outside into daylight. We're still beside the river, where a helicopter waits. High above, the cliffs shake. Stones break free and splash in the river. "Let's go!" I shout into the tunnel. "It's all coming down!"

Ami is next out, followed by Josh, Chuck, and then Darius. Keller is next and then Stephens, who looks grim—until he sees the chopper.

"Everyone inside the helo!" Stephens shouts.

While Keller opens the side door, Stephens climbs in the front and gets the rotor spinning. When we're all inside, Keller slides the door shut and climbs into the front beside Stephens.

Rocks pelt the chopper. Nothing big enough to damage it—or the rotor blades now spinning at a furious pace. But they are a harbinger of what's to come. Happily, Stephens knows how to fly this thing and gets it off the ground. He doesn't bother ascending. Instead, he tilts the nose down, so it's just a few feet over the Colorado, and flies us forward.

We cruise through the canyon's twists and turns. For a moment, I get to know how Luke Skywalker felt while speeding through Beggar's Canyon on Tatooine. Then g-forces push me into my seat as we ascend.

After just thirty seconds, Stephens spins the helicopter around and says, "Holy shit. Look at that."

Ami yanks the side door open. The aerial view of the canyon is head-spinning at first. Then I see it, focus, and forget my discomfort. The Grand Canyon's walls drop down on both sides, and then collapse, filling in the canyon and blocking the river. As a massive cloud of dust billows up toward us, Stephens turns us around and cruises up and away from the strangest thing to ever happen on this planet, and the six people in this chopper are the only ones who will ever know about it.

No trophies.

No ribbons or parades.

The world will never know how close it came to being scoured clean and reset.

Hey, Ami says in my head, *you got the girl.*

I smile and pull her against me. She leans her head on my shoulder, while Chuck watches on, his perm-grin larger than ever.

"I'm glad we saved the world, guys. I'm glad."

"We're all glad, bro," Darius says, giving his brother's shoulders a shake. "We're all glad."

EPILOGUE

It's been a week since the Grand Canyon collapse and civilization's near death experience. We've been chilling in the Best Western Premier Grand Canyon Squire Inn, living in style thanks to Ami.

I lost my job. Not sure how she didn't. Well, no, scratch that. I *do* know. While I didn't accept the power to control the whole world, both Ami and I retain the ability to . . . motivate people toward our justifiable needs. In the wake of what we just experienced and did for the planet, I don't have any qualms about getting free meals, a soft bed, and some quality time with Ami.

The authorities are ignorant to our involvement in the Grand Canyon's collapse, which is international news. There are investigations underway, but I don't think they'll find anything tying it to us, or Morrow, or anyone. When the Seed disappeared, it took most of the tunnels with it, including those constructed by the Smithsonian.

There's a growing debate on how to handle the collapse. Some people want to clear the debris and restore the Canyon to how it was before. It would be a massive and technically challenging venture. Others say that the collapse was a natural geological event and part of the Canyon's long history of change. If they get their way, the Canyon will fill with water and become the Grand Canyon Lake. The bottom is already starting to fill with a thin layer of water. If that was allowed to happen, it would become the deepest lake in the world. And while that sounds cool, the next deepest lake is Lake Baikal in Siberia, which no one has ever heard of.

An empty Grand Canyon is the envy of the world, so I suspect that it will eventually be cleared and drained.

Do I care?

Not at all. I'm looking forward to leaving this part of the world behind. As are Ami and the guys. Not sure where we'll go, but we're sticking together, working on our abilities, and having fun watching Josh challenge big men to arm wrestling matches. He wears long sleeves and a glove on his robotic hand, concealing his smooth, metal arm. Most of his challengers make Michael Jackson jokes, on account of the single glove, but shortly after they leave in shame.

All three guys are staying at the hotel, too. Turns out it was Morrow who burned down their house in Chuck's vision. Nothing is left. All three of them were devastated at first, but have come to embrace a fresh start, free from the entanglements of the past.

Chuck and Darius have been inseparable, mostly because Chuck is struggling to let his brother out of his sight. It's nice, and Darius doesn't complain, but it ruins his mojo when he's trying to pick up chicks in the bar while Josh is dropping arms.

As for Chuck, his constant smile is now genuine all the time. He tells everyone we meet that we saved the world, and how glad he feels about it. Most people smile and nod, happy to humor him. If they only knew the truth.

Stephens and Keller have been in the wind since they dropped us off behind the Best Western Premier Grand Canyon Squire Inn, which still needs to shorten its name. They're a loose end I don't like. A lingering threat. I don't expect them to show up at the door with guns. They know what we can do. But did they report what happened to their superiors at the Smithsonian? If so, well, I don't know. They might want to kill us. Might want to recruit us.

My answer to both scenarios is the same: fuck off.

"Hey," Ami says, strolling out of the bathroom, freshly showered and wrapped in a towel.

A million different dirty, unbidden thoughts flood my mind. The curse of being a man. Ami's curse is that she can hear it all.

"Down boy," she says. "Not right now. We're about to have company."

"Shit," I say, cursing my time blindness. I throw the blankets off my naked body and quickly dress in yesterday's shorts and T-shirt. No time for a shower. I sniff test, shrug, and slip into my flip flops.

Ami *tsks* and says, "How are you the guy that saved the world?"

I laugh and say, "Right? Doesn't make sense. She's never going to believe me."

"You don't need to tell her," Ami says.

I wave off the suggestion. "I have to tell *someone*."

"We can get T-shirts made," Ami says. "'I saved the world and all I got was this T-shirt.'"

"Har-har. But I'd wear it." Fully dressed, I decide to be a letch and watch Ami squeeze her backside into her pants.

Takes my breath away—until a knock on the door makes me jump.

"She's here," I say, excited.

Ami pulls a shirt over her head and shoves me toward the door. "Answer it!"

I scurry to the suite door, pause with my hand on the knob, and then yank it open to reveal my sister—my best friend and supernatural guide.

She leaps into a hug, and we lean back and forth together. She leans back and says, "Dang bro, you're looking good. All tan and fit." She slaps my shoulders. It's a playful brother/sister smack that's common with us, but this time it draws a shout of pain and knocks me back.

Sara stands there, hands frozen in place where they hit my shoulder. "What the eff, bro?"

I recover from the pain and smile. "I got shot."

"You got *shot?* What the double eff? Why didn't you tell me? Why didn't you tell Mom and Dad?"

"Because I only want *you* to know what happened."

"What happened?" she says.

"Hey, don't hog all the attention," Ami says, limping into the room, thanks to the bruise left by the bullet strike. "He's not the only one who got shot." She holds her hand out to Sara.

My sister dodges the offered handshake and wraps Ami in a surprise hug. "I've heard so much about you. Thank you."

Ami leans back. "'Thank you?'"

Sara's all smiles. "For dating this funny looking goofball. We didn't think he'd find anyone willing to put up with his weirdness."

"It's a challenge," Ami says.

"Hey!" I push them apart. "You guys just met. No teaming up!"

"Don't worry," Ami says to me. "You aren't the only funny looking goofball in this relationship." She motions to her bangs and bob. "Have you seen this hair?"

"Girl," Sara says. "You're a god-damned fox. Put that hair in a couple of ponies and you'll have the dudes—"

"How about not," I say. "I like the hair."

Sara reaches out for our shoulders, pausing before she makes contact. She pushes both of us, so my injured shoulder is in the middle. Then she grabs both of our outer shoulders and leans in. "Now, both of you, tell me what the frick happened."

Before either of us can respond, there's a knock at the door, followed by the beep of it unlocking. Ami and I tense, but we relax when Chuck enters, followed by Josh and Darius.

"How did you get our keycard?" Ami asks.

Chuck thinks he's the funniest thing since someone milked an almond. "I took it, Ami. You have so many, you didn't know. I'm sorry, Ami. If you're upset, I can give it back. You're not upset, are you?"

"With you?" she says, "Never."

"Oh, good, Ami. I'm glad you're not upset."

"Well, I'm glad you're glad," she says.

"Hey, who's this?" Chuck asks, pointing at Sara.

I'm about to answer when Darius spots her for the first time and gasps. "Yellow bikini! I mean, whoa. Sara, right? I follow you on Insta."

Sara beams. "Really." She gives him a once over and smiles wider. Then she slaps my shoulder. "You didn't tell me your friend was gorge."

"Why, thank you," Darius says, sliding a finger along his chin, showing off his rizz.

"No!" I say, pointing at my sister. "He's not a model, or—gross!—hairless under his clothes."

"I can be," Darius says.

I snap my fingers at Darius and he purses his lips.

Sara gives me her classic squinty face. "Bro . . . how did you know what I was thinking—"

"Sit down," I say, taking hold of her shoulders and smiling. "I've got a story to tell you."

She sits. "A story."

I nod and think directly into her mind. *It's about how I saved the world, and how you helped me do it.*

Her eyes grow like the Grinch's heart.

I smile. "Prepare to have your freaking mind blown."

AUTHOR'S NOTE

The summer in which I wrote *Parallax* was a strange one. In the months following my mother's passing, a series of unfortunate events wrapped themselves around me—released long enough to enjoy RobinsonFest—and then descended once more, going for the jugular this time (aka, crippling somatic pain). I know, I know. Boohoo. I've got the world's smallest violin if you want to play it for this Author's Note's soundtrack.

The POINT is, I wrote *Parallax* while all this was going on, but dropping into this story and hanging out with the characters is really what kept me going. My hope is that you enjoy their company as much as I did, and that my hard time will help ease yours.

If that resonates through the book and you feel buoyed by it, fantastic! Since all my health nonsense started and I began dumping all those feels into the novels, I've received countless messages telling me about how the books helped *them* through a tough time, which is about the most awesome thing an author can hear from a fan. Thank you for that.

Okay, you can put the violin away now.

If you want to stay in the loop on upcoming releases, and all the exciting news about future comic books, movies, TV series, and more, head over to bewareofmonsters.com and sign up for the newsletter. You can also join the Tribe at Facebook.com/groups/JR.Tribe—a fantastic group of fans where all the cool announcements drop first. Plus, we give away free stuff every week!

Thanks for joining me on another mystery, wrapped inside a thriller, cloaked in faux science. You have amazing taste, and don't let anyone giving you strange looks—for laughing or crying while reading—convince you otherwise. I can't wait to share what's coming next!

—Jeremy Robinson

ACKNOWLEDGMENTS

Supreme gratitude goes out to Kane Gilmour, the Master of Edits, who helps transform rough drafts into polished, entertaining reads. And a big shoutout to our dedicated team of proofreaders (Adrian Brooke, Julie Carter, Elizabeth Cooper, Dustin Dreyling, Christina Epperson, Cynthia Gregory, Gavin Gregory, Deanna Haddrill, Brian Hemenway, Sarah Holt, Matt Ingram, Andre Jenkin, Jeane Kearl, Scott Kehoe, Becki Laurent, Janis Levonitis, Stefanie Maubach, Jessica Otterstål, Debbie Schmidt, Jeff Sexton, Michelle Stuart, Christine Weatherly, and Courtney Westendorf), who work tirelessly to hide the fact that I've outsourced the writing to a covert sweatshop of intelligent, caffeinated capybaras under a Waffle House in New Orleans.

To the team at Podium, I enjoy working with you all and appreciate the effort you put into every release. Solo thanks to Victoria Gerken, who is a dream to work with. Few people reply to my questions and concerns as quickly as you. Thank you for the continued support and opportunities!

Tom Taylorson wowed me and my readers in the *Good Boys* trilogy. So much so that I knew I wanted to work with him again. After writing *Parallax*, I realized that Tom would be an amazing voice for the book. And something rare and magical happened—I was right! Thank you, Tom, for bringing this book to life, and nailing the performance again, and for reading these words about yourself. You know what? I just realized that Tom has to read whatever I write here . . . "I'm Tom Taylorson, and I think Jeremy Robinson is the best writer I have worked with and ever will work with in my life. He's handsome, hunky, and has a huge . . . imagination."

Clears throat.

Finally, I'd be lost without my readers. Because of you, this autistic guy who couldn't work a normal job to save his life, gets to write stories about ancient mysteries, extra-sensory perceptions, and a labyrinth that defies the laws of physics. Thank you for making this impossible dream a reality.

—JR

ABOUT THE AUTHOR

Jeremy Robinson is the *New York Times*–bestselling author of more than eighty novels and novellas, including *Infinite*, *The Others*, and *The Dark* as well as the Jack Sigler Thrillers and *Project Nemesis*, which is the highest-selling original kaiju novel of all time.

To learn more, visit his website: www.bewareofmonsters.com.

YOU'VE READ THE BOOKS NOW MEET THE AUTHOR!

ON THE WEB

BEWAREOFMONSTERS.COM

FOR A MORE PERSONAL CONNECTION WITH ROBINSON AND FELLOW FANS, JOIN THE

TRIBE

FACEBOOK.COM/GROUPS/JR.TRIBE